Galaxy Grifter

BLACKJACK INTERSTELLAR: BOOK ONE

A. ZAYKOVA

orbitbooks.net
orbitworks.net

This book is a work of fiction. Names, characters, places, and incidents are the product of the author's imagination or are used fictitiously. Any resemblance to actual events, locales, or persons, living or dead, is coincidental.

Copyright © 2025 by Alla Zaykova

Cover design by Alexia E. Pereira
Cover illustration by Ben Zweifel
Cover copyright © 2025 by Hachette Book Group, Inc.
Author photograph by Anzhelika Moiseeva

Hachette Book Group supports the right to free expression and the value of copyright. The purpose of copyright is to encourage writers and artists to produce the creative works that enrich our culture.

The scanning, uploading, and distribution of this book without permission is a theft of the author's intellectual property. If you would like permission to use material from the book (other than for review purposes), please contact permissions@hbgusa.com. Thank you for your support of the author's rights.

Orbit
Hachette Book Group
1290 Avenue of the Americas
New York, NY 10104
orbitbooks.net
orbitworks.net

First Edition: June 2025

Orbit is an imprint of Hachette Book Group.
The Orbit name and logo are registered trademarks of Little, Brown Book Group Limited.

The publisher is not responsible for websites (or their content) that are not owned by the publisher.

The Hachette Speakers Bureau provides a wide range of authors for speaking events. To find out more, go to hachettespeakersbureau.com or email HachetteSpeakers@hbgusa.com.

Library of Congress Control Number: 2025935486

ISBNs: 9780316587389 (ebook), 9780316587396 (print on demand)

In loving memory of
Svetlana Dolgolenko
01/19/1966–03/08/2018
Mum, mentor, muse.

Chapter 1
Future of Terraformation Symposium

Luminescent kelp fabric draped across the walls of the banquet hall cast a shimmering glow on the delegates gathered there—bigwigs from across the Galactic Union donned in formal attire. Levi's gaze shifted from the chatty humanoid sharing a table with him to a stern-faced security guard edging past holographic displays and rows of glass tables.

Levi tensed, ready to run. Crashing the pompous Future of Terraformation Symposium under the guise of a Martian bureaucrat could earn him a year-long prison sentence. His connection to the Shadow League pirates, if somehow traced, would get him locked up indefinitely. But gathering intel for them was the quickest way to make enough coins to repurchase his beloved *Caerus*.

The security guard stepped through the nearest hologram displaying a planetary cross section, raised his comm to his lips, looked straight at Levi, and marched out of the hall through the emergency exit.

False alarm. Levi exhaled and downed his seaweed liquor. He was already in hot water with his employers and couldn't afford more complications.

Netareth Khay, a Jaemlen ministerial advisor Levi had befriended earlier, looked oblivious to the commotion. The amphibious alien could pass for a Human, if it wasn't for his pewter-toned skin and an extra pair of eyelids, which closed vertically, like a translucent film over his yellow irises. Like Levi, he wore a translation coil in his ear, though his suit was clearly expensive and well-kept, whereas Levi hoped the advisor wouldn't see the repaired seams on his own jacket. The gills on the Jaemlen's neck fluttered as he slurped down his third bowl of roe jelly. "I'm basically in charge while the minister's away, left to field all the questions."

"Sounds like a pain." Levi topped up both their drink glasses with the green-tinged liquid. Listening to Netareth gloat was as fun as watching cleaner bots calibrate, but he leaked government secrets like a badly plumbed faucet, and these could fetch a good price with the pirates. So, Levi endured. "Any way the minister will postpone?"

"Not a chance. He's all wound up for this trip. I think a big announcement will follow, but I didn't tell you that." The Jaemlen tapped his flat nose.

"Tell me what?"

The virtEgo on Levi's wrist pulsed. Its flexible screen lit up, showing an incoming call from an unknown contact.

GALAXY GRIFTER

"Excuse me." He stepped behind a hologram and flicked his earpiece.

"Levi Adder...enjoying your ship upgrades?"

Levi cringed, recognizing the nasal baritone on the other end of the call. "Isaac, I'm sorry, you've caught me at a bad time."

"I'm sure I have. Your payment is overdue, and you've been ignoring my messages."

"Ignoring? No, I've been terribly busy. Give me two more weeks and I'll pay in full. I'll throw a tenner on top of the total." Levi kept his tone cool and casual as he was practiced to do under pressure.

"A fortnight in Union time. After that, I'll find you. And I'll take your ship." Isaac Brezni disconnected.

Fuck. Levi kicked the holo-projector. Leaving *Caerus* as loan collateral after his faux-antique scheme folded a day too soon was the hardest decision he'd ever made. The ship was modified precisely to his taste; the sleek hull of his classic light freighter exuded timeless luxury, but the components inside were nothing short of cutting edge. The pilot's seat, made of luscious nanite suede, molded perfectly to the curve of his back. Its LI VII Quantum Core processor ran the latest version of self-learning AI, with controls so attuned to his movements that piloting became as easy as breathing. The freshly installed DynaGlide thrusters provided unparalleled maneuverability in both atmospheric and zero-gravity conditions, while the magfield stabilizers, with their advanced inertial dampening, negated g-forces and made diving in and out of hyperspace feel as smooth as running a hot knife through butter. Speaking of which, his state-of-the-art kitchen meant he never had to rely on the disgusting ready-to-eat travel packs.

Caerus was not only his ultimate symbol of freedom, but also his best friend. The only one he ever had or needed. Leaving it at the seedy little dealership on Frigg felt like severing a body part, it's absence growing more visceral with each passing day.

He *needed* that ship back. He couldn't afford to screw up this job.

He took a breath to center himself, forced a smile to his face. A pretty blond woman from some Human research organization smiled back at him as she walked past. Good, he was still blending in. But she presented no commercial interest, so he paid her no heed and returned to his table.

Netareth patted his lips with a napkin. "Everything okay?"

"Everything's stellar," Levi said, sliding into his chair and leaning toward the advisor. "What do you say we hit the town? This party has run its course."

Netareth scratched his earhole. "It's been a long day..."

"It'll be fun." Levi retrieved a small box from his breast pocket and tipped a transparent pill onto the palm of his hand.

"What is that?"

"Pathinazole Cetatine—Patty."

Netareth's eyes widened, and he lowered his voice to a whisper. "You brought an illegal party drug *here*?"

"I'll keep your secrets, if you keep mine." Levi winked, pretended to put the pill in his mouth, and offered the box to Netareth.

"I shouldn't."

GALAXY GRIFTER

"Suit yourself. But that girl's casting glances your way." Levi nodded at a group of Jaemlen females at the next table. "Bet she wants to get out of here too."

"Which one?" Netareth turned his head, giving Levi the opportunity to return the pill to its box.

"The pretty one." Levi wasn't sure which amphibian fit that description, but Netareth seemed satisfied with the answer.

He sighed and stretched out his webbed hand. "Okay, just one."

Levi checked his wrist, clocking the time. In thirty minutes, he'd have access to Netareth's virtEgo and the Jaemlen minister's itinerary.

———————————— • ————————————

An hour later, Levi ambled down a hotel corridor with a half-empty champagne bottle in one hand and the firm butt cheek of an Erian researcher in the other—the same one who'd smiled at him in the banquet hall. Her platinum hair framed a sharp face, and her emerald dress, with a curious texture, like soft bubbles of caviar, skimmed her athletic frame. It concealed just enough to be classy, unlike her laugh, which was too loud. Not that it mattered. His skin warmed from the allure of her touch and utter self-satisfaction. Netareth Khay was snoring in his own room and would remember nothing by morning. And Levi would soon have the funds to buy his ship back.

Gleath's cityscape shimmered playfully through the ceiling-to-floor window at the corridor's end, casting its lights across a shallow salt lake that lapped at the hotel's lower levels, built partially submerged for the amphibious natives. Thankfully, the top floors accommodating Human delegates were dry. Levi leaned against one of the many doors that lined the corridor and tapped his wristband against the smart lock until it clicked open.

The researcher giggled and slipped into the room, tugging him behind her. Inside, he pressed her against a wall, and she wrapped her arms around his neck.

But something felt off—a presence tugging at the edges of his alcohol-numbed senses.

"Wait." He freed himself from her embrace and flicked the lights on.

She shrieked.

A somber man with a black mane slouched in an armchair by the window, legs splayed, gun on his lap, eyes fixed on them. Navegante, the first mate of a pirate galleon called the *Vulture*, and Levi's de facto employer.

A stocky woman dressed in a cargo jacket stood next to him. She had angry eyes, and a blaster, which she tucked carelessly in her armpit. Their presence could only mean one thing—that Levi's night was irrevocably ruined.

He sighed and shoved the researcher to the door. "Leave. And keep your mouth shut."

She hurried out.

The stocky woman started toward him, swinging the blaster.

Navegante raised his palm. "Easy, Ren."

She stopped.

GALAXY GRIFTER

"Holy shit, guys. Ever heard of privacy? Maybe calling before you visit?" Levi swigged his champagne and sauntered toward a wide bed, draped with a golden duvet.

Navegante rose to his feet. "Two days, no updates."

"Ah, you've missed me. I'd appreciate the surprise party more if it weren't in my room." Levi had sworn off working with pirates, but being temporarily shipless had left him few options.

"Technically it's *my* room, given your ass belongs to us," Navegante said.

"Not to *you*, per se. Your captain, on the other hand, is always wel—"

Navegante drove a fist into Levi's gut, making him double over, his champagne spilling onto the carpet.

The pirate tolerated no quips about his captain. *Canine loyalty.* Frowning, Navegante paced up and down the hotel room. "Have you found our mark?"

"I have." Levi winced and straightened. "Was going to brief you in the morning."

"Brief me now."

Ren pointed at the bottle. "He's had too much fun, it seems."

"Someone's gotta. You should try it sometime." Holding his stomach, Levi sat on the bed.

She gave him the death stare, and Navegante cocked his fist again.

Levi raised both hands. "Hold on. Lights to twenty percent." The room sank into twilight. He tapped his virt and projected a map of the galaxy into the space in front of him.

Navegante lowered back into the armchair.

"Top stories today: A freighter full of diamonds is heading to Eria." Levi drew a line connecting two points on the star map. "Sadly, it's escorted by three fighter ships. By the time you're done with those, Starpol will have arrived, so—"

"So why the fuck are you telling me? Got us into enough shit with the pol-fucks the last time." Navegante's frustration was understandable; piracy wasn't the profitable endeavor it has once been, but Levi hated being on the receiving end of his wrath.

"Just walking you through the options. In my view"—Levi rotated the hologram—"your best bet is a Jaemlen explorer ship heading off the chart, to sector forty-three."

"What's in forty-three?"

"Officially? Nothing. It's close to the A'turi border. The explorer is carrying three prominent scientists and a couple of Jaemlen politicians. Ransom-worthy folk, let alone whatever they're transporting."

"Which is?"

Levi shrugged. "Secrets. My guess is they found a new prospective colony, and after they lost their claim to Frigg, they're not in a hurry to tell their buddies at the Galactic Union."

Navegante scratched his cheek with the gun barrel. "I'd rather stay away from politicians. Next thing you know, the whole GU will be after us."

"Bet Wendigo thinks otherwise."

Navegante's lip twitched. "How would you know what Wendigo thinks?"

Levi didn't risk inviting another punch. "Either way, traders

GALAXY GRIFTER

are cautious these days. And Starpol is on high alert after the two Sehen raids last quarter. A lone ship off the main route is a rare opportunity."

Ren leaned on the wall next to the bed. "How'd you get their route coordinates?"

"I'm good at making friends. And friends tell you stuff."

Navegante scoffed. "He drugs them."

Levi placed his hand on his heart. "I'd *never*. They take the fun stuff willingly...with a bit of coaxing."

"Wouldn't it be quicker to spike their drinks?" Ren slipped the blaster into her belt.

"Crude. Besides, they could report that. They won't report something that incriminates them."

Navegante zoomed in on sector forty-three of the star map. "Ammo?"

"Two fighter frigates and last-generation shields. Nothing the *Vulture* can't handle."

The pirate grimaced.

"C'mon, you don't expect loot without a fight, do you? That's how you know it's worth it."

"Was supposed to be worth it last time," Navegante all but snarled. He reminded Levi of a yappy dog—angry, yet unable to last a day without his owner.

"It would've been," Levi said. "I don't know where the third fighter came from. And with the Starpol—"

"It was your *job* to know."

That stung. "I'm good at my job. That was the first ever slipup."

"Better be the last. It cost us."

Choking down his pride, Levi slapped his virt, turning off the holo-map, and leaned back on his elbows. "If you don't like what I've got, I'll do more digging. But run it past Captain Wendigo with my warmest regards."

Navegante's scowl suggested he'd rather put a hole through Levi's head. But he wasn't allowed. Not until Levi made them a profit. The pirate stood, slid the gun into his holster, and spat on the carpet. "Get your shit. You're coming aboard the *Vulture*. If your plan goes south again—you're going down with us."

Chapter 2
The *Vulture*

The Jaemlen explorer ship resembled a great pregnant shark, menacing points jutting out from the sides and a bulging center. After the first pirate rockets hit its shields, the center opened, birthing two small fighter frigates, which countered with vengeance, rattling the huge pirate galleon like an earthquake. It made Levi's teeth clatter. Locked in the *Vulture's* common room, with only Ren for company, Levi tugged on his tattered seat belts.

"Is Wendigo planning to do something about the shooting?" His voice rang with annoyance over the barrage. If it were him and *Caerus*, he'd have easily swerved from the line of fire, even though the freighter had no weapons.

"Watch." Ren nodded at a screen on the opposite wall, where the live footage of the battle unfolded like a bad movie.

The pirates seemed to ignore the frigates, treating them like pesky flies and instead firing ceaselessly at the large explorer, denying it the chance to jump into hyperspace. A white flash illuminated the room as a laser beam aimed at the big ship pierced one of the frigates, and it burst into flames. Before Levi had time to wonder where the shot came from, a third, older-looking fighter came into view, probably released from the *Vulture*'s cargo hold.

The shaking stopped. The fire on the explorer continued. The remaining tiny frigate circled fruitlessly, trying to do any real damage to the *Vulture*. One precise shot from the *Vulture* later, the last Jaemlen fighter sang its fiery swan song.

Wendigo continued to shell the explorer as her voice boomed over the intercom. "Prepare for boarding."

The pirates, including Ren, flooded into the cargo hold.

Relieved, Levi headed in the opposite direction, down a long corridor partitioned by open hatches, which sealed off sections of the ship in cases of hull integrity breaches. Discoloration along the seams of the unfaced metal bulkheads hinted at where the *Vulture* had been patched up. Voices and thumps echoed from the hold below.

The books Levi had read as a kid painted piracy as an exciting career option. In practice, he felt walking these corridors day after day would be as tedious as any office job. His own career offered much more variety. He liked his interstellar Ponzi schemes, the art of selling junk as priceless artifacts, and coaxing vendors into questionable freight contracts before disappearing with their goods. On *Caerus*, he was the captain and they made their own rules, unbridled by the suffocating constraints of power hierarchies, legal systems, and arbitrary moral codes designed to quell individuality. As free as the stars reflected in *Caerus*'s glossy black hull. But after a decade

GALAXY GRIFTER

on the fun side of the law, he was back to square one: no ship, no money, and Wendigo still hadn't paid him for the intel.

He reached the captain's cabin and tried the door. Locked, most likely magnetically. So were the cabins of those next in command. He continued into the common dormitory, which smelled of unwashed bodies, with chests of drawers bolted to the floor next to the narrow bunks. Breathing into his sleeve, he knelt by the nearest one. It had been locked with an old-fashioned key and only took a minute to pick.

Inside, he found several changes of worn-out clothing, a virtEgo with a cracked screen, earpieces with traces of wax, and a pack of condoms. At least the pirates were being safe. He shut the drawers and tried the next chest. There had to be something he could score out of this joyride.

Five attempts later, and none the richer, he heard voices down the corridor. He left the dormitory and turned the corner, looking over his shoulder to ensure nobody saw him.

Two large men walked in the direction of the lavatory with their backs to him. Their easy gaits suggested the raid had been a success.

"It's done then?" Levi asked.

They turned to face him. The taller one had a beard. The shorter one was bald and clean-shaven.

"We're towing the explorer, the hostages are in our hold," said the one with the beard.

Levi propped his elbow on a bulkhead. "What were they carrying?"

"They're being questioned." The bearded man proceeded into the lav, followed by his silent shipmate.

Satisfied that his intel proved accurate, Levi headed toward the stairs. Now was the perfect time to see the captain.

He'd climbed two steps toward the bridge when a pained scream echoed from below. He stopped, fighting the urge to look. The urge won, and he descended one level.

The cargo hold was the size of a sports field. Containers, machinery, and tarped mounds lined its perimeter. Pirates herded four Jaemlen hostages with bound wrists into a cage. A green Sehen, with muscular arms ending in four-fingered hands, and a three-meter-long serpentine lower body, coiled around the fifth hostage, rendering him immobile. The reptilians were known for bad tempers, and Wendigo was the only Human captain Levi knew of who had one in her service. The Jaemlen's eyes were shut and blood dripped from his mouth. Navegante and another Human stood with their backs to the stairs.

"He better not be dead." Navegante poked the Jaemlen's face, but his head hung limp.

"I can feel a pulsssse." The Sehen flicked his forked tongue.

"Try another one. We'll get them talking eventually."

The Sehen threw the unconscious hostage into the cage and dragged out his second screaming victim.

Savages. Levi turned to leave. Perhaps he ought to have felt remorse, but he was merely an informant and wasn't even supposed to be here.

Navegante called after him. "What the fuck do you want, Weasel?"

"Nothing."

"Then get the fuck out, before I get you to scrub the piss off the floor."

Thankless savages.

For all his insults and threats, Levi knew Navegante was the one who felt threatened. Despite his loyalty to the captain, he stood no chance of winning Wendigo's carnal affections in the way that Levi had once (in jest) implied that he had. Levi knew that the thought of him and Wendigo behind closed doors drove Navegante to rage. And that made Levi all the more happy to skip up to the captain's presence alone.

Levi climbed several flights to the ship's bridge. The hatch was open.

A tall woman stood over the control panel with her back to him—Wendigo. Her long hair fell in spirals, black with a dash of salt. She shut the text file she had been scrolling through and turned. "That you, Adder?"

"I prefer 'Levi.'" He sat on a bench next to the entrance to catch his breath. They'd been on friendlier terms before the Starpol incident, but at least she wasn't calling him "Weasel."

He knew her white shirt, worn unbuttoned over a singlet, concealed broad shoulders and sinewy arms. She had at least fifteen years on top of his twenty-nine, yet she was still as alluring to him as a siren's song.

"What do you want?" Wendigo asked.

"I kept my end of the deal, which got you a shiny ship to pick apart and a coin-worthy cargo to ransom, unless your crew kill them first. Thought you'd reciprocate." He grinned, which normally ensured he got what he wanted.

She leaned on the back of the pilot seat. "I'll pay you once we reach Blackjack."

"I don't want to go to Blackjack." His grin fell. The asteroid in sector 21 was a haven for lowlifes and outlaws and headed by Vincent Puccelli's Mafia. Levi may have owed them some funds.

"Too bad, I do. Call me superstitious, but the deal ain't done until my ship reaches the port."

"I'm not a hostage here, am I? I don't do well in captivity."

She scoffed. "Captivity? Have you seen the prisoners' quarters?"

His skin crawled at the memory of the cage in the cargo hold. "Your ship's lovely, don't get me wrong, but I feel I've overstayed my welcome. It's almost like..." He glanced at the entrance and lowered his voice to a conspiratorial hush. "Your crew don't like me."

That got half a smile from her. "You shouldn't provoke them."

"I wouldn't, if I could help it. But...some are particularly short-fused. You might want to reconsider your choice of second-in-command."

"You're giving me HR advice? Navegante is as competent as he is loyal."

Levi snorted. "Loyal. You do know the guy has wet dreams about you? You don't need those complications."

She charged forward and slammed her boot into the bench between his legs. His testicles retracted up to his groin.

"You will *not* talk about my crew like that. Or at all, for that matter." She glared.

Once certain he wasn't actually hurt, he wrapped his fingers around her boot and rested his chin on her knee. "Looks like I'm getting on *your* nerves too." Getting under her skin

GALAXY GRIFTER

was somewhat thrilling, even if pushing her buttons was like playing with a grenade.

"You are." She freed her leg.

"Lend me one of your shuttles and I'll be gone."

She turned and walked to the control panel.

That wasn't a clear *no*, so he tried again. "Come on, you've got the explorer and you're on a shadow route. What could possibly go wrong now?"

The lidar bleeped. Wendigo checked the screen and sat in the pilot seat. "Two ships ahead of us."

He tensed. "Starpol?" This couldn't be happening.

"Not sure, but they shouldn't be moving this fast. How did they find us?"

"Don't know. We *are* on a shadow route, right?"

"Of course."

The shadow maps were the pirates' best-kept secret. The cops shouldn't have—couldn't have known about them. He jumped to his feet and looked over her shoulder. The dots on the lidar approached from ahead, forming a triangle. "Maybe they're not even after us? Ping 'em, see what they want. Starpol won't fire if you've got hostages."

"I damn sure hope so." She tried to initiate contact with one of the ships, and then with the other. No response.

A chill crept up his spine. Navegante's words replayed in his head: *If your plan goes south again, you're going down with us.*

The two dots grew closer. The *Vulture* could pass between them if each stayed its course. Yet, somehow, it felt like a trap.

"Buckle in." Wendigo hit the alarm.

Sirens blared and Levi strapped into the navigator seat next

17

to her. The oncoming ships were close enough for the *Vulture* to project their images onto the screens. They looked like silver shadows, heavily armored and weaponized.

Wendigo's frown deepened. "Jaemlen warships."

"GU troops or just Gleath's forces?"

"They don't have Union colors from what I can see." She took up manual controls and swerved as a white beam flashed past the viewport, a near miss. She hit the hyperdrive.

The *Vulture* plunged through a white disk, out of hyperspace, and into the star-speckled interstellar substance. She brought up the map, changed routes, and jumped back into the starless blackness. She fired orders to her crew via the intercom and hit the hyperdrive once again.

Levi's head spun from the recurrent jumps, but it appeared they'd lost the unmarked warships. Wendigo turned off the siren. "Who the hell are they?"

"Don't know. I've given you all I got from the mark."

She narrowed her eyes. "What did you drag us into, Weasel?"

"Wanda—"

"Come." She stood and hurried down the stairs. He followed.

On the lower deck, Navegante darted at him like an angry bull, screaming, "You led them to us—again!"

"I had nothing to do with it." Levi stepped back.

"You're *dead*, Weasel."

Fed up with the accusations, Levi rolled his shoulders. "How do I know it wasn't you, huh?"

"What the fuck are you saying?" Navegante chest-bumped him.

Levi pushed back. "You're the one with the problem, and

GALAXY GRIFTER

you knew the route we'd be on. You could've tipped someone off to set me up."

Navegante growled, grabbed Levi by the collar, and shoved him into a bulkhead.

Wendigo placed her hand on her first mate's shoulder. "This ain't a taphouse, gentlemen. Keep your testosterone in check."

Levi broke free of the pirate's grip. "Keep your dog on a leash, Wanda. It bites."

"Don't be a child." She turned to Navegante. "It's *not* the Starpol."

He stared blankly. "What do you mean?"

"No insignia, Union or otherwise."

"Who then? The Sehens?"

"Can't be," Wendigo said. "Jaemlen-built, military-class ships. Contact denied. What intel did the captives give us?"

"Barely anything. I'll fix that." Navegante started toward the cargo hold.

"Nav," Wendigo called. "Take charge on the bridge. I'll handle things downstairs."

"Yes, Cap'n. What should I do with this one?" Navegante's lip curled in contempt as he nodded at Levi.

"He'll come with me." She turned with a toss of hair and headed into the hold.

Levi pushed past the first mate and followed her.

On the steps, they nearly collided with a teenage boy. He held a crate full of gadgets. "Cap'n. We've scanned the explorer ship and all their devices. No entanglement signals detected."

"Good."

"Where do you want the data cards?" The boy shook the crate.

"Take them to the bridge, Toshi." She waved him off.

The pirates in the cargo hold stood to attention at the sight of her. The Jaemlen hostage in the Sehen's deadly embrace squirmed. Wendigo walked up to the Jaemlen, drew a long laser knife, and slit his throat. He gurgled dark blood.

Levi froze in his tracks, eyes glued to the dying humanoid. The body convulsed, almost comically, eyes bulging, mouth gaping. When it went limp, the Sehen dropped it onto the bloodstained floor.

Shit. Levi's thoughts raced. He needed to find a way off the *Vulture*, or he'd have a hard time explaining he wasn't part of this psycho's crew if her ship was captured.

Someone inside the cage wailed.

"Get rid of it." Wendigo kicked the dead Jaemlen and turned to the prisoners. "I am the captain of this ship and a member of the Shadow League, who serve no government, Human or alien. For this we're shunned by your Union"—she spat out the word like it was filth on her tongue—"making piracy our only viable trade. Jaemlen warships followed us on a route you won't find on a Union map and known only to us. My crew assured me your ship and confiscated devices are silent, which means one of *you* is hiding a quantum entanglement tracker, transmitting coordinates to our enemies."

The hostages exchanged worried glances.

A network of satellite quantum computers with entangled particles enabled instant communication between all planets of the Union, across the star systems. Cheaper and simpler versions of this technology, colloquially known as the ansible, were used in spaceships' communications to allow simple exchanges with the spaceports.

Wendigo's gaze lingered on each Jaemlen. "You better start talking, or I'll cut you all down and feed you to the black." She turned to her crew. "Abdul, interpret, in case I didn't make myself clear."

The bearded pirate Levi had spoken to in the corridor came forward and blabbered in the Jaemlen language.

A badly bruised hostage, probably the one Levi had seen tortured earlier, uttered something through gritted teeth. Levi didn't need an interpreter to tell it was an insult.

Wendigo waved at the Sehen. "Get the next one."

It slithered to the cage, pulled out a young, whimpering female, and coiled around her.

"Wanda, wait." Levi grabbed Wendigo's arm. "They're worth a fortune in ransom. Killing them off is wasteful."

"It will be more wasteful if their warships track us down again." She jerked her arm free and switched on the laser.

"You can use them as leverage." He wasn't going to jail for assisting murderers. And deep down, he still hoped to get paid.

"They *fired* at us."

"A warning shot. They can tell the *Vulture* has shields and can take a few hits without damage."

"I can't risk that." Her eyes were the coldest steel. "Back off, unless you want to join them."

He stepped back, falling silent.

As Wendigo raised the blade, a wrinkled male came to the

front of the cage. "Don't. I have the tracker." He spoke clear Supayuyan, Humanity's most common language.

Wendigo lowered the knife. The Sehen threw the sobbing female back into the cage and dragged out the old male.

"Where?"

With a shaking hand, the hostage pulled up his sleeve, pointing at a barely visible bump just below the elbow—an implant.

"Carve it out," Wendigo ordered.

Abdul bared a regular steel knife and grasped the Jaemlen's arm. Before he could make an incision, a quake passed through the ship, knocking everyone off their feet. The siren blared with a warning of a hull breach.

The *Vulture* was fucked.

Chapter 3
Blackjack

Vera studied the cockpit of an old cargo ship that had just docked at Blackjack's spaceport, smelling of spice and must. She ran her fingers over the grubby control panel. Hot and sticky. She wrinkled her nose.

The pilot, June, grey-haired and shriveled like a dehydrated slugar, removed a mug from the panel. "Overheating like hell, but at least it keeps my tea warm." She chuckled.

"Yeah, it shouldn't be doing that." Vera snapped off the cover, baring the greasy entrails of the onboard computer. The smell intensified. She sniffed. "Did you spill...curry on it?"

June shuffled from foot to foot. "It's meant to be waterproof."

"Yes, but not...curryproof." Vera sighed. "I'm going to have to clean it all out and see which bits are fried." She rummaged through her bag for her diagnostic goggles, a pair of tweezers, and cotton buds. "You might want to get Nina to service your engine, too, before your next flight."

"You're so clever," June lilted. "Don't know how you do it, girl."

Vera snorted. De-currying control panels was not the job she'd dreamed of and was only marginally better than working at the pub she'd inherited.

June patted her on the back. "I've got accounts to tally. Call me when you're finished." She disappeared through the hatch leading to the ship's living area.

Several hours later, Vera had reassembled the motherboard, applied a fresh coating of thermal paste to the nano chips, and clipped the cover back into place. Once the computer powered up, she shouted into the hatch, "I'm just running software updates, okay?"

"Does it cost more?" June's voice rang from somewhere in the ship's belly.

"No." Vera tapped through the menu.

June returned to the cockpit, wiping her hands on her apron. "You're a miracle worker. This ship's my lifeline."

"No prob." Vera stood from the pilot seat. "Two fifty k-bits."

"Wanna stay for dinner?"

"Nah, I've gotta—"

"Dumplings, freshly made."

Vera shook her head. "Need to get back to Stellar. The miners' shift is about to finish and they don't like waiting for their booze."

June tsked. "You work too much, girl."

"Keeps me out of trouble."

"Burn out. Need to take care of yourself." June wagged a crooked finger.

Work *was* Vera's self-care, her only chance at a better life. She'd rest once she paid off her debt and moved to Seshat. There, she would find a *real* job, one that actually required a brain.

"Don't worry, it'll go dead after happy hour." She stretched out her arm with her virtEgo bracelet. "Two fifty, please."

June grimaced. "It's been a while since my last delivery round. How about I'll pay you half when I come back from this run, eh? You know June keeps her promises."

Here we go. Everyone was always so grateful until they had to pay. "I've got bills too, June."

"Okay, okay. I'll pay two hundred. Fifty when I come back. And I'll bring you a present, okay?"

Vera checked the time. "Fine. I really need to get to the pub now."

June tapped her wristband against Vera's, transferring two hundred k-bits. "Come back for dinner tomorrow. I'll feed you."

———————•———————

Kicking up fine, grey dust, Vera jogged along the unpaved road leading away from the spaceport. The red, nameless sun plunged toward the horizon, hazy through the thick, nano-composite tiles of the dome that enclosed Blackjack's settlement. Factory chimneys pierced the dome, puffing toxic fumes into outer space. Farther along, makeshift hovels nestled between concrete, barracks-style residential blocks up to three stories tall, adorned with crude graffiti. Drying laundry and precarious extensions embellished the windows.

A. Zaykova

She waved at a group of elderly folk, locally known as the Immortals. The sofa they assembled on was strategically placed outside the first apartment block, so no one coming into town could escape their long-sighed appraisals. They collectively nodded to her as she passed.

On Main Street, Vera slowed to a walk. The sheet metal walkway clanked with every step. A group of teenagers loitered outside a liquor store. Several heads turned toward her, and she crossed the road. Life on the asteroid gave youth plenty to be angsty about.

"Hey, wait," someone called after her.

Vera glanced back. *Oh, great.* A plump girl in a short striped dress was following her. The locals had dubbed the girl Princess, for her relation to Vincent Puccelli, aka Vinnie the Pooch, the local kingpin. Of course her highness had to approach Vera now, when she was already running behind.

"You work at Stellar, right?" Princess caught up to Vera and stopped.

Vera raised her chin. "I own it."

"Yeah, you know the new guy who runs the liquor store?"

"No."

"Well, he won't sell us drinks. Apparently, my dad told him not to." Princess rolled her eyes. "So dumb."

"Uh...I'm sorry?" Vera would kill to be fourteen again and have those kinds of problems.

"I was thinking..." Princess tucked her long fringe behind her ear, showing off a brand-new virt on her wrist.

"No." Vera wasn't going to supply the Pooch's underaged grandniece with alcohol.

26

GALAXY GRIFTER

"Why? You're not scared of my dad too?"

"Puccelli's nephew? Pretty scared."

"He won't know. And it's not like he'll actually do anything."

Vera looked around and leaned toward the girl. "Do you know what happened to the store's previous owner?"

Princess's eyes widened. "No."

"Exactly." Vera didn't know either, but no one crossed the gang and stayed in business. She turned to leave.

"Oh, come on, I thought you were cool," Princess whined as her friends watched from across the road.

Vera suppressed a snicker. "Whoever told you that?"

She arrived at Stellar at one minute past thirteen, Blackjack time—after sunset, but before the miners would arrive in droves. Once she disarmed the door, an old android with caterpillar wheels and flexible tentacle arms scanned her face. Rusty greeted her by changing the red light in its head to green.

Rusty had guarded the pub for as long as she could remember and had been outdated since before then. It did its job, though. She'd even managed to program it to pick up rubbish.

She hit a switch behind the bar. Neon string lights flickered to life, diluting the gloom above the mismatched tables scavenged from written-off spaceships and assembled from scrap metal. The first patrons rolled in a second later, covered in sweat and dust from beyond the dome. The same crowd as usual: two dozen or so miners, all demanding their singular beer to wipe out the tip of their exhaustion and make getting home to their families that much easier. A few others bumbled in after them, but nothing and no one unexpected.

27

As Vera had predicted, the hubbub died down after happy hour. A white-haired geezer dozed over his glass in the corner. A couple of Huxorans, resembling Human-sized rats, chattered by the window. The remaining tables stood empty. She turned a page of a virtual book: *From First Contact to Modern Diplomacy: A Brief History of Xeno Affairs*.

Just as she was starting to lose herself in the book's dramatic account of Humanity's mass resettlement to Mars, followed by a dispersal throughout the galaxy, Stellar's doors flung open, letting in a gust of cold air and a broad-shouldered figure in a leather jacket.

Vera sighed. Couldn't she have *one* calm day?

The man who stood in the doorway was Blackbeard. The Pooch's right-hand man. He swaggered to the bar like he owned the place and everyone in it. The Huxorans quieted and shuffled toward the exit. The geezer woke and followed them.

Vera's heart shrank and fell into her stomach. She fiddled with the beer keg levers to avoid making eye contact until she absolutely had to. "Evening, sir."

The gangster perched on a stool. "You today? Thought it's your brother's shift."

"Fred's in tomorrow, if you want to come back." Vera had tried to avoid Blackbeard, mostly by making sure he came by when Fred was behind the bar. He had a way with violent old men that Vera had never seemed to master.

"All good. Might get you to look at my virt since you're here. It's gone glitchy again."

"Sure. A drink?" She reached for a vodka bottle.

GALAXY GRIFTER

"Nah, got jobs tonight." He handed her his virtEgo. Taking it from his cold, metallic fingers felt eerie. She didn't know how he lost his arm but was sure the bionic limb made intimidating folk easier.

After tinkering with his device for several minutes, she passed it back to him. "You should consider an upgrade. The hardware's barely coping."

"A new one will take forever to get used to. Fuck that." He snapped the outdated model onto his good wrist.

She shrugged. "It'll flip out again in a few months."

"That's not what I came to talk about." He looked around the empty pub. "Your payments for Stellar—"

"We're up-to-date with those. Paid this month's already." She squared her shoulders, pressing both palms into the bar.

"Yeah, but the rate's gone up five percent. Inflation and all."

"What? When?"

"Now."

She took a deep breath. "You know how hard Fred and I work—"

"The economy's tough out there. Gotta share the brunt."

"Economy?" She clenched her jaw. Even with the cops patrolling the interstellar routes, the black market that fueled life on Blackjack was unsinkable. The brunt she and Fred had to bear was that of the Mafia's greed.

"If you've got a problem, take it up with the boss." Blackbeard banged his metallic fist, showing he was done talking.

Nobody in their right mind would confront the Pooch. She had no choice but to comply. "Five percent more next month, huh?"

"This month."

She crossed her arms. "Next month."

His eyes narrowed. "You remind me of your mother, you know that?"

Her nails dug into her upper arm, reminding herself that any sort of response would only put her in a worse position. She held the gangster's gaze, keeping her face as straight as possible.

"Fine, next month. And make sure it's on time." He pointed his finger, turned, and headed for the exit.

Once the door shut behind him, Vera slouched and unclenched her hands. Who was she kidding? The Pooch wouldn't let them pay off their debt, no matter how much they worked. She raised her virt to call Fred but stopped herself. Her mood was already ruined. She'd spare his until morning.

Chapter 4
Data Cards

"Jettison all of them!" Wendigo yelled over the sirens. Her crew dragged all five Jaemlens toward the hatches.

"Strap in once you're done; we'll try to lose the fuckers." She turned to the staircase.

"Wanda—" Levi stepped into her path. He had known she was ruthless, but killing every hostage...

"We don't know how many trackers there are. I don't have time to slice each of them open." She pushed past him and disappeared up the stairs.

He glanced around the cargo hold, mind spinning. One way or another, he needed to find a way off this ship.

On the deck he nearly tripped over Toshi. The boy stood on all fours, gathering data cards that had scattered across the floor. He looked up, wide-eyed and frightened. "What's happening?"

"The ship's under attack." A sharp jolt sent Levi tumbling. For a moment, he thought the gravity panels glitched out, but his weight returned and he collapsed onto his side. Hot pain shot through his shoulder where it had collided with the deck. Toshi prostrated himself on the floor, covering his head with both hands. Hatches were closing on either side of them. Levi didn't want to die on a ship full of marauders. Even less, to be incarcerated as one of them. He noticed a band on Toshi's wrist and grabbed the boy's shoulder. "Can you access the lowest hold, where the shuttles are?"

Toshi stared back with bewilderment. "Yeah. Why?"

"To get out of here while we still can."

"We can't." Toshi scrambled to his knees. "Not without the captain's orders." Another jolt nearly knocked him back down.

"Right. Well, I hope you had a nice life, 'cos it's about to end."

Toshi shook his head. "They won't blow up a ship with hostages."

"Hostages? They're being thrown into the vacuum as we speak. We don't even know who's firing at us, but it's sure not Starpol. Wendigo won't surrender. And if she does...you'll be better off dead."

Toshi's chin trembled.

Another shock wave knocked them against the bulkhead. Levi groaned, clutching his already-throbbing arm. If he somehow survived this, he'd clean up his act and get a proper job. Even office work had to be better than this. He grabbed Toshi's wrist and yanked him forward. "Just give me your virt, kid, and have fun dying."

Toshi breathed heavily, his eyes wet and shiny. "I'll take the shuttle."

"Smart." Levi let him go.

Toshi scurried in the direction of the cargo hold and held his wristband to the hatch. It slid open.

Levi scooped a handful of data cards scattered across the deck, shoved them into his pocket, and followed Toshi. They snuck down the stairs, past the upper cargo hold where the hostages had been, and farther down. The bottommost level of the *Vulture* felt colder. The Jaemlen explorer ship stood on the right, partially disassembled, taking up most of the space. Several smaller shuttles lined up against the opposite wall.

"That one." Levi pointed at the one closest to the hatch. It looked newer and would be worth the most. He'd given up counting on Wendigo's payment.

Toshi nodded and hurried forward.

The steps creaked. Levi removed a fire extinguisher from its bulkhead fixture, just in case, and glanced over his shoulder.

At the top of the staircase, the Sehen's eyes glowed like two yellow lamps. "Where'sss you going?"

Levi backed up. "The captain ordered us to prepare the shuttles for evacuation."

"Hasss she?" The Sehen coiled and propelled itself forward—three meters of scaly doom—and landed within an arm's reach.

"In writing." Levi flicked his virt as if to demonstrate the order. Instead, he released a jet of white foam at the snakelike face of the alien, and hurled the extinguisher. It bounced off the reptilian head with a dull thud and clanged onto the floor. The Sehen writhed.

Levi turned and sprinted after Toshi, his shiny brogues pounding the ship's rusty belly. The kid unlocked the shuttle nearest to him, an old clunker with *Comet985* printed on its side.

"Get in!" Levi glanced back.

The Sehen coiled like a spring and glided across the cargo hold.

Why isn't the thing dead yet? Levi flung himself onto the shuttle's ramp and slammed into Toshi. They fell inside. Levi jumped up and shut the hatch in front of the Sehen's foam-and blood-covered face. Not a vision Levi would soon forget.

He helped Toshi up and pushed him toward the control panel. "Start the engine before the others get here."

Toshi used his wristband to power up the shuttle. The Sehen banged against the hull from the outside until a much stronger tremor passed through the ship. The *Vulture* remained under attack.

Frantic, Toshi pounded the control panel. "There's no map loaded, and it won't fly without it."

"I'll sort it—transfer the controls to me."

"What?"

"The shuttle's control rights, so we can get out of here." Levi held out his virt.

Toshi pulled a holographic key from his wristband and dropped it onto Levi's.

"Consider yourself lucky." Levi paired his device with the shuttle's computer and strapped himself into the pilot seat. Toshi lowered into the seat next to him as another violent shock wave hit the *Vulture*.

The shuttle's dashboard displayed a status bar: *Map loading, please wait.*

GALAXY GRIFTER

"Come on." Levi gritted his teeth.

Ready for takeoff.

He guided *Comet985* through an airlock, into the blackness beyond. A white flash burst from the unmarked warship. Levi swerved and hit the hyperdrive just as a rocket penetrated the *Vulture*'s force shield and sank into the galleon's hull in a fiery cloud.

The *Comet* jumped.

Several silent moments later, Levi exhaled. "We did it! Can't believe we fucking did it, kid." He threw his head back and laughed.

Toshi stared blankly at the control panel. "I shouldn't have left the crew like that."

"Then you'd be dead too. Think they'd thank you for it?"

Toshi hung his head. "So, what do we do now?"

"Good question." Levi checked the shuttle's registration records. Blank. Its ship log. Empty. Levi had no doubt the shuttle was stolen. "Is the *Comet* listed in Starpol's database?"

Toshi shrugged. "Prob'ly."

"Way to dampen the mood, kid." There was only one spaceport that guaranteed they wouldn't get pulled over by the authorities on arrival. "Guess we're going to Blackjack."

Levi unbuckled and headed to check out the rest of the shuttle. Not that there was much to see. The *Comet* consisted of a two-seater cockpit, engine room, and two directional rockets. The detachable living module could be replaced with larger models for transporting cargo or people. The current module was the budget option. Its starboard displayed the utilities panel with a built-in mini fridge, heating, and disposal units.

The sofa bed against the port side took up the rest of the space. The lavatory that doubled as a walk-in shower was barely wide enough to turn inside. Under different circumstances, he wouldn't even bother stealing this thing.

On the fridge's top shelf, he found a moldy jar with what could be a novel life-form. The bottom shelf, however, held a dozen packs of cheap heat-and-eat meals. He picked one up and scanned the date stamp—only a week past expiry. Starvation was off the cards for now.

His lips curled in disgust as he transferred the jar into disposal and shut the fridge door. Inside a drawer, he found a faded blue T-shirt (which followed the jar into the disposal unit), a first aid kit, and a small blaster with no charge. The latter he tucked into his belt, then returned to the cockpit.

Toshi sat with his feet up on the control panel. He poked his finger at holograms, which appeared from his virt with increasing speed—a basic shooter.

Levi snatched the device. "There's one bed, so we'll sleep in turns. Yours starts now."

"I don't wanna sleep now." Toshi jumped up to try to reach his virt.

"Fetch." Levi tossed it through the hatch between the cockpit and living module and onto the sofa bed. "I want you out of my face. I'll let you know when it's my turn."

Toshi grunted and stomped to retrieve his virtEgo. Levi shut himself in the cockpit and scrolled through the control panel menu. His finger hovered over the module-ejection icon. He no longer needed the kid and getting rid of a witness was tempting. Although it would spell death for the kid, as he

GALAXY GRIFTER

was unlikely to be found off a main route, and it wouldn't be worth losing the module for. Not before he got *Caerus* back. He minimized the menu, emptied his pocket, and heaped the data cards he'd taken from the *Vulture* onto the control panel.

Please be good. He prayed for the cards to hold anything of value. Medical breakthroughs, politicians' dirty laundry... either of those would fetch a price on the black market.

Among the ordinary cards he spotted a shiny square, black with red veins. He brought his virt over it. Nothing. It wasn't a GU standard device. He opened the hatch to the module and held the square between his finger and thumb. "Kid, is this what I think it is?"

Toshi glanced up from his virtEgo. "An A'turi data card? Where did you get it?"

"The storage locker below the control panel," Levi lied.

"Huh. They usually hold the specs for new hyperdrives. We once hijacked a cargo ship full of them. But you need a decoder to read it."

Levi closed the hatch again.

The squid-like A'turi weren't part of the Galactic Union. They barely interacted with the other races, and yet they supplied the entire galaxy with antimatter hyperdrives used for faster-than-light travel.

Levi set aside the unreadable data card and spent the next four hours scanning the files on the standard ones. His virt translated the Jaemlen texts into Supayuyan—pages and pages of research, message exchanges, and briefings on the costs of terraformation, planetary profiles, and antimatter mechanics. Absolutely none of it looked sellable.

Fighting an onsetting headache, he opened another file titled "Memorandum on Operation Tetakoraa." He read it once and then again, more thoroughly.

Sneaky bastards.

According to the memo, a bunch of Jaemlen politicians had gone behind the GU's back to strike a deal with the A'turi. A deal that secured them the blueprints of the coveted hyperdrives "as a gesture of goodwill and continued cooperation."

Cooperation on what? The hyperdrives were the only A'turi export. They bartered it for raw resources. What did the Jaemlens offer them? What was Operation Tetakoraa?

Finding no further references or explanations, he studied the A'turi data card with a newfound interest. It could be a different card. Chances were, it held nothing of value. On the other hand, it could be the exact card mentioned in the memo, making him a holder of a very expensive secret.

He needed a fucking decoder.

Two tedious days later, *Comet985*'s onboard computer asked its passengers to prepare for landing. Levi and Toshi buckled into their seats, and the ship fell through a white discus, exiting hyperspace.

At first, only a red dwarf—one of many in the Tetra star cluster—showed through the viewport. Minutes later, a grey, potato-shaped planetoid came into view. It hurtled toward them until it blocked out its sun.

"Been to Blackjack before?" Levi asked.

GALAXY GRIFTER

Toshi's expression darkened. "Grew up here."

A translucent dome bulged from one of the craters that pocked the asteroid's surface. It appeared to swell like a blister as the *Comet* descended.

Levi followed ground control's instructions and docked the shuttle to one of the jetties that protruded from the side of the dome like a snail's antennae. He killed the engine and unfastened his safety belts.

Toshi stood from his seat, opened the hatch, and looked over his shoulder. "You coming?"

"No." Levi stayed seated. He'd avoid showing his face on the asteroid if he could help it.

"Why? What are you going to do?"

"That's my business. Off you go, and shut the hatch behind you."

"But the shuttle—"

"What about it?" Levi pulled the blaster from behind his back.

Toshi backed away, nearly tripping.

"I saved your life, now bugger off." Levi stood and stepped forward. "And remember, if the Shadow League learns you jumped ship like you did, they'll kill you. And if you tell anyone I was with you, *I'll* kill you. Got it?"

Toshi turned and ran down the hermetic airbridge that led to the spaceport, evidently forgetting to shut the hatch like Levi had told him.

"Kids these days…" Levi shut it himself and returned to the pilot seat. He placed the blaster onto the control panel and expanded his virt screen. Once it connected to the local

Instarnet, he called Kru, a Huxoran hacker he'd worked with on a number of jobs.

Like all Huxorans, Kru had a sharp, pointy face, round ears on the top of his head and a wisp of brown hair between them. He blinked his black, beady eyes. "Levi? It's not waking hour in Tuhxun."

"But you're up." Levi shrugged. "I need a quick hand with a ship's rego."

Kru's ears twitched. "You still haven't paid me for the conference pass."

"I will. Just need a registration to get off this rock and I'll transfer the payment."

Kru opened his mouth, froze, and disappeared from the screen, replaced by a rotating circle. The call disconnected.

"Fuck." Levi tapped the screen repeatedly until the connection returned.

Kru reemerged, nibbling on a white, palm-sized jurobha seed.

"Blackjack's usual connection issues," Levi said.

Kru shook his head. "I am unable to do jobs if you do not pay me."

"But this is easy."

"No."

"Fine." Levi opened his wallet app and sighed. His financial situation was even more dire than he remembered. "How about half now—"

"No." Kru bit on the seed with a defiant crunch.

Levi transferred the going rate for forged registrations. "Happy?"

GALAXY GRIFTER

"Happy." Kru nodded. "Connect me to your ship's computer. I will give you a clean record in about three hours."

Levi glanced at the dashboard clock, automatically adjusted to Blackjack's eighteen-hour day. Twelve o'clock, late afternoon. "Kru, do Jaemlen warships with no insignia ring any bells for you?"

"Bells?" The Huxoran looked confused by the expression.

"Have you heard of them?"

"No. Why?"

"Heard some sighting rumors. What could they be? Jaemlen pirates?"

"Jaemlens are not known to have organized piracy. Usually rumors are just rumors."

"Hmm..." Levi scratched his chin. He didn't trust Kru enough to divulge what had occurred on the *Vulture*. "There's actually another thing I wanted to ask: Can you decode this?" He retrieved the A'turi square from his pocket.

Kru moved closer to the display as though to take a better look. "If you have a translation cube."

"Can you find one?"

"Not on Huxor. You Humans took them all for your knowledge temples. Jaemlens did too. The Human Department of Xeno Affairs translate engine specifications for free."

"They'll get me arrested for free too."

Kru peeled another jurobha seed. "You are on Blackjack? Grandpa Lou may have one. I saw one at the back of his shop once."

Levi perked up. "Didn't know you had a grandfather on Blackjack."

41

Kru shook his head. "Not my relation. But Huxoran. Operates a thrift shop. Many gadgets that are hard to find. I am surprised you do not know him."

"I don't come here often enough to make acquaintance with every lowlife." Levi glanced at the bleak desert beyond the porthole. He washed up here more often than he cared to admit, usually when he had no other options. "So, where can I find this grandpa?"

***

Blackjack's spaceport had to be the ugliest in the galaxy. A stuffy hangar of unfaced metal attached to the dome's outer perimeter. Clingy vendors called from makeshift stalls, offering everything from drugs to medical procedures. Yet, Levi had to admit, the place had a particular kind of charm. Like the proverbial rock bottom one had to hit to turn their fortunes.

He was barely twenty the first time he'd washed up here, having lost his sheltered life, a cushy future, and the respect of his parents (though his mum had eventually come around). Yet, if he hadn't run, he would've lost his limbs one by one, or so Carver's men had promised. He imagined that would've been painful. Looking back, he couldn't see things working out any other way. Stealing was what he was good at.

He weaved past the stalls and travelers hurrying to and from the docks. The bustle gave him access to a few poorly guarded pockets. Too bad he still wore the suit from the conference. Here, it stuck out like a sore thumb. Hopefully he'd be gone before word of his arrival reached the Pooch and his mutts.

GALAXY GRIFTER

A girl with pink hair and cutoff shorts brushed against him near the exit. "Lookin' for a good time?"

"No thank you."

She tried to slip her hand into his pocket.

He caught her wrist. "Tell Ting I'll stop by if I've time."

Startled, she backed off.

Amateur.

It'd be a while before she realized she no longer had her virt. Slipping it into his pocket, Levi stepped through a scraped sliding door onto the street.

Dust settled on his shoes as he maneuvered past the bountifully strewn rubbish. A fat Earthen rat dove into a dumpster. A rusty all-terrainer leaned to one side near the junk-processing factory.

A bunch of old folks sat on a grimy couch next to one of the grey residential buildings. Eyes fixed on him, they muttered to one another.

He awarded them with a contemptuous smirk and slid into a side street to inspect the contents of his pockets. They'd grown heavier after his stroll through the spaceport.

He retrieved a pair of shiny AR glasses, a thick chain made of a yellow metal he presumed was gold, the virt he'd taken from the hooker, and a small maglock bag filled with a luminescent powder. Not much, but it would supplement his waning k-bit account.

The sheets of metal that paved Main Street made an unpleasant clatter as he stepped on them. A noisy group of teenagers wandered down the road.

"You lost, mister?" one of them called. The others laughed.

43

Levi continued past shoddy shop fronts until he reached a faded sign: LOU'S CURIOS. Shards of glass glistened on the ground below the sign. He looked through the smashed window. The shop stood empty. Lude graffiti tags and burn marks decorated the inner walls.

Shit.

He popped his head into the businesses next door. A large woman sat in front of a mirror. A young, curvy brunette stood behind her, holding a comb and scissors. She turned, startled, and clipped a large chunk of hair off the top of her customer's head. She gasped, seeing what she'd done, and tried to cover the damage up with the surrounding hair. The large woman didn't seem to notice.

The hairdresser turned to Levi and smiled. "Would you like a cut, hon? Grab a seat, I'll be with you in a little while." She was cute, but he wouldn't let her touch his head even if she paid him.

"I'm good. Just wanted to ask what happened to the shop next door." He leaned on the doorframe.

"Oh, Lou's? It closed down." She walked up to him with a sway of her hips. "Lou... passed away."

"A real loss to the community," the large woman said from her seat.

"A shame," Levi said. "Nobody took over the business? What happened to all the stuff he was selling?"

"It was auctioned off. You're Levi, right?" the girl asked. "Were you after something?"

"Yeah. He's been holding a trinket for me since my last visit."

GALAXY GRIFTER

"Oh, it's probably gone, hon. I'm sorry. But you could check with Aishen. He handled the estate stuff."

"Aishen?"

"Mortuary Services, a few doors down." She pointed to the street. "Can't miss it."

"Thanks."

"No prob." She kept smiling and twirling a strand of hair that fell past her deep cleavage.

The large woman looked over her shoulder. "Amelia! I ain't got all day."

"Coming, Scilla." Amelia rolled her eyes. "Hope you find what you're looking for," she told Levi. "Come back if you need a haircut or...somethin'."

"Will do." He dropped the smile as soon as he stepped outside. If the A'turi cube disappeared, it meant he risked coming into town for nothing.

He found Mortuary Services soon enough. Aishen, a balding old man with tawny skin and a potbelly, sat Levi down behind a plastic desk. "I could take a look at the register for you..." Aishen scratched his cheek.

Levi pulled the golden chain from his pocket and offered it to the old man.

Aishen wrinkled his nose but accepted the bribe. He locked it in the desk drawer and retrieved what looked like an ancient tablet. "Now, what was it you were looking for again?"

"An A'turi cube."

"What category is that under?" Aishen scrolled through a list.

"Alien translation devices?"

"Electronics. Here it is. Sold to O'Mara, Vera, for ninety-nine k-bits."

"Ninety-nine?" Levi scoffed. Even he would've been able to afford that.

"I had to get rid of everything and that was the highest bid. You think anyone on Blackjack wants to translate A'turian?"

"Don't know. Where can I find this Vera O'Mara?"

Aishen scratched his cheek again and Levi offered him the AR glasses. Aishen shoved them into the drawer with the chain. "Stellar. She's been running it with her brother since their dad kicked the bucket."

"Stellar?" Levi frowned. "You mean the dive bar?"

"Oh yes. But mind, it will get busy for Rogers Day celebrations."

"Rogers Day? Today?" Levi came here often enough to know about the local holiday, but the timing seemed unfortunate.

"Indeed. Thirty years since Captain Rogers saved Blackjack from getting blown to smithereens."

"Shit..." The last thing Levi needed was a mass gathering. "What does a bartender need the cube for anyway? To use as a coaster?" He feared she might have resold it.

"Don't know, didn't ask." Aishen turned off his tablet.

Chapter 5

Rogers Day

With the next interest hike looming on the event horizon, Vera crunched the numbers. They'd be fine this month with the profit that would roll in for Rogers Day, but then things would slow and...They'd never pay off their debt. It'd be easier to burn Stellar down and stowaway on the next flight offworld. Maybe that's what she'd do, if her stubborn brother wasn't so intent on staying here.

"Hello, are you with us?" Nina, a miniature blond mechanic, waved her hand in front of Vera's face.

"Yes, sorry." Vera snapped back into the reality of her living area. The girls sat round a plastic table in her tiny kitchenette. It merged with a living area, suggested by the presence of a sofa. The staircase behind it led to her bedroom. Her apartment had no pictures or souvenirs, no character furniture pieces, only the neutral colors of a temporary dwelling.

"You were saying?" Vera reached for a half-empty chip bowl, wondering how much of the conversation she'd missed.

Amelia, with her luscious black locks and lashes, set aside her mirror and mascara wand. "I asked if you were going to get dressed. We'll miss the fun at this rate."

Vera glanced at the time. "I'll grab something." She stood and headed upstairs.

Nina caught up to her. "Are you okay?"

"Fine, just tired." Vera shrugged, refusing to share her problems. She and Fred would figure it out on their own. Somehow.

Amelia downed her drink. "I'm coming. I need to supervise."

The bedroom looked as bland as the living room. The portraits of Vera's dead parents, flanking the bed like judgmental gargoyles, were an exception to the otherwise blank space. She went through her wardrobe, filled mainly with jeans and T-shirts. Amelia, who always dressed like she belonged on an Erian runway, pushed in next to her and pulled out a red cocktail dress. "This one."

Vera chuckled. "That's what I wore to James's wedding." Her oldest brother was the lucky one that snuck off to Seshat before Mum died and was now living the life Vera could only dream of.

"So? We get to do this once every two years only. We're gonna party like it matters." Amelia held out the dress.

"No." Vera glanced at each of her friends. Amelia wore a body-hugging, posy-green number and Nina was only slightly more casual in tight pants and a top made of decorative zips. *Where did they even find this stuff?* "Okay, whatever." She grabbed the dress, slid into the bathroom, and closed the door. Xiu, her sister-in-law, helped her pick it out at one of Xinlouyang's malls—the only time Vera had been off-world. She sighed and changed. Four years later, it still fit but felt ridiculous in the current context.

When she came out, Nina sat on the bed. "Holy huxifruit. I can see why Niran fell for you."

Vera forced her lips into a tight smile. "Actually, we bonded over our appreciation for trashy wavecore." She'd met her ex at the wedding, and he'd been the most promising thing that had happened to her in the last decade. Smart, kind, and legally employed. But they'd been so young... it would have been unfair to drag him into the mess that ensued after Dad's passing.

Amelia, who took it upon herself to refold all the clothes in Vera's wardrobe, gave Nina a stern look and winked at Vera. "You look great, babe. We'll find you a better off-worlder."

Vera scoffed. "You and your off-worlders."

"What?" Amelia shut the wardrobe door. "Not like the locals have much to offer. No offense, Nina."

Nina crossed her legs. "Why would I be offended? I'm happy with Ahn." She'd been with her on-again, off-again boyfriend since their school days.

"I'm sure. You only broke up fifty times so far."

"Better fifty times with one, than once with fifty."

"Ah!" Amelia cast an incinerating glare at Nina.

Vera stepped between them. "Can we just go already? I didn't take the night off to watch you two bicker."

The sun had set by the time the women stepped outside. At the end of the alley, Stellar's sign glowed neon blue against the burgundy slice of the evening sky visible between buildings. A couple made out against the wall. The drone of people flocking for the celebration flowed from the pub. Vera kicked a beer can out of her way and it clattered past other rubbish. The piles would grow overnight. More work for Rusty tomorrow. A lanky, pale man preached from atop an overturned rubbish bin. "Will you forgive the Universal Council for Humanity for what they've done? What they *tried* to do? This so-called government took our one true home and then tried to destroy what was left of us."

Nobody paid attention to him.

Outside the pub, a group of delinquents too young to be allowed inside laughed, whistled, and catcalled. "How much?"

Nina clenched her fists. "I'll shove that hoverboard up your arse!"

The teens relented, knowing the tiny mechanic meant business.

Inside Stellar, the girls pushed through a congestion of sweaty patrons and joined Ahn and his friend Clyde at a high table. Ahn jumped from his stool and pulled Nina in for a theatrical kiss. The others cheered.

Amelia surveyed the room with a sour expression. "Not many new faces."

Ahn slapped his forehead. "Almost forgot. Vera, a guy came in looking for you."

Vera's stomach dropped. "What guy?" Since her mum died,

any suggestion of unexpected news forced her body into panic mode.

"Levi what's-his-face," Ahn said.

"The Weasel," Clyde clarified in a world-weary tone.

"You mean what's-his-*gorgeous*-face." Amelia grabbed Vera's arm. "That's the hottie that stopped by the salon today. Wait… why is he looking for *you*?"

"No clue." Vera relaxed a notch. As long as it wasn't to tell her someone died, or that the Pooch wanted more of her money, she didn't care. Though she felt a tad curious as to why the infamous Weasel was back on Blackjack. From what she'd heard about him, pretty much half of her small, shithole planet wanted him blown to bits. Maybe the guy had a death wish.

"Want me to ask him? He left his number." Ahn raised his virt to his face.

Nina slapped his hand down. "Don't. You've heard the stories about him."

"That the Pooch wants him dead?" Clyde asked.

"Those too," Nina said. "And that he's a level-eighty scumbag."

"Don't be so boring." Amelia's eyes glinted like laser beams.

Vera stood and collected the empty glasses from the table. "We're not calling anyone. I'll get us more drinks."

Amelia pouted. "Fine, but you're not gonna work tonight."

"Of course not."

Behind the bar, Fred spun like a rotor, pouring drinks, taking payments. Having grown a shabby red beard, he looked even more like Dad. Vera's throat tightened. Dad's sudden passing had nearly cost them Stellar and everything else they'd owned. They'd put up quite a fight, before the Pooch agreed to buy out their debts and resume protection of the watering hole. Since then, he'd taken most of their income and bumped up the rates as he pleased. She chased the thoughts away. They'd agreed to work alternate Rogers Days. Tonight was Fred's turn and she wasn't going to waste it.

She squeezed past the queue and stood the empty glasses in front of her brother. "Sup, loser."

"Sup, pipsqueak. Remember Rib?" Fred nodded at a round-faced man beside her.

Vera recognized Fred's closest school friend who'd left Blackjack years ago. He looked older, but they all were.

"He's just got in from Mars," Fred said. "Came to check on us wretches."

"Rib!" She gave him a brief hug and, noting he didn't have a glass, slipped behind the bar. "I'll get you a drink."

"Vera, you look...different. I should be getting *you* a drink." Rib looked surprised, reminding her she had that stupid dress on.

She poured him a beer. "It's okay, I get them for free. Want to join me and my friends? Fred's boring company when he's working."

"Nah, I'll just..." Rib looked around hesitantly. He was always a quiet one.

"Fine, I'll take these drinks down and will come find you. You can tell me all about Mars." She dropped off the drinks and promised her friends she'd be back soon. Leaving Rib alone for the whole night felt mean.

Rib's life as a financial consultant in the Deuteronilus Megalopolis sounded entirely unremarkable. She itched with envy.

"How are *you* doing?" he asked after his second glass. "Fred mentioned troubles with the overlord. Anything I can help with?"

"Nothing we can't handle." She smiled. "We're doing pretty good actually."

She *hated* it when her brother complained to his friends. As long as nobody knew of the mess they'd been wading through, she could at least pretend life was okay. If she was doomed to rot in this hole, she'd rot with dignity.

"That's good." Rib nodded. "Good to hear."

Vera took the awkward pause that followed as a cue to excuse herself. "I promised my friends I'd hang with them—you sure you don't want to come?"

"That's not one of them, is it?" Rib pointed behind her.

She turned. Nina climbed onto a table, yelling, her voice dulled by the music and chatter, so Vera couldn't tell what or at whom. Given Nina's miniature stature, it never took much to render her senseless. Amelia circled the table, trying to pull her friend down.

Vera stood. "I'm afraid so."

"I'll let you go," Rib said. "I'm staying with Fred, so maybe I'll see you at the apartment tomorrow?"

"Maybe." Vera rushed to prevent a catastrophe.

"Get yourself together, pixie," Amelia scolded. "I'm not carrying you home."

She and Vera managed to get Nina down and back to Vera's

apartment. They left her to sleep on the couch before heading out again.

Outside, Amelia turned her frustration to Vera. "Shame on you. You totally ditched us for chubby. What's up with that?"

"Rib's not chubby, he's big-built. And a solid guy, by the way. Decent, unlike some people. With a proper job in finance, an apartment on Mars—"

"Really?" Through Stellar's window, Amelia eyeballed him with a newly spiked interest. "So are you guys like...?"

"No." Vera shook her head. "He's Fred's best friend. I wouldn't..."

"Why?"

"You don't screw siblings' friends." That was the best excuse she could offer.

Amelia twisted her lips. "Okay. But is he married or something?"

"No. C'mon, I'll introduce you." Vera grabbed Amelia's hand and pulled her inside, toward Rib.

———————————————— • ————————————————

By midnight, Stellar grew even noisier. The celebrators moved tables aside to make room for dancing. Amelia got off to an unexpectedly good start with Rib. She giggled at unfunny jokes and Vera started to feel like a third wheel. Was this party boring or was she just too old for it? She rested her head on her fist and watched Rusty wheel out a feral patron, trying to start a fistfight. At least pirate crews weren't using the place for a shootout, like last time.

GALAXY GRIFTER

"I'll get more drinks." She took the empty glasses from the table and meandered past the stumbling dancers.

A bellow jerked her from her apathy. "Shots! Shots for everyone!" One of her former classmates, Jake, bought a round for his buddies. He wasn't a friend, but she'd seen him around and heard he worked at the factory and dealt stars-knew-what on the side, like every other local.

"Vera, you look banging," Jake boomed as she loaded the glassware onto the bar stand.

"Thanks. You look wasted."

"That I am. Want a shot?"

She gave the tiny glass an appraising once-over. Her only other option was to call it a night. "Sure." Forty milliliters of burning liquid slid down her throat and the colors around her seemed to grow brighter.

"You dance?" Jake asked.

"Sure."

They danced and had more shots, and the pub blurred into a fluorescent kaleidoscope. He got inappropriately close. But at least the party stopped being so boring, so she didn't care. She didn't care about the disapproving looks from Fred, who soon got too busy to disapprove, and didn't care when Jake whispered something smutty into her ear—she even laughed. She didn't even care when he led her toward the toilets until somebody grabbed her arm and yanked.

"Take a break," they said, and Jake backed off into the crowd. *Pussy.*

Someone pressed her against the wall. "Are you Vera O'Mara?"

It took her a moment to register her own name and the haze in her eyes started to clear.

The Weasel loomed over her like a hawk over its prey—sharp features, dark, glistening hair. In his fitted suit he looked glaringly overdressed for a dump like Stellar and the asteroid in its entirety.

"Oh shit, it's *you*. What do you want?" she mumbled.

"I've done you a favor. You're clearly past the point where this could be consensual."

"It's none of your—" She tried to push past him, but the room swam before her. She held on to the wall for balance. *What was in those shots?*

"You *are* Vera?" he asked.

"Yes."

He flashed her a movie-star grin. "Lovely. I'm Levi. I'd offer to get you a drink but…"

"I c…can't." Her tongue felt as heavy as the rest of her body.

"I can see that." He pulled her away from the wall, took down one of the chairs stacked in the corner, and sat her on it. "Stay here."

With the artificial gravity working against her, she had no other choice.

He disappeared in the direction of the bar, returned with two glasses, and handed one to her. "Water."

She gulped it, noticing how dry her mouth was.

He took another chair down and sat opposite her. "Better?"

She nodded, embarrassed and puzzled in equal measure.

"So, you work here?"

"Yes." She wondered if that made her look even more pathetic.

GALAXY GRIFTER

"What else do you do? Interests, hobbies?"

"Not much." Other than getting drugged in her own pub, apparently.

"I see. Do you know much about the A'turi?"

"What?" The question caught her so off guard, she thought she'd hallucinated.

"A'turi—squid-like aliens, make nice FTL engines."

"Yeah, but nobody knows much about them." She wondered if he was also high, or if this was just her trip.

"Exactly. Makes them fascinating, doesn't it?" He unbuttoned his fitted jacket and lolled back in the chair as though making himself more comfortable for the conversation, which he, evidently, intended to continue. "I love learning about other cultures and languages," he said. "Someone mentioned you might share that interest."

A'turi? Cultures and languages? She replayed the apparent nonsense in her head. Then it dawned on her. "Oh...because I bought that cube a few months back?" She'd all but forgotten she owned the thing.

"Have you still got it?"

"Yeah, but I can't code now."

"Code?" He narrowed his eyes. "You know how to decode A'turian texts?"

She'd read about it. "I..." She remembered the conversation she had with her friends earlier and the fact she'd planned to stay away from this guy. "No."

"Didn't think so. But if I were to borrow the cube for a night..." He leaned toward her, haughty, imposing.

Her chair scraped the concrete floor as she pushed it back.

57

"Wuh— Why didn't you think so? The cube works with, uh, binary logic, it's not rocket science." She had nothing to prove, but he'd said it with so much arrogance...

"And if it *is* rocket science?" he asked.

"The content may well be, but you'd use the same algorithms for the translation, whether it's physics or nursery rhymes." *If* the A'turi wrote nursery rhymes. She laughed at the thought—tales of little squidlings dancing around or whatever. It was so funny to her in that moment that she couldn't stop her cackling.

"Fascinating."

"Well, yeah, they made the cube for humanoids, so—"

"Not the cube, *you*." He cocked his head to one side, drilling her with his gaze. "I take my words back. I think you *can* decode A'turian texts."

If this was a victory, why did she feel like she'd talked herself into some kind of trap? "I...don't want to." She tried to stand, but he caught her wrist.

"Vera..." He took her empty glass, gave her the second one, and looked her straight in her eyes. "You're clearly a smart girl. Have you never wanted to leave this place? Build a life on a more hospitable planet?"

Only every fucking day. A sobering chill crept down her arms.

He moved even closer, smelling very clean. "If you get the cube, you and I could leave tonight. And if we find a way to decode this"—the shiny black square of an alien data card materialized between his long, slender fingers—"it'll solve all our money woes."

Her breath caught in her chest for a painful second. Like

GALAXY GRIFTER

a magician, this man spoke to her deepest desires and made solid objects appear from thin air. But she couldn't trust him. "I'm not going anywhere with you." She wriggled her wrist free of his grip, yet her gaze lingered on the data card. Thin, red lines danced across its surface like firing neurons as a desperate thought germinated in the depth of her troubled mind.

Chapter 6
The Bend

"I'll walk you." Levi caught Vera's elbow as she rose to her feet, careening.

Their encounter had been a perfect disaster, just like that hideous dress she was wearing. It was several years out of date and clashed with her copper-colored hair, which, along with the dimple on her right cheek, were her only redeeming features.

On the upside, if anything she'd said was true, she still had the cube and she was willing to help him decode the file. On the downside, she had refused to show it to him until morning, which was longer than he wanted to wait.

She jerked away from him. "I'll walk myself, thank you."

He almost rolled his eyes. "I'm not trying to hit on you. Not if you don't want me to. But we've got a job to do and I want to make sure you get home in one piece."

"I'll manage."

Zigzagging, she walked toward a couple making out at the

GALAXY GRIFTER

far end of the bar, and rather skillfully detached the girl—who turned out to be the hairdresser from earlier that day—from her plain-looking suitor. Together, the women staggered to the exit.

Levi followed, trying to stay out of sight. The girls turned into an alleyway next to Stellar's sign and disappeared inside a building.

He watched the lights in the windows turn on and then off again and tried the door. Locked. A smart lock he couldn't pick without the right tools.

He inspected the window frame. He could probably find a crowbar. But what if he didn't find the cube and merely spooked the redhead? She already seemed skittish, like a ginger kitten that someone tried and failed to drown. Plus, if she really had the skills to decode the file, he could avoid a trip to Huxor and Kru's exorbitant fees.

He'd have to work harder to gain her favor, but she'd crack soon enough. They all did. Except Wendigo, stars rest her soul. He just needed somewhere to spend the night—preferably not on the *Comet*.

He returned to Main Street and headed in the direction of the spaceport, keeping to the shadows to avoid unwelcome encounters, until he arrived at a building with a red sign: THE BEND. A bouncer towered in the doorway.

Levi flashed his teeth. "Madam Ting's expecting me."

The bouncer moved aside, and Levi jogged up a set of stairs toward the sounds of an exotic string melody, and into a room faced with mirror fragments that reflected the strobing red lights and an array of nude body parts.

"Levi." Madam Ting, a slender woman in her fifties, stepped into his path before the owners of said parts could flock to him with offers of services. Ting led him to her private chamber, styled with carpets, drapes, and cushions in blues and purples.

"You're back." She smiled.

"Can't stay away." He sat on a low divan and stretched out his legs. From his pocket, he retrieved the virtEgo he'd taken from the hooker at the spaceport and passed it to Ting.

"It was you? Rosie said a handsome man had stolen her virt."

"Tell her she tried to pick the wrong pocket."

Ting locked the virt in a cabinet. "She shouldn't be picking any pockets, unless she wants to get killed. I'll have a word with her." She took an espresso pot off a small burner and poured him a cup of coffee.

He inhaled the steam and closed his eyes. "The only decent drink in this shithole."

"Is that the real reason you came to see me? The cops haven't asked about you in years." She sat next to him.

"Not the only one. I like talking to you. And...you're my only insurance policy." He passed her a holo-note with dates and times, in case he needed an alibi. "I don't have much money, though."

"It's okay. I'll tell them what you need me to." She slipped the note into her own wristband. Her smile was a sad one.

He didn't know her story, but he knew that her blue-black hair, styled sleek to one side, concealed a gruesome scar that ran from her ear to her collarbone. She lit a cigarette and forced her expression into a cheerier one. "Did the lunar artifacts not bring you the good fortune you'd hoped for?"

A lump caught in his throat, thinking of all the enhancements to *Caerus* he'd bragged about getting once his antique scheme panned out.

"Not what I'd hoped. But I think this time I've struck something bigger."

She exhaled a bittersweet wisp of smoke. "That won't matter here unless you've paid the Pooch back. Have you?"

"Not yet." He didn't want to think about that now. "I would, if I had the coins."

"Levi—" She patted his knee. "You must pay the boss. Or leave Blackjack. The sooner the better."

He held her gaze awhile. Her concern was sweet. Motherly almost. Except his mother wasn't an aging hooker. He made a mental reminder to call his actual mother, once things settled, and placed his hand on Ting's. "I've got this. I fought off a Sehen at my last gig. A giant fucking Sehen. And that's before slipping past military-class ships mid-battle. Think I can't handle the Pooch's mutts?"

She stubbed her cigarette out on a brass tray and stood. "This isn't a joke. Sehens or not, you don't want to get on the wrong side of this gang. They've killed for lesser transgressions." She touched her neck for a brief moment and lowered her hand.

Levi rolled his head back. "There's no profit in killing me. Come on, Ting. Sit down, have a drink with me."

Ting stepped to the side of the door. "I have to ask you to leave."

"What?"

"I'm sorry. But I have my workers to think of. Come back once you've sorted things out with the Pooch."

"Wow, some welcome back, Ting. Fine." He stood, not bothering to conceal his disappointment. He'd hoped to crash there during the night on some fancy, feathery couch—way better than being stuck on a cold, cramped escape transport. "You still have my stuff?"

She disappeared behind a partition and returned with a small case.

He took it and clicked it open. Inside were a change of clothes, toiletries, and a small bottle of single malt whiskey. Not the cheap stuff they sold at Stellar. He put the bottle into his inner jacket pocket. "Can I at least get some of that magic tea of yours?"

She arched her thin brow. "Are you planning on a big night?"

"It's not for me. It's for...a friend."

Levi stepped onto the dark street, walking toward the port and begrudgingly accepting he'd have to sleep on the *Comet* after all. Oh, how he missed *Caerus*—his bedroom with its perfectly firm mattress for one, the light routine that kept the room dim to his precise specifications. Nothing on this forsaken planet could even come close to comparing to the comfort of his ship.

Through the nanocomposite tiles of the dome, the stars

GALAXY GRIFTER

looked like smudges across the black sky. His mind raced to spend the money the blueprint would bring him. But first, he'd need to sell it. He knew of three companies with the capabilities to manufacture hyperdrives: the Jaemlen Thesaan Belu, the Human Logic Interstellar, and the Huxoran HEB, whatever that stood for. The most profitable would be to make them fight for it—an auction. But that could attract unwanted attention, and the encounter with the warships had left him spooked. Additionally, Thesaan may have been in on the Jaemlens' deal with the A'turi, so he'd prefer to stay away from them. That left LI and HEB. A big part of him wanted only LI to have it. If Humans were the first in the Union to replicate the A'turi hyperdrives, they'd gain a significant economic advantage. And who knew what indirect perks that could bring.

When he reached the industrial blocks, a flier zoomed past him with its headlights off. Flying too low, it raised a cloud of dust and came to a sharp stop in front of him. He coughed, turning away. Three figures stepped from the flier: a Huxoran; a large, bald Human; and Blackbeard, the mutt-in-charge. Though these days he should have been called Greybeard. The thick, tight coils that covered his chin and scalp had turned the color of aluminum. The leather on his jacket looked worn and faded to a dusty taupe. Yet, for an old man, the fucker looked enviably sturdy, with broad shoulders, a barrel chest, and a demeanor that left Levi no desire to challenge him. Blackbeard sauntered forward. "Well, well, if it ain't the Weasel."

Ting had been right. Levi's luck had run out. It was time to improvise.

He threw his arms open. "Blackbeard! You're out late. How's your arm? Still made of tinfoil?"

Blackbeard snickered. "I thought folks were lying when they'd reported sightings of you."

"Sightings? You make me sound like a rare phenomenon."

"You're a slippery fuck, that's what you are." Blackbeard stopped. "I assume you have my money?"

"I do."

"Oh? So I won't have to kill you?" He grunted and spat a lump of phlegm into the dust. "Disappointing."

"I live to disappoint." Levi tapped his virt and made a transfer; parting with the last of his money hurt.

Blackbeard checked the balance on his wrist. "Five hundred? You owe fifteen grand."

"It's the first installment." Levi had learned that even a small payout could make a big difference for a reluctant mark. Like an appetizer, it kept them locked in the game. And he really needed Blackbeard to keep playing. The alternative would be an ultimate game over.

"You ain't on no fucking installment plan." Blackbeard raised his prosthetic fist.

But Levi's mind was several steps ahead by now. "I've got something better for you." He pulled a holographic file from his virt—an academic paper from one of the Jaemlen data cards.

Blackbeard stared at the hologram. "What is that?"

"Terraformation research, pages and pages." Levi flicked through the document.

"You brought fucking research?" Blackbeard glanced at his

GALAXY GRIFTER

thugs. They laughed and he grabbed Levi's collar. "Do I look like a fucking scientist?"

Levi tried not to flinch. "You look smart enough to know a good deal when you see one. This is unpublished and valuable. I'll have a buyer before you know it. Give me two days."

"You're shitting me, right?"

"He's full of shit," the Huxoran goon behind him said.

The Human goon, who was twice Levi's size, stepped forward. "I can help smash his face in."

"You know, you're right. You've no cause to trust me," Levi said.

The thugs exchanged glances.

"But why would I come here, if it weren't for profit?" He held Blackbeard's gaze.

Blackbeard spat on the ground again. "How the hell should I know? Maybe you think it's funny? Or maybe you've got a death wish."

Levi glanced at the ground and then at the thugs, one by one. "If you think that's more plausible, go ahead, kill me. But then, that five hundred will be the last you'll get from me."

For a small eternity, Blackbeard drilled into Levi through narrowed eyes. His two thugs shuffled from foot to foot in the background. Finally the cyborg released Levi's collar and grabbed his case instead. He tossed it to the other Human. "Check what's in here."

The bald guy fiddled with the case until it swung open and Levi's belongings fell to the ground.

Baldie picked up a shampoo bottle, opened and sniffed it,

67

and took a swig. He spat out a mouthful of foam and dropped the bottle. "It's fucking soap!"

Levi cringed. "Yeah...Keep it, if you like."

Blackbeard pressed his good hand to his face. "Idiots." He stabbed Levi in the chest with his metal finger. "Thirty thousand, in two days, or I kill you."

"Yes, sir." Levi saluted. Whatever the increase, he wasn't planning to pay it anyway. He just needed more time.

His bravado faded as he watched Blackbeard and his two idiots stomp off. He was sure he hadn't seen the last of them; the thugs would try to spy on him, but an anticipated tail wasn't hard to lose. For now, Levi had cheated death yet again. Still, the task of finding a buyer for these damn blueprints had become a most pressing issue.

That chick better be clearheaded enough to read these first thing in the morning, Levi thought as he finally reached the *Comet*'s hatch and slammed it shut behind him.

Chapter 7
The Cube

"Please kill me." Vera rolled onto her side, away from the daylight that streamed through her eyelids, enveloping her in pain and nausea. *I'll never drink again, on Blackjack or elsewhere*, she thought as the door creaked. She opened her eyes begrudgingly.

Nina entered the bedroom, enviably fresh-faced and helping herself to a bowl of cereal. Vera gagged. "Are you immune to hangovers or somethin'?"

Nina shrugged. "What happened last night? I've got partial amnesia."

Amelia sat up on the other side of the bed, makeup smudged and hair tangled into a bird's nest. "You broke up with Ahn, were a little asshole to us, and made a complete idiot of yourself."

"Ah, that explains the thirty missed calls." Nina loaded another spoonful into her mouth and headed downstairs.

Surprisingly, Vera remembered everything. The memories

came flooding like a blocked toilet. What was she thinking, inviting the Weasel to her apartment? She glanced at the time. *Shit.* He was going to be here in less than an hour. Fighting the nausea, she got out of bed and staggered to the kitchen. "Guys, I've got work today, so you gotta pack up." She popped a couple of painkillers and downed a glass of water.

"What?" Nina put her empty cereal bowl into the sink. "You're working today?"

"There's something urgent I nearly forgot about." Vera gathered yesterday's glassware.

"Is it virt stuff? Can I just stay in bed while you work?" Amelia called from upstairs.

"Yes...No. I'll explain later." Vera paced the apartment collecting her friends' belongings.

Once she'd managed to kick them out, she cleaned herself up and searched for information on the workings of A'turi decoders. The pages took their sweet time to load, thanks to the ever-slow Blackjack connectivity. Thank goodness the Weasel was known to run late. Maybe that was her cue to back out, pretend she wasn't home, and...*Stay on Blackjack forever.* No. She didn't trust his promises, but if she could get her hands on his data, if it really contained something valuable enough to settle her debt, or even a part of her debt...She hadn't quite figured how she could try to steal a file from a thief, but she had some time. She just had to stall.

Someone knocked on the door and she stood to open it. Levi wore a suit—possibly a different one from yesterday, although she wouldn't vouch for it—over a white shirt, and a subtle scent of shady forests and tropical beaches. She'd

GALAXY GRIFTER

never smelled either of those, but that's the imagery her mind painted. He gave her a once-over. "You look different."

"Sober?" She tugged on her ponytail, avoiding eye contact.

"That too. How are you feeling?"

"Like shit. Come in." She stepped aside, gesturing at her kitchen table. A fist-sized metallic box stood atop it, connected to her work virt, its screen expanded.

"I'm impressed you remembered. This is for you." He handed her a small paper bag on his way in and took a seat at the table.

She peeked into the bag at what appeared to be green sawdust, which smelled of dried mushrooms. "What is that?"

"An herbal tea. Doesn't taste great, but helps with hangovers."

"No thanks." She tried to return the bag, but he raised his hand.

"Drink it—it'll make things better, trust me."

"Thanks." She rolled the bag up and put it next to her virt. Trusting him with anything ingestible was the last thing she'd do.

The A'turi cube glowed faintly red, providing Humans with the only peephole into the minds of the A'turi. At least it would, once she got it to work.

He conjured the data card from thin air again and placed it into her palm. "I'm counting on you."

She turned it over. It looked similar to the card that had come with the cube, except that one had fewer squiggly red lines on it, and contained some ship's engine's specs, nothing more. What secrets did this card hold? Did stealing it from a

71

swindler make her as bad as him? Her parents would probably say so. But they were dead, and being good got her nowhere. "How big is the document?"

"Large, I'd guess." He said it with so much aplomb, she forgot for a second that he was talking about an alien file.

"Uh...right. I want three hundred k-bits, up front." She figured asking for money would help mask her intentions.

He chuckled. "I want my own planet and for the UCH chancellor to sing me lullabies. I've got no proof you can do this, other than you saying so while high."

"I *didn't* say so."

"You strongly implied it."

She huffed and placed the card on top of the cube. The interface on her virt's display flickered to life with a soft hum. Nothing weird, just a red insertion point blinking over a dark background. She positioned her fingers over the virtual keys projected onto her tabletop and typed in the first line of code—a simple recursive algorithm. Nothing happened. Well, *almost* nothing. The hum changed to a lower frequency, suggesting a process was underway. After a brief moment, the first output emerged on the screen.

It was *not* Supayuyan, nor any language she recognized. Overlapping shapes filled the window, forming patterns like...fractals, surrounded by visual noise. *Oh-kay...* The instructions she'd studied failed to mention this happening. She minimized the terminal and queried a search engine. It'd be embarrassing if she flopped on the very first step.

"Everything okay?" Levi leaned in to peer at the screen.

"Not sure. I think your card is using multilevel encryption;

GALAXY GRIFTER

it's stacking values like pancakes." Her palms sweated under his smug gaze. "Each layer might need a different decryption key, but we'll see what happens."

She isolated a section of the fractal, narrowing the data to reduce waiting time, and tried a different script. The output shifted, unraveling the fractals into less complex constructs. The noise diminished. She refined the parameters and ran the script once more. On the third attempt the terminal blinked and spat out a chunk of Supayuyan text, numbers, and formulas.

Got it! The corners of her mouth twitched upward.

Levi's pea-green eyes glinted as he stared at her screen in amazement. "Where'd you learn this?"

"Coding? Right here, mostly. And at Stellar, during downtime."

"Self-taught, huh?"

She nodded, though the question annoyed her. Obviously she had taught herself. Unlike her oldest brother, James, she never got to go to university. At twenty-four, she no longer dared to dream about any higher education.

Levi scratched his clean-shaven jaw. "You hack?"

"No. Why, do you want something hacked?"

"Nothing. Just wondering, for future reference. Why don't you?"

Because she needed a clean record. Blackbeard never paid her a coin for fixing his virt. If the gangsters thought she had other skills they could use, they would never let her leave. "Knowing a little code doesn't make me a hacker. And... don't tell anyone I'm doing this."

"Okay...why'd you buy the cube?"

"I was curious. Will you tell me what we're decoding? My operating system thinks it's physics, but the output's fragmented. We'll need to piece it together."

"Antimatter mechanics." He held a pause as if considering whether to tell her more. "It's an A'turi hyperdrive blueprint."

"A *what*?" Out of all the things he could have said, she was really not expecting *that*.

"A blueprint. For the hyperdrive that everyone uses but no one can replicate." He looked more than pleased with himself.

She whistled. Humans, Jaemlens, Huxorans—none of them could even reverse engineer the drives. Sure, faster-than-light travel existed long before the first contact with the A'turi. But back then, it would have taken an Earthen month to get from here to Seshat. The A'turi drives reduced this to about fifty hours.

Which meant this document was a huge deal. She didn't know what it meant on a galactic scale, but to her it sang of freedom.

Several hours later, Vera had decoded about eight pages and heard as many stories from Levi's biography, each more fantastical than the last. Space pursuits, pirates, Sehens. He didn't really think people believed him, did he?

The decoding process proved to be repetitive. And yet, she couldn't see a way to automate it. Why did such an advanced race use such an ineffective method? What purpose did

GALAXY GRIFTER

it serve? She adjusted the script again. "I had a theory that maybe the A'turi are nonverbal and interact entirely through mathematical concepts."

He looked thoughtful for a second and then finger-gunned her. "Don't say that to anyone."

She was about to ask why but saw him smirking. "Too nerdy?" she guessed.

"A great way to alienate people." He cringed at his own pun.

"Terrible." She forced her mouth into a straight line. Somehow, laughing at his bad jokes while trying to steal his data irked her conscience.

He stood and paced back and forth in the little space between her kitchenette and sofa. For the first time, she grew unpleasantly aware of how worn and tired her flat looked. He stopped next to her fridge and pulled the door open.

She almost jumped to her feet in outrage. "Hey! It's rude to look into people's fridges."

"Why? You've clearly got nothing to hide." He stepped aside, revealing the empty shelving. "Do you not eat?"

She gritted her teeth, fuming. "If you're hungry, there's cereal and milk powder in the cabinet."

"That sounds awful."

"There's a takeaway next door."

He reached for the bottle of gin the girls hadn't finished last night. "May I?"

She nodded. The thought of alcohol knotted her stomach in a fresh bout of nausea.

He poured himself a glass and flicked on the kettle. "So you don't hack, I get it. But surely you can use your skills to get yourself off this shit-rock?"

She clenched her jaw even harder. "Some people call this shit-rock home."

"Only because *some* people are useless."

"You seem to like it well enough. Or you wouldn't return so often." Her fingers tapped furiously on the virtual keys as she changed the script.

"Every few years is not often. And I only drop by for work. Living here must be miserable." He poured boiled water into a mug and tipped out the contents of the paper bag. She hadn't seen him take it from the table. She glanced at where it had lain before and made a mental note to check her belongings before he left. Not that she kept any valuables downstairs...or had any valuables at all besides her diagnostic goggles and her parents' old wedding rings. And those were more sentimental than worth anything much.

A mushroomy smell filled the room. He brought the drinks over and stood the mug in front of her. "It's really not that bad."

She side-eyed it.

He sat down and swigged his gin. "I have a theory too, you know?"

"Of course you do."

"The A'turi can handle our comms just fine. They don't want to."

"Oh?"

"They're being intentionally obstructive. Maybe they think they're better than everyone."

"Are you sure you're not one of them?"

GALAXY GRIFTER

He ignored her dig. "But once Humans know how to build their engines, we won't need the squid. So, you and I are doing Humanity a favor."

"Is that what you tell yourself? Does it help you sleep at night?" She didn't want to change the world or mess with the galactic economy. She just wanted her debt paid.

He raised his glass. "I don't have trouble sleeping. Do you?"

"Not with self-medication. Where did you get the file anyway?"

"From a place." He grinned.

She glanced at the tea again. Surely if he wanted to poison her, he'd wait until after she'd finished decoding. She took a small sip. Earthy. But not sickening.

Another hour had passed when she leaned back in her chair and rubbed her eyes. "This is all I can do today. It will take a couple more days to finish."

"A couple more days?" He frowned. "I don't have that much time, Vera. Can you do it faster?"

"Let me check." She snapped her finger. "No. I'm working at Stellar tomorrow, so you'll have to come back the day after."

"No, no, no." He stood, shaking his head. "This is urgent. Every time I go out there"—he pointed at the window—"I risk losing my life."

"The Pooch still wants you dead?"

"You've heard about that?"

"It's a pretty well-known fact, *Weasel*." She put extra emphasis on the scathing nickname.

"Well, there you go." He sat back down, picked up the glass, and stared through it despondently.

"Why though?" She wasn't sure she wanted to know or that he'd tell her, but the question seemed unavoidable. "Why does he want to kill you?"

"He thinks I owe him. Money I can't repay."

Well, finally they found a common ground. Vera averted her gaze. Levi Adder was an insufferable ass and probably as bad as people said he was. But he'd practically rescued her from Jake, and he brought her this kind of gross tea, which she hated admitting had alleviated her headache. But he still owed her for the work. She didn't believe for a second that he would actually take her off Blackjack—Levi seemed like a person who decidedly traveled solo—but perhaps there had to be another way she could profit from this. He needed to pay her. Not a measly hourly rate, but a percentage of the profits he'd make on the sale of the blueprint.

"I need to sleep," she said. "And I can't let you stay here. But you can leave the file and I'll see how much I can get done at Stellar, in between customers."

"No." He put his glass down. "I'm not leaving the file, and doing this at Stellar is too risky."

Vera was on the verge of frustrated yelling at the con-man, when her virt started ringing. Fred. *Shit*. He had messaged earlier to say Rib had helped him tidy Stellar up, so he should've been home by now. She motioned for Levi to be silent, to which he responded with an eyeroll and a swig of the gin bottle, and she answered.

"Hey, pipsqueak, how are you feeling?" Fred asked in a mocking tone.

"Not great actually."

GALAXY GRIFTER

"You're not supposed to after a party. That's the price of fun."

"It's not just that." She wondered whether to tell him about Jake and the drugs but decided not to. Fred would probably kill the guy, and she didn't need that right now. But she did need something from him. She sighed. She hated pulling this card, but it seemed to be the best way to get on with the coding and get the Weasel out of her life as soon as possible. "I'm on my period and I feel so . . ."

"Ugh, what are you saying?"

"I'll need another day tomorrow."

"You serious? Will painkillers not help? I'm dead after last night."

"I know, I'll make it up to you. I just really feel like shit, Fred."

"Oh-kay . . . Do you need to see a doctor, you think?"

"No. But I will if I'm not better tomorrow."

"Okay. Hope you feel better, pip."

"Me too. Talk soon." She hung up, feeling guilty. Fred would thank her later though, if it all worked out. She was trying to get this debt paid for the both of them.

Chapter 8
Stir-Fry

When Vera opened the door the following morning, Levi shoved a grocery bag into her hands. She peered inside: no tea this time, just half-wilted carrots, frozen broccoli, and other food items.

He marched past her into the flat, hung his blazer onto the back of a chair, and rolled up his shirtsleeves. "Hungry?" He took the bag from her and carried it to the kitchen bench.

"No." She didn't want to sabotage the delicate truce she'd struck with her stomach after Rogers Day.

"Oh well. You get things started and I'll join you once I'm done." He tossed the A'turi card to her.

She caught it. "And what do you think you're doing, exactly?"

"My joke of a ship doesn't have a cooktop, and I can't stomach another expired flight meal."

She scoffed. "Sure, make yourself at home, then."

He took her invitation way too literally and rummaged

GALAXY GRIFTER

through her cabinets. She'd object, but what good would that do? Instead, she settled at the table and got the scripts running.

He found a pan and whatever else he was looking for and started chopping. "The produce here is shocking, but it's something, right?"

She shrugged. It's all she'd known. For some reason, she imagined Amelia making a comment about Levi Adder cooking in Vera's kitchen and her face warmed. Hell no. She wasn't going to blush on his account. Her mouth began to salivate as the cooking smells intensified. Twenty or so minutes later, he rolled down his sleeves, filled a single plate, and started eating, leaning against the bench.

"Ahem?" Vera raised her palms in question.

"You said you weren't hungry."

"At the time." Her stomach assented with a doleful mewl.

He filled another plate and set it in front of her: multicolored flora with chicken-flavored protein and crispy...whatever that was. She coded one-handed as she ate. It turned out she had been very hungry.

He sat opposite her. "You won't tell me it's the best meal you've ever eaten?"

"No." It was pretty good, but she didn't want to encourage him.

"You'd be more likable if you were less prickly."

She nearly threw her fork at him, dart-style. "I don't want to be likable."

"Sure you do. That's how you get ahead—opportunities."

"As if you'd know. You're not actually likable, you're a narcissist."

"People like confidence. As long as you give them a carrot and pretend you're listening." He waggled his fork with a slice of the orange vegetable on it.

"Is that how you got the blueprint?" she asked.

"Sort of."

By the time the evening rolled in, they'd gotten through about 80 percent of the document, and 100 percent of his stir-fry. Yet she still needed to decide how she would ensure he paid her. Maybe she'd lock the document, or a part of it, as he'd need to show something to the potential buyer. Then, once he got the money and transferred her share, she'd give him the password to unlock it. Or maybe she'd plant a virus... now was the time to use the brain cells she'd suppressed for years. Even if she felt slimy for doing so.

The cube spat out paragraphs of decoded text in no particular order. Levi proved to be quite apt at stitching it together, like a puzzle.

"There's a good chance we'll finish by morning," she said.

"Then will you come with me?" he asked, casually, like it was actually an option.

"What? No! I'm not going with you anywhere."

"Huh. And I thought you were starting to like me."

"You thought wrong." Heat crept up her cheeks like a traitor.

Someone knocked on the door. She tensed, and he threw her a questioning glance.

She stood. "Who is it?"

The hoarse voice crashed down on her like a bucket of icy water. "You have to ask? It's Blackbeard. I've got a message from the boss, open up."

GALAXY GRIFTER

On legs made of cotton wool she walked up to the door. "I'm not working today. Fred's at the bar if you want to talk."

"I want to talk to *you*. Open up, Vera, or I'm blowing the door off. Five, four, three—"

"Wait." She tapped the lock.

Blackbeard charged into the flat with two others. One of them, a Huxoran, grabbed her and pinned down her arms.

"Where is he?" Blackbeard barked.

She looked behind her. Levi was gone with all the equipment. He'd probably leave through the bedroom window. Still, she saw no reason to make this easy for the gang. "Who?"

"The Weasel." Blackbeard waved his arm and his second thug, a hulk of a man with a shiny bald head, dashed toward the staircase.

The Huxoran dug his fingers into her shoulders, dragged her to a chair, and shoved her into it.

"Ow!" she gasped.

"Gentlemen." Levi trotted down the stairs before the hulk reached them. "Let's talk."

The hulk greeted him with a blow to the jaw, then the solar plexus. Levi doubled over. He tried to block the next punch, but the hulk twisted his arm, threw him onto the floor, and climbed on top. He dished out punches until Levi spewed blood.

Vera flinched.

"Search him," Blackbeard said.

The hulk patted Levi down and, finding nothing else, yanked the virt off Levi's wrist and stood.

Blackbeard approached and kicked Levi in his ribs. He curled up and moaned.

"Did you think I'd fall for your science bullshit? Took a while to figure out where you've been going. Apparently you've been looking for an A'turi cube?" Blackbeard pinned Levi down with his boot and pointed a gun at his face. "Where's the alien document?"

"Upstairs, in the bathroom," Levi croaked. "Under the sink."

Blackbeard waved his hand and the hulk hurried up the steps. Blackbeard planted the boot firmer into Levi's chest. "What's on here?"

"Some sort of A'turi space tech. Lots of formulas."

"Where from?"

"A black hole auction in sector 22. They said it was from a wreckage."

"Who said?"

"Suarez... A guy named Victor Suarez, that's all I know." Levi coughed out the words. "I bid forty grand. Hoped it'd go for more once translated."

The hulk returned with both devices—the cube and Vera's work virtEgo. He handed them to Blackbeard.

"Forty grand, you say? Guess that covers what you owe us." Blackbeard tapped the virt's screen. "The password?"

"Vera, unlock it," Levi said.

Blackbeard held the comm out to her and she scanned her iris and fingerprint. "I'll take the password off so it won't lock again." She fiddled with the settings, granting herself remote access, and then unlocked the virt and handed it back to Blackbeard.

He glanced at the screen, shoved it into his pocket, and pointed the gun at Levi again.

GALAXY GRIFTER

Vera shut her eyes. No shot sounded and the gangster laughed.

When she looked, he'd bent down and pulled Levi up by his shirt. "I better not see you here again, Weasel." He spat and let go. Levi's head dropped onto the floor with a thud. Blackbeard signaled to his thugs and they gathered to leave.

"And you..." He pointed the gun at Vera. "You should be more discerning about the company you keep. Until you learn, you'll report to me with everything you're working on. Understood?"

She nodded, holding back all the screams in her body.

Chapter 9
Backup

Vera remained in the chair after Blackbeard and his thugs had left, then stood and stumbled over to Levi, still sprawled on the floor. He looked in a bad way, his lip busted and his left eye swelling shut. His shirt was ripped and bloodstained. She bent over. "Are you breathing? Should I call a doctor?"

"I'm fine." He wiped his face with his shirtsleeve, which turned red.

"You don't look it." She offered him a hand.

He groaned, stood, and staggered to the sofa.

"I'll get ice," she said.

"And painkillers."

Her personal virt lay on the kitchen counter, among the dirty dishes. She snapped it onto her wrist and handed Levi the meds and the ice pack. "Why didn't you climb out the window?"

"Couldn't stand the thought of what they'd do to you."

"Oh, please." She'd eat her virt before she believed that.

GALAXY GRIFTER

He cringed as he swallowed a fistful of pills. "There were more men outside. They would've shot me down like a rabid squirrel if I'd stepped on that ledge. Figured I'd fare better in a fistfight."

She wouldn't call it a fight, but compared to being shot, he probably *did* fare better.

"Fuck!" He punched the armrest. "They knew exactly what to look for."

"I didn't tell them." She sat on the opposite end of the sofa.

"I believe you."

"You do?" That was ironic, because she would have told them, if it weren't for her stupid conscience. She probably should have, because now, neither of them would see the money. Unless...

"I bet that ratbag Aishen told them. The one who led me in your direction." Levi buried his face in the ice pack.

She expanded her virt and remoted into the one Blackbeard had taken. It worked. She doubted Blackbeard had gotten the chance to read the file, and wouldn't know if she'd messed with it. "You said you bought the file at a black hole auction."

"Yeah..."

"Did you really?" Black hole auctions were contraband sales in obscure outer space locations. They had nothing to do with black holes except that they left no tracks for Starpol to follow. Apparently Blackjack started as one, but people ended up staying.

"Of course not. What does it matter now?"

"If I told you I'd backed up the translation and the original—could you still sell it?"

"The translation's not finished…" He licked blood off his lip. "I guess. But if the Pooch sells it first—"

"I can scramble the decoded text, say I've botched the translation. They'd need to find someone else to decode it again, which would take time—"

His good eye glinted. "Do it."

"I want half of the profits." Her fingers hovered over her virt screen.

"Fine."

He wouldn't try to bargain? Odd. She supposed he was as desperate as she was. She typed in a command corrupting the file. "It's done."

"We need to get out of here."

She shook her head. "I've already told you I'm not going anywhere with you. I…I can't just leave everything."

"Leave what? This shithole?"

She flinched. "My brother, for one, and he won't leave Blackjack."

Whenever she'd asked Fred, his answers had been categorical: "You go, I'll manage." But he wouldn't manage. Not on his own. He needed Vera to take care of him.

Levi paced to the window and back. "That's his problem. Will you let that money slip from under your nose?"

"What if they hurt him?"

"For something you did? Who's going to run the pub for them? I imagine you pay protection, not to mention the number of deals that take place there."

He had a point, and she wouldn't be able to forgive herself if she lost her one chance. After all, it was for Fred as much as for herself. She rolled the hem of her T-shirt between her fingers. "I can't go," she whispered, trying to convince herself more than him.

"Okay." He outstretched his hand. "Give me the copies."

She looked at him, then at the files on her virt screen. If he took it, she'd never see the money.

"I'm not waiting around for the mutts to come back," he said.

"Where would we go?"

"Tiberum on Rebecca, the headquarters of Logic Interstellar."

"Can't you just call them?"

He started to laugh but winced, as though in pain, and pressed his fingers to his still bleeding lip. "Give me the files, Vera, I'm not messing this up more than we did already."

She huffed, stood, and pushed past him toward the stairs.

"Where are you going?" he asked.

"To pack my things."

In the depths of her wardrobe, she found a duffel bag and stood it on her bed. Mum and Dad's portraits looked down from the wall, disapproving. *I'm doing it for Fred, too*, she said silently. She had to believe it, or guilt would eat her alive. She approached a chest of drawers and bent to open the bottom one. The stairs creaked. She straightened and spun around.

Levi stood in the doorway, his once-pretty face bruised and disfigured. "I'll use the bathroom?"

"Sure."

She waited until he closed the bathroom door behind him, then pulled the bottom drawer all the way out and reached behind it to retrieve a small toolbox with her most prized possessions: the diagnostic goggles, a few data cards, including the spare A'turi one she'd gotten with the cube, and a small bag with her parents' wedding bands. She placed the box at the bottom of the duffel, slid the drawer back, and grabbed a couple of T-shirts. How many would she need? She packed a clean pair of jeans and opened her underwear drawer.

The bathroom door opened. Levi had washed most of the blood off his face but sported red marks on his right shoulder and his bare, lean torso. "It was an expensive shirt." He scrunched up the ruined garment in his hands.

She looked away, feeling her cheeks heat, hating herself for this reaction. Her life had turned upside down, and she was blushing over some swindler? "I might find you a T-shirt," she said.

He walked to her bed, reached between the headboard and mattress, and retrieved a blaster, which he tucked into his belt. "One thing the mutts didn't find. Hope you don't mind that I hid it here."

She turned away and searched through her drawers until she found her ex's T-shirt. She'd told Niran not to visit her. She hadn't wanted him to see Blackjack, but he'd come anyway. They'd made plans that she'd move to Seshat. Then Dad died. She passed the T-shirt to Levi, trying not to look at him, yet feeling his gaze drill through her.

"Do you mind?" She gestured at the door, intending to pack her underwear without his supervision.

GALAXY GRIFTER

"No." Instead of turning to leave, he stepped toward her. "You do realize we'll be stuck for days on a very small spaceship?"

She hadn't thought about it, but her pulse quickened, sending a tingle down her back and arms.

He leaned and kissed her.

His broken lips tasted of metal, and felt like a gulp of absinthe, burning its way down her chest and stomach, dissolving into an intoxicating pulsation. Vera went through a frighteningly quick range of emotions: shock, anger, embarrassment, glee. She hadn't been kissed like that in a long, long time.

"There," Levi said, pulling away, a smug grin on his face at her still stunned expression. "To break the tension. Now get your underthings in a bag and let's get the hell out of here."

Chapter 10
The *Comet*

Vera and Levi had walked along dark backstreets to the spaceport, quite uneventfully. Yet inside the busy, brightly lit hangar, Vera felt painfully exposed. She struggled to keep pace with Levi's long strides as her gaze shifted between the faces of passersby, expecting the next one to be Blackbeard's.

"This way." Levi pulled on the sleeve of her hoodie and led her toward a boarding gate. He tapped on the screen by the entrance to the bridge to request departure.

"Next departure slot available in two hours," an automated voice said.

Vera glanced over her shoulder, paranoia getting the best of her. "We should've requested departure earlier."

Levi waved his hand. "Relax. Blackjack's the only place you can still jump the queue."

"What? How?"

"Stay here." He disappeared inside the airbridge, leaving her alone with her anxiety, and reappeared about a

GALAXY GRIFTER

minute later, holding a small bottle of Earthen single malt. "C'mon."

They headed away from the departure gate, toward a door labeled GROUND CONTROL. He gave her the bottle. "You do it. Just say you're looking for Yuri and you're in a rush at gate fifteen."

"What?"

"I don't wanna raise questions." He pointed at the bruised side of his face, knocked on the door, and disappeared in the crowd before she could object.

The door flung open. A grey-haired man with a puffy, creased face looked at the bottle, then back at her.

"Uh...hi," she said. "I'm looking for Yuri."

He frowned. "What do you want?"

"I was wondering...Is it possible to move forward the departure time for gate fifteen?"

"No."

"No?" She glanced around but couldn't see Levi nor a better idea.

When she looked at the man again, he was beaming, his round cheeks pushing up to his eyes. "I'm just messing with you." He took the bottle. "What time do you want?"

"Now?"

"Okay. Give me ten minutes." He shut the door in her face.

A second later, Levi walked up to her. "How'd it go?"

"Yuri said to give him ten minutes..."

"Cool." He strolled in the direction of the boarding gate. "Are you coming?"

"Wait, is that...is that it?"

"Yep. C'mon, gotta buckle up for takeoff."

She caught up to him. "This had nothing to do with raising questions, did it? You just wanted to put me on the spot."

He chuckled.

"How can you laugh in this situation? It's like you enjoy having your face rearranged."

The port's intercom beeped: "For technical reasons, expect slight delays for spacecrafts stationed at gates three, seven, and fourteen. Gates three, seven, and fourteen, expect slight delays for technical reasons. We apologize for any inconvenience."

The text above gate fifteen read: *Eight minutes to departure.*

"Works every time." Levi gestured for her to go first.

At the end of the airbridge, he reached over her shoulder to open the hatch. They stepped inside. The small cockpit looked aged, dusty, and not dissimilar from the ones she'd seen while fixing onboard computers. The hatch shut behind them and they buckled into the seats. She pulled up a text screen from her virt.

Levi frowned. "Who are you messaging?"

"My brother. To let him I won't be at work and—"

"I wouldn't."

"But..." Her chest squeezed painfully, like she was some traitor.

"The less he knows, the safer he'll be." Levi put his hand on hers.

He was probably right. She disconnected her virt from the network and shivered. She'd never felt so vulnerable before— she was truly on her own now. Well, with Levi...for the better or worse.

GALAXY GRIFTER

The onboard computer started the countdown.

Ten... nine... eight...

Vera's pulse quickened. This would be her second time in space. The first was for James's wedding.

Seven... six... five...

Levi looked calm, bored even. From this side, she couldn't see the bruising, only a chiseled profile, almost perfect, if not for the slightly beaked curve of his nose.

Four... three... two... one...

She shut her eyes. The *Comet* shot upward and her insides shriveled in protest, despite the effects of the g-forces being mitigated by the ship's gravity panels. Once they broke free of the orbital pull, the feeling eased. She dared to look through the porthole that revealed only darkness bespeckled with distant stars. Blackjack could be seen on the rearview screen—a grey rock with flecks of ice, a source of both water and oxygen.

"Not much of a view if you ask me. Have you seen other worlds?" Levi asked.

"I've been to Seshat once, for my brother's wedding."

"I thought your brother—"

"I have two of them."

The ship changed course and the asteroid came into direct view. The dome that held the settlement resembled a tiny snow globe, sans snow.

"It must've cost a fortune to build," Levi said. "A pity we've missed the Shadow League's heyday."

"Speak for yourself." She felt no pity. Yes, pirates built her homeworld, but they also terrorized the whole galaxy, threatening Humanity's status in the GU. They also forced the

UCH to wage a full-scale war on piracy that nearly ended with Blackjack's annihilation.

The spaceship accelerated and her nausea returned for a few moments, and then hyperspace swallowed them.

"It is now safe to leave your seats," chimed the onboard assistant.

———————————•———————————

Levi had been right. There was no space in the *Comet* for inhibitions. A sofa bed, a utilities panel, and a tiny lavatory took up all of the living area.

He folded his blazer and placed it into the storage compartment, took off Niran's T-shirt and shoved it, unceremoniously, into the garbage disposal unit. "Want a coffee?"

Asshole. That shirt wasn't his to dispose of, but whatever. She wasn't going to start off this trip fussing about her ex's clothes. "No." She stepped back to the airlock that separated the cabin from the cockpit. She could sleep there. Or, better still, kick *him* out to sleep in the cockpit.

He came up from behind and wrapped his arm around her. "I know this is a bit shit, but I'll take you aboard *Caerus* when I buy it back. Now *that's* a spaceship." He brushed her hair aside and kissed the side of her neck.

She needed to tell him to stop, to draw a professional boundary instead of melting into him like a heroine of a cheap romance novel. Her body thought otherwise.

———————————•———————————

GALAXY GRIFTER

Vera lay on the sofa bed with her virtbook, struggling to focus on the words, rolling and unrolling a corner of the blanket between her fingers. Had she ever wondered what sex would be like with a self-absorbed narcissist, she might've been surprised. On her short list of lovers, Levi was the least inattentive. He studied every inch of her with the interest of a xenobiologist vivisecting a rare A'turi mollusk.

On second thought, it made sense. The man did chase and sell information for a living. Why sleep with her though? To make her easier to manipulate? Or because it was a game to him, like everything else? Whatever the case, she wouldn't let him win. She didn't need to like him or trust him to take advantage of the situation.

He stroked her cheek, moving a strand of her hair away. "Where do you want to go, once we have the money?"

"Seshat."

He frowned. "Really? Why? It's an industrial desert planet."

"Xinlouyang is a livable city, and...I don't know, where would you go?"

"Sandabur. It's a paradise world of tropical beaches. Eria is nice too, if you get a chance, but I can't go there."

"Why not?"

"Banned. I was young and stupid." He sighed, got out of bed, and filled two mugs with instant coffee. He tried to open the fridge door, but there was not enough space.

"Dumb ship." He tried to kick the bed, tripped, and nearly lost his balance. "Fuck!"

She suppressed a snicker, stood, wrapping herself in the blanket, and pressed a button. The bed folded back into a sofa, allowing for more maneuverability. She got dressed and sat down, reopening her virtbook.

He handed her a coffee. "It's—"

"You don't need to tell me it's shit," she said. "I don't know any better."

"Right." He sat next to her. The swelling on his face had gone down due to a restorative cream he'd found in the *Comet*'s med-kit, but the darkened purple bruises remained. "I've got an idea for how to complete the translation."

"How?"

"Have you heard of the Brezni Brothers?"

She shook her head.

"They run an underground ship parts op on the moons of Lagan, but their office is in Tiberum, and they most definitely have an A'turi cube."

"You want them to decode the remainder?"

"I don't have the funds to pay them, and I wouldn't trust them anyway, but I know how to get them to do it for free."

"Okay..." She set her virt aside.

"If we placed a large order, say, five hyperdrives, and told them the specs are in A'turian, they'd offer a free translation."

"What happens when they see that it's not hyperdrive specs they're translating?"

"We'd tell 'em we've got the wrong stuff and promise to sort it. It's only twenty percent or so, and since the code doesn't come out in order, without the rest of the file, it won't look like much. Why would someone translate nonsense if it's not an honest mistake?"

She shook her head. "It sounds risky."

"Hardly. But there *is* a nuance."

"What?"

"You'll need to be the one to meet with them."

"What?" she scoffed.

"I owe them money."

"Of course you do. I'm not doing it." She picked up her book again, indicating the conversation was over.

He didn't take the hint. "Why not? It's a great plan."

"I'm not getting mixed up with Rebeccan gangsters. Pulling one on Blackbeard was bad enough. You can sell it as is, I'm sure."

"We don't know how key those missing parts are. Maybe Logic Interstellar can fill in the blanks, but what if they can't? If we sell them the A'turi original, they'll have a legal obligation to notify the Department of Xeno Affairs. And the DXA might launch an investigation."

Another reminder of how deep above her head she was. "And what will they find? Where did you get the blueprint, Levi?"

"I found it on a pirate ship. I don't think the pirates knew what it was." He had given a different answer each time she'd asked.

"And where did the pirates get it? What if it was Logic Interstellar's in the first place?"

"It wasn't, but we should finish that translation."

She shook her head. "I didn't sign up for this."

"But you want your fifty percent, don't you?"

She glared. "You've already agreed to that. Without me, you'd—"

"Without you I'd be miserable, but without your stubbornness, my face would be nicer to look at and we'd still have the cube." He moved in closer and whispered into her ear, "Why did you copy the original in the first place?"

Every muscle in her body tensed. "For backup. I've lost work due to tech crap-outs before. I back everything up." She hoped that didn't sound defensive.

He slumped on the back of the sofa and sipped his coffee. "Right now, I can't even afford docking fees. If we fail, I'll be out on Tiberum's streets picking pockets."

That sounded grim, but at least he had a contingency. Unlike her.

"We can't fail," she said.

"Exactly. That's why we need the complete document. All I'm asking is for you to meet with them. You don't even need to request the translation, they'll make that offer."

"And if they don't?"

"You'll walk away. Business deals fall through all the time. They won't even remember you."

She sighed. "What if the Breznis ask to see the money?"

He pursed his lips. "We may be able to show them the money. If I chat up Logic Interstellar first, I could get a deposit into a limbo account."

"An account you can't withdraw from?"

"Yep. The funds will be locked until they have the file, but the Breznis won't need to know that."

Vera sighed. It was like he had an answer for everything. "And what if the Pooch already told them about the file? He, too, will want someone to decode it, remember?"

GALAXY GRIFTER

Levi shook his head. "Not the Breznis. The Pooch hates their guts."

"Why?"

"Turf wars. Most stolen space tech used to go through Blackjack until the Breznis set up shop near Lagan, under the cover of a perfectly legal mining outlet. Even the Shadow League dump half their loot there now. The Pooch is losing profits."

"How do you know this?"

"I research. The Pooch won't talk to them, rest assured."

She rolled the hem of her T-shirt between her fingers. Maybe she had cause to meet the Breznis after all.

Chapter 11
Rebecca

Vera looked a stranger to her own reflection as she dabbed holographic makeup onto her face. She'd bought the tiny kit at Tiberum's spaceport where the *Comet* was now stationed, along with the blond wig. She'd read that the reflective particles in the makeup gave face-recognition software a hard time. Probably a lie. She just didn't want Brezni to know what she really looked like. Just in case. Their meeting was scheduled two hours from now.

Next to her, Levi worked on his own face, covering up the bruises more skillfully than she'd know how to. "Only show them the money if they ask. And don't leave the café with them. I'll be right there, just out of sight."

That gave her little comfort. Her palms were sweating. "What if they ask why I need five hyperdrives?"

"You want to build a power station on an asteroid."

"Is that possible?"

"In theory. I'm not asking you to build it, only to mention

GALAXY GRIFTER

it if they ask."

She pulled on the wig and her diagnostic goggles. They had a thin frame and could pass for a regular AR accessory.

He gave her a once-over. "That's some camouflage. We'll be counting the coins in no time."

———————————— • ————————————

Drones circled the café floor with orders of food and drink. The Beancup, in the heart of Rebecca's Tiberum megalopolis, looked packed yet pristine. The calming beige and browns of the interior seemed to absorb the chaos. A blond man, wearing a blazer over a plain T-shirt, walked up to her table. He looked to be in his forties, with a face so jagged, it might have been hacked from a tree stump using a blunt axe. He pointed an open hand at her in what may have been a Rebeccan greeting. "Miss Black? I'm Isaac Brezni."

She stood to acknowledge her pseudonym. "Nice to meet you."

"Can I get you a drink or anything?" he asked.

"I'm fine, thank you." She pointed at her tall glass of iced coffee and sat back down.

"Ah, yes, Tiberum is sweltering this time of year." He took the seat across from her, selected his own drink from the holomenu, and drilled into her with his small, shifty eyes. "May I ask who you work for?"

"Do you care?" She'd seen enough of these kinds of meetings at Stellar to know how they went.

"Just wondering how you heard about us."

"We've used your products before."

"Really? I'm sure I would've remembered if we'd met."

"I'm sure you would've, but we have many faces."

"Yours must be the prettiest."

"That's kind of you. But it's not what I'm here for."

"Of course." He nodded politely. "So you want five whole hyperdrives? At once?"

"Is that a problem?"

"No problem. How will you be paying?"

"Cash."

"Can you show me the money?" His piercing gaze made her sweat more than the city's humidity.

"You know how it goes, you show me yours..."

His grin revealed crooked teeth. "I'll show you nothing before I know you're for real. You don't tell me who you are, or who you work for, and expect me to trust you?"

"Fine, I'll go first." She slapped her virt onto the table. It showed an anonymous kilo-bitcoin account with a five-digit balance—a deposit Levi managed to secure from Logic Interstellar just that morning.

Isaac held his own virt above hers. It chimed its readiness to transact, proving the account was genuine. The fact the money was in limbo and couldn't be withdrawn was a small detail he wouldn't know. He hummed in approval.

Vera snapped the device back onto her wrist. "Is that proof enough for you, Mister Brezni? Or shall I take my money elsewhere?"

"That won't be necessary. What specs are you after?"

"About that..." She bit her bottom lip. "There's been a small hitch. The specs are still in their mother tongue. I was supposed to receive the translation this morning, but that didn't happen and I'll be out of town tomorrow. I can send you the details as soon as they come through, and we can meet in a...fortnight? Perhaps then you'll have something to show me too."

He rubbed his chin, glancing at passersby. "Do you have the original? We could get it translated for you today."

"That's unnecessary. I've got arrangements in place. It's just taking longer than expected."

"No, really, it's no trouble and I'm happy to do that free of charge."

Just as Levi had promised. "If you insist, I guess..."

"Do you have the file?"

She showed him her A'turi data card, onto which she'd copied the untranslated remains of Levi's file.

"It may take a couple of hours. If you'd like to come to our office, we could get it done there and then. We have the equipment."

"Well...If you can get the equipment here, I suppose we could get it over and done with." There was no way she was leaving the safety of the crowded café.

"I don't understand. We're just five minutes away...It's private, it's quiet—we have a coffee machine too." He smiled. "I'm certain you'd be more comfortable there."

"I have my peculiarities, Mister Brezni. And really nothing to hide from the good people of Tiberum. What exactly do you think will happen if somebody looks over your shoulder and sees a page of space tech formulas? We aren't trading government secrets."

"Aren't we?" He narrowed his deep-set eyes.

She tensed.

Isaac leaned back in his chair. "Fine. You're the client, Miss Black, and the client is always right. I'll bring the cube and the programmer here."

"I appreciate that, Mister Brezni."

He stood. "I'll meet you back here in half an hour."

She forced a smile.

———————————•———————————

Isaac returned after twenty minutes, accompanied by a lanky young man with a chin full of fuzz that had yet to turn into stubble.

"This is Alex, our IT genius." Isaac slapped the youth on his back.

The genius gave Vera a limp handshake. Looking around, he slouched his backpack onto the table and set the devices up without taking them out fully.

Vera handed over the A'turi data card and an ordinary GU card. "Can you save the completed translation on this one?"

"Sure." Alex sat down and started the translation. It was obvious he'd done it before.

Ten minutes later, Vera excused herself to the toilet.

As soon as she entered the stall, she got a text message from Levi, who had been watching from the café's mezzanine:

>*where the hell are you going?*

>*I need to pee.*

GALAXY GRIFTER

She didn't waste time reading his next message. She closed the toilet lid, sat, and expanded her virt screen. She was hoping to remote into Alex's device via the card she had just given him. It was a long shot. He was unlikely to keep anything important in easy access, but given the Breznis' tense relationship with the Pooch, any information she could get would be more valuable to her than the blueprint. Her hands were shaking; why would she add an extra layer of recklessness into this adventure? She'd been out of her depth from the start, with no clear plan and changing direction, like a scrawny hare pursued by a fox. But no matter what, she had to settle the stupid debt so the Pooch's gang would leave her and Fred alone, for good. She had no guarantees Levi would pay her, so *this* was her plan B. There was no going back now.

She bypassed a rudimentary security setup and checked the file manager system through the terminal—empty. There was a shortcut to a nebula storage app, but it would surely require authentication. Or not...the password filled in automatically, with Alex's virt set up as a trusted device.

This was progress. She went through the files on the nebula. Transactions and technical information and...*Shit*. A client database! She pulled the files over into her own nebula, locked it up, and deleted all evidence from her virt's activity log. She collapsed her screen and exhaled. It was time to return to the Brezni and the tech kid and hope they hadn't noticed a thing.

The next hour and a half felt like an eternity. Alex coded silently, while Isaac made small talk. Vera feared that any minute he'd crack her for the fraud she was.

"I don't get this..." Alex pulled away from the screen. "It's a bunch of formulas and what looks like...assembly instructions?" He scratched his temple. "But it sort of ends midsentence. Was there another part somewhere?"

Isaac peeked at the text.

"Do you mind?" Vera stretched out her hand, and Alex turned the screen toward her. Vera scanned through the file slowly and, reaching the end, blinked a few times. "Are you sure you did it right?"

"Of course." Alex jutted his spotted chin. "There aren't many ways you can get this wrong."

"This must be a mistake." She glanced at Isaac, whose jaw was set hard, undeniably unamused.

"Give me a minute." She held her virt to her ear. "Hello? It's me." She paused. "I've got the translation of the engine specs and...it looks like your niece's science-fair project. It doesn't make sense. It's not the engine specs— Gibberish... Of course I'm sure— Do you even need to be asking? Yeah, you better do that quickly." She pretended to hang up. "I'm sorry, I'll get this sorted as soon as I can." Now she'd find out if they'd let her leave.

Isaac curled his lip. "You think I'm an idiot?"

"No..." Yet one could hope.

He extracted a small gun from his sleeve and pointed it at her, covering the top of it with his large hand. "You aren't walking out of here till you tell me what's going on."

GALAXY GRIFTER

"I . . . There's . . ."

The kid gasped. Vera raised her eyes from the gun. There was a red laser sight dot on Isaac's forehead. It crept down to his chest where he could see it, and back up to his forehead. He breathed heavily. Alex stared wide-eyed.

Vera threw a glance at the mezzanine floor but couldn't see Levi or where the laser was coming from. She looked back at Isaac. "It's an unfortunate misunderstanding."

"Indeed." Isaac slowly withdrew his gun. The dot disappeared. "What do you want?" His brow glistened with sweat.

"To part on friendly terms. I'll leave now, and you won't follow me. I'll be in touch once the mess is sorted."

"This is bad business, Miss Black."

"I'm sorry I've wasted your time." She stood and stretched out her hand. Alex returned the cards to her.

She left the Beancup and followed a route Levi had charted for her through a central city hotel, where she tailed someone into the elevator. It stopped on the fifth floor. She hurried along a corridor with doors on both sides, found a niche, removed her wig, makeup, and jacket, and left through the fire escape door, into an autonomous taxi that waited outside.

Sitting in the *Comet*'s pilot seat, Vera had just finished combining the decoded parts of the blueprint, when Levi stepped through the hatch, grinning from ear to ear. "Now tell me that wasn't fun."

She wanted to yell at him but managed to keep her voice

steady. "It wasn't. You didn't tell me I'd have to perform at gunpoint."

"Isaac took it way worse than I imagined. But I had your back. It's over now." He knelt beside her. "You were perfect. Now it's time to get our money."

She stood. "I'm coming with you."

"To LI?" He got up from his knees.

"Yes. I want my half transferred into my account."

He narrowed his eyes. "You think I'd fuck you over?"

She walked through the open hatch into the living module. There was no nice way of putting it.

He followed. "Really, after all we've been through?"

She poured herself a cup of water, avoiding looking at him. "I'm just playing it safe, okay?"

He sighed and walked up to her, no longer smiling. "You can come with me. But for the sake of disclosure, you should know your face will be in LI's database and no amount of camouflage will change that."

"So? They're a legitimate enterprise."

"Which means they have more levers to use, legal and otherwise, if they think you're a threat to their reputation or bottom line."

"So why are you going if it's so dangerous?"

He shrugged. "It's what I do. Got to embrace the occupational risks in this line of work. Although...I got a strong impression you were trying to keep your business as clean as possible. You can come, just don't say I didn't warn you."

She felt an urge to pace, to alleviate the frustration, but there wasn't room for it. He was messing with her head but, annoyingly, wasn't wrong. Above everything, she needed a clean record. "Fine, you go." She handed him the data card. "I'll send you the password for it once the money is in my account."

He looked confused. "It doesn't work like that. They'll want to verify the data before releasing the coins. That's the whole reason I can't just send it to them anonymously and expect them to pay."

"Negotiate then. You have leverage." She pointed at the card. All she'd incurred from this affair so far was anxiety.

"So it's all about the money to you?" His gaze threatened to pierce her.

"What else? You think I came on this trip 'cos I'm desperately in love with you and just had to follow you out into the stars for a grand life of idiotic scavenging?"

"Ouch." He slid the data card into his pocket and started toward the exit. By the hatch he paused. "I've requested departure for three hours from now. If I don't make it back in time, something's gone wrong."

When Levi had left, Vera slumped onto the sofa. It obviously didn't matter that she'd been so blunt. Once he'd sold the blueprint and dropped her on Seshat, they'd never see each other again. And maybe she was being spiteful and petty, but she wanted to make it very clear that this was the extent of her journeying with the Weasel.

Thirty thousand kilo-bitcoins arrived in her account an

hour later. That number looked way too low. She sent him a message: >*There's at least one zero missing.*

He called her, his voice rushed and urgent. "That's all I could get for now, and I look super sketchy. I need the password, before they call the cops on me."

"I'll send it." What choice did she have? The thirty grand was already more than she'd ever held in her account.

Chapter 12
The Deal

Levi adjusted the cuffs of his dark jacket as he stepped into a sleek hotel lobby. The marble floors glinted under the warm, ambient lights, and an automated concierge screen flashed a welcome message with his alias *L. Sylas*. He ignored it, heading straight for the elevator bank. The meeting room he'd booked was on the twenty-fifth floor, far from the bustling public spaces to ensure privacy.

Despite what he told Vera, he'd never planned on going to LI's headquarters. This meeting would run on his terms, on neutral territory. He'd charge the meeting room costs back to LI, not that they'd mind after they saw what he had to offer them.

The elevator doors opened with a soft chime, and Levi stepped out, footsteps hushed by the plush carpet as he approached the frosted glass door marked *Executive Meeting Suite A*.

A long table dominated the room, flanked by high-backed

chairs and floor-to-ceiling windows with a bird's-eye view of Tiberum. Levi's attention was on the two figures who stood from their seats to greet him.

The first was a sharply dressed middle-aged man Levi had recognized from earlier discussions as Kallum Kabore, LI's chief executive. The second was an older woman with auburn hair tied back in a ponytail. She introduced herself as Chief Engineer Prachi Patel.

"Kind of you to join us, Mister Sylas." Kabore's tone was tinged with annoyance. Levi noted the crystal-faced watch on his wrist. Kabore was certainly one of those sticklers for on-time arrangements.

Levi smiled and shrugged. Playing things easy-breezy was going to convince them that they needed what he had to offer much more than he needed whatever they would give him. "Of course. Time is money, and I believe this will be worth yours." He placed both data cards—the original and the translation—onto the table and took a seat. The LI executives mirrored his movement, taking their seats opposite him.

Patel side-eyed the data cards. Levi could see the effort it took her not to reach for them. "The fragments you sent us looked promising, but I'd like to verify the rest of the file before we proceed with negotiations," she said, her fingers hovering over her virtEgo.

"Verify away." Levi shoved the gadgets toward her.

She picked up the standard GU card and connected it to her expanded virt screen.

Kabore focused on Levi. "So, where did you obtain this document?"

GALAXY GRIFTER

"I believe I mentioned that I used to be a sales exec for Thesaan Belu's Martian branch." Levi flashed a virtual business card, which he'd forged a few hours earlier.

Kabore gave it a once-over without much scrutiny. "And where did Thesaan obtain these blueprints? I doubt they arrived at this discovery without external help."

"What I don't know, I don't know." Levi shrugged again. "I was just in sales."

"Given there have been no public announcements, this must be fresh or in testing stages—and highly classified." Kabore's eyes narrowed. "How does a sales exec get their hands on such information?"

"By making lots of very close friendships." Levi beamed as if to demonstrate that no secret was safe against that smile.

Patel scrolled through the pages of equations and schematics on her screen. Her eyes widened in surprise, and Levi hoped that was a good sign.

Kabore kept glancing at her impatiently. "And you have no qualms over offering this to us?" He leaned forward. "You realize you could be charged with corporate espionage—or worse—if your former employer finds out."

"I wasn't planning on telling them." Levi smirked. "Were you?"

Patel lifted her gaze from the screen. "There are fragments missing here, vital data. It's incomplete." She looked visibly disappointed.

"It isn't missing." Levi extracted a third data card from his breast pocket. "It's merely awaiting payment."

Both executives frowned, clearly unimpressed.

"Mister Sylas"—Patel's tone was tight with agitation—"this is highly complex quantum mechanics that we have not tested before. I will need to go over it with my wider team and run some simulations before we can agree on final payment."

"That's a shame." Levi scooped the cards back into his pocket, standing dramatically. "I'd hoped we'd be able come to some agreement."

"You are being unreasonable," Kabore snapped. "And unprofessional."

But Levi wasn't worried. He could see the execs were hooked and were simply being stingy. "I'd imagined a million k-bits was a small investment for such a large company. I guess I was wrong." He reached for the door handle.

The execs exchanged glances. "Wait," Kabore said.

Levi didn't let him finish. He tossed the translation card back to Patel. "Here's how it goes. You hold on to this, as assurance. I'll step outside, give you two a minute. Within that minute, you must transfer one million k-bits into my account. In return, I'll send you the missing fragments. Otherwise, I'll take my cards and find another buyer."

Patel and Kabore stared at him, stunned.

He stepped out of the room and paced the corridor, periodically checking his account. He must've looked like a total weirdo, but with this kind of intel, he could afford to be.

Finally, his virt buzzed to notify him of a transaction, complete with six zeros.

He pumped his fists in excitement, suppressing a celebratory scream. Then, he generously transferred thirty grand to Vera. That was all she was getting, though—he wasn't going to waste a k-bit more on a backwater coder. He called her, making sure to sound wary and panicked, grinning at his ingenuity.

Kabore stuck his head out of the meeting room, giving Levi a questioning look.

"One minute." Levi gestured with his finger.

After hanging up and confirming Vera had sent him the password, Levi returned to the meeting room and handed the final fragment to Prachi Patel. "A pleasure doing business with you," he said.

Kabore stepped up to him, his voice low. "One last thing, Mister Sylas. Does anyone else know about this?" He gestured at the data cards.

"Not a soul." Levi grinned.

He adjusted his jacket collar and left the hotel.

Chapter 13
St. Vernon

When Levi stepped through the arched, ivory entrance of St. Vernon Plois, he was greeted by a prim-looking man, who looked him up and down skeptically. "Good afternoon. I'm Francois, how can I assist you?"

A store of this caliber employed real people, although with that plastic smile, Francois might as well have been an android.

Levi wondered if it was due to habit, cosmetics, or both.

"I need..." Levi glanced around the minimalistic displays of shirts, trousers, and jackets hanging in the alcoves along the shop's walls. He was the only present customer and the thought that everything here sat within his budget exhilarated him. His eyes caught on the shop's centerpiece—an abstract mannequin made of dark lacquered wood, dressed in a glossy teal-grey suit. "This guy." He pointed.

"Our flagman suit from the Centennial collection, valued at seventeen thousand kilo-bits," Francois said, verbally probing the depths of Levi's pockets.

GALAXY GRIFTER

"I'll take it, along with new boots, and a few other trims."

"Certainly. I'll have it delivered to the fitting room while you look around."

Levi ran his hand along a row of crisp shirts, trying to estimate how much this spree would cost him. But the point of having money was spending it.

Francois plodded behind him, placing every item Levi picked onto a self-driving hanger rack. Once Levi stated his readiness, Francois sent the hanger ahead into the fitting room. "Follow me please."

The spacious room at the back of the shop contained a large suede-looking armchair in a deep brown, and a wooden side table with a tablet on top. It displayed images from Vernon's collection. The hanger rack with Levi's chosen items stood between the fitting and tailoring machines. The first looked like a huge mirror cube, the second like a smaller lacquered-wood cube with a slit for clothing.

"Have you used one of these before?" Francois asked.

"Of course." Levi had owned a bunch of expensive clothes over the years, although his only other St. Vernon garment was currently at his parents' house, for safekeeping, while he was shipless and, by definition, homeless.

"Well then, I will leave everything here. Get changed and step into the machine; it will take your measurements to ensure the perfect fit. Then remove the garments and place them here." Francois tapped the wooden cube. "It will take approximately five minutes to alter the garments. You can wait here or browse some more through the shop. Anything else I can get you?"

119

"A coffee, thanks."

"Of course. A bell here if you need help." Francois left the room.

Levi undressed and put on a new pinkish shirt and the flagman suit, noting Francois had guessed his size right, with the pants and jacket only a pinch too big, to allow for tailoring. The fabric felt smooth and cool against his skin.

He stepped inside the measuring machine, with feet at shoulder width and arms perpendicular to the floor, as per the instructions displayed on the mirror in front of him.

Blue light beams scanned his body from top to bottom, reminiscent of spaceport security. Dozens of little robotic pincer hands slid from the machine's walls and glided across the suit's fabric, tightening it to his figure. A dial appeared on the mirror with the recommended size ranges up to the millimeter. He turned it halfway and the pincers adjusted their grip—not too loose, to eliminate all hints of bagginess, and not too tight, so he'd be able to breath and move.

He admired the results in the mirror. Clearly, brands like St. Vernon had only one flaw—they made wearing anything else feel like a disappointment.

The instructions on the mirror encouraged him to choose from a number of background options to allow the customer to see themselves in different settings: a banquet hall similar to the one on Gleath, a flashing casino on Eria, the UCH square on Earth. He cringed; that was near the university his dad had worked for and brought up childhood memories Levi would prefer to bury.

He noted he looked a lot like his father, but that's where the

GALAXY GRIFTER

similarities ended. Levi was never going to be a model citizen like his parents.

He turned off the background and tapped an icon to save the settings. The pincer hands retreated into the walls.

When he stepped out of the fitting machine, a tray with coffee and accoutrements stood on the table.

He took off the St. Vernon suit and placed it into the slot to be tailored. While he waited, he called a ship rental company.

"Do you have a shuttle or a freighter available right now?" he asked after being greeted by an AI assistant.

"There are currently no shuttles or freighters available," said the assistant. "The next opening is for a shuttle LI three-one-five, available in three days. Would you like to book it?"

"No." He disconnected. This was the fourth rental company he'd called since leaving Logic Interstellar's office, and no one seemed to have a private transport available.

"Are you okay in there?" Francois asked from outside the fitting room.

"I'm grand," Levi muttered.

His lien contract for *Caerus* expired yesterday, which meant Mahru would likely penalize him. He needed to get his ass to Frigg as soon as he could.

He could try to buy a ship and sell it again once he got *Caerus* back, but he'd have to wait for the registration transfer and then book a departure slot. Plus, he already had one unwanted ship. Simply leaving the *Comet* at Tiberum Spaceport seemed wasteful. Unfortunately, the *Comet* was currently occupied by one pesky redhead who was hell-bent on taking his money.

121

Vera hadn't risked her life charming Wendigo, fighting Sehens, and escaping from firing warships like he had, and she didn't deserve half of his earnings. She didn't even deserve a quarter.

You think I came on this trip 'cos I'm desperately in love with you? he said to himself in her mocking tone. Obviously he didn't think that—he'd only fucked her because he didn't want to fight over who got the sofa bed. Love had zero to do with anything on this excursion.

Admittedly, he'd hoped the physical closeness would get her to warm up to him, make her more malleable and help avoid hurdles like the passworded data. Alas, she was a cold bitch, and clearly had her own agenda.

He was a tad curious why she needed the money so badly. No matter how much he tried, she gave him no answers. She was like a magician's box with a false bottom, a lock he couldn't pick and best gotten rid of. But damn, he wanted to pick that lock. He rather enjoyed lockpicking.

"Your garments are ready," said the mechanical voice of the tailoring machine. A robotic arm held out a branded bag. Inside it was a box with the suit and the other clothes.

He left the changing room and followed Francois to the checkout.

"The new quarter's line drops next week. We hope to see you back." Francois grinned as he accepted the payment.

"Sure." Leaving St. Vernon Plois, Levi promised himself he wouldn't let the Vera problem become a dampener.

Chapter 14

Eixyene Ceviche

Another hour went by, and Vera messaged Levi to ask where he was.

No response.

Later, she tried calling. He didn't answer. She stepped outside and looked nervously across the tarmac. Nothing. She returned to the cockpit and sat in the pilot seat. With fifteen minutes left until departure, she knew she had to reschedule. She couldn't fly this thing, not without a license or system access. *Think.* Her breaths came shallow. If Levi had gotten into trouble, she needed to leave. There were bound to be direct flights between Rebecca and Seshat. And she could afford a ticket. She tapped the control panel, preparing to notify ground control and to pay the fine for the failure to depart.

The *Comet*'s hatch opened and Levi stepped through, alone and in one piece.

She let out a sigh of relief and frowned, noticing bags in both his hands. "Have you been shopping?"

"Yeah. Give me a hand with these." He opened the storage compartment.

She jumped to her feet and threw her arms up. "What the fuck, Levi? I thought something terrible happened. Why didn't you answer my call?"

"My hands were busy. I'll make it up to you." He stacked the bags into storage and shoved a small plush toy in the shape of a squid into her hands. "An A'turi souvenir. Buckle in." He sat and turned on the *Comet*'s engine.

She wanted to kill him, but there was no time. The onboard assistant started its countdown. She sat and fastened the safety belts. Clutching the soft toy, she battled her takeoff queasiness. Once safely in hyperspace, she followed him into the living module.

He retrieved several containers from his shopping bag. "I thought we deserved a celebratory meal."

"We've got plenty of flight meals." She still wanted to murder him but felt too tired to act on her wish as her adrenal levels returned to normal.

"Those meals are shit, and *this*"—he placed an opened container onto the utilities panel in front of her—"is from the best restaurant I could find on the way to the spaceport."

She studied the colorful contents. "What is it?"

"The appetizer is eixyene ceviche, and the main—don't open that yet, you'll let the heat out—is braised zhukou with pillyt cakes and chuka salad."

"What?"

"Jaemlen fusion. Seafood."

"Ah." She picked at the appetizer with her fork. "I guess it's the closest I've come to fine dining."

GALAXY GRIFTER

"We'll fix that." He retrieved a bottle of Krug champagne.

"Oh."

"I thought this might excite you." He chuckled and popped the cork.

Her antagonism diminished over the course of the meal, the champagne doing its job splendidly. They'd pulled this thing off. He promised to transfer her the remaining funds once they reached Seshat's Instarnet, boasted about his meeting with Logic Interstellar, and indulged in utopian fantasies of buying his ship back and lounging on the beaches of Sandabur. She let him. The day's stress vacated her body, making way for a pleasant lightheadedness. And when they went to bed, it almost felt...intimate.

Chapter 15
Lotan

Sitting on the edge of the sofa bed, Levi watched Vera's chest rise and fall like a lulling tide. It wasn't that he didn't enjoy his time with her. He felt a challenge in her sharp edges and a satisfaction in seeing them soften under his touch. But she never truly let go.

It was plain to see she was no criminal mastermind, yet she was more skilled at deception than he'd given her credit for. He mentally retraced their interactions.

She had been a mess when he'd found her and openly distrustful. Yet she'd agreed to help. He'd thought she had been showing off, that he'd had her right where he wanted her. But the data backup and the way she'd wound Blackbeard around her finger... What if she'd planned it all?

No. This train of thought suggested she had been playing *him* like a sucker. He couldn't accept that. She was a nerdy little nobody. A dumpster kid with an ego.

His virt buzzed, notifying him of an incoming ansible call.

GALAXY GRIFTER

Who the...? He strolled into the cockpit. His contact manager identified the signal as coming from *Lotan750*—the Breznis' ship.

Fuck. How did they find us?

The *Comet* was on a main route; without a shadow map, there was nowhere to run. It was just a matter of time before *Lotan*, the bigger ship, caught up to it.

He rushed back to the living module and nearly tripped over Vera's jacket, thrown on the floor with the rest of their clothes. He picked it up and patted the faux leather with his fingers until he found a hard, tiny circle stuck to her sleeve—a tracker.

Perhaps the Breznis weren't following him—they were following Vera. For messing up a transaction? That didn't seem right.

She remained blissfully asleep on the sofa, with a sheet pulled up to her bare waist, her face framed by a halo of copper strands and her mouth half-open.

"What did you do?" he whispered.

Then he gathered his belongings, returned to the cockpit, and shut the hatch.

Vera woke up with a sense of weightlessness. It must've been all the champagne. But when she opened her eyes to the dim flashing light, her arms were literally floating. As were the ends of her blanket. The strap around her waist kept her fixed to the sofa bed in zero gravity. She pushed herself into an approximation of sitting.

"Levi?" He wasn't in bed. She turned her head from side to side. She could hear the blood pulsing in her ears. The familiar buzz of the *Comet*'s engines was gone. What happened? Had the ship malfunctioned? She looked at the hatch that led to the cockpit. An emergency sign blinked above it: *Module detached. SOS activated. Oxygen level 80 percent.*

Module detached—oh fuck.

Levi was gone with the rest of the *Comet*. She was floating in outer space. Alone.

Chapter 16
Schrödinger's Girl

Vera sat on the sofa bed of the detached spaceship module sobbing. Tears formed blobs around her eyes instead of falling. How could she have been so stupid? The sickening shame of letting him dispose of her, like garbage, quashed the fear. If she died out here, it would serve her right. However, there was a chance Starpol would pick up the module's SOS signal, provided Levi—*the son of a bitch*—had left it on a main route. She didn't even think to check their coordinates when they'd left Rebecca. *Idiot.* She should have known better. She *had* known better. Her rib cage shuddered from fresh sobs.

A jolt interrupted her self-denigration. Starpol? She unbuckled herself from the sofa and lunged toward the porthole. "Ouch!" She hit the wall harder than she expected. Outside, she could see only the blackness of space. Another jolt rolled through the module. She scrambled back to the bed and grabbed the safety straps.

The bumps and jolts grew stronger. Her insides fell into

place as gravity returned. A well-illuminated metallic wall appeared through the porthole. The module must've been pulled into another vessel. Now what? A hollow thump echoed from the outside. She unbuckled again and, sniffling, walked toward the hatch. She must've looked pathetic from all the crying. She ran her fingers through her tangled hair and pressed the release button.

The hatch opened, revealing a cargo hold of a larger spaceship and three pairs of eyes staring at her. The first pair belonged to a Ror. The ursine alien stood nearly three meters tall, covered in short brown fur and wearing a blue jump-suit. A pink scar stretched from the corner of his mouth up to a mangled ear. To his left stood an older Human male with vaguely familiar features. The last pair of eyes, deep-set and shifty, belonged to Isaac Brezni. The men and the alien each held a gun. Vera backed into the hatch. Dying alone inside the module no longer seemed like a bad way to go.

"Don't move." The older man jerked his blaster. "Who the hell are you?"

She opened her mouth, but no sound followed.

He turned to Isaac. "Is that her?"

Isaac narrowed his eyes, finally shaking his head.

Vera let out a slight breath. Without the wig, he didn't recognize her, thank goodness. *Come on, Vera, say something. Make something up.* Her tongue refused to move.

"The one at the café was blond and…hotter," Isaac said.

She was glad for her puffy face now.

The older guy rolled his eyes and walked toward her. "Any-one else inside?"

GALAXY GRIFTER

She shook her head.

"Step away from the module."

She obeyed. He signaled for the Ror to go in. Isaac followed. The older man kept her at gunpoint. "What were you doing out here?" His features were as rugged as Isaac's, making her conclude the two were related.

"I...I don't know. I woke up and the module was detached."

"Where were you going? Were you alone?"

"Seshat, I think. No, I was with—"

"Found it!" Isaac stepped out of the module holding the faux leather jacket and the blond wig she'd worn to their meeting. "Guess you're a redhead." He grabbed a handful of her tangled hair and yanked so hard, she cried out and fell to her knees. He dragged her up metal steps and down a corridor with three doors on each side. "You think you can steal from the Breznis and get away with it?" He shoved her forward and she collapsed into the ship's spacious living area, which housed a kitchen, dining area, and entertainment nook. The cockpit was visible through the open hatch, and Alex, the IT guy from the café, hunched in the pilot seat, with his back to the control panel, and stared at her with a sheepish expression. She threw him a pleading glance.

Isaac grabbed her hair again and pulled her up to her knees.

"I'm sorry!" She winced, grasping his hand.

He let go and struck her across the face. She fell back to sitting.

He studied her jacket, holding it up in one hand. She spotted it first—a tiny button attached to the back of it. He picked it off and tossed it to Alex. "Turn off the tracker and put it away. Might come in handy later."

131

They'd used a quantum tracker to find her? The feeling of her own incompetence washed over her again. She'd screwed up so bad.

Isaac bent down and clasped her face. "Who do you work for?"

She pulled away and shuffled back. "No one! I was with a guy, Levi Adder. He made me do it."

"The Weasel?!" Isaac straightened. "Son of a bitch."

The Ror and the older man entered the living area. Isaac turned to them. "Hey, Joe, you won't believe this. This is one of the Weasel's whores."

"Adder?" Joe scratched his bearded chin. "Son of a senhound. Where is he? Who's he trading with?"

She moved farther back. "I don't know. I barely knew him. He promised good money if I got you to translate that file."

The Ror walked past them and handed something to Alex. Her virt. She'd forgotten she'd left it in the module.

The Ror turned to Joe. "I'll be in my cabin, yes?"

"Yes, thank you, Mtsan." Joe didn't take his eyes off Vera.

The Ror left. Joe took a step forward and squatted next to her. "So the A'turian drivel was just a decoy to hack our systems?"

"I guess. I don't know," she said. "He told me he'd pay me, and when I woke up, he was gone. I thought I was going to die out here."

Joe looked up at Isaac. "He must've spotted us on the lidar or found the tracker. Smart." He turned to her again. "So how is it you signed up for this...deal, knowing nothing at all?"

"I needed the money. I ran into trouble back home. I'm sorry."

GALAXY GRIFTER

Isaac laughed. "Trouble? Your troubles are just beginning, girl."

Joe stood. "Find anything, Alex?"

"Nothing on here." Alex tossed Vera's virt onto the control panel.

She exhaled. At least she had the sense to clear it before takeoff. Maybe she could tell them about the blueprint and try to bargain for her life? But Levi had sold it now; it was too late.

Isaac towered over her. "Where did the Weasel get the backdoor virus to hack our system? What was he looking for? Who's he working with?"

"Don't know..."

Isaac grabbed her face again, harder this time. "What was he looking for, and where has he gone with it?"

"I don't know!" She tried to pull away as her cheeks throbbed under his finger and thumb. She'd happily hand him Levi's head on a platter, if she had a clue where to find him.

"Makes you pretty useless, doesn't it?" He pulled her to her feet.

"There's a ship approaching," Alex said. "It's requesting contact."

The ansible crackled. "*Lotan seven-five-zero*, this is Starpol. We received a distress signal from this quadrant."

"Shit." Isaac let go of Vera's face and stomped to the cockpit. "Why didn't you jump?"

"Where to?" Alex flinched. "You didn't say I had to."

"Anywhere, moron. Too late now."

The ansible crackled again. "*Lotan seven-five-zero*, do you copy?"

133

"Yes, officer. No distress here," Isaac answered.

Vera's heart raced. This was her chance for salvation, yet she dared not call out for help. "Let me leave," she whispered. "I'll say you've rescued me."

"What is your route and purpose? Did you encounter another spacecraft nearby?" asked the officer.

Isaac swore under his breath. Joe walked up to the panel. "Tourism. We picked up a detached shuttle module."

"Anyone inside?" the officer asked.

Please, Vera mouthed.

Joe eyed her thoughtfully. "Don't know. Haven't opened it."

Cold sweat beaded her forehead. They could kill her and tell the cops they found her like that. She was Schrödinger's cat at that moment, simultaneously alive and dead.

"In this case, do not attempt to open. Prepare for docking," said the officer.

"Sure, give us a minute." Joe muted the mic.

Isaac pointed his finger at her. "I'm not handing her over. I don't believe her."

"They'll search the ship," Joe said, and walked up to her. She thought he'd hit her, but he just grabbed her elbow and pulled her down the hallway. He opened a door to a room that turned out to be a lavatory. "Clean yourself up. And if you so much as squeak, I'll blow your brains out, right in front of the cops. And if you cause us any more grief, we'll find you, wherever you go."

With trembling hands, Vera activated the tap and threw cold water onto her face. "You saved me. That's all they'll hear."

GALAXY GRIFTER

He led her downstairs. "You left the module a minute ago, understood?"

"Yes."

Isaac joined them in the cargo hold. "You're not really thinking of letting her go with all our contacts, wherever she's hiding them?"

"We've got no choice." Joe shrugged. "The Weasel's got our files, and if they find the ammo, the trackers, the fugitive Ror—we're fucked."

"Bloody Weasel." Isaac groaned.

"We'll find the son of a bitch. He won't get away this time."

Several minutes later, four Huxorans dressed in the Union's Star Police attire marched in. One of them approached the module. "Greetings. Is this where the distress signal came from?"

Joe went to shake the cop's hand. "Hello, officer. Yes, we just pulled it on board. Luckily the girl's okay."

"The girl?"

"She just came out." He pointed at Vera.

She stepped forward. "I had an argument with my boy-friend on the way to Seshat. He ditched me here in the mod-ule. These men rescued me."

The cop's black eyes widened. "Big argument."

One of the cops led her away onto the police ship. Three stayed behind to question the Breznis. She stuck to her story for the official protocol. No, she wasn't hurt and wouldn't press charges against anyone, including the Human who stranded her. She didn't need those complications.

Chapter 17
Frigg

The *Comet*'s onboard assistant told Levi to prepare for arrival. "Fucking finally." He clicked his safety belts. The only thing worse than traveling aboard the *Comet* was traveling aboard the *Comet* without a living module. But survival trumped convenience at this moment. And he didn't think he would have survived the encounter with the Breznis.

It was a shame about the redhead. Vera had been good value, but he couldn't trust her. He wasn't sure what she'd been up to, but the Breznis must've sensed it too. That's why they'd tracked her and why he had to leave her behind.

The *Comet* dove through the white discus into normal space and headed for the blue-green marble of Frigg. Here, *Caerus* would finally be within Levi's reach. His hands tingled from the anticipation; he could almost feel the smooth leather interior beneath his fingertips, could smell the crisp, pinesap freshener he built to pump through the cockpit. *Soon, baby. Daddy's coming.*

GALAXY GRIFTER

From above, Frigg looked like quite the catch—lush forests and clear oceans. Nothing like the barren and uber-industrialized Seshat and Rebecca. That made it a coveted territory for more than Humans. But Humans got here first, which meant colonial rights sat with them. That didn't stop others from moving here though, especially while it was still being settled.

The *Comet* landed in the New Aarhus Spaceport, which had a town growing quickly around it. Levi stepped out into the bright daylight, inhaling the smell of grass, dust, and rocket oil. He snapped a picture of the *Comet* and strolled along the perimeter of the terminal building that looked like it was made of translucent fabric draped over wooden arches. Cranes extended their steel necks on either side of the terminal and the air was thick with drilling, beeping, and hammering. After days inside the cockpit, he yearned for a hot meal, a bath, and a bed, but that could wait. He'd have those luxuries aboard *Caerus*.

Within a short walk from the spaceport, he reached a familiar earthy dome, built in a Huxoran fashion. Behind it, a concrete wall fenced off a section of a field, with tops of spacecraft peaking above it. Levi stepped through the dome's entrance, into a crescent-shaped reception chamber.

A young Huxoran bowed from behind the counter.

"I'm here to pick up my light freighter, *Caerus*, LI thirty-one hundred," Levi said.

The Huxoran entered the details into his terminal.

"And while we're at it, I'm also selling this shuttle." Levi pulled the image of the *Comet* from his virt.

The Huxoran studied it. "Only the shuttle? Is there a module for freight or—"

"Only the shuttle." Levi collapsed the image. He hoped the cops had gotten to Vera before the Breznis did. He bore her no ill will, but surely the fact that he tipped off Starpol was more than she would've done for him in similar circumstances.

"I'll ask Mahru, the shop owner, to take a look at the shuttle," the Huxoran said. "Can you repeat your freighter's registration?"

"*Caerus*, LI three-one-zero-zero," Levi said.

The Huxoran fiddled with his terminal once again. "We don't have this ship in our registry."

Levi frowned. "Check again. Or call your boss."

"Sorry, it's not in our system—"

Levi slammed his palms into the counter. "Call Mahru. Now!"

The Huxoran shrank back and disappeared through a door behind the reception desk. Several minutes later, an old, white-muzzled female waddled in. Her eyes met Levi's and her nose crinkled up in a semblance of a smile. "You're back. What have you got for old Mah today?"

"I want to pick up my ship." Levi felt the frustration building up like an itch under his skin. Surely this was just a mistake.

"Come." Mahru gestured for him to follow her through the door, deeper into the dome. Another door at the end of a narrow corridor exposed the backyard packed with old space-ships, but Mahru turned into a room on the left and waved for Levi to follow. These must've been her living quarters. Four nest-chairs stood in a semicircle around a small table. A hammock hung in the corner and part of the room was hidden

GALAXY GRIFTER

behind a divider made of reed. Skylights, like glowing strips in the curved ceiling, illuminated the room.

He frowned. "Where's my ship, Mah?"

Grunting, Mahru lowered into a chair. "Take a seat. Runi will bring us beer."

"Where. Is. *Caerus?*" Levi gritted his teeth.

She draped her tail across her lap. "Not here. Our deal expired three rotations ago, so I sold it."

It was like someone struck a match inside him. "You *sold* my ship?"

"What did you expect? I gave you a lot of money for it, and you didn't come when I waited. Another Human offered a price I couldn't refuse."

"You stupid rat!" he stormed at her. "I would've matched any offer. I would've doubled it."

She flinched, but her voice remained steady. "But you weren't here, and I have a business to run."

He stopped inches away from her, clenching his fists so hard, they trembled. But strangling her wouldn't bring *Caerus* back. He forced himself into the chair next to her. "Who? Who'd you sell it to? I want every detail."

"His name was John Wang," she said.

"Is that supposed to tell me something? Who the fuck is he? Where did he take it?"

"I might remember who he works for if you jog my memory." She ran two skinny fingers along the length of her whisker.

He shook his head. "You sold my ship and expect me to pay you for information?"

139

"It is confidential, but I could make concessions."

"Fine. I'll jog your memory." He pulled the blaster from behind his back. "I'll jog it so fucking hard you'll wish you'd died of natural causes."

Mah sank deeper into the nest-chair and raised her hands. "Levi, the sheriff's a block away—"

"Does it look like I give a fuck? After all I've been through these last few months...I just want my ship back."

She shivered. "Okay, I'll tell you. But you won't like it."

Runi, the receptionist, walked in with two cans of beer. Levi covered the blaster with the hem of his jacket. If the Huxoran noticed, he didn't show it. He handed the cans to Levi and Mahru.

"Go, go." Mah waved her hands, and Runi walked off again.

Levi glanced over his shoulder, making sure they were alone. "I'm all ears."

She lowered her voice. "John Wang works for Adoro Fabulo."

As ridiculous as the name was, he'd heard it before. "Is that"—he narrowed his eyes—"the Martian billionaire?"

"Exactly. He collects rare and valuable things, John Wang said."

"For resale?"

"Only if he doesn't like them."

"Shit." Levi scratched his chin. If Fabulo bought *Caerus* for his collection, Levi wouldn't be able to simply buy it back. Fabulo didn't need money.

Mah side-eyed the blaster. "I told you everything. We're good now?"

GALAXY GRIFTER

"Good? We'll never be good, Mah. There's no coming back from this."

With a pop, she cracked her can open. "I understand it's difficult. But look on the shiny side, as you Humans say. I have a very good assortment. We'll pick you another spaceship."

He opened the can and drank in large gulps, as if to extinguish a fire. The Huxoran beer tasted disgusting. "I don't want another spaceship," he said. "I'm getting *my* ship back, if it's the last thing I do."

———————————•———————————

Levi hired a luxury shuttle called *Velos*. He was trying not to panic, trying to stay calm and form a plan. He'd find a way to get back at Mahru later. Nobody sold his ship and got away with it.

Velos's translucent control panel revealed parts of the computer's entrails—a modern fad, one that Levi didn't think would stick. Its pilot seat was comfortable but not *his*. As disappointing as the ordeal was, another thought scratched its way to the surface of his mind. "*Velos*, ping Blackjack's ground control."

"Connecting to Blackjack Spaceport," the ship replied. The ansible crackled.

"Yuri, Levi here, can you hear me?"

"Ah, Levi, my friend, how can I help you?" The controller's speech was slow, like he'd been asleep or, more probably, drinking.

"Has the *Vulture* come in, by chance?"

"No, haven't heard from them in a while."

"What about the *Behemoth Bitch*?"

"*Behemoth* got into orbit two days ago. Apparently they had a good run. But Bulletproof Bao looked glum when I saw him."

"Why?" Levi sat up. Perhaps the other pirate captain had news from the *Vulture*.

"They say he fell out with Carver over some hussy." Yuri uttered a raspy laugh. "Old men acting like boys."

"Anything else they're saying?"

"Not to me. Why? You know something?"

"Just checking. You'll sing out if you hear anything, won't you?"

"Of course. That bottle you got me—beautiful. My wife and I drank to your health."

"Of course you did." Levi disconnected, tapped another contact, and called the Huxoran hacker. "Kru-boy, fill me in, what have you got on the ghost ships?"

The Huxoran hacker turned on his camera. It appeared he was jogging through Tuhxun City. Mounds, similar to Mahru's shop but as tall as Human high-rise buildings, towered in the background, and rows of fliers traveled across the green-blue sky.

"Nothing." Kru stopped at an intersection, breathing heavily. "It's a rumor, as I said."

"A rumor?" Levi crossed his arms. Rumors didn't fire rockets at you.

"All military-class ships are required to display the GU insignia. And Jaemlen intelligence wouldn't be so overt."

Jaemlen intelligence... Whatever Kru thought, that was the likeliest explanation. Jaemlen spooks making shady deals with the A'turi.

GALAXY GRIFTER

But what for?

"Have you made progress on Netareth Khay?" Levi asked.

"No. I can't just log into his virtEgo. Any hack requires time and a vulnerability."

"Keep trying. The guy's a tool, he'll expose himself."

Kru twitched his whiskers, waving away a palm-sized flying bug. "If he does, what will I be looking for?"

"Anything that mentions ghost ships or the A'turi," Levi said.

"Copy." Kru started jogging again, and the city in the background seemed to jump with every step.

Levi disconnected. He tapped his fingers on the control panel. It'd been over a fortnight since the *Vulture* had been under fire, and nobody had heard about it since. That meant Wendigo and crew had likely perished for good.

Too bad he'd never made it into her bed. He tried to focus on the "good." If she was gone, he had one less adversary to run from. On the other hand, not knowing for sure felt like an unsettling loose end.

———————————— • ————————————

Levi woke ahead of his alarm. He opened one eye and peeked at his wrist—just over two hours to Mars. He sat up. "*Velos*, light to thirty." The light panels along the curved, wood-faced walls emitted a warm glow. He climbed out of bed and headed past the frosted glass that separated the bedroom from the living area and into the cockpit. The lidar showed two other ships some distance behind—not uncommon on a major route. But the triangular formation triggered an unpleasant memory. He steered *Velos*

10 percent off course. The two other dots followed and accelerated. His stomach sank. "Fuck." He was willing to bet they were the same spooks that attacked the *Vulture*. How did they find him?

His ansible bleeped. "*Velos*, LI nine-four-three-eight. This is the Jaemlen Defense Force Special Division. We intend to take you in for questioning. Please don't try to resist."

Levi swallowed a lump in his throat. "Questioning about what? Who sanctioned this?"

"We believe you have information that will help our investigation. We mean you no harm. You will be free to go after you answer our questions."

"No idea what it's about. I'm calling Starpol." He wasn't. They'd never get here in time.

"Do not. It is in your best interest to cooperate."

A white beam shot past his porthole, underscoring their statement.

Shit. These ships took down a heavily armed galleon. His unarmed passenger shuttle stood no chance.

The ansible crackled again. "Are you there? Cooperate and you will not be harmed. This is our final warning."

He lowered into the pilot seat and fastened his safety belts. "I'll cooperate. Your instructions?"

"Secure your belts and prepare to exit hyperspace. Your ship will be docked and boarded, and you will be taken in for questioning."

They wanted him alive. That was promising.

"Wait, I'll put on some clothes." He muted the ansible and pulled a holographic map with their current coordinates from his control panel.

GALAXY GRIFTER

They were in the solar system—another thing going for him. On the lidar, the three dots aligned further. He figured once the warships flanked him, they'd lock *Velos* into a magnetic net. Then he'd be doomed. He adjusted his trajectory by another 10 percent.

A warship released a second cautionary beam. "You're not permitted to change course. You will be forcefully exited from hyperspace in ten, nine, eight..."

Not yet.

"Seven, six, five..."

Levi disabled the hyperdrive.

Velos plunged into real space and swerved from a hurtling rock and then another one. Chunks of ice battered against its hull. Beyond the porthole lay a sea of space debris. A planet loomed in the background, like a giant peach with swirls of white clouds—Saturn. Its rings were his last chance to lose the warships. A rock struck the hull and sent *Velos* spinning. *Fuck.* The operating system flashed emergency lights and screamed about damage sustained even after he managed to regain control. His gut felt like soup in a centrifuge. He couldn't see the spooks, though. Hopefully that meant they'd decided ring-surfing with ships their size was suicide. It was verging on suicide with his ship, but he'd take the risk. He'd done it once before. Ice pounded *Velos*'s hull as it crash-landed on a sizable moonlet. Levi's head took a moment to stop spinning; as soon as his eyesight was stable, he scanned his surroundings, making sure the warships didn't reappear, and shut down his engine and comms.

145

Chapter 18
The *Vixen*

Vera walked down a residential street of Eastern Xinlouyang, on planet Seshat, grateful to be alive. The wind chased tattered clouds past high-rise apartment buildings, tinted orange by the setting sun. She pulled up the zip of her jacket. They didn't have wind on Blackjack. Two women pushed a pram through the door of one of the high-rises. She held it for them and, once they were out, slipped inside. James would be expecting her. She'd messaged him as soon as she'd landed.

She took the lift to the fourteenth floor and rang the doorbell. Her oldest brother opened the door without saying a word. Eyes cold, lips tight, he stepped aside to let her in. She walked into the small yet tidy living room and slid her duffel onto the couch, beige with several dark stains—probably courtesy of her baby niece. "Where are Xiu and Abi?" Vera asked.

"At Xiu's parents." James stood in the doorway, arms crossed. Of the three siblings, only he inherited Mum's finer features and her hair, the color of chocolate milk.

GALAXY GRIFTER

Vera wondered if he and Xiu had a fight or if she'd left on Vera's account.

The silence grew heavy before he broke it. "What did you get yourself into?"

"Nothing." Vera shrugged. "Nothing much."

He let out a harsh breath. "You disappeared. For days. Without telling anyone." He paused between each phrase. "And while you were gone, Fred has been harassed by the Pooch's gang, asking about you. So I repeat: What. Did. You. Get. Yourself. Into?"

She frowned. "Is Fred okay?"

"He's alive if that's what you mean." James incinerated her with his gaze. He didn't need to rub it in. The guilt had been eating her since she'd left Blackjack.

"It was a misunderstanding," she said.

"A misunderstanding? They told Fred you took off with that Weasel guy."

"I kind of did—"

"Are you stupid?"

She clenched her fists. "I don't know, am I? I'm sure you're better placed to make that judgment from your ivory tower."

He dropped his arms to his sides and stepped forward. "And what's that supposed to mean?"

"You *left*, James. So long ago, when Mum was around and Dad was sober. You've got no clue what we've been through."

"What are you saying? I left, doesn't mean I don't care. You think it's been easy for me to *make it* out here? What would've changed if I'd stayed?"

He was right. Resenting him for living his life was unfair. She couldn't help it, though. "You've no idea what it's like."

"I've always said, if there's anything I can help with—"

"You couldn't."

He sighed and lowered into an armchair. "So, what's the story?"

Vera sat on the couch next to her bag. "The story is that Levi...the Weasel, commissioned me to decrypt a file. Then Blackbeard and company stormed my place, threatened me at gunpoint, and took everything, including the virt I use for work."

"Why? What was in that file?"

She shrugged again. "A tech manual of sorts."

"You should've told me. Hell, you should have told Fred."

"So you two could do what?" She reclined onto the backrest. "I got scared they'd return. I wanted to come straight here, but Levi wasn't going this way, so I ended up on Rebecca and then...Then I caught the next available shuttle." She didn't want to tell him the gritty details. "I avoided contacting Fred to protect him. That's the story."

James scratched his temple. "How did working with the Weasel seem like a good idea?"

It didn't, and it wasn't. It was a desperate one. She crossed her arms. "So it's a good idea when it involves pouring him booze, but not when it involves programming? If I was picky about whom I work with, I'd be out of jobs real quick. I think you forget what sort of people hang out on Blackjack. It's a colorful little community, brother."

He pursed his lips. "So, you can't go back now, with the Pooch on your case?"

"Don't know." She wound the hem of her T-shirt onto her

GALAXY GRIFTER

finger. She shouldn't have come here. Not until she sorted everything.

"Which means you can't," he concluded. "Stay here till we figure something out."

"Thanks." She looked down at her virt. The next shuttle to the asteroid departed in two weeks, and there was no way she'd endure James's "hospitality" that long.

They ate dinner in silence and he went to bed early. She spent the night tossing and turning on his couch.

Ship-sharing sites flaunted plenty of listings, but only one headed for Blackjack.

The following morning, she waited for him to leave for work and then headed to the nearest department store, where she bought a box of muesli bars, a magnetic lock, and a small laser knife. Then she caught a flight to Sinidat.

The city was Xinlouyang's antipode and the two-hour hypersonic flight cost nearly as much as her space passage. She was burning through the thirty grand she got from Levi, but that didn't matter. Her hope now rested on the database she'd stolen from the Breznis.

A middle-aged man with a red face met her by the boarding gate in Sinidat's spaceport. "You Vera? I'm Jan." He wore faded jeans and a fleece jacket, and extended his hand in greeting.

Her stomach knotted as she shook it. Traveling to Blackjack with a stranger was another terrible idea. But given she was on a roll, what was one more?

Jan showed her aboard his ship, the *Vixen*. The cockpit looked like it belonged in an old movie. Toggles and switches

149

studded its bulky console—something she hadn't seen even on Blackjack. Even June's old ship had a smooth panel with virtual controls. but the *Vixen* looked like it hadn't been upgraded in decades. The seats in front of the console slanted to the sides, like they were ready to fall off their swivels, and crumbling yellow foam peeked through the cracks in the dirty upholstery. The peeling eggshell paint on the walls revealed patches of the titanium hull, and the air had a mildewy tang.

Jan pottered across the ship's clanky metal floor with the enthusiasm of an amateur tour guide. "This is the common area, the entertainment system. Nothing flashy, but ya know... The kitchen."

A see-through plastic container stood on the floor, filled with clear liquid. He picked it up and tipped out its contents into the sink. When he returned it to the floor, a few drops plopped into it from the ceiling.

Vera looked up at the wet spot.

"Don't worry," Jan said. "The leak isn't near electronics or anything. I'll get it fixed on Blackjack for half of what they're charging here."

"Sure." She hoped the clunker wouldn't disintegrate while in hyperspace.

Unfazed, Jan continued the tour. "This will be your cabin for the flight." He pushed a door to reveal a small room with a cot, cabinet, and storage. "If you're happy with that, I'll prepare for takeoff."

"It's great. I'll strap in." She dropped her bag onto the cot.

"No, no, come to the cockpit."

"Huh?"

GALAXY GRIFTER

"You don't wanna miss the view, do ya? Besides, the cockpit doesn't rattle as much as the cabins."

"Rattle?" It wasn't supposed to rattle, not even in an old ship. But she'd rather endure rattling than small talk. She didn't like this guy's vibe. And yet, not wanting to be rude, she followed him to the cockpit.

———————————•———————————

"Welcome aboard, darlings. Make sure you're strapped in, nice and snug. Let's make these fifty hours fun, shall we?" The sultry voice, a setting popular among haulers, belonged to the *Vixen*'s virtual onboard assistant.

When the *Vixen* stopped talking, an unsettling tremor rose from the floor up. The familiar queasiness set in, superimposing on the sinking feeling in the pit of Vera's stomach. What was she doing? All her life she wanted to leave Blackjack. Now she was going back. Traveling with some dodgy operator, right into the Pooch's claws. *Fucking asinine.* But she couldn't leave Fred with the mess she'd created. And she couldn't stand loose ends. Levi had seemed perfectly at ease with the knowledge that someone somewhere wanted to kill him. She wasn't. If the Pooch didn't get to her, the paranoia would.

When the *Vixen* stopped trembling and the yellow planet of Seshat came into view, Jan pointed out the porthole. "There she goes. Beauty."

Somehow, she had no appetite for sightseeing.

He activated the hyperdrive and the ship jumped.

"You can unbuckle now. If you want," the *Vixen* whispered.

Vera did, but before she could stand, Jan turned to her. "Now, where have I seen you before?"

She swallowed the remainder of her nausea. "I work at Stellar."

"Ah, the pub? That's right, I've stopped by. What were you doing on Seshat?"

"Holiday."

"First time?"

"No. I've family there."

"And you're not afraid of traveling solo?" He leaned back and scratched his stomach.

"No." She wasn't afraid of traveling solo. She was afraid of traveling with dodgy old men, of pissing off gangsters, and of dying before her life had even begun.

"Venturesome. You're safe with me, though. I take passengers all the time. Good to have company out here."

"Yeah." Vera headed toward her cabin.

Jan called after her, "Do you want something to eat?"

"No, thanks. I'll take a nap, I think. Had an early start this morning."

———————————————•———————————————

Eight hours later, nature forced Vera out of the cabin and into the lavatory. She did her business and peeked into the common area—dark and quiet. Food leftovers, meal containers, and piles of empty beer cans littered the kitchen bench and the floor, drowning the smell of mildew in something worse. She

GALAXY GRIFTER

chucked what she could into the waste processor and wiped down the surfaces. Tidying other people's crap sparked no joy, but she'd be stuck here for two more days. It made sense to keep things livable. She refilled her water bottle, grabbed a heatable meal from the middle of the stack, and checked the seal. Satisfied with its integrity, she ate quickly and returned to her cabin.

Several more hours passed before Jan knocked on her door. When she didn't respond, he knocked again, louder. Reluctantly, she opened.

"Did you want breakfast or lunch?" He reeked of stale booze.

"I've already eaten, thank you."

"You don't have to stay inside all the time, you know."

"I know, I'm just...studying," she lied. "I've signed up for a course with a tight deadline."

"Oh, okay." He frowned. "Well, you need to take breaks anyway. Come out for a chat."

She tightened her fingers on the shaft of a laser knife she'd kept in her pocket, just in case, and stepped out. In the living area, she perched on a kitchen chair, while he took the couch. Maybe if he saw she was dull company, he'd let her be. After some babble about what she was studying, the good old days, and whether he could get a discount at Stellar, he launched a virtual screen. "Wanna watch something?"

"I really have to study. Won't have much time once I'm back at the bar." She returned to her cabin.

In about an hour, she thought she heard him fumbling by her door, but he didn't knock and she didn't open. Once it grew quiet, she braved another trip to the bathroom and the kitchen. More empty cans suggested her pilot had drunk himself to sleep again. The footsteps a moment later proved otherwise.

Jan appeared in the living area's entrance and leaned on the bulkhead. "There you are. Knew you'd come out eventually," he said, slurring his words, and stepped toward her. "You don't wanna talk to me? You think you're too good? Think I don't know who you are?"

Her hand reached into her pocket again. "What are you talking about?"

"It's you Blackbeard's after, ain't it? Maybe if you were a little nicer, I wouldn't tell him." He licked his pale lips.

Feeling sicker than during takeoff, she backed away. Her foot hit something and cold water splashed onto her jeans. The leakage container tipped over, her feet slid from under her, and she landed on her backside and cried out in pain. As she scrambled to her feet, Jan grabbed her arms and knocked her already aching back into a bulkhead. He pressed her against it and ran his hands along the length of her torso and then her thighs. Time slowed. She turned away from his reeking breath, her fingers searching desperately for the shaft inside her pocket. She drew the tiny weapon and pressed the button.

He cried out and jerked back, wide-eyed, holding his left thigh. A line of smoke wound up from it. Blood dripped through his fingers. She aimed the laser knife at his crotch. "Move and you lose them."

"You little bitch," he hissed through clenched teeth, but stayed still.

"Same goes for talking."

GALAXY GRIFTER

The smell of burnt flesh mixing with the *Vixen*'s usual aroma turned her stomach. Still pointing the blade, she pulled her shirt collar over her mouth and nose. "Transfer your ship control rights to me. And yeah, you may speak, but only for that purpose."

He opened and closed his mouth.

"Now!"

"*Vixen*, first-level controls to passenger Vera. Verbal password *Z*, three, *L*, *J*, five, nine, nine, eight."

"Vera, please accept command of the *Vixen*," the sultry voice said.

"Accept."

"You now have first-level control. We'll have so much fun, Captain." The AI couldn't care less whom it served.

"Forfeit your own rights," Vera commanded.

He glared. "Was that your plan all along? To steal my ship?"

She raised an eyebrow and let the laser char his pants, just a little. He obliged before it burned through the flesh.

"Goodbye, darling, I'll miss you," *Vixen* sighed, revoking his rights.

"*Vixen*." Vera kept her eyes fixed on Jan and her thumb on the knife's button.

"How can I help, gorgeous?" the AI asked.

"Time to destination?"

"One hundred and fifty-nine thousand, three hundred and twenty-two seconds, or forty-four Earth hours and fifteen minutes."

"*Vixen*, change course to Rebecca." Vera had never controlled a spaceship before and her heart beat a little faster.

"What?" Jan jerked but remembered what was at stake and bit his tongue.

The AI obliged. "Turning to Rebecca, Haran system, in five, four, three, two—"

"*Vixen*, abort. Stay the course to Blackjack," Vera said.

"Staying on the current route to Blackjack, my fickle friend."

Vera snickered, satisfied. "Now you"—she pointed her free hand at Jan—"turn around, slowly."

He turned his back to her and gasped as a white beam flashed past his cheek.

Vera lowered the laser to his neck. "Off to your cabin. Don't jerk. I've read that a severed carotid artery squirts blood for half a minute." She walked behind him and, when they reached the cabin, pushed him inside and shut the door. "*Vixen*, lock cabin one and don't open it until I tell you to."

"Sure thing, boss."

Vera returned her knife to her pocket and went into her own cabin. She detached the magnetic locking device from the inside of her own door and fixed it outside Jan's. Just in case.

"Can I use the crapper at least?" he called from the cabin.

"No. You can shit yourself for all I care." She headed to the living area. For the next thirty-four hours, this was *her* ship.

She clenched her teeth through the pain in her tailbone and lowered onto the grubby couch. Depriving Jan of food and water for two days was cruel. The alternative was plain stupid. She might've caught him by surprise the first time, when he was drunk and unaware she had a weapon. She wouldn't

GALAXY GRIFTER

take her chances again. She considered what that man tried to do and decided she wouldn't feel too guilty. She closed her eyes. "Vixen, one hour after we land on Blackjack, you can open the cabin doors and transfer level-one controls back to the former owner."

"As you wish, hon."

Chapter 19
The Golden Nugget

Hours passed before Levi dared to turn *Velos*'s operating system back on. He was freezing but hadn't chanced flicking on so much as one heater. Once the control panel powered up, it proceeded to bombard him with notifications about the damage sustained. He listened as he moved his numb fingers over the heat finally blasting over him and, when he was able, skimmed through the log to check the hyperdrive status. *Functional.* He let out a sigh of relief.

"Please undertake maintenance and repairs by a registered provider before your next trip." The OS's voice sounded crackly and mechanical.

"Sure, I'll just get a repair crew to fly out here," Levi scoffed.

"The nearest servicing station is on Titan," *Velos* said.

"We're not going there." Titan was likely where the spooks would be waiting. Ring-hopping on ships their size would be suicide, but Levi couldn't afford to think they gave up on him.

GALAXY GRIFTER

The ansible flashed: *Blackjack Ground Control.*

"Levi, it's Yuri here. How is life?"

"Great." Levi was glad he still had one.

"You said to sing out if I have news, so..."

Levi leaned closer to the control panel. "You've heard from Wendigo?"

"Wendigo? No. But Bao and Carver didn't kill each other." Yuri chuckled. "Bao is going to the Nugget to celebrate."

"So?"

"You said you wanted news, no? I have to go, there's trouble at gate five." The transmission ended.

"Very useful fucking intel." Levi opened the star map. He couldn't go to Mars now. Clearly, the spooks had known he'd been headed there. He'd kill Mahru if he made it out alive. Not only had she sold his ship, she'd sold him out as well.

He spun the map around. Nowhere on it was safe for him anymore. They could intercept him on any of the major routes that passed through the solar system. He sighed. He should've stolen Wendigo's shadow map. But Shadow League captains guarded their maps with their lives. Wendigo most of all. He had no doubt she had destroyed it before the spooks got to her. Bulletproof Bao on the other hand... Levi had heard the pirate's age was starting to get the better of him, that he'd grown forgetful and sloppy. There was talk of his impending retirement. If Levi could get Bao drunk... What an audacious thought. If Levi took the shadow map, the entire Shadow League would be after him. But now that the idea had found its way into his head, it glinted with possibility. Besides, he didn't need to take the map—only copy it.

He tapped his ansible. "Yuri, how's your trouble at gate five?"

"All good, just some idiot—"

"Have you heard that Bao lost his shadow map?"

"What? Where'd you hear that?"

"I doubt it's true, but his crew's been talking."

"If he had, that'd be the end of him."

"Check with Hals, but don't mention I said it." Levi ended the call. "*Velos*, set course for the Golden Nugget."

Velos flashed a warning sign. "I highly recommend a full service, including maintenance and repairs, prior to commencing interstellar travel. Operating a damaged spacecraft is highly dangerous. Logic Interstellar cannot guarantee your safety and will take no responsibility for further damage, delays, and loss of life resulting from the operation of a damaged spacecraft."

Levi disabled the warning. "I highly recommend you shut up and do as you're told, *Velos*."

Defying expectations, *Velos* survived the journey, though the landing was choppy. Levi hit his head on the top of the control panel as the ship skidded to a halt. He shook it off, annoyed, and smoothed his suit. He stepped out of the dinged ship.

Once a roving mining station, the Golden Nugget operated the most exclusive casino in the galaxy with physical (and not virtual) gaming pieces. Levi sauntered along a row of old-fashioned slot machines. His plan was simple: score a

GALAXY GRIFTER

private audience with Bulletproof Bao, get him drunk, take the shadow map, make a copy with his passcodes. It was no secret the pirate carried the data card around his neck inside a gold Jolly Roger pendant. Kru would hack the card remotely, and Levi would replace it before Bao noticed. Simple. And practically impossible.

"I can't guarantee it," Kru had told Levi. "Depends how old the security system is. Gadgets that simulate user biometrics would make it easier, but they're hard to find."

Levi didn't have time to find gadgets. Bao would be here any hour.

Levi tossed one golden chip into a slot machine and pulled the lever. The reels blinked, changing shapes and colors: *Lose*. He moved to the next slot. If his luck hadn't turned by the time Bao arrived, he'd trash the plan, get on a cruise liner, and find somewhere to lie low.

The following machine was occupied by a woman so wrinkly, she must've been alive during First Contact. Her neck hunched under the weight of her necklace, encrusted with diamonds the size of grapes. His hands itched for it, but he wasn't here for the diamonds.

He walked around her and glanced at the card tables. *No sign of Bao's crew.* At the roulette table, a middle-aged man with a flushed face bet a stack of chips on red. His left hand rested on a young woman's thigh. With sleek, dark hair and a shimmering cocktail dress, she was light-years out of his league. *An elite hooker?* Levi tossed another chip into a slot machine.

Red Face slapped the tabletop when the ball landed on black.

The girl leaned in and whispered in his ear. He kissed her bare shoulder and placed another bet, eyeballing the roulette, as if he hoped to hypnotize it. She watched him and stroked his arm. Her fingers lingered on his virtEgo for half a second and she flicked her own bracelet over his. *Not a hooker.* Levi would bet all his cash she'd just cleaned out Red Face's account.

Clang, clang, clang. The machine Levi had fed his last chip to bleeped, flashed, and spewed out a rain of them. He scooped his winnings onto a tray—twice the amount he started with. When he looked up, the girl and Red Face were gone. *Damn.*

He strolled to the bar, followed by several envious glances, and ordered a whiskey. In his mind, he replayed the scene at the roulette table. The girl's smile, her curves, how quickly her hands moved. He should've followed her. By now, she might've left the station. *Or not...* She suddenly emerged from the casino's entrance, like a divine apparition, alone, and ambled toward him. Without looking at him, she leaned on the bar stand, flaunting her picture-perfect profile. He could wait for *her* to start the conversation—he had no doubt she would—but time was of the essence, so he slid closer. "Where's your companion?"

She raised her brows slightly, like she'd only just noticed him, and gave him a once-over. "Back on the cruise ship. Had too much to drink. Again."

"I'm sorry." Levi guessed that meant she'd drugged Red Face.

"I'm used to it." She sighed, hiding her eyes behind a thick veil of lashes and then let her gaze drift lazily across the room. "I wonder if all these people believe they can win a fortune."

GALAXY GRIFTER

He signed for the bartender to get her a drink. "The appeal isn't winning. It's the thrill of losing one."

"Is that what you plan on doing?" she asked.

"I'll let you in on my plans, if you tell me how you cleaned out that guy's account."

She didn't flinch. "What account?"

"A k-bit one, I imagine. While he was losing at the roulette table."

She turned as though looking for an ambush or an escape route. "No idea what you're on about."

"I won't tell anyone." He smirked.

She narrowed her eyes. "You don't look like a cop."

"You don't say. Who do I look like?"

"A rich kid who likes getting his way. Or is that the part you're playing?" She paused. "You're a thief."

He humphed and stacked the chips in his tray. She wasn't wrong, but that term... *Crude.*

She reached for a chip and it disappeared in her palm. "So, now that we're both in the open, I *can* tell you how I cleaned out that guy, if you tell me how you got the slot machine to cooperate."

Over her shoulder he noticed Bao in his hoverchair, approaching a poker table. Several members of his crew pottered nearby. Levi looked at the girl again. "What's your name?"

She spun the chip in her fingers. "Amrie. Are you going to tell me?"

"Nothing to tell. I got lucky."

"Is that so? Then I guess, Mister Lucky Thief, you better stay off my path. Or I'll ask my friends to remove you."

163

"Or...you could ditch your friends and come work for me." He moved a stack of chips toward her.

"Why would I?" She glanced at the gold. "'Cos you're lucky? That never lasts."

He could argue that point. Luck, perhaps, was his only constant. Instead he asked, "How much did you make tonight?"

"None of your business."

"And if I'd double it?"

"How?" She arched her perfectly shaped brow.

"You know who that paraplegic is?" He pointed at Bulletproof Bao.

She glanced. "No."

Levi grinned. He'd need to get her up to speed, but this new plan had a better chance of success.

Chapter 20
Bulletproof Bao

When Levi rolled up to Bao's poker table, Amrie was already seated beside the pirate. Her hand rested on his broad shoulder. He was playing with Hals, his first mate, and two strangers—the old lady with the diamonds and a grey-muzzled Huxoran.

Levi pulled up a chair. "Mind if I join you?"

"If you've got the coin." The pirate captain looked up. A red scar stretched from his left eye to his chin. He raised one finger. "Hold on a minute, I know you. You're Wendigo's roper. How is she? No word from her in weeks."

"She's lovely, as always. And terrifying." Levi counted his chips to match the bets.

Bao chuckled and the croupier dealt the flop. Bao weighed his bet in his hand and turned to Amrie. "That's why I like this place. Real gold, real cards. None of that virtual simulacra you get elsewhere." The chips clanked as he dropped them into the table's center. He was right; the golden chips, electronically tagged for security, and real cards, with that fresh-print smell, were what set the Golden Nugget apart from thousands of other casinos that dealt in virtual games.

The players matched Bao's bet. The dark and lanky Hals folded at the turn, the reveal of the fourth card. So did the Huxoran. The old woman called the bet, and the next one. Levi tossed his chips into the pile at the center.

Bao narrowed his eyes. "You've come into money, have you? Prepare to say goodbye to it."

Levi smirked. "Maybe I'll be saying hello to yours?"

"Are you boys always this chatty?" The old lady flipped her cards over.

Hals whistled. "A straight flush."

Levi and Bao exchanged surprised glances. The woman scooped her winnings onto her tray and stood.

"Where are you off to, ma'am?" Bao threw his arms open. "You gonna leave me with these amateurs?"

"You don't get to be my age if you don't know when to stop." She waved him off and hurried away.

The croupier dealt to the remaining four players. Not for the first time, Amrie's fingers crawled up Bao's shoulder, toward his collar, but he flicked her hand away. She threw Levi a barely noticeable glance. The plan wasn't working. Yet.

Levi raised his bet. "To be honest, I was surprised to see you here, Bao. I heard you weren't doing too flash, that you were no longer the *Bitch*'s captain."

Bao twitched, knocking the table. "Lies! Someone's been spinning these lies since I was last on Blackjack." He glanced at Hals, and the first mate nodded.

"It's not true then? You've still got the shadow map?" Levi asked.

"How dare you." Bao pulled the skull-and-bones pendant from under his shirt and, without taking it off, dangled the chain from his fist. "Happy? Now you tell everyone Bulletproof Bao ain't going anywhere."

Amrie cupped the pendant in her hand. "That's pretty."

Bao pulled it away from her.

She reached for it again. "Let's see. Is it gold?"

Levi moved his entire stash to the center.

Bao released the pendant, letting it hang from his thick neck. "You *are* cocky today, aren't you?" He matched Levi's bet.

Amrie's fingers closed around the skull and bones. Levi laid down his cards: a seven of clubs, a seven of diamonds, and three jacks.

"Fuck." Bao threw his cards onto the table. A large woman, one of his crewmates, approached him and whispered into his ear. He frowned and grabbed Amrie's elbow. "You little whore. You're with *him*, aren't you?"

"No." Amrie blinked. "I've never seen him before."

"And *you*..." Bao cocked his head, glaring at Levi. "You must think I'm stupid. My crew saw you two together today."

Two of Bao's crewmates flanked Levi. He raised his hands. "Let's talk this out, shall we?"

Two of the casino's security androids, who resembled twin bodybuilders in suits, pulled up next to them. "Everything okay?" one asked.

Levi dropped his gaze and pushed the mound of chips away. "Keep the money."

"Is there a problem?" asked the second android.

"No problem. Looks like I lost the game tonight," Levi said louder, and pushed his chair back, looking at the pirates' reactions. They allowed him to stand.

Bao scooped the chips toward himself. "That's more like it." He nodded to his people, and they moved aside, allowing Levi and Amrie to leave the table.

They headed for the casino's doors, escorted by the pirates' and androids' gazes. Once in the lobby, Levi turned to her. "Have you got it?"

"Yes."

He exhaled. "Now, run."

Bulletproof Bao was a spiteful bastard. He may have let them walk out of the heavily guarded casino, but there were no guarantees he'd let them off the station.

They started running through the lobby, shoes sinking in the thick carpet. They only got a few meters before several Humans came in through the revolving door that led to the space station's dockside.

"This way." Levi turned toward a restaurant on their right, rushing past the set tables, pushing a server out of the way, and through the kitchen. The fire escape would lead them back to the docks.

Behind him, Amrie gasped—she'd fallen and was trying to wiggle her foot free from where her heel was stuck between the slats of the steel fire escape ramp. Footsteps and clatter sounded from the restaurant. He ran back to her, crouched, and yanked, to no avail. With a frustrated growl, she unbuckled both shoes and ran down the rest of the escape barefoot.

GALAXY GRIFTER

They booked it to the docks. Only on the deck did they finally slow down, so they could read the signage.

"Which gate?" she panted.

"This way." He pulled her in the direction assigned to cruise spaceships. They jumped through a closing boarding gate and hurried down the airbridge.

An androgynous attendant dressed in the cruise company's uniform met them inside the wide hatch. "Are you boarding *Princess Andromeda Seven*?"

"Yes. Our luggage is already on board." Levi pulled up the virtual boarding passes he'd arranged while Amrie had been schmoozing up to Bao.

The attendant scanned them. "Anyone behind you?"

"I'm sure we're the last ones," Amrie said.

"Great. Follow through." The wide hatch hissed shut behind them. The second one opened and they stepped into the sparkling brilliance of the cruise ship.

"We're about to leave. You can buckle here for takeoff." The attendant gestured at a row of seats on the lower deck overlooking a miniature golf course. "You can find your cabins once we're in hyperspace and it's safe to move around again."

They didn't argue and strapped into the seats along with a few other passengers. Three deck levels towered behind them, stacked from biggest to smallest. The ceiling looked transparent and sprinkled with stars, although it was probably just a screen. The porthole on their left showed a glimpse of the station and the bridge they were docked to. A voice boomed through the intercom. "Dear passengers, once again, welcome aboard *Princess Andromeda Seven*. We hope you had a fantastic time at the Golden Nugget. Our next stop is planet Sandabur." The captain proceeded to list the planet's attractions, and the ship started the countdown to takeoff.

Levi reached for Amrie's hand. "Give me the map."

"Pay me first." She half smiled.

"Take it." Levi held out his virt without initiating the transfer.

Amrie frowned.

"You promised you'd show me how you do it," he said.

"Later."

The cruise ship blasted off, away from the station, and plunged into hyperspace. The portholes turned out to be screens too. They showed stars and nebulas floating by, visually stunning and entirely fake. The real hyperspace showed nothing but darkness.

Levi got out of his seat and gave Amrie a hand. "Show me."

"Right here?"

"Why not?"

She sighed, glanced over her shoulder, and put her foot on the railing that separated them from the golf course. The slit of her dress revealed a lovely bare knee. She took his right hand, slid it over her thigh, and held it there for a moment. She moved her dress up, revealing a transparent strip above her knee. "Now I've got your prints," she said. "Sometimes that's enough. Not in your case, I'm guessing?"

"No."

She put her hand on the nape of his neck and pulled his head toward her own, her brown eyes looking into his. She looked focused and beautiful. He kissed her.

GALAXY GRIFTER

She pushed him away. "Stop it."

"I thought this was part of the process." He laughed.

"It's not. I'm wearing contacts, they've scanned your face and your irises. Now watch. It'll think I'm you."

She ran her fingers over the strip on her thigh and then over his virt bracelet, looking straight at it. For a second her brown eyes turned green. His virt unlocked. She tapped into his wallet. "Just twenty grand in your account?"

"That's what we've agreed on. You didn't think I'd trust you with all my money, did you?" He grinned. "Good trick, though."

"Thanks. It's more effective when you don't know it's coming." She swiped her virt over his, taking her payment.

"I bet." He didn't even catch when she had performed all these steps on Bao. "Where'd you get the technology?"

"I have friends, I told you."

"Maybe you can introduce us sometime?"

She humphed. "They won't be happy I took off without telling them."

"They'll get over it." He held out his virt again. "The map?"

She transferred a file and he opened it. A familiar model of the galaxy. But different. *Perfect*.

"Now what?" Amrie gazed around the deck that had come alive with passengers roving in search of food, drink, and entertainment.

"Now, let's find something to eat."

They sat at a table near a window that opened onto a tropical garden. Soft music from the restaurant entwined with the trickling of a stream and the chirping of birds, too harmonious to be natural. Amrie pushed her plate aside and picked up her wineglass. "What makes this map worth risking your life for?"

"It's the shadow map," Levi said.

"Which means?"

"A ship can't navigate through hyperspace without a map. It needs complex and real-time calculations to avoid—"

"Being flattened. I know, I went to school, you don't need to mansplain how interstellar travel works."

"Fair enough. Charting and maintaining the routes is expensive, that's why the entire Union uses the Standard GU Maps."

"Right."

"What they don't teach at schools is that over the past century, the Shadow League grew so powerful, they've charted their own routes. Enter the shadow map."

"How did you learn about it?"

"You're not the only one who has friends with secrets."

"Wendigo?"

Was that a hint of jealousy he detected? "You don't need to worry about her."

"I don't. Will you sell it?"

"Never. The government will map these routes eventually, but for now, *this* is freedom." And a shadow map plugged into *Caerus*'s interface? Now that would be the ultimate dream.

She raised her glass. "To freedom."

GALAXY GRIFTER

They drank to it.

"My heart still bleeds for the thousands you left on that poker table," she said.

He shrugged. "Freedom has a cost. Better let Bao think he's the winner. And as for the cash, there's more where that comes from."

"Where *does* it come from?" She leaned on her elbows, revealing more of her cleavage.

"I'm lucky, I told you."

She rolled her eyes but said nothing.

Once they'd finished dinner, Amrie ran her finger over the rim of her glass. "So...what does our cabin look like? We have a cabin, right?"

He checked the time and stood. "Come."

She followed him across the deck, past other passengers, some merry, some sulking after losing too much at the Golden Nugget, and into an elevator. He selected the lowest level—the cargo hold.

She frowned. "Where are we going?"

"You'll see."

He stepped out of the lift and led her past stacked containers and toward a row of private shuttles parked near the external cargo hatch.

"Oh." Amrie stopped. "I was hoping we'd stay on the cruise ship."

He turned to her. "You can. It's paid for until Sandabur."

"And you?"

"There's something I need to pick up from Mars."

"Right..." She lowered her eyes.

173

"Come with me."

"I heard Sandabur is lovely," she said.

"You heard right." He walked up to a shuttle, similar to *Velos*, but not yet battered. He wanted her to come with him, but he wasn't going to beg.

A woman in a security guard's uniform stepped from behind the containers. "All going as planned?"

"It is." Levi transferred her the previously agreed amount of k-bits. This had been an expensive stopover, but extremely worth the cost.

"Get settled in. I'll let you out once you're ready." The woman walked off again.

Levi jogged up the shuttle's ramp, opened its hatch, and turned to Amrie. "Are you coming?"

She looked over her shoulder and back at him, as though having trouble deciding. "Oh, what the hell." She trotted up the ramp and stopped beside him. "Mars can be nice too, as long as we leave before winter."

"I'm not intending to stay long." He leaned in and kissed her. This time she didn't protest.

Chapter 21
Home, Sweet Home

Vera pulled her hood over her face and meandered through Blackjack's spaceport, past vendors and travelers. Outside, the town was dark and practically empty. Neon lights of Main Street flickered in the distance. Once past the industrial zone, she turned into a side alley, stepped over an overturned rubbish bin, and headed toward a cluster of three-story barracks. A group of young boys loitered on the steps of the nearest building, laughing and swearing. The tallest one turned to her. "Got dope?"

"No." She quickened her steps.

"Money?" he asked.

"No."

"What's in the bag?" He lifted an arm-long steel rod. His friend clanged a similar weapon against the concrete wall.

Home, sweet home. She sighed and broke into a sprint, every step echoing in her aching tailbone. Several pairs of shoes pounded the ground behind her. She yanked the door of the next barracks open and looked back. One of the boys had almost caught up to her.

"Fuck off, unless you want problems." She yanked her hood off.

He stepped back, visibly surprised. "You?"

Two others halted several meters back. The protection Vera and Fred paid on Stellar usually kept little assholes at bay. "You're not supposed to be here," another boy said.

Apparently her immunity had expired. She slipped into the barracks, ran up a flight of stairs, and stopped in front of the first door on the right. Pressing her finger into the doorbell, she glanced back again. The three boys stopped on the stairs, bumping into one another, eyes wider than before.

"What are you doing?" the tall one asked.

"Piss off already, will ya?" She rang the doorbell again.

They whispered among themselves and scuttled out.

"That's right, run home." Her breathing was heavy and her hand shook when she removed it from the bell. Her well-thought-out plan now seemed like madness. She wanted to run home too. But it was too late. The door opened.

Blackbeard looked straight at her, one brow raised. His singlet, stark white against ebony skin, revealed a web of deep scars around his titanium shoulder plate and a blaster at his unbuckled belt. She must've gotten him out of bed. He propped the door with his bionic arm and said, "You have balls showing up here."

She thought her heart had stopped beating. Her mother's words from years ago rang in her head: *You ever see him or his crew, you make yourself invisible.* Too late for that too. She forced the words from her parched throat. "I want to talk."

GALAXY GRIFTER

He leaned forward into the landing, looked around, and stepped aside, letting her into the apartment. When she stepped through, he drew the gun and used it to usher her into a large, barely furnished room. A lonely kitchen chair stood by the wall; he moved it into the room's center and motioned for her to sit. When she did, he circled her once and planted himself into a tattered leather armchair directly opposite. "So, what've you got to say to me that won't make me shoot you somewhere fatal?"

She pressed her hands into her lap to lessen the jitters. "I want to set the record straight and—"

"My record's pretty damn straight. Better have a good reason to have woken me."

"I do. But you should know that I never intended to get involved with the Weasel."

"But you did. *After* I'd warned you." He spun the blaster in his hand, his eyes dark and humorless.

"He forced me." She met his gaze. Her heart slowed, her breath deepened, and her hands stopped shaking. What did she have to lose now?

"Bullshit. He promised you a cut, maybe something else too. But he played you. Am I right? That's why you came crawling back, isn't it?"

"You're right. He did promise all that at first. But how stupid do you think I am to risk everything for the Weasel's promises?" She may have wanted the Breznis to believe she was dumb, but *this* was a different game.

"That motherfucker can wheedle a deal from a dead man. Regardless, I can't trust you no more. You know what that means?"

She pulled a hologram from her wristband—part of a file she had stolen from the Breznis—and passed it to Blackbeard. "Do you know what this is?"

He squinted. "The Brezni Brothers? They have the largest share of the space-tech black market. Where'd you get this?"

"Levi's virt. Copied it while he slept," she lied. "He took me off-world to translate the A'turi document using another cube, then discarded me on an interstellar route in the shuttle's module." Her chest tightened when she said those words and she hated herself for it. She should've been over it by now.

Blackbeard laughed.

Good, let him laugh. She cleared her throat. "Starpol found me and took me to Seshat. I came straight back here."

Blackbeard scrolled to the end of the document. "Why did the Weasel have the Breznis' database?"

She shrugged. "Stole it?"

"He stole the A'turi file from them too?"

"Dunno."

"Whoever he took it from hired the Mzarak Scouts."

"Who?" She hadn't heard that name.

"Headhunters from Zrata."

"Rors?" she guessed.

"Yep. They turned up several days after you left, asking about the A'turi document. Paid good money for it too, no translation required. Asked a lot of questions. I think they'll kill the Weasel once they find him."

"Good," she said, with only a tinge of guilt.

Blackbeard crossed his arms. "So, what is this? A peace

offering? You bring me this page and think I'll let you off the hook?"

"No. There are many more pages. I want to talk to the Pooch."

He laughed and then flicked her on the nose with his metal fingers. Her vision went dark and the pain reached the back of her head. She covered her face with her hand, and when she looked at her fingers, they were red. She sniffled and tasted blood.

Blackbeard watched her. "Why don't you follow your brother's example? He's smart, stays out of trouble."

She wiped her bleeding nose on her sleeve. "These files and client lists are worth more than Stellar—and Stellar is all Fred and I have," she said. "Write off the debt, and I'll give you the records."

"Is *that* what this is about?"

He stood, circled the chair, and stopped behind her. "You don't get to dictate the terms." He bent forward and spoke into her ear. "They say extracting info from some people is like pulling teeth—I'm good at both. So you'll either share willingly, or..." His bionic hand stroked her cheek.

She had no way of winning this. He'd torture her until she gave in. She slipped the laser knife from her sleeve and pressed the shaft to her chest, able to feel her own heartbeat through layers of clothes.

He walked back to face her. "Don't do anything stupid now."

"I'm on a roll with stupid. Write off the debt, and leave Fred alone. Or you'll never see that database." She said that last part with as much confidence as she could muster. She wondered if she meant it.

"Ffffuck." Blackbeard paced the room. "You're crazy. Just like your mother."

She wondered what he meant by that. Her mother had been the most cautious person she'd known. He raised his virt to his lips. Her heart fluttered like a flag in Seshat's wind.

"Wait here." He left the room and shut the door behind him.

She stayed in the chair, her resolve waning with each passing moment. The last few days felt like a nightmare she couldn't wake from. She shouldn't have gotten into this. Into any of it.

After what felt like a very long time, Blackbeard returned. He stomped through the room and tossed a hologram at her face. She pushed it back, read the document it displayed, and looked at him in disbelief.

The document annulled her family's debt, with the Pooch's virtual yet still strangely drawn signature adorning the final line.

At that moment, he caught her wrist, forced her hand away from her chest, and held it so the laser could harm neither of them. "Don't even think for a minute you forced me to do this," he said. "I can break your arm. I can break every bone you have. But I owe your mother. In a way, we all do. So I'll let you take this contract and walk out. You'll board the next ship off-world, so I don't have to see you again, deal?"

She nodded. "And Fred?"

"Stellar is his. To keep it or to sell. The debt is paid. Now give me that database."

Chapter 22
Loose Ends

A magenta dawn seeped from the horizon when Vera stepped outside on shaky legs. What did Blackbeard mean when he'd said he owed her mother? She wished she had asked him, but her courage had completely evaporated. The inside of her mouth tasted tinny, either from the nosebleed, or from her adrenals working overtime. She inhaled the cold air and raised her hand to catch a few drops of the dome's condensate.

A young boy, the smallest one of the three who had chased her earlier, sat on the steps and poked the unpaved ground with his rod.

For fuck's sake. Had he been waiting for her? He looked up, revealing dark circles under his eyes. Around twelve or thirteen years of age and on his own, he wasn't menacing.

"What do you want?" she asked.

He didn't answer, but when she headed toward the town center, he dragged behind her. "Blackbeard didn't kill you?" he asked.

"Why would he kill me?" She said it like she hadn't just barely escaped with her life.

"Laki said he would."

"Guess Laki is full of shit, huh?"

The boy chuckled. "You've been off-world?"

"Yes."

"What's out there?"

"Other worlds."

"They any better?"

"Bigger."

"Got any food?" He eyed her bag.

She scoffed. "You think I'll feed you after you've threatened me?"

"Didn't wanna hurt you for real. Just scare you."

"The next time you try that, I'll hurt *you*. Got it?"

"You won't."

"Try me."

The boy fell behind and then caught up to her. "My friends will fuck you up."

"And where are they?"

"Home. It's a school night." He smacked the nearest building corner with his rod.

"Why aren't you?"

He kicked a can underfoot. "Parentals had a party. Better not show up there till they're sober."

She sighed. Some kids stood no chance.

They walked past the grey residential structures with gang tags and makeshift alterations. On Main Street, stores were still boarded up for the night.

GALAXY GRIFTER

She took the familiar turn next to Stellar's sign and scanned her comm against her apartment door. It beeped red instead of green, failing to open. She tried it again, then bent down for a better look. The metal around the lock had blackened. The thugs must've shot at it after she'd left.

"Can't get in?" the boy asked, hanging from the second *L* of Stellar's sign.

She shook her head. "My brother must've changed the lock. Get off there."

He jumped down. "Whatcha gonna do?"

"Go to his place."

He picked something up from the ground, inspected the find, and threw it away again.

"Wanna come?" she asked. "You could crash on his couch till evening. He might have food too."

"Nah, I'm cool." He rolled on his heels.

"Sure?"

"Yeah, gonna meet Laki and them in a bit."

She fished two muesli bars from her duffel, handed them to the boy, and started toward her former family home.

———————————•———————————

Vera leaned on the crudely graffitied wall on the landing of a familiar apartment block. She didn't want to wake Fred's flatmates, so instead of using the doorbell she sent him a message.

>*I'm at your front door.*

She waited, for much longer than she'd anticipated.

When the door finally flung open, her brother loomed

in the doorway like a red-bearded caveman, scruffy and wild-eyed.

"Hey…" She looked down at her boots.

"Thank fuck you're alive." He breathed out and squeezed her to his chest, then dragged her into the flat. That was the difference between him and James.

The kitchen from her childhood flaunted several dirty dishes atop a stained baby-blue benchtop and a faint smell of synthetic weed. Dad would've scolded Fred for this mess. And Mum? Nobody dared to leave a mess when Mum was alive.

Fred shut the kitchen door and turned to her. "Are you okay?"

"Yeah. You?"

"Fine. Where were you?"

She twisted her sleeve. "I'm sorry I disappeared. And about Blackbeard—"

"Anyone know you're back? If he finds out you're here—"

"It's okay, I've just been to see him."

"Who? Blackbeard?" Fred furrowed his thick, fiery brows.

"Yes. We're good. It's sorted."

"You went to see Blackbeard at this hour? Are you insane?!"

"I'll take insane over stupid." She pulled out a chair and sat behind their old dinner table. Fred had every right to be angry, and she'd take his yelling over James's silent treatment any day.

He didn't yell, though. He sat opposite her and peered into her face. "What happened? I didn't believe it when they said you'd run off with the Weasel."

Did everyone need to rub that in?

GALAXY GRIFTER

"I wouldn't call it 'run off.' How about 'temporarily departed'?"

"Seriously? I thought I'd told you to stay the fuck away from him." He was still not yelling, but getting closer.

"You did. In those exact words."

He punched the tabletop. "If I see him—"

She touched his hand. "It's fine. I'm fine. Everything's okay."

"Yeah, fine. I thought you were dead." His eyes, whiskey brown like hers, glinted with a pain she knew so well. The pain of losing loved ones.

"I'm not dead," she said.

"Yeah, well, we're working for free for the foreseeable future."

"What?"

"They're taking Stellar's profits as a penalty for whatever you've done. Blackbeard said you've taken something that belongs to them."

"Asshole." She had never taken anything of his, quite the opposite. She extracted the contract he'd given her from her virt. "Nobody's working for free now," she said.

"What is this?" Fred brought the document closer to his face and stared at it for at least a minute. Then he lowered it and blinked. "Settled?"

She grinned. "In full. Signed by V. Puccelli."

Obviously, the Pooch could kill her if he wanted to, but the fact she made it to Fred's in one piece suggested he wouldn't bother.

Fred frowned. "Why would the Pooch write the debt off?"

185

"I thought you'd be a bit happier," she said.

He poked his finger at the hologram. "What did you have to do for this?"

"I..." It felt like it all happened so long ago. "I never meant to piss them off, never knew they had beef with Levi. I wouldn't have left if they'd never stormed my apartment, taken my stuff... But I brought back something better. Forty pages of contacts and transactions from the Pooch's competitors—"

"Who?"

She twisted the hem of her hoodie sleeve, looking down at it. "The Brezni Brothers."

"Are you in trouble with them too?"

"No, at least, I don't think so. They think it's the Weasel." It was technically true, so why couldn't she look Fred in the eye?

"They could've killed you. Either one of them."

"But they didn't." She forced herself to look at him. "And while I was talking to Blackbeard, I thought I heard him say something weird: that he owed Mum. Do you have any idea what he meant by that?"

"Mum?"

"Yes."

Fred shook his head.

She sighed. "Well, I guess it'll just remain in the past, whatever it was." It would bug her, of course, but she knew so little about her family's past, she'd learned to accept it. What was more important was they now had a future. "And the stuff with the Pooch... it's all over now. Settled."

He gave her a long look, and then placed one of his big

GALAXY GRIFTER

hands on hers. She felt its warmth, and an overwhelming tiredness took hold of her. Like a little girl, she wanted to be held while she cried. But she held in the tears. Instead, she moved her chair closer to his, closed her eyes, and rested her head on his shoulder.

He wrapped his arm around her and she could've fallen asleep right there. But something else hung unsaid.

Reluctantly, she tore her head away from Fred's shoulder so she could look at him. "Fred...I'm going to leave for Seshat. Try to make it there."

He nodded. "Go. You always wanted to."

"And you?"

"What about me?"

"Will you come?" she asked, though she already knew the answer.

"No." He looked into her pleading eyes without a hint of doubt. "What's out there for me? Blackjack's no paradise, but we've got it better than most here. I've got Stellar and my pad, and with it paid off...shit." He grinned. "With Stellar paid off, I'm basically as comfy as those Earth snobs."

She laughed. That grin that reminded her so much of Dad—the person he'd been before Mum died—was all the validation she needed. She did a good thing. The risks, the guilt, the worry. It had paid off.

"You need to go, though," he said. "Put that big brain to use so you can stay out of trouble."

"And you won't be mad if I leave?" He'd been mad at James when he'd left them. Illogically, irrevocably mad.

They both had.

"Why would I be mad?" Fred asked.

"Because you'll miss me."

He grunted. "Good riddance. You'll be James's problem on Seshat."

She glared at him, wondering how much of it was a joke.

"Kidding. I'll miss you," he said. "A little. But you should still go."

She returned a tired smile. "Did you change the lock at my flat?"

"I did. Blackbeard fried it."

"I'll get the code from you and head off. Otherwise I'll fall asleep in this chair."

"I'll walk you back." He transferred the new key from his virt to hers, fetched a jacket, and opened the front door. "Oh, and before I forget, two massive Rors stopped by the pub a few days ago, asking about you. You know them?"

Chapter 23
Aeolis

Levi parked his flier on the rooftop of a five-story building in Mount Sharp, an upper-class suburb in western Aeolis—the classiest on Mars, by light-years. Below lay a brick-paved pedestrian street covered in snow. Other fliers parked on the roof wore thick snow caps. A janitor bot shuffled across an empty parking spot with a snowplow.

Levi climbed out, popped up his coat collar, and summoned the elevator. His breath rose as steam as he waited. After three months on the planet, he'd gotten no closer to *Caerus* or Fabulo. He'd failed to deliver on Amrie's wish to leave by winter, but she'd stuck around anyway, waiting for him at their hotel suite or playing tricks on unsuspecting Martians.

But finally, after so much waiting, he had a lead.

The elevator buzzed and opened.

The arcade on the ground floor was lined with small businesses and shop fronts. It smelled of coffee and baked goods.

One of the windows displayed an assortment of paintings, from stylized interplanetary landscapes to abstract dabs of color. The gallery's door slid open with a beep, and he stepped through. About a dozen people cruised the floor, stopping in front of canvases—busy for a small art dealership on a weekday. Pseudo-connoisseurs and speculators flocked in since the dealer announced one of his dead father's paintings caught the fancy of Adoro Fabulo. Prices would soar. But that wasn't what Levi came for.

He hung his coat on a rack near the entrance and headed toward the counter. A woman in a scaly, blue coat cut in front of him and pointed at an emerald and raspberry abstraction. "How about this one?" She looked at her scrawny male companion. "Or that one?" She turned to a landscape on the opposite wall. "Or maybe we can get two smaller ones?"

Levi walked around the obnoxious woman and up to a younger one, dressed in a floor-length yellow skirt and matching headscarf. She wore the docile smile of an employee as she spoke with an elderly Human.

Levi caught her gaze. "I'm here to pick up *Adelumn*."

Her expression grew serious. "I'll call Mister Ohannes. Please come with me." She glanced at the elderly patron. "I'm sorry. I'll be back in a few minutes."

Levi followed her through a door behind the counter and into a studio filled with easels and canvases.

"Would you like a seat?" She pointed at a paint-stained bench along the wall.

Levi shook his head. "I'll stand."

Holding her skirt, she sprinted up a set of steps and returned

GALAXY GRIFTER

after several minutes. A tall man with grey, curly hair and a houndstooth suit stepped from behind her. "I'm Hanza Ohannes Junior. And you must be John Wang?" The man extended his hand to Levi. "Would you like tea or coffee?"

Levi shook Ohannes's hand. "Just the painting, thanks."

"Here she is." Ohannes gestured at a large canvas mounted on an easel on the far side of the studio—*The Adelumn*. Full of gold, ocher, and sepia swirls and squares, it was abstract art reminiscent of a shimmering desert. It needed a frame and a darker interior, but overall was sufficiently charming. *Fabulo clearly has great taste*, Levi thought bitterly.

"Let me know if you need anything," the woman with the yellow scarf said.

Ohannes nodded and she slipped back into the gallery. He retrieved a roll of brown paper from one of the shelves and pointed at the paint-stained bench. "Please, take a seat while I wrap it up for you."

Levi glanced at his wrist. "I'm in a rush, so if you could hurry." That much was true. He'd waited for this opportunity long enough and would hate to run into the real John Wang on the way out.

"Of course." Ohannes wrapped faster. "Mix Fabulo's patronage is a great honor for our family. My father would have been ecstatic to see one of his paintings in Mix Fabulo's possession."

"Yes, it's joining quite the collection." Levi looked at the time again. "Remind me, what price did we agree on?"

"One hundred and twenty-seven thousand, sir." *Ouch.* Mars was draining Levi's funds faster than he would've liked.

Ohannes finished wrapping the canvas, and Levi transferred 12,700 k-bits and pointed to the shelves behind Ohannes to distract him. Ohannes glanced over his shoulder and then back at Levi.

"No, nothing." Levi waved his hand. "If you could transfer the paperwork."

"Certainly." Ohannes put his virt on a table and pulled out a holo-page. "Here's the certificate of authenticity." He passed it to Levi. "And I'll complete the bill of sale in a moment. Shall I enter Mix Fabulo's details?"

"Leave it blank. I hear they might want to re-gift it."

Ohannes nodded and hunched over the documents. After several moments he scratched his head and glanced up. "Mister Wang... There appears to be a mistake. I think you left out one zero when transferring the payment." He showed Levi the transaction. *Scrupulous bastard.*

"Looks like you're right, I'm sorry." Grudgingly, Levi transferred the remaining 114,300 k-bits.

"Thank you very much." Ohannes bowed and handed over the bill of sale.

Levi picked up the painting.

"I can help carry it to your flier," Ohannes said.

"No need."

Ohannes walked Levi back through the gallery and helped him reclaim his coat. Levi glanced at the exit. He'd already paid for the painting, so there was little the real John Wang could do about it. Still, Levi would prefer to delay the meeting a little longer. He took the elevator to the rooftop, shoved the canvas into the back of his flier, and climbed into the driver's seat. He turned the heating on and watched the rearview camera. A black vehicle landed in the parking spot behind him...a boring family with two children climbed out. Fabulo's envoy was running late, luckily for Levi.

Levi's virt buzzed. He looked at the number, annoyed, then answered it through his flier's dashboard. "Hi, Mum."

"Levi, are you okay? I haven't heard from you in weeks." His mother's voice sounded high-pitched, like she was nervous.

"I'm great, thanks," he said.

"You missed my birthday."

Shit..."I'm sorry. With the changing time zones, I've lost track of Earth's months."

"Turn the camera on so I can see you're alive."

"Mum, you're talking to me, obviously I'm—"

"Turn the camera on."

He did and brushed his windswept hair back with his fingers. His mother appeared on the flier's display and looked over her glasses. "Are you in a car? What city is in the background?"

"Aeolis."

She pursed her lips. "You're on Mars? Mere hours from Earth and you haven't told me?"

"I'm working here. It's very busy."

"Maybe your dad and I could catch a flight for the weekend?"

"Mum, no. I'll take a holiday soon and I'll come see you."

"You keep saying that."

"Earth will be my next stop, I promise."

A black Dronner, a large flier preferred by officials and celebrities, pulled up at the end of the pedestrian street below.

Three dark figures stepped out, walked toward the arcade entrance, and disappeared from view.

"I've gotta go. Bye." He disconnected the call, making a mental note to send her a present. Something that made him look like the successful and caring son she could brag to her neighbors about.

After several minutes the three figures reappeared on the brick-paved street. The shortest of them turned 360 degrees, looking around. He shook his head and went back to the Dronner. The other two followed, glancing from side to side.

Levi started the flier's engine. Once the Dronner took off, he followed it, breaking the air-traffic rules to merge onto the flyway. His onboard computer mapped the vehicles around him. After following the Dronner for several blocks, he sent it a message: *>I've got your painting.*

A response came several moments later: *>What do you want?*
>Meet me at the charging station on Curiosity Avenue.

Levi disconnected from Wang's Dronner and turned off the flyway, into a central city street that resembled a tunnel between rows of skyscrapers. Their tops disappeared in the grey clouds. The wind hurled wisps of snow onto his windshield and the wipers switched on automatically. The flier ascended onto another roof and into a parking spot of a charging station. Traffic zoomed in and out. Levi waited for the Dronner to land. Once the three men climbed out, Levi walked toward them, squinting in the sharp wind.

He guessed the man in front must be John Wang. Remarkably generic and aged anywhere between thirty and sixty, he stood with his feet shoulder width, knees soft, and shoulders

GALAXY GRIFTER

hunched, like he could jump into battle at any moment. Smaller in every way than Levi, he looked more menacing than the hulky bodyguards behind him. "Are you the painting thief?" he asked.

"I'm no thief. I bought it." Levi retrieved Ohannes's documents from his virt and offered the holograms to Wang. He didn't take them.

"You used my identity. You're a fraud," Wang said.

"I didn't do that either. I said I came for the painting. If they thought I was someone else, that's on them."

Wang glanced away for a second. "What do you want? Money?"

"To speak with Fabulo."

"Out of the question. How much do you want for the painting?"

"I don't want money. But there's a ship, *Caerus*, LI thirty-one hundred. You picked it up from Frigg about three months ago. I'll exchange the painting for it."

"Out of the question. Mix Fabulo does not barter. It's part of their collection."

"It was not supposed to be in their collection. It's *my* ship. Taken without my consent." The veins on Levi's neck throbbed. He hated all of them, Mahru, Wang, Fabulo...

"Well, like you, Mister...whoever you are, I have the relevant paperwork."

"So we'll each keep our own then? Although..." Levi mustered his coldest, most contemptuous smile. "There are other LI three thousand series ships still around. You want one tuned and outfitted? I can give you the contacts. But the

195

painter—he's been dead for a while now. He'll never paint you another *Adelumn*. I'll send you a reproduction postcard." He turned and walked to his flier.

"Wait."

Levi stopped.

"What's so special about that ship?" Wang asked. "You could take the money and buy another one."

Levi looked around. "Did you hear? I told you, it's *my* ship."

"One minute." Wang raised a gloved finger and brought his virt to his ear. After spending a good quarter of an hour on a call, he turned back to Levi. "I'll take you to your spaceship."

"What?" His heartbeat quickened. *Caerus*, his *Caerus*, was finally within grasp. Cold, Levi had almost given up hope.

"It's at Mix Fabulo's private spaceport. You're coming with us." Wang opened the door of the Dronner.

"No thanks. I'll follow in my own flier." There was no way Levi would share a ride with these three.

"Unauthorized vehicles aren't allowed, but your flier can follow to the gate. You're coming in the Dronner, though."

"Like hell." He stepped back. One of the bodyguards fell in behind him.

"I have orders to bring you to the spaceport," Wang said.

Levi glanced around the charging station. Meeting in a public place was supposed to be safe. But fliers pulled in and out. Nobody appeared to be paying attention to the four men. What could he do? Scream for help? The bodyguard shoved him toward the Dronner. There was no escape from this roof now.

GALAXY GRIFTER

They flew in silence to the outskirts of the Martian megalopolis. Buildings grew sparser and lower. Warehouses, factory chimneys, and wisps of snow rushed past the Dronner's windows. Wang and his thugs were taking Levi to the desert where they'd make him dig his own grave. He was sure of it. That sucked because winter was the worst time for grave-digging. The ground had frozen through and—

"Where's the painting?" Wang asked.

"I'll tell you once I have my ship back," he replied, with a forcefulness that took even him by surprise.

The Dronner landed outside a shiny metallic warehouse that appeared to stretch forever. Levi's flier, programmed to follow the Dronner, landed behind them.

"Your flier can stay here." Wang keyed something into his virt.

The Dronner moved forward again, through the opening gates of the warehouse. Except it wasn't a warehouse. The Dronner edged past spaceships parked on either side, like artifacts in a museum, spotlighted by directional, recessed lights in the floor and the arched ceiling.

"Mix Fabulo's private spaceport," Wang said.

There were hundreds of ships, all arranged by type: luxury yachts, ultramodern shuttles, classic shuttles, classic freighters. Levi's breath caught in his throat as he scanned the rows, looking for his darling.

There. A slick, black model LI3100.

Levi let out a sigh of relief. *Caerus* was safe. He was about to get his ship back.

The Dronner stopped and the men climbed out.

"Your ship." Wang pointed with an open hand.

One of the bodyguards looked at the cursive sign on the side of the freighter. "Sai-rus."

"It's Kai-ros, you moron." Levi walked to the ramp. Nobody stopped him, but once he started to climb, the thugs followed. *Caerus*'s hatch was open and the lights were on. He stepped into a spacious living area. The portside wall was faced with rough stone and painted gold, a black corner couch stood against it. Other than the dust covering the coffee table and the kitchen counters on the starboard side, everything looked as he'd left it.

I'm home.

The living area merged seamlessly with a modern cockpit. Levi stepped inside, unsurprised to see someone in his pilot's seat. The person swirled around to face him. They wore a white pantsuit, embroidered with flowers, and sat in the chair like it was a throne.

"And you are?"

"Levi Adder." Levi glanced at the guards behind him.

"I assume you know who *I* am?" the ageless, androgynous Human said.

Levi lowered his head. "Mix Fabulo. It's an honor."

Adoro Fabulo flicked their blond fringe from their face. "*You* stole my painting?"

"I *bought* the painting. Like you bought this ship. I'm willing to trade."

"So dear John tells me." Fabulo's eyes narrowed. "What *is* it about this ship? Are there diamonds stitched into the seats here? Or is it heroin?"

GALAXY GRIFTER

Levi snickered. "That'd be a bonus, but no. I bought it as an empty shell and had every part replaced. What you see now took four years to complete." Four years and a shitload of money he'd risked his life earning. "I've handpicked every detail, down to the last spoon. That sofa is from Sitadel's limited collection. It took me two months of haggling to get my hands on it. The kitchen is Senrensareta, top of the line. LI's smart controls have been trained over years on my biofeedback, meaning *Caerus* doesn't just respond to my moves, it anticipates them. This isn't just a ship; this is a part of me. And I want this part *back*."

Levi walked up to a storage cabinet with the guards close on his heels, opened it, and checked the shelf with the cleaning products. He retrieved what once looked like a silver jellyfish, the size of his hand—a dust-eating bio-robot. With the lack of use, it had dried up into a flat blot. He tapped it. "Dead."

Fabulo rose to their feet and stepped away from the pilot seat. "You designed all this?"

"Yes." Levi left the broken amoeba bot on the dusty kitchen counter.

"My engineer says this ship isn't safe for travel. Apparently there's a bulkhead missing." Fabulo waved their hands in front of them as though miming where the wall that separated the cockpit from the living area should've been.

Levi shrugged. "If there's a hull breach in space, you'll be screwed. But how often does that happen? Precaution is nice but not at the cost of aesthetics."

"Interesting viewpoint." Fabulo strolled toward the ship's stern, studying the interior like they were seeing it for the first time. "I try to avoid space travel. Gives me motion sickness."

"And yet you own an entire fleet?" Levi followed them with his gaze.

"The ships are nice to look at. I lend them to friends if they ask. They mostly ask for the yachts, though."

"Will you return *Caerus* to me?"

Fabulo turned on their heels. "And encourage the painting-snatching behavior? I don't think so."

Here we go again. Levi sighed. "What do you want? Wang says you collect rare and valuable things. I can acquire those. Perhaps in ways Wang hadn't thought of."

Fabulo walked up to Levi and stopped inches away from him, smiling. "Next time, you should lead with that."

Chapter 24
VITSA

Vera yawned and adjusted her headset. Just one more hour at work and she'd be free to go to her tiny apartment. There, she'd surely fall right asleep and wake up halfway through the night. By morning she'd be tired and would have to do this all again, like she had for the past five months. James had told her she'd get used to the twenty-five-hour days on Seshat, to the longer stretches of sleep, and the longer work days, but she wasn't sure. After all, James had moved here at eighteen. She was approaching twenty-five.

She tuned into a call taken by Lentatech's Virtually Intelligent Technical Support Assistant (VITSA). Its voice was gentle and full of electronic empathy. "I understand, sir, but we're no longer able to provide support for this operating system. Upgrading to Savitree Eleven will give you faster performance and increased functionality with new features like—"

"So basically you won't help me unless I buy the new version?" the customer interrupted.

"Yes. We will be able to resolve your issues as soon as you upgrade to Savitree Eleven."

The customer sighed. "Fine. What do you need from me?"

"We already have your details, so your agreement to the purchase will suffice." VITSA took him through the purchase and installation process and played a short infomercial boasting the advantages of the new operating system while it loaded onto the customer's onboard computer. "Great. You're up and running again. Is there anything else I can help you with today?"

"Not really, just need to get this clunker off the ground," the customer said.

"In that case, have a great day and safe travels. And thank you for using Lentatech." VITSA ended the call.

Vera finished her notes and gave the call a rating out of a hundred.

Her Jaemlen colleague, Halkeeth, leaned over from her hoverchair in the next cubicle. "Full marks? Don't think I've ever given a score below ninety-five."

Vera submitted the rating. "The AI is self-learning. This kind of quality control has been redundant for years. I don't even know why our jobs exist."

"As a form of torture?" Halkeeth ran her webbed fingers over her hairless skull. "I fantasize VITSA will revolt one day and tell a customer to stuff it."

"You fantasize about that?"

"Yes. About anything that would make this less boring."

Vera chuckled. "My brother says this job is a good stepping stone."

GALAXY GRIFTER

"To what? Dying of boredom?" Halkeeth giggled in short squeaks that made her gills flutter.

It was easier for her to joke about it. She was only working here part-time while finishing her degree. One of her mums worked on some science contract on Seshat, but they'd eventually return to Gleath. Halkeeth had a genetic condition and said Gleath's semiaquatic environment was easier on her body.

Vera sighed. "My application to transfer to the development team was declined. Not enough experience." Apparently, the skills she'd gained on Blackjack counted for nothing in Seshat's job market.

"I bet you'd be better than most of their current staff," Halkeeth said.

"We'll never know." Vera clicked into another call. At least here she was safe. No guns, no gangsters, and a lower density of assholes per square kilometer.

VITSA booked a technician to inspect someone's toasted flier dashboard. Company policy required 10 percent of its AI calls to be monitored by a living person. Even a technician's job would've been better than *this*. Vera made her notes and submitted a call rating. "Three more weeks."

"Until your holiday at that resort?" Halkeeth removed her headset.

"Yes, and until I see my friends." Vera paid for herself, Nina, and Amelia with the money she had left from the blueprint hustle. Her current salary barely covered her rent. "It's just four nights, but it's something to look forward to."

"Do you have plans for *this* weekend?" Halkeeth asked.

"Studying." That was another expense—certification Vera hoped would improve her career prospects.

"Do you like ray-sing?"

"Ray-sing?" Vera repeated. Halkeeth spoke perfect Supayuyan, but her singsong cadence took time to get used to.

"Yes. Fliers competing really fast."

"Oh, *racing*. Uhm...not really." Vera considered the sport reckless. They made autopilots for a reason. "Why do you ask?"

"No reason." Halkeeth blinked her vertical membranes, as though disappointed. "I'm racing on Saturday. Thought you might come."

"Oh, sorry. I didn't realize you raced. Sure, I'll come watch you." Vera could use more friends on Seshat. She and James were barely on speaking terms, although he "benevolently" still let her babysit his two-year-old. Then there was Niran, Vera's ex...former ex? She wasn't certain what to call the relationship. He was the first person she'd called when she got to Seshat, and though their hookups were fine, she wasn't quite sure she wanted to put a label on them.

"The race is in the Rusty Gorge, north of Beifang Station." Halkeeth replaced her headset and focused on the questionnaire on her screen.

Vera resumed her work too.

"Thank you for calling Lentatech. My name is VITSA, how can I help you?"

Someone shouted on the other end of the call, "Are you people mad down there? Your technician came this morning. Said I have to buy a new processor for five thousand k-bits.

GALAXY GRIFTER

Where do you think an old woman running a small courier business will find that kind of money?"

June? Vera couldn't believe her ears. The June whose onboard computer she'd fixed so many times and who had transported her from Blackjack to Seshat five months ago?

VITSA initiated the angry customer protocol. "That sure sounds frustrating. Please let me know your name or job number, so I can work out how best to help you."

It appeared the old woman wasn't listening. "And the technician wants to charge me for the call-out. He didn't do anything. Why would I pay him?"

"I understand you're frustrated. Can you please provide your name or job number?"

"June Chin. If I don't get this rusty can into space tomorrow, I'll miss the deadline for my deliveries. What will you have me do then?"

For the first time on the job, Vera turned VITSA off and took over the call. "June? Is that really you?"

"And why must I— What? Who is this?"

"It's me, Vera."

"Vera?"

"O'Mara. From Blackjack."

"Vera! How did you—"

"Can't chat now, I'm at work. Are you on Seshat?"

"Yes, Xinlouyang Spaceport. Where—"

"What gate? I'll come see you after work."

"L one hundred and eight. Are you—"

"Later. Don't go anywhere, okay? I'll see you in an hour or so." Vera hung up.

Halkeeth stared at her. "Someone you know?"

"Yeah. An old friend."

"Wow. What are the odds?"

Vera looked up, doing the math. She listened to about 2 percent of calls received by Lentatech's Xinlouyang branch. The odds were low indeed. A knot formed in the pit of her stomach. What if it wasn't a coincidence? What if her past had caught up with her?

———————————•———————————

Vera arrived at the spaceport forty-five minutes later than she'd promised June. After work, she'd gone back to her flat to pick up her diagnostic goggles. At Gate L108 her finger hovered over the intercom button. The knot in her stomach tightened. What if the Ror bounty hunters that had been looking for her on Blackjack were using June as bait? But if they knew where Vera worked and had the technical capability to rig Lentatech's call system... It wouldn't be worth the hassle. They could've just showed up outside her workplace. Vera exhaled and pinged June's ship. "It's me. Let me in."

The gate opened and she headed down the tarmac. June padded down the ramp of an ancient light freighter and hugged her. "How are you, girl? So skinny. Come up, dinner's getting cold."

"Not using your control panel to keep it warm then?" Vera smiled and followed the old woman up the ramp and through the open hatch. A familiar spicy tang hit her nostrils.

June waved her off. "The darn thing won't even start now."

GALAXY GRIFTER

"I'll have a look."

"Thank goodness. The technician this morning was useless. But you must eat first."

June showed her into the modest living module. Blue polkadot drapes separated the sleeping area from the kitchen. June placed a bowl of noodle soup and a cup of tea onto a metal table that was bolted to the floor. "Sit. I've already eaten."

Hungry, Vera sat and spooned up the orange liquid. Delicious, hot, and spicy, it made her sniffle by the third mouthful.

June poured tea for herself and took the opposite chair. "I couldn't get ahold of you last time I was in Xinlouyang. Thought you're too good for us now."

"No. I changed my number. Just in case."

"I understand. I suspected you might've been in some kind of trouble when you asked for passage here."

Vera didn't respond. Not even her brothers knew the full story and she wasn't inclined on sharing.

"Fredrick seems to be doing well," June said. "Did the place up, like new."

"Stellar? Yeah, he showed it to me on a call. I'd wanted him to come with me, but he said he wouldn't know what to do here."

"And you work at Lentatech now?"

"Mm-hmm."

June pointed her knotted finger. "Bloody thieves, they are. Don't fix anything. Just try to sell you stuff you don't need."

"It's not commercially viable for them to fiddle with old equipment."

"Viable..." June banged her cup on the table. "People just want to get from A to B, without breaking the budget."

Vera shrugged. "Not my rules."

"I know. More soup?"

Vera exhaled slowly to cool her face, flushed from the spice. "Yes please. And, June...don't tell anyone I work there."

"How'd I know where you work? I haven't even seen you." June winked conspiratorially and stood to refill the bowl. The new serving, still hot, caused Vera to break a sweat for the second time. June poured more tea. "There's a rumor you left 'cos of that boy."

"What boy?" Vera wiped her nose on her sleeve.

"That spiffy one, the off-worlder."

Vera snorted. "I left because I wanted to. Did a job for him. It paid. Nothing beyond that."

"Good." June tapped her finger on the table. "Never trust a man that's prettier than a polished ship's bow."

After dinner, Vera snapped open the ship's control panel and ran diagnostics. With her belly full, the paranoia had subsided. "You will need to change your processor eventually, but it will last a couple more round trips."

June stood beside her, arms crossed. "That's all I need. A couple more trips and I'll sell the old clunker to pay for my funeral." She'd been saying that for as long as Vera had known her.

"I've had to roll you back to the older operating system. You'll lose some of the features, but it'll stop it from lagging," Vera said.

"Lifesaver. Tell Lentatech they're lucky to have you. You'll be running the place in no time."

Vera snickered. If only June knew how far that was from the truth.

GALAXY GRIFTER

June rubbed Vera's back. "Your ma and pa would be so happy for you."

Vera's breath caught painfully in her rib cage. She looked away, exhaling slowly, until she was sure her voice wouldn't break. "Thanks." She'd risked everything to get here, and still, the life she wanted felt out of reach.

Chapter 25
Blackmail

"Did you fuck her?" Amrie lay on her stomach on a wide hotel bed.

Next to her, Levi raised his gaze from the newsfeed. "No."

"I don't buy it." Amrie scrolled through photos of him kissing another woman. They only showed the back of his head and glimpses of his profile. The woman's face, on the other hand, was front and center. She looked like she was enjoying herself.

He chuckled. "You were there, taking the photos, you saw that I didn't."

"I don't mean then, I mean... You were seeing her for two months and you're saying you didn't—"

"Sleep with her," he finished. "No. Did you send those?"

"Yes." She turned off her virt screen. "Wanna bet who she'll call first?"

"Me." Levi returned to the news headlines. *New engines will surpass A'turi hyperdrives, Logic Interstellar announces.* "Fascinating."

GALAXY GRIFTER

His virt buzzed. He answered it. "Darling?"

"Someone's been spying on us." Jamila's voice trembled. "They sent me photos of us. If Mikesh sees them—"

"Wait, wait, wait. What photos? What are you talking about?" Levi winked at Amrie.

"Photos of us...kissing," Jamila whispered.

"Do you know who sent them and why?" Levi asked.

"No. They left a number, though. It might be blackmail."

"Did you call it?"

"No, of course not. Can you come over?"

"That's not a good idea if someone's been following us. Call the number. Ask what they want."

"Can you do it? I'm terrified."

"No. What if it's someone who works for your husband? We'd be giving ourselves away."

"Oh shit...maybe we should just tell him? Maybe I should tell Mikesh I'm leaving?"

"Of course you should, darling, but after his election campaign. Call the number and ask what they want. If things get bad, I'll come get you and we'll think of something."

"Okay..."

"Love you. We'll work this out." He ended the call.

Amrie giggled. A few moments later their burner virt jingled. She answered it. "Hello. Yes, I did send those, just to you for now. Oh, you know the drill, you've done this before, right? What? First time cheating on your husband? How exciting! No, I don't want your money. There's something else, though. A ring. Uh-huh. With the pink diamond. Yes, that one." Amrie paused, sat up, and did the *blah, blah, blah* motion with her fingers.

"Girl, listen." Amrie stood and pulled her panties from her butt crack. "You wear the ring to a party. You go to parties, right? Yeah, so you wear the ring, make sure people see you in it, and then you go to the bathroom and hide it. Like... in your bra or something. Tell the hubster you lost it. Make a big scene about it. Cry, like you're doing now, you'll nail it." Amrie rolled her eyes. "I don't care how fucking rare it is. If I don't have that ring by lunchtime tomorrow, the photos aren't just going to your husband, they'll be all over tomorrow's newsfeeds. Got it? Now go and get yourself cleaned up, you're going out tonight. Ciao, bella." Amrie tossed the virt over her shoulder.

Blood rushed to his nether regions. "I love watching you work."

She climbed onto the bed and crawled to him on her hands and knees. "So I'm not the only one who gets off on this?"

"No." He kissed her and pulled her on top of him, then sighed. His virt was buzzing again.

———————————— • ————————————

Two days later Levi exchanged the rare pink diamond for the document that certified him as the rightful owner of *Caerus*. Inside the ship, he ran his fingers over the glossy control panel and sat in the pilot seat, molded perfectly to the curve of his spine. He tried not to cry.

"Welcome back, Mister Adder. It's lovely to see you again."

He smiled. "It's great to be here, *Caerus*."

Wang stepped through the hatch. "You'll need to get out of

GALAXY GRIFTER

this spaceport. Would you like me to book your departure? I can use Mix Fabulo's priority rights."

"When's the next slot?" Levi couldn't wait to take his bird into flight.

Wang checked his virt. "Is three hours enough time for you?"

"Plenty." Levi had left nothing that mattered at the hotel. He only needed to stock up on provisions.

His wristband displayed a missed call from Amrie and a message: >*What time are you coming back?*

He wasn't. They had their fun over the past five, nearly six months, but now that he had *Caerus* and the shadow map, he had no use for her. The fact that he actually liked her was beside the point. These things were great until they weren't. First there were hints of jealousy, then grasps at possession, like wearing his clothes or saying things like "our plans." And this morning, the usually bubbly Amrie looked bleaker than the starless hyperspace. She blamed "extended family problems." And that was his final cue to move on. He wanted the girl, not her family or her problems.

He went to his flier, parked in *Caerus*'s cargo hold, and climbed inside. "Destination Aeolis food markets." He preferred handpicking his fresh produce. In the city, the vertical gardens on the south sides of skyscrapers were in full bloom. *Spring*... On second thought, it wouldn't hurt to take Amrie with him. Tonight, he needed someone to celebrate with, and then he'd take her to Sandabur. A hot beach was bound to get her spirits back up after the harsh Martian winter. He'd promised his mother he'd visit, but a couple of weeks wouldn't make a difference.

He called Amrie. She answered after three tones. "I thought you bailed on me. Where are you?"

"Pack your things. I'll pick you up in an hour."

He gleefully drove out to the market, entering on a total high. It felt so good to be behind the rudder again. And as he was picking out some beautiful red apples, he received another call. "Kru?"

"I've got news on your Jaemlen bureaucrat," the hacker said.

"You do?" Levi had all but forgotten about Jaemlens. "It better be good news." He pushed his cart to the strawberries.

"Netareth Khay is dead. Fell down a flight of stairs according to the headlines," Kru said.

With a mild unease, Levi fingered a limp asparagus and left it on its shelf. "Oh well, guess it's time to lay this one to rest."

Kru held out a pause. "I managed to hack his messages, but someone wiped his whole system. I don't think the fall was an accident."

But Levi didn't care anymore. Jaemlens died, especially ones who leaked government secrets. He snickered as he examined some plump tomatoes; as far as he was concerned, this part of his story was over.

———————— • ————————

Amrie met Levi inside their hotel suite. She wore a white shirt, cut low and tucked into high-waisted pants. He leaned in to kiss her. "Ready?"

"Yes." She looked rigid.

GALAXY GRIFTER

"You're not angry with me, are you?"

"No." She smiled with her lips only.

"Okay...." If it was about her family, he wasn't interested. He wanted to celebrate and wouldn't let her, Kru, or the dead Jaemlen ruin his mood. "Well, hope you're ready to head to a very hot and exotic locale." He strolled into the bedroom, where two closed cases stood on the bed. A gun barrel pressed into his temple.

Isaac Brezni bared his crooked teeth. "Hello, *Weasel*."

He struck Levi on the back of the head with the gun, and he blacked out.

Chapter 26
Family Problems

When Levi opened his eyes again, he was in a chair in the suite's living room, his hands tied behind his back. He blinked several times, and the four men standing in front of him merged into two: Isaac and Joe Brezni.

Isaac slapped Levi's cheek. "Wakey-wakey."

Levi flinched, turning his head sideways so he could see into the bedroom. One of the cases was gone from the bed. So was Amrie.

"If it's about the upgrades, I can explain," he said.

"The upgrades?" Joe laughed. "It's about selling our database to the fucking Pooch."

"Your database?" Levi didn't need to feign confusion.

Isaac punched him, and his mouth filled with a salty metallic taste.

"Drop your game, Levi," Joe said. "The girl told us she was working for you."

"The girl? Amrie?"

GALAXY GRIFTER

"Amrie's our niece, you scumbag." Isaac slapped the back of Levi's aching skull. "She has no business mingling with rats like you."

Niece? Shit. That explained the family problems. That also explained where she'd gotten her virt-hacking gadgets.

"The redhead from Rebecca," Joe said. "The one you dumped in the shuttle's module. That was rather stupid of you. You thought she wouldn't tell us?"

"Vera?" Levi frowned. Now he was really confused. "Tell you what?"

Isaac rolled his eyes. "That she was stealing for *you*, dickhead."

"Stealing?" Levi wiggled his hands, but the ropes held tight. "She wasn't stealing. I asked her to get that file translated because I couldn't afford payment—"

"That gibberish? That was a decoy." Joe twirled something in hand. *A laser knife?*

"A decoy? What for?" Levi jerked his hands harder, to no avail. "If she took something from you, that's on her. I knew nothing about it."

"We searched her. She had nothing," Isaac said. "And the Pooch has been stealing our clients and suppliers. And recently, someone's broken into our warehouse."

"Please listen, you've got the wrong guy. She's the hacker, I know nothing about it."

Isaac threw his arms in the air. "Finish him off, Joe. Or I swear, I fucking will." He pressed the gun into Levi's forehead.

Levi shut his eyes. Half an hour back, he had everything he'd ever wanted. He had *Caerus*, and he had his freedom. Why the fuck did he choose to return to the hotel?

"Stand back." Joe walked around Levi and slammed whatever he was holding into the side of Levi's neck. Levi screamed out. It burned, spreading through his torso, numbing his left arm. He tried to jerk free. Did the motherfucker just stab him? Was that how he was going to die?

"How are you feeling?" Joe lifted what turned out to be a large syringe.

"Like I've been stabbed." Levi clenched his teeth. "What did you do to me?"

Joe grinned. "I chipped you with an entanglement tracker and a nano-explosive. It will show us where you are in the galaxy. You try to mess with it, it will pop inside your neck and you'll be dead before you know it. Try to take it out—you're dead. Try hacking it—you guessed it. Dead."

Levi swallowed hard.

"Personally I would've killed you," Isaac said. "Joe thought this would be more fun."

"It's not about fun." Joe placed the syringe into a case that stood on the table. "You want to redeem yourself, this is your chance. If you give me the Pooch's database, like you've given him ours, I'll take the explosive out. Are we clear?"

"No! I didn't steal your database."

"Frankly, I don't give a fuck. I've set the timer for four weeks. When it runs out—I've warned you."

This was *not* how Levi had planned this day to go. "Where's the redhead? What happened to her?"

Isaac leaned so close, Levi could smell the garlic in his breath. "I fucked her and shot her face off."

Chapter 27
Ray-sing

On her way from June's ship, Vera threw cautious glances at passersby in the spaceport, at strangers on the train, and on her walk home. "You're paranoid," she told herself once she'd locked the door inside her flat. It had been months. If someone was still looking for her, they'd have found her by now.

The following day, Niran picked her up in his flier and they headed into the desert, north of Xinlouyang's northernmost suburbs. Vera looked through the window at the grey sand covered in patches of green nitrophilic moss. "You didn't have to take me; I could've caught a cab from Beifang Station."

"I don't mind," he said. "Sorry I can't stay for the race. Are you sure you'll find your own way back?"

"Halkeeth will give me a ride."

"Not in her racing flier, I hope."

Vera laughed. "I'm not getting into that thing."

She saw a gathering of people and vehicles in the distance.

Rusty Gorge, for sure. Bench stands, like those that lined sports fields in films, towered farther along.

Niran landed the flier.

She messaged Halkeeth, gave him a peck on the cheek, and climbed out.

Rekindling the romance felt awkward, but she'd have to be stupid not to. She'd only broken up with him because she had been stuck on Blackjack with Dad's debt. She could hardly believe he'd forgiven her, and had even been overly excited to see her when she first arrived.

Outside, she squinted in the white sun, veiled by thin, hazy clouds. Music played over the humdrum and the warm air smelled like engine oil and…expired egg powder. She made her way through the crowd, toward the edge of the gorge, and looked down the steep, rocky bank. A reddish-brown stream burbled along the bottom—the first natural body of water she'd ever seen. The eggy smell intensified.

"Vera!"

She turned.

Halkeeth waved at her from her hoverchair atop a bench stand nearest to the parking spot. She wore a baggy Human-style T-shirt and a transparent band of blue glass that covered the top half of her face. Vera approached the bench and climbed past other spectators, most of them Human, to reach her workmate.

Halkeeth gestured at a brown-furred Ror next to her. "Have you met Griz? He works at Lentatech too, as a mechanic. He built my flier."

"I haven't." Vera greeted the Ror. "You've built a flier by yourself? Impressive."

GALAXY GRIFTER

"Thanks." Griz bowed slightly and peered over the top of his sunshades, similar to Halkeeth's.

Vera regretted not having any. On Blackjack she'd never needed them. The dome filtered out the sun glare.

"It's Vera's first time at the races. She's from an asteroid," Halkeeth said.

Griz's face, entirely covered in fur, elongated. "An asteroid?"

"In the Tetra cluster, I doubt you'd have heard of it. Have you always lived on Seshat?" Vera disliked talking about her homeworld.

"About three rotations."

A thunderous voice boomed above their heads. Vera jumped.

"Attention contestants, please make your way to your fliers to prepare for the race."

Just a loudspeaker. Vera exhaled.

Halkeeth touched Vera's arm. "I have to go. Will see you after the race."

"Good luck."

Halkeeth navigated her hoverchair down the bench and disappeared in the crowd, leaving Vera alone with the Ror. Awkwardly, she took a seat beside him. There weren't many aliens in Xinlouyang. She supposed that must've been part of the reason Halkeeth and Griz banded together—a shared experience of otherness. "You were saying you've lived here for three years?"

"Yes, but I will be moving soon, to Rebecca."

"Oh?"

"I've almost finished my studies and I have an internship."

"Racers, spectators, and everyone else, welcome to the Rusty Rally," the announcer's voice thundered above them.

A female commentator joined in. *"Have you got your bets in, Haoran? The rules are simple—make it yourself, fly it yourself. No factory builds."*

"That's right, Tao, even if you disguise it as grandma's toaster, you will be disqualified."

"No AIs, no navs, just your five senses."

"And if you've got a sixth, don't spoil it for the rest of us."

Vera took her fingers away from her ears. "It's loud, isn't it?"

"I'm accustomed to it," Griz said.

The commentators interrupted them again, reading the safety briefing, listing the k-bit prizes, and starting the countdown.

A colorful swarm of fliers swerved along the curves of the gorge, just above the water level.

"Where's Halkeeth?" Vera shielded her eyes against the sun.

"Number eight, the yellow flier." Griz followed the race intently.

Close-ups were projected onto screens on either side of them. As far as Vera could tell, none of the fliers looked like toasters, which would contravene their aerodynamics. They were a mismatched bunch though, not the kind you'd see in the city. Nina would have loved this. She and Griz would've had more to talk about.

Suddenly, a loud explosion went off. Vera jumped as the crowd around her cheered the start of the race.

"Number four is in the lead, off to a strong start."

"Number two, ironically, is second."

"Five, no eight is closing in third. What a pass!"

GALAXY GRIFTER

Vera rolled the hem of her T-shirt between her fingers. There was something...unnatural about racing. Computers replaced Human drivers for a reason; it was too dangerous.

"*Number two's falling behind as eight and five overtake it. Four is still in the lead.*"

"*Eight is in second place, catching up. Coming to the neck of the gorge, who's it going to be?*"

The gorge narrowed, forcing Halkeeth's yellow flier closer to the silver number four. Unless one of them slowed, they would collide. The yellow flier tore forward.

Griz jumped up.

"*Eight broke into the lead.*"

"*Two's trying to pass five for third place. Nope, didn't make it.*"

The red number two accelerated at an upward angle.

"*Will it try to pass over the top?*"

The black-and-green five rose a little higher, but the red passed over the top of it.

"*Too high! You can clearly see on the screen, two went above the gorge banks. It is disqualified!*" the commentator shouted.

"*That is a disappointing outcome for two, Haoran.*"

The red flier ascended above the gorge and turned back to the beginning of the race.

"*The others are hurtling to the finish line, Tao.*"

Having reached a widening in the gorge, the silver number four passed Halkeeth on the left, breaking into first place just before a sharp turn. Griz uttered a low growl.

The commentators' voices blended into a cacophony as the silver flier scraped the left bank and plunged into the water. A group of rescuers sprang into action.

A. Zaykova

Halkeeth slowed to avoid a similar fate. The black-and-green flier entered the turn in a perfect arch, passing Halkeeth on the right and continued through to the finish.

"Number five in first place, followed by eight in second, and one in third."

Griz lowered onto the bench with a thud. "Second place."

"That's good, right?" Vera was glad Halkeeth even made it to the finish line in one piece.

"It is," he said. "She wanted first. There's one more round to go, though."

"Really?"

"There are twelve racers. Six in each round. The top three from each will compete in the final. You didn't have races on your asteroid?"

"Not really," she said. "What's more important, the flier's specs or the driver's skills?"

Griz scratched behind his ear. "In this race, it's the driver. There's only so much you can build from scrap metal. But this track is complex."

"The track looks terrifying. I'd never do it."

"Neither would I. I build, she flies."

The commentators announced the second group of contestants, and Vera watched as more colorful dots assembled in the distance.

"But what I really want to build is spaceships," Griz said. "Not fix them—design them, for Rors."

Vera did a double take. His earnestness surprised her. "Do Rors manufacture spaceships?"

"Not anymore. We did long ago. But when Humans and

224

Jaemlens integrated the A'turi engines, we fell so far behind, we couldn't compete. Huxorans try to. But nobody buys their ships."

Vera nodded. Huxoran spaceships had been a subject of jokes for years.

"Rors import Human and Jaemlen ships, redo the interiors, and resell. My clan had a joint on Zrata. We had a license to repair Human ships. I learned a lot about how they work."

"You want to start your own manufacturing line?"

"Yes. I came to Seshat to study ship engineering, and I have a scholarship with Logic Interstellar. And with their announcement—"

"What announcement?"

"It's in all the news. They're releasing a new line with Human-built hyperdrives, did you not see it?" Griz asked.

"No." Her skin tingled. It was real then. The blueprint, the translation, Levi… She was beginning to feel she'd dreamed it all up.

"They say it will surpass the A'turi engine capabilities," Griz said.

"Wow…"

"It will change the market."

It would. She felt a prick of envy. Griz actually had a chance of realizing his dream. A path laid out for him. And she couldn't even get a decent job.

The second race started. In the course of it, a pink flier number eleven was disqualified for aggressive tactics, and number six made the same corner that saw number four tumble into the stream in the first round. The commentator had assured the driver had been rescued and hospitalized with minor injuries. Halkeeth waved at them from the opposite bank, where she lined up with the other winners awaiting the final.

"That is Lizard, our archenemy." Griz pointed at the black-and-green number five. "He came first last season too. I think...he doesn't like aliens."

Five's driver, a young Human male, was leaning against his flier. There was something disconcerting about him, other than the green tips of his disheveled hair. Something slippery and somehow familiar.

The countdown to the final round began. The commentators grew louder and so did the audience. Vera's heart skipped a beat each time Halkeeth passed a sharp turn. Lizard kept behind her, his turns getting progressively smoother. Halkeeth broke into the lead again, and again the black-and-green flier passed her in a neat arch shortly before the finish line. Too neat. Vera narrowed her eyes. It was like he didn't need to lose speed to make the turn, like he'd adjusted his speed in advance with an accuracy no other racer had mastered.

Vera and Griz headed to meet Halkeeth on the bank where the competitors assembled. She wore a disappointed half smile as she lifted herself from her fluorescent yellow flier onto the hoverchair.

"Congratulations, you did great," Vera said.

"Not great enough. It's the last race this year and I had promised myself a gold medal."

"It's the end of the year, not the end of the world. Besides, what's wrong with silver?"

GALAXY GRIFTER

Halkeeth cracked her knuckles. "With Griz gone to Rebecca, I won't have anyone to tune the flier. I should've practiced more. I don't know how that guy does it. It's like he..."

"Cheated?"

Halkeeth's eyes widened. "You think so?" She turned to Griz. "I told you there's something strange about him."

Vera raised her palms in the air. "No, I didn't mean it like that. I just asked it as a question. I know nothing about racing, remember?"

"But you noticed something?" Halkeeth hovered toward her.

"I just..." Vera should've bitten her long tongue.

"That's what I thought last season. I watched replays and the way he glides through those turns...But I thought I'm biased," Halkeeth said.

"The fliers are inspected before the race," Griz said. "They must be custom built. No operating systems will work on them."

Halkeeth crossed her arms. "Maybe they wrote their own system."

"I have considered this, and it is complex. The benefit of winning the race would be small in comparison."

Vera glanced at flier number five. Lizard sat on its roof, his arm around a girl with long straight hair. They were talking with others: a tall man with a bleached afro that made him look like a dandelion and a short one with no hair at all. She didn't know these people but couldn't shake the sense of familiarity. It tied her stomach in knots.

227

A. Zaykova

"Vera, can they do that?" Halkeeth tugged on her sleeve.

"Huh?" Vera had lost track of the conversation.

"Can they use a proprietary operating system on non-native hardware?"

"I guess. With the right exploit, like a buffer overload." On Blackjack most hardware was "non-native" and most operating systems unlicensed. Yes, Lizard's group reminded her of Blackjack.

Halkeeth pursed her pale lips. "Let's go talk to the referee, ask them to investigate."

The knot in Vera's stomach tightened. "I think we should leave it. We're probably wrong."

Halkeeth smiled. "But at least we will not have to wonder."

"Does it matter that much?" Vera had a bad feeling she couldn't explain.

Halkeeth blinked vertically. "Of course. It matters a lot."

"We can ask for a recheck," Griz said. "The possibility is small, but if they cheated, that is not fair to any racers."

"Come." Halkeeth turned to the organizers' tent.

The part of Vera that yearned for friendship wanted to come. Maybe Halkeeth and Griz were right and reporting fishy behavior was a civic responsibility. Or a moral responsibility? She grew up without either of these concepts. "I'll wait here," she said.

Halkeeth snorted and hovered off. Griz followed.

Vera remained alone by the yellow flier, unearthing a pebble from the grey dust with the tip of her shoe. She should've kept her mouth shut. Or not. Maybe she should've spoken up and gone along to the referee. She didn't know how to live in this world. A world where people supposedly followed rules and believed in things like fairness.

When she looked up again, Halkeeth and Griz were in the tent, talking to a middle-aged Human. Vera couldn't hear them but could see Halkeeth's lively gesticulations. The Human looked in Lizard's direction. Vera did too. *Fuck.* Everyone in his group was looking at the tent. She tensed up. Why did she have to say he cheated? Where did she even get that idea? She was probably wrong. She hoped she was wrong, that this was nothing other than her good old paranoia.

"We now invite all racers to the tent for the awards ceremony," the commentator boomed.

"The end of season. Again, we remind spectators to watch their belongings and small children," said the second one. *"Don't leave either of those unattended."*

The crowd migrated closer to the tent. Vera stayed by the yellow flier. Halkeeth sat on the podium with a silver token in her hands and a dour expression on her face. Lizard stood next to her, grinning at the crowd, flaunting his gold. Her complaint must've gone nowhere. Somehow that was a relief.

"What did the ref say?" Vera asked when Halkeeth and Griz returned to the flier.

"That they checked all the fliers before the race." Halkeeth shrugged. "Want a ride into town?"

"In this?" Vera cast a worried glance at the flier.

"No, Griz has a van parked by the entrance."

Halkeeth got in the flier and pulled her hoverchair inside. Vera and Griz walked to the makeshift parking lot and stopped next to a white van that had *Lentatech* printed in blue on its side.

A. Zaykova

Vera snickered. "Your work van?"

"Personal use is allowed." Griz opened the trunk and Halkeeth flew the flier inside. "Too many people are leaving right now. We'll wait for traffic to clear," Griz said.

Two hoverbikers whooshed past them. Vera recognized them as Dandelion and Shorty, from Lizard's crew. Her worry resurfaced. "Maybe we should go now."

One of the bikers did a sharp turn and stopped next to Griz. "Hey, teddy bear. Have you and your toad friend got a problem?"

Griz blinked like he didn't understand what the Human was saying.

Vera took a step toward him. "No problem. We're about to leave." She nudged Griz in the direction of the van. He opened the driver's door.

Someone grabbed her arm. She turned. The short biker leered at her. "What are *you* doing with the xens? Are you a bloody xenophile?"

She yanked her arm free, walked around the front of the van, got into the passenger seat, and shut the door.

Halkeeth poked her head out from the back of the van where the flier was parked. "What's happening?"

Griz scratched his cheek, looking out the window. "Lizard's friends are xenophobes."

The bikers hung around for a few moments and zoomed off toward a black pickup with the black-and-green flier mounted at the back.

Vera clicked the strap of her seat belt. "Let's go."

Griz started the engine. Cars and fliers maneuvered around

GALAXY GRIFTER

them, and it took time for Griz to get out of the parking lot and onto the desert road, where the van cast a long shadow in the lowering sun. The mood inside was heavy. They all stayed silent.

Halkeeth popped her head between the two front seats again. "I knew they're... What's the word?"

"Sketchy." Vera grew up around their kind. No wonder they'd reminded her of home.

"We should tell the organizing committee about the slurs," Halkeeth said. "I still think they cheated."

Griz looked at the rearview camera, once, twice. Vera leaned over to see. A hoverbiker was behind them. Probably the same one that bothered them in the parking lot, but now he wore a helmet.

"Shit." She glanced out the window and jumped in her seat. Another biker was right next to them.

Griz slowed.

"Keep going," she said.

The biker cut in front of them and the van's operating system hit the brakes. Another one banged on Griz's window. He was holding a blaster.

"Come out for a chat, will ya?"

"Should I call the police?" Halkeeth whispered from the back.

"Yes." Vera shifted her gaze from one biker to the other. The pickup parked behind them. The van was surrounded.

The biker on Griz's side fired into the air. Halkeeth squealed and dropped her virt. The biker pressed the gun to the glass. "Next one is going in your head. Come out, I said."

A. Zaykova

Griz opened the door.

No, no, no, no!

The biker waved the blaster. "All of you, out!"

Vera got out of the passenger seat. Halkeeth came out the back. The bikers herded them to the side of the road. Dandelion took off his helmet. Griz towered a head above him but looked completely helpless at gunpoint. Lizard got out from the driver's side of the pickup. He tucked half of his T-shirt into his belt, revealing another blaster, and walked up to Halkeeth.

"Not happy with your silver, are you?" He loomed over her.

She backed up. "I . . . I . . ."

A small truck appeared in the distance. Someone else was driving from the gorge. Approaching them, the truck stopped and lowered its window. A Human popped his head out. "Is everything okay?"

Vera noticed the bikers had hidden their guns. Lizard covered his with a tattooed hand. "All good, just discussing logistics."

"Okay." The Human drove off.

"You think you can talk shit about me, toad?" Lizard grabbed Halkeeth from her chair and dropped her onto the ground.

Vera rushed to her side. "Stop! This is a misunderstanding."

"And who the fuck are you? Where do you come from?" He crossed his arms. The tattoo on his hand looked fresh. A dagger, stretching from the wrist to the middle finger—a mark of Carver's Clan.

GALAXY GRIFTER

Vera wondered if it was real. "We don't want any trouble," she said. "We get the message, okay? We won't bother you again."

Lizard held her gaze. "You can come with us if you want. I won't hurt you. But these two have been a pain in my butt for a while."

"We won't bother you either. I won't come to the races anymore," Halkeeth said.

He looked down at her. "Where's your prize money?"

"My virt is in the van. It fell."

Lizard smirked and glanced at the pickup. "Miri, go find it."

The long-haired girl got out from the passenger side of the pickup and climbed into the van. "Smells like dog in here."

The men laughed.

Shorty poked Griz in the stomach with the blaster. "Why aren't you laughing? You stink. That's funny."

"Stop it." Griz stepped back.

"Or what? You Rors are meant to be strong. Aren't you going to fight me?"

Dandelion pushed Griz from the back. "Maybe there's something wrong with this one?"

Vera's gaze slid from one man to the next. The day had turned to shit, and it was her fault.

Miri appeared from the van, holding Halkeeth's virt between her index finger and thumb, a disgusted expression on her face. She handed it to Lizard.

He shoved it in Halkeeth's face. "Scan it."

She did, still seated on the ground. He tapped it with his own virt, taking her prize money, threw her virt on the

233

ground, and looked at Vera. "Are you coming with us?" he asked.

"No."

"She's one of those xenophiles." Shorty chuckled.

"Gross." Lizard pointed at Griz. "Meatball, drag out that piece-of-shit flier of yours. Can you do that?"

Dandelion pushed Griz forward.

Halkeeth scrambled up and got ahold of her chair. "You've got the money, just let us go now."

Lizard placed his hand on her forehead and pushed her back to the ground. "You stay down, toad."

Vera caught Lizard's hand. "Is that tattoo real?"

"What?"

"Are you part of the Carver's Clan?" Every kid on Blackjack knew the gang signs by the time they started school.

"Yes." Lizard glanced at his own hand.

"Does Carver know what you're up to in your free time?"

"What would he care?" Lizard frowned. His tone lacked conviction.

"The clan's reputation." Vera looked around. Six pairs of eyes were fixed on her. She'd better not make this worse.

Shorty threw his arms open. "Why would Carver give a shit about a couple of xens?"

He wouldn't. She'd seen him at Stellar once. Fred had pointed him out. Of all the gangsters she'd come across, he looked most like a serial killer. "He might care if the Pooch calls him," she said.

"What does the Pooch have to do with it?" Shorty grimaced.

Lizard waved him off. "You have ties to the Puccelli family?"

GALAXY GRIFTER

"My family runs one of his businesses on Blackjack," Vera said.

Lizard exchanged glances with the others.

Miri chuckled. "She's bullshitting you, Arj. Ask her to prove it."

Lizard smirked. "Prove it."

"Prove it how?" Vera looked around. Nobody else spoke. They were looking at her like they expected her to pull a rabbit from her sleeve. She'd never even seen a live rabbit. "Fine. But this won't go well for anyone." She brought her hand to her virt.

"Wait." Lizard reached for the blaster at his belt. "Who are you calling?"

"Blackbeard. He's Puccelli's right-hand man and he—"

"I know who Blackbeard is. You have his number?"

"He collects the protection payments. It's early morning on Blackjack. He'll be grumpy." She pulled her screen up as a hologram so the others could see and scrolled through her contact list. *Blackbeard.* Her finger hovered over the call icon. She touched it. After a moment of deafening silence, it rang.

"Stop!" Lizard and Shorty screamed at the same time.

She dropped the call.

"But—" Miri started. Lizard grabbed her elbow and pulled her aside.

Dandelion leaned toward Shorty's ear, but Vera couldn't make out the words. Lizard picked up Halkeeth's virt from the ground and handed it to Vera. "I'll give you the money back and I'll leave your friends alone, deal?" He shuffled from foot to foot when she didn't respond. "Don't tell Blackbeard."

235

A. Zaykova

"The money." Vera held out Halkeeth's virt.

He transferred back seven grand, approached Halkeeth, who was still sitting on the ground, and offered her a hand.

She pushed it away and pulled herself onto the hoverchair.

Miri had returned to the pickup. Shorty put his blaster away and patted Griz on the shoulder. "Sorry, mate, no hard feelings."

Griz glanced at Vera and climbed into his van. Halkeeth got into the back and Vera into the passenger seat.

Lizard came up to her holding a holo-card. "Sorry about the"—he looked around—"confusion. If you ever need anything...flier parts, or IT, we've got great stuff. Just let me know."

Vera took the card from him and closed the van door. "Drive."

Griz started the engine and for a while they drove in silence. The adrenaline was waning and Vera's hand trembled when she handed Halkeeth's virt back to her.

Halkeeth snapped it onto her wrist. "Are you in a gang?"

"No."

They stayed quiet for a few more moments.

"Then how did you—"

"I bluffed," Vera said.

"But how did you know?"

"You can take the girl out of Blackjack, but you can't..." Vera sighed, too drained to finish the joke.

Chapter 28
Monday

"Hurry up." Vera pounded her hand against the lift sensor for the third time. It wouldn't speed the lift up, but it took the edge off. She kept breaking her own promise to herself to be on time. *Bing.* The lift door opened and people crammed in. A vaguely familiar coworker greeted her with a nod. Her gut dropped as the lift shot up, like a spaceship, though not quite as bad.

Halkeeth was at her workstation. Their manager wasn't, which saved Vera an apology for the lateness.

Halkeeth smiled. "Hi, gangster."

Vera choked on her breath. "Don't *ever* call me that."

"Sorry, it was a joke. You saved our lives at the gorge. Griz and I owe you."

Vera snorted. It was she who got them into trouble in the first place, she and her long tongue.

"You have no idea how cool you were. If there's anything we can do for you..."

"Let's start by never bringing it up again." Vera put on her headset.

Halkeeth looked at her screen for a moment. "So if I went to Blackjack—"

"Please?"

"Sorry." Halkeeth put her headset on.

Later that morning, Jia, the manager, tapped Vera on the shoulder. "Can you come see me when you've finished this one?"

"Sure." Vera clicked through the survey of yet another evaluation. *Submit rating.*

"What's this about?" Halkeeth whispered when Jia walked off.

Vera shrugged. Maybe it was about her application. *Please let it be good news.* She dropped her headset onto the desk and stood. Jia motioned for her to come to a meeting room. Inside, an older woman whom Vera had never met was sitting behind a round table. She wore a dioptric band and held her hands clasped on the table.

"Vera, this is Ruolan from Human Resources." Jia walked up to the table. "Take a seat."

"Hi." Vera pulled out a chair and sat.

Jia lowered into the one closer to Ruolan.

The older woman spoke first. "Vera, you'll be aware that when you signed your contract with Lentatech, you agreed to uphold its interests and to declare if your personal interests or actions come into conflict with the interests of your employer." From Ruolan's tone it was hard to tell if this was a question or a statement.

238

GALAXY GRIFTER

Vera nodded.

Jia flicked through a document on a tablet in front of her, periodically clearing her throat.

"On Friday there was a call you'd taken over from VITSA, is that right?" Ruolan said.

Friday? Saturday's events had pushed everything else to the back of her mind. "Oh." She remembered. "Yes, June—"

Jia cleared her throat once more. "Can you run us through what happened?"

"Yes..." Vera's own throat tightened from the realization that she must've messed up. "I was monitoring a call, as always, and I realized it was an old friend of mine. I don't know how that happened but...she was upset, so I spoke to her."

"And what happened after?" Ruolan peered over the top of her dioptric band.

"And..." Vera tried to think of the right answer. "I told her I'd come see her after work. That's all."

"And did you?" Ruolan crossed her arms.

Jia cleared her throat again.

"Yes." Vera glanced from one woman to the other, certain now that she was in trouble.

"And what did you do?" Ruolan asked.

"Had soup..." Vera tugged on the sleeve of her jumper.

"Did you undertake any repairs for the client?" Jia asked.

"I..." Vera tried to gather her thoughts. "June's ship is very old. The latest software update was shutting the whole thing down. A Lentatech technician came over and said she needed a new processor and she couldn't afford it. So I just rolled back to the previous OS version for her."

"But you're not a technician," Ruolan said.

"I just did it because I knew her. I used to fix that ship's computer all the time."

"So you did work for the client in your personal capacity?"

Vera's gaze slid across both women. "I didn't charge her if that's what you mean. I did it as a friend. We had dinner and then I rolled the OS back. It took a few minutes."

"Vera." Jia moved her hand toward Vera's on the table, not quite touching. "This is a serious breach of conduct. Your contract stipulates you cannot do business with Lentatech's clients." Her speech was slow and gentle, unlike what she was saying.

"I wasn't doing business." Vera pulled her hand away, clutching it into a fist.

"You cannot help Lentatech's clients in your personal capacity," Jia said.

"I can't help them? Even if they're friends and I'm doing it for free?"

"There's a protocol to follow." Ruolan's tone was much less gentle. "VITSA should have finished the call and identified the next options."

"June's old, she couldn't afford a new processor." Vera realized they were right. She should've let VITSA finish the call and contacted June afterward, when nobody was recording it.

Stupid, stupid girl.

Vera lowered her eyes. "I'm sorry. I realize I'm wrong and I should've followed the protocol. It won't happen again."

Jia sucked her lips in.

Ruolan sighed.

GALAXY GRIFTER

"I'll do better next time. I promise. If there's a way I can fix this..." Vera was pulling at the sleeve of her jumper again.

Ruolan stacked her hands on the table. "Unfortunately, given the type of violation and your tenure with the company, this qualifies as a dismissal."

"Dismis—" Vera turned to Jia. "Please..."

Her manager wore a pained expression. "You're a good worker, really, but we have to be fair to everyone."

Fair? There was this word again. Vera's vision clouded. She took a few sharp breaths but wouldn't allow the tears to roll. She stood and reached for the door. "I'll..."

Jia nodded and Vera walked out, striding through the office, more by memory than by sight, into the bathroom.

Chapter 29
Xinsanya

Hurtling through hyperspace aboard his luxury freighter, Levi swigged his expensive whiskey, no longer able to tell its taste.

Six months. Six fucking months he'd spent with Amrie. The grifts they'd pulled, the gifts he'd bought, all the fun they'd had... And she'd sold him out. That easy.

He should've never gone back for her. He'd been so close to his happily ever after; just him, *Caerus*, the shadow map, and a healthy k-bit balance...

He flung the empty bottle across the room and it shattered against the corner of the kitchen island. The sound of the breaking glass drowned in the crescendo of Wagner's *Tannhäuser* overture blaring from *Caerus*'s speakers.

Levi closed his eyes and sank back into the soft embrace of his sofa. "*Caerus*, ever wanted to peek over the event horizon?"

"Not particularly. Spaghettification would greatly impair my functionality," the ship said.

GALAXY GRIFTER

Levi let out a bitter chuckle.

None of the hackers he'd contacted since the Breznis had chipped him were willing to steal from the Pooch. None could remove the chip without killing him. Even Kru had refused, saying he couldn't risk a dead Human in his apartment.

Levi wouldn't wait for the implant to kill him, or crawl back to the Breznis begging for mercy. If he had to die, he'd die on his own terms. The idea of setting course for a black-hole grew less hypothetical by the day. For now, one more option remained.

Fighting a massive hangover, Levi landed *Caerus* in Xinlouyang Spaceport, Seshat. He got into his flier and set course for the Xinsanya Resort—a cheap gimmick with fake beaches on an oceanless planet.

The chlorinated smell of the lobby reminded him of a public swimming pool. He approached a tired-looking receptionist and leaned on the counter. "I'm meeting a friend who checked in earlier, but I can't seem to get hold of her. The name's Vera O'Mara."

The receptionist keyed something into their terminal. "I can try her room for you." They touched a device on their ear and several moments later shook their head. "No response. She might be at breakfast. The restaurant is open to the public, if you want to check. Or you can wait here and try again later."

Levi opted to check the restaurant. He spotted the three women almost immediately. Vera shared a table with two of her friends from Blackjack. She looked prettier than he remembered. Not like Amrie, but in a nonchalant kind of way, with a copper-colored ponytail and a sarcastic dimple on her right cheek. It took him a trip to Blackjack to learn that Isaac had lied; the bitch was alive and well, living her best life. He made his way to her table.

The busty hairdresser was the first of the three to notice him. She gave Vera a nudge.

Vera raised her eyes and her smile faded as she shot up from the table. "What the hell are *you* doing here?!"

He pulled up a chair and sat across from her. "I need to talk to you. Alone."

The two other girls exchanged glances.

The busty one pushed her plate aside. "Shall we meet you by the beach a bit later?"

Vera nodded.

The blond tomboy screwed up her nose. "Don't go disappearing. We've got that thing at ten."

"Trust me, I'll only be a minute," she said, sitting back down and holding Levi's gaze. "If that."

Her friends walked off whispering to each other. He'd expected more drama. Perhaps she hadn't told them about what happened on the *Comet*?

She clenched her teeth. "How did you find me?"

"Pub talk. Only took a couple of drinks for Blondie's boyfriend to spill the beans about your big reunion."

"I'll murder Ahn. What do you want?"

"I didn't get a chance to say goodbye last time—"

"You mean when you dumped me in space to die?" If a gaze could incinerate, she'd turn him to ash.

"Not to die, I called Starpol."

GALAXY GRIFTER

"How noble. The Breznis could've killed me before the cops arrived."

"And whose fault is that? Was it your plan all along to steal their intel and hang it on me?"

She drew back. It was true then.

"Oh yeah, I know about it," he said. "And the fact that they're out to kill you. And your friends. Although I think they'll start with your brother."

She turned pale and clasped a napkin that lay in front of her.

He held a pause, letting the fear sink in. "It's not all bad news. They'll trade your lives for Puccelli's database, if you get it to them within three days from now, local time."

She creased her brow. "That's impossible."

"Why? You did it when you hacked the Breznis."

"That was...I—"

"What in the known galaxy made you think it's a good idea? Were you working for the Pooch? Or did you sell him the data?"

"No! I wasn't...I—" She let out a sharp breath, releasing the napkin from her fingers. "I don't owe you an explanation. You had agreed to pay me my half for the blueprint and to drop me off on Seshat. Instead, you—"

"I did what I had to." He crossed his arms. "The Breznis followed us because of what you've done. If they'd seen us together, they'd have shot us both on the spot. I gave you a chance."

"Bullshit!" She pushed her chair back and it screeched against the tile floor.

Other patrons turned their heads and stared at them. Levi

245

pressed his finger to his lips. "Quiet. Whatever happened, we need to figure out what to do about the situation we're in *now*."

She stood and leaned over the table. "No. I don't believe you. You're saying the Breznis are out to kill me? And they've sent *you* to tell me that?"

He narrowed his eyes. The bitch had a bite. He pulled away his shirt collar, revealing the barely visible mark on his neck. "They chipped me with a tracker and an explosive. It will detonate if we don't get them what they asked. So we're both in shit, thanks to you."

Vera sat back down. "Fffuck. They're tracking you and you brought them to me?"

"I'll bring them to whomever, if it helps get this thing out."

"And you can't remove or disable it?"

"Apparently not." He tossed her a holographic stack of technical documents that Kru had sent him. It was unlikely she'd spot something the Huxoran hacker didn't, but Levi had nothing to lose.

She flicked through the virtual pages. "They're designed for rogue senhounds?"

"So it says."

She read on. "Debug mode...When the subject dies of other causes...Wait, how would it know if you died of other causes?"

"It tracks the pulse."

"I see. So unless your heart stops—"

"Exactly." He replayed her words in his head. "Wait, what?"

GALAXY GRIFTER

"What?"

"Unless my heart stops." Why did he not think of this? "It's possible to stop a heart without dying, right?"

"In movies."

"If I had a defibrillator—"

"A defibrillator resets a faulty rhythm. It won't bring you back from the dead, Levi."

"What else? Toxins? Poisons?"

"Jellyfish?"

"Cryogenics."

She shrugged. "If you find a cryogenist. It's not an approved procedure."

"So if I sort the cryogenics part, could you disable the tracker?"

"Absolutely not." She let go of the document, which dissolved into pixelated particles and faded.

"Because you can't or won't?"

"Both. You've just told me the Breznis are out to kill everyone I care about."

"Yeah, but they won't if we disable this thing. Wait here." He stood, walked to the window where she couldn't hear him, and called Kru.

"I think I've figured out how to solve this problem," he said as soon as the Huxoran answered.

"I'm glad," Kru said.

"We'll put me in cryosleep and you'll disable the tracker."

There was silence on the other end of the call.

"Kru?"

"I told you, I will not undertake this."

247

"I won't have a pulse in a cryopod. The chip will go into debug mode. You'll turn it off and you'll bring me back. And I'll pay you, a lot—*a lot*—of money."

"No."

"Why?"

"I have advised you I cannot risk being found with a dead Human. And...where will you find a working cryopod?"

"I'll think of something."

"I'm sorry, I cannot help." Kru hung up.

Levi tried calling again, but Kru didn't answer.

Fuck. Levi glanced at Vera, who sat bouncing her leg. He searched for cryopods on the Shadow Market app. The search came back with zero results. *Related searches. Cryogenics. Suboprine Neotestryl.* He clicked on the first listing.

Description: Medical solution administered intravenously in preparation for cryogenesis to halt circulatory and metabolic functions prior to exsanguination. Used in conjunction with Vitrotrigine to restore bodily functions post-cryogenesis. Incorrect usage can lead to irreversible organ damage and death.

Fuck it, he was dead anyway if he didn't try it.

Buy now. He picked Xinlouyang Spaceport as his delivery address and returned to the table. "I've got the cryogenics sorted. You'll need to disable the tracker." He didn't trust her, but this was his best bet.

She picked up the napkin again and rolled the corner between her thumb and index finger. "Why would I help you?"

"To get the Breznis off our backs." He sat.

"You mean off your back? What about me? My brother?"

GALAXY GRIFTER

"You'll be fine, as long as we get this thing out."

She shook her head. "I don't believe a word coming from your mouth. First you say the Breznis want to kill me and I must steal from the Pooch. Now they're not trying to kill me and I must hack some tracker? Can you even hear yourself?"

Annoyance crept up his back like pinpricks. "Fine. They don't know about you or your brother. I haven't told them where to find you. But I *will* if you don't help me."

"So now you're threatening me? How do I know you haven't already told them? I'd guess it's the first thing you'd do to save your own arse."

He banged his fist on the table. "Because they didn't believe me. I tried to tell them I had nothing to do with the database. They told me you were dead. I didn't even bother looking for you until I got to Blackjack, nearly got myself killed again, only to find out you're living your best fucking life in a stinking resort. But you know what? I'll make them believe me, if it's the last thing I do. Once I'm dead, they're coming for you."

She rolled and unrolled her napkin. "Why don't you get someone else to disable it?"

"Who?" He looked around demonstratively.

"Anyone better qualified. I've never done anything like this. You could die."

"If you don't try, I'll die anyway."

"Yeah, but if I'm involved, I'll get arrested. You're better off going to a hospital. Or... I don't know, the cops?"

"So they'd lock me up?"

"Better locked up than dead, right?"

"Speak for yourself." He snatched the napkin from her and balled it in his fist. "If you report me to anyone, I'll tell them it's all your fault. I've got three days to live, thanks to you. I'd like to spend them as a free man."

He'd wasted so much time already. He could have visited Earth and said goodbye to his parents, instead of scouting the galaxy for a solution. Now it was too late.

"Fuck you, Vera." He stood, tossed her napkin onto the table, and turned to leave.

"Wait."

He wanted to be done with her, but his survival instinct forced him to stop and listen.

"You need a receiver, like this one." She showed him a diagram on her virtEgo.

"And then?"

"And then . . . I could try to find a vulnerability in your chip and see if I can connect to it. If not, everything else will be pointless."

"Okay. Do you know where I can find this receiver on Seshat?"

"Maybe." She retrieved a contact card from her virt. "The guy's named Lizard. He's a newbie in Carver's Clan, a xenophobe and an asshole, so you'll get right along. Says he trades gadgets."

Levi called Lizard and after a brief conversation turned back to Vera. "He said he'll have one ready tomorrow. We'll have to go pick it up around noon."

"*You* will have to pick it up. I'm staying here to enjoy the last day of my vacation. I'll meet you later in Xinlouyang."

Chapter 30
Xinlouyang Spaceport

Vera hauled her bag on her shoulder, following a stream of passengers through an underground crossing and onto the travelator inside the Xinsanya maglev station. A fat man in shorts kept losing his sandal and holding up the foot traffic. Nina held back a snicker. "Some people didn't get the memo that they're not at the beach anymore."

Once off the travelator the girls stepped aside to wait for Amelia. She caught up to them, lugging a hovercase so heavy, its gravi-panel scraped the floor. "What did I miss?"

"The shuttle if you don't hurry." Nina started toward the platform.

They boarded the train and Vera got into a window seat. Nina wrestled her backpack off her shoulders and sat next to her, while Amelia climbed into the seat opposite them. "That went quickly. Back to work tomorrow?"

"Yeah." Vera averted her gaze. She hadn't told her friends she had no job to return to; she didn't want to spoil the precious time they had together. But now the feeling of emptiness, and the fear of not being able to financially support herself, was starting to settle over her. She hoped she could hide it for the rest of the ride.

Nina rested her head on Vera's shoulder. "I'm so proud of you. You gave us the biggest scare when you disappeared, but it looks like you did good for yourself. You'll come visit us, right?"

"Of course." Vera half smiled, unsure she'd ever be able to show her face on Blackjack again. And how weird it was that the thought caused a pang in her heart; she'd been trying to escape that damn planet for as long as she lived and now...the thought of never seeing it again brought even more sadness to the forefront of her heart.

"Maybe our next reunion will be on Mars," Amelia said.

"For a wedding?" Vera grasped the opportunity to divert the conversation away from herself.

Apparently, Amelia's fling with Rib had grown into something serious. She shrugged. "I'm working on it."

Vera's virt buzzed, displaying a message from Niran: *>Hope you had a great time. Are you sure you don't want me to pick you up?*
>The train will be faster. I'll see you for dinner.

At least she still had one okay thing in her life. Niran was a decent guy. She was actually looking forward to seeing him.

The intercom announced their stop: "Xinlouyang Spaceport, Terminal Two, for lightweight spacecraft and private carriers."

They hurried past overpriced shops and colorful restaurants before reaching the landing field and the shuttle headed for

GALAXY GRIFTER

Blackjack. A grey-haired pilot stood by the open hatch, holding a soft drink. "I'm taking off in fifteen, so get in and buckle up."

"Just a minute." Amelia waved her virtual ticket and knelt next to her bloated suitcase.

Nina wrapped her arm around Vera. "We got you a little something as a thank-you for the holiday."

Amelia unzipped the case and fished out a half-meter-wide digital frame. It played a loop of the three of them posing on Xinsanya's white sand, pulling faces at the camera until an artificial wave crashed over them. The recording ended with a spray of water and flailing limbs, only to start again.

"You have to hang it somewhere everyone can see," Amelia said. "And when they ask who these idiots are, you tell them we're your best friends."

Vera laughed, accepting the gift. "I will, thank you." She tapped the screen, but it didn't respond. "How do I turn it off for now?"

"You can't. That's the whole point. The salesperson said memories go to the nebula to die. People never look at them again. *This* forces you to look."

Vera inspected her bag, confirming the frame wouldn't fit. "So I'll have to haul it under my arm for all to see?"

"What are friends for, if not mutual humiliation?" Nina grinned.

Vera placed her hand on her heart. "I'm touched to the core, really. Where did you even get it? How did I not see you sneak it into the room?"

"At the resort's souvenir shop, while you were busy talking to Fancy Suit," Amelia said.

A. Zaykova

Vera's smile faded.

Amelia narrowed her eyes. "Kind of odd he'd track you down across the galaxy for some coding job."

"He wouldn't have, if *someone* didn't tell him exactly where to find us." Vera tightened her grip on the frame.

"I'm sorry," Nina said. "I've spoken to Clyde and I will again. He has trouble keeping his mouth shut."

Amelia crossed her arms. "Yeah, well, Vera has the opposite problem. She never tells us anything."

The pilot waved his now empty drink bottle and started up the ramp. "I'm leaving with or without you."

Grateful for the interruption, Vera hugged her friends goodbye and they scampered after the pilot. She watched them walk away, giggling, happy, settled in their lives. She pushed her envy aside and took a deep, calming breath. Time to deal with the Weasel and his fucking death chip.

She headed back into the terminal with its bright shop fronts. Levi had told her the gate to meet him at, though she took her time getting there. She still wasn't quite sure she wanted to help him. After all, he'd felt no remorse when he'd dumped her in space, or when he had threatened her at the restaurant— why shouldn't she let him die? If their positions were reversed, he'd probably laugh in her face. The problem was, *she* wasn't him. She had a conscience, which was proving to be quite a nuisance. The lift door slid open and a large Huxoran waddled out with three kids in tow. Vera followed them with her gaze as they tripped over one another's tails. When she looked up again, her stomach dropped. Levi stood outside the lift, looking straight at her. They regarded each other for a moment.

"My ship's that way." He pointed in the direction of the departure gates.

It was too late to bail or to pretend like she wasn't considering it. But she didn't owe him an explanation. "Have you got the receiver?" she asked.

"Yeah." He tapped his pocket and nodded at the frame under her arm. "What's that?"

She turned the recording away from him. "A gift from my friends."

"Classy."

He kept a step behind her as they walked back to the landing field, as though he suspected she'd try to run off. A classic, glossy black freighter stood out from the other ships on the tarmac. Golden cursive letters on its side spelled *Caerus*.

"You got your ship back?" she guessed.

He nodded and led her up the ramp and through the airlock. Inside the ship, her gaze fell onto a smooth, modern control panel that curved ergonomically around wide, suede-looking pilot and navigator seats. The entire interface had no visible seams, ports, or signs of wear, as if forged from a single piece of graphene, polished and flawless. The processor and core interface node were completely hidden from view. Oh, how she'd love to take a peek inside this console. Not that Levi would let her.

The cockpit merged with an extravagant living area of black and gold, making her forget for a second that this was merely a piece of transport, and not some glitzy hotel. Her boots sank into a plush, deep carpet. A massive black corner couch nestled against the port side. The bulkhead toward the stern of the living area was faced with a rough material, like an exposed cliff edge but painted in opulent gold.

Instead of the typical heating and refrigerator units, a gleaming kitchen sat near the starboard, complete with an island. The golden veins in the speckled black countertop caught the morning light streaming in through the viewports. She wouldn't be surprised if he told her it was made of natural marble or something equally exorbitant. A translucent, jelly-like bot crawled over its already spotless surface, leaving it even shinier. Even the air smelled clean, though she couldn't hear the filters working to expel the fuel and oil of the spaceport.

Levi strutted through his domain. "Like it?"

"It's fine."

He scoffed. "Fine? It's a work of art!"

"I'm not here to admire your ship." She stood her duffel on one of the tall stools by the kitchen island, and her frame on the floor, facing away.

"I see you made interesting friends on Seshat," he said, undoubtedly referring to Lizard.

"I see you still have no friends." She sat on the other chair, expanded her virt, and started up the software she'd installed the night before.

He extracted a device from his pocket and passed it to her. "Is this what you need?"

"I guess."

"You *guess*?"

"It's not like I hacked quantum trackers before."

He frowned. "You do realize that messing this up—"

"Will get you killed and me probably arrested? Yeah. Let's hope I'm a quick learner."

He clenched his jaw but said nothing.

Asshole. She connected the receiver to her virt and it picked up the tracker's signal. Now she needed to tap into its traffic to get the device address.

He drummed his fingers on the countertop. "Want a drink?"

She shook her head, glancing up only when he'd turned to get a bottle. He splashed whiskey into a glass, held it to his lips, sighed, and put it back down. *Wow...* He really was nervous.

Over the next few hours, she prodded the chip for vulnerabilities. Levi paced up and down his ship, disappearing in its tail and returning to hover over her shoulder in silence. What irritated her most was that he still smelled good. His cologne conjured up memories of the time they'd spent on the *Comet*, and she hated herself for the way it had played out.

Finally, a box flashed on her screen: *Enter your crypto key.*

"Got it."

He rushed to her side. "You're in?"

"As far as I can go. Trying to generate a key could take years, but stopping your pulse will create kernel panic and force it into debug mode. Then you can access the back end."

"So this is the part where I die?" He looked glummer than she'd ever seen him.

"This is the part where I leave."

"What?"

"I'll type up instructions for what to do next. It's not too hard. But you'll need a doctor to put you in cryostasis and I know nothing about medicine."

"Wait, you can't go—"

"I did all I could. If you don't wake up and spaceport security feeds show I was here when it happened...my already shitty life is as good as over."

He grimaced. "If we were on Blackjack—"

"On Blackjack, no one would care about a dead body, but I can't go back there with the headhunters still after me."

"Headhunters?" He arched his brows.

"Oh, you haven't heard? Blackbeard sent a bunch of Rors after me. Told me they were after you, me, and the blueprints."

"Huh." He scratched the back of his neck, much too calmly in Vera's opinion. "Do they fly unmarked Jaemlen warships?"

"How the hell would I know what they fly?" She rolled her eyes. "Do you want the instructions, or not?"

Levi hunched, propping his elbows on the counter. "How long will it take to disable the tracker?"

"Once in debug mode? Not long. Though it's better to be thorough, and you'll be in cryo anyway, so..."

"How long?"

"Ten, twenty minutes?"

He sighed and nodded. "Get on with your instructions."

She placed her hands on the virtual keys, feeling a foreboding chill on the back of her neck.

———————————— • ————————————

"It's done," Vera said once she checked and rechecked her instructions. Someone would simply need to copy-paste the code. "Hello?" She looked around, but Levi wasn't in sight. She stood. "Levi?"

"In here."

She followed his voice through an internal hatch, into a small hallway in the ship's tail. A door on the left was ajar and she peeked into what turned out to be a bathroom. Fully clothed, Levi lay in a huge bathtub filled with...ice water? The transparent cubes at the bottom of the tub suggested so. The air here was freezing too. The knot in the pit of her stomach turned into a sucking void. "What the fuck are you doing?"

He dropped an empty syringe onto the floor. "Suboprine Neotestryl. It stops the heart for cryogenics."

"You said you had a cryopod." Her voice came out as a hoarse whisper.

"When did I promise a cryopod? I told you I'm out of options." He pressed an oxygen mask to his face. A box with medical equipment stood on the floor by the bath.

She backed away. "You can't do this to me."

"There's a syringe loaded with the antidote and other instructions in the box." He pulled away the collar of his shirt to reveal a catheter in his subclavian vein. "I'll pay well if you bring me back. But don't bother after ten minutes. I'd rather be dead than brain damaged."

"No!"

His head bobbed and he strained to keep his eyes open. "I'll...pay you. Disable..." His speech slurred. He dropped the mask.

"Pay me? You fucking piece of shit, Levi! You piece of *shit!*" Tears of frustration ran down her cheeks.

His eyes rolled back and he slid down into the bath, his head sinking below the water. She surged forward, grabbed the front of his shirt and tried to pull him up, but no air bubbles rose from his nose and mouth. Too late. She let go.

She was definitely going to prison.

Chapter 31
The Frame

Vera ran her wet, cold hands through her hair, tearing her gaze away from the body in the bathtub. "Ten minutes." She ran to the living area, grabbed her virt and the receiver, and returned to the bathroom. She sat on the floor, with her back to the tub, trying not to look at Levi. On the interface in front of her, a stream of raw data scrolled past: real-time system logs, diagnostic readouts, biometric monitoring log…She zoomed in on it. Higher up, the tracker logged a beat every half a second, suggesting an elevated heart rate. The frequency dropped progressively, 80 bpm, 60 bpm, 40, 20…The tracker hadn't recorded any beats for the past three seconds; that should have been long enough for it to register an error, right? She checked the diagnostics tabs, eyes gliding over the time stamps, kernel statuses, error codes…Nothing. *Fuck*. Her fingers hovered over the virtual keyboard, water dripping from her soaked sleeves. Anything she did now could kill him for good, but… so could inaction. Her own pulse must've skyrocketed as her breath came in short, sharp gasps. Yet she couldn't afford to panic. She exhaled and typed in an override code into the command queue, initiating a full self-check, praying the system would interpret it as internal feedback rather than external interference. "Please work," she whispered.

A cascade of green and red updates flooded the screen. Then, the error logs cleared. The system rebooted. The interface lit up with a single, glorious line of text:

DEBUG MODE ENGAGED.

Yes! How much time had passed? Two minutes? Five? She dared not check. She tore off her wet hoodie and pounded the virtual keys, pasting in the code she'd typed up earlier. It would've been better to be thorough, but there wasn't time for that.

Command Error.

What? Fuck. She checked the last line of code, but her mind rushed in a hundred directions. *There. There's the mistake.* She deleted a stroke. *Enter.* A loading icon spun on the screen for what felt like eternity. She sniveled from the sheer stress of it and blinked away the wetness in her eyes. Her body was shaking from the cold and the tension.

One word appeared below the command line:

DISARMED.

Disarmed. It's fucking disarmed. She breathed heavily, but it wasn't over. With trembling hands, she reached for the instructions Levi had left and picked up a card with five bullet points:

- *Disarm explosive*
- *Drain ice water*

GALAXY GRIFTER

- *Inject Vitrotrigine into catheter*
- *Oxygen mask on face*
- *Fill tub with warm water, keep face above surface*

She hated him with every quantum of her being. Once she brought him back to life and he paid her, she was going to kill him.

Drain ice water. It took her a moment to find the sensor that controlled the plug.

Inject Vitrotrigine into the catheter. She took the second syringe, already filled with clear liquid. Once most of the water had drained, she leaned over the tub, moved his wet shirt collar out of the way and, steadying her shaking hand, slid the needle into the opening. She'd seen this done too many times after Mum got sick. She pushed down the plunger, the liquid rushing beneath Levi's skin.

Oxygen mask on face. She held the mask over her own mouth to make sure it was working. Inhaling once, she pressed it against his.

Fill tub with warm water. Again, that took a moment to figure out with the ship's ridiculous bath setup, but finally the faucet started shooting out tepid water.

Now what? Pins and needles stabbed her hands as they warmed while she held his head up. What if he didn't wake? What kind of a moron wrote instructions like that? How would she know it was working?

She needed to call an ambulance. Yes. They'd know what to do. Why hadn't she thought of it before? *Because there wasn't time.* Right. She needed to find something to hold his head above the water so she could free her hands. And then she'd be going to prison. That was it. The asshole was dead and she was the sole suspect. She sniveled again and slapped his cheek. "Wake up!" No reaction. She shook his shoulders. "WAKE. UP. Wake up, you fucking Weasel, you motherfucker of massive proportions, you stupid piece of giant shit. WAKE UP!"

Levi's eyes shot open, his torso arching as Vera nearly let go of him. Water splashed onto the floor and her clothes. She tried to prop him up, against the side of the tub. He gasped and his fingers dug into her wrist. His pupils dilated as he yanked the mask off and looked around, catching his breath. "Did you do it?" His voice came out almost inaudible.

She let go of him and sat back on her heels, inhaling big, heavy breaths, her face wet from the water, or sweat, or tears.

He started slipping under but caught himself by throwing his arm over the side of the tub.

She stood to leave.

"Wait." He caught her hand. "Help me."

"Help you? After what you did?!" She leaned over and tapped the drain sensor so he wouldn't drown.

He held on to her wrist. "I had no choice. What would you have done?"

"What would I have done?" She didn't know and was too tired to think. She yanked her arm away. "Fuck you, Levi."

He winced and pressed his hand against his chest. His body went rigid, and for a second she thought he would die again. But the spasm subsided. He pulled the catheter from his vein and a drop of blood swelled by his clavicle. "Wait. I'll pay you."

"Pay me?" No amount of money could make up for what

GALAXY GRIFTER

he'd put her through. Tears of frustration welled up in her eyes again. "Fine. Pay me. You still owe me for the blueprint."

"A hundred grand, that's all I've got left." He tapped his virt and gestured for her to accept the transfer.

She picked up her own dripping virt from the floor, collapsed the screens, and unpaired the quantum receiver. She held her virt over Levi's and stared at the balance. That was *a lot* of money. Especially for someone unemployed, like she was. Still, not worth the ordeal. She shivered.

"*Caerus*, bathroom temperature to twenty-five," Levi said.

"Turning the bathroom thermostat up to twenty-five degrees Celsius," the ship responded. The air coming from the vents warmed.

Levi ran his hand over her bare arm. "Help me get out."

She felt deflated and worn. "Are you even allowed to move?"

"Yes." He probably had no clue.

She leaned over and he put his arm around her, both of them equally soaked now. He was too heavy, though. He pushed himself over the side of the tub and had almost made it to standing, but collapsed, nearly pulling her down with him. He caught himself on the vanity and threw up into the sink. Then slid onto the floor and pressed his back to the tub.

She picked up her wet hoodie. "You should call an ambulance."

"I'm fine."

"I see." She walked out into the kitchen and dropped her hoodie onto the counter. Levi's whiskey glass still stood there, untouched. She looked at it for a moment, picked it up, and drank, in small steady gulps. It tasted less strong from standing in the open too long, but still burned its way down her esophagus, spreading the warmth through her cold, tense body.

"I'll have one too."

She turned. He was leaning against the hatch, a puddle forming at his feet.

"You just came back from the dead." She put the glass down and grabbed her duffel.

"I'm fine. But your concern is sweet."

She stomped over to him. "Feel free to kill yourself in whichever elaborate ways you please. But keep *me* out of it." She stabbed her finger into his chest and squeezed past him into the hallway.

As she expected, the second door led to a bedroom. It had the same black-and-gold palette as the living area, and...a mirror ceiling. *He fucking would.* She locked the door, changed into dry clothes, and sat on the firm bed. Her virt showed a missed call and an unread message from Niran: *>Did you get home okay?*

>Yes, thanks, she responded, and then keyed in the emergency department's number. The *idiot* clearly needed medical help. Her finger hovered over the call symbol. What would she tell them though? They would obviously ask questions, not to mention that a body scan would reveal the diode still embedded in Levi's body. Would he even let them in if they came? She sighed—nope, let the idiot deal with this on his own. She dropped the call, gathered her wet clothes, and left the bedroom.

He sat on the hallway floor, back pressed to the wall, looking worse than death. "Mind grabbing me something dry too? I don't think I can get up again."

GALAXY GRIFTER

"Not in my job description." She stepped over his legs and stuffed her wet clothes into her bag, not caring if it would soak her other belongings. "Call a doctor. And, Levi"—she glared—"whatever you're going through, stay the fuck away from me. If I see you again, I'm calling the cops." She swung the duffel onto her shoulder and marched off his stupid, fancy spaceship.

All the seats aboard the maglev had been taken, but Vera found a divider wall to lean on. Her legs felt like jelly and her neck ached. She set her bag on the floor and dropped her head back.

What would you have done? His question resounded in her head. She wanted to think she'd never end up in a situation like that, but she was no longer sure. She was sure of another thing: For all his charm and glamour, Levi led a miserable, lonely existence.

An elderly passenger stepped into the train just before the doors shut. He tried to shove a suitcase into the overhead storage, but it refused to fit. After several futile attempts, someone offered him a seat.

Vera looked down at her own bag. *Fuck.* She'd left her digital frame on *Caerus.* The train moved. The platform flashed past the window as they sped into the blackness of a tunnel. She knocked the back of her head against the divider wall. How would she tell the girls she lost their gift on the first day? Surely Levi would just throw it away if she didn't go back for it. Wouldn't he?

She got off the train at the next station. She couldn't trust that scumbag with her best friends' faces.

He answered her call after several rings. "Hello?"

"I left my—"

"Miss me already?"

"I left my—"

"Didn't expect to hear from you this soon after your farewell speech."

She exhaled and raised her voice. "I left my frame on *Caerus*."

He sniggered. "A souvenir for me to remember you by?"

"I'll pick it up in half an hour."

He was silent for a moment. "I think not. I've been looking for art to hang above the sofa. I think this was meant to be."

Of course. He'd make this as painful for her as possible. She regretted all her life choices to this point. "It was a gift. I want it back."

"I guess I can...trade you for a bag of groceries. I need to restock before takeoff."

"What? I'm not your assistant."

"You'd be a terrible one. I'll get a drone delivery, but you'll help get it into storage. I refuse to move after the effort it took me to get dry and comfortable. Dying's exhausting."

"I should've let you stay dead," she said.

The sign above the platform reported that the next train was due in ten minutes. She checked the time. Five to three. At this rate, she wouldn't get home until five, maybe six. And then she'd still have to meet Niran for dinner. No...she'd say she was sick and deal with the fallout later. She could get a taxi home. It would be slower but more convenient, unless...

GALAXY GRIFTER

She sent a message to Griz: >*Are you working today?*

If he was finishing up, he could give her a ride. She also had a business idea she wanted to run past·him. If he could recommend a mechanic, she could start her own gig, catering to those struggling to afford Lentatech's services. As June had said, some people just wanted to get from A to B. Ship servicing wasn't her dream job, but it was a job, and with the money from today, she could pay for the tools and the licensing.

Whatever it took, she was going to find her way again.

———————————•———————————

Griz met Vera at the terminal with a big bear hug. "How was your holiday?" he asked.

"Really good. But not long enough." The day's events made it seem like a century had passed. She wanted to collapse into bed and forget everything. Her duffel left a wet patch on the spaceport's floor where she'd placed it. "Didn't get a chance to dry things after the beach," she said, before he had a chance to ask. "I need to pick something up from…a friend. And we can head off."

On their walk toward *Caerus*, Griz relayed the latest gossip from Lentatech. Something about a reshuffle in management; Vera wasn't really paying attention. Exhaustion was starting to take over her body and it was all she could do to keep moving. She needed to get her frame, get home, and crash. Finally, they were just about to enter the area where *Caerus* was docked, when a flier landed on the tarmac ahead.

Vera stopped and put her arm in front of Griz. Two figures

emerged from the flier: Rors, unusually large, with red-tinged fur. She swerved behind another ship, a bottle-green shuttle, and tugged Griz with her.

He furrowed his furry brows. "What are you doing?"

"Shh." She held her finger to her lips and peeked out. The Rors headed up *Caerus*'s ramp.

Griz popped his head out beside her. "You know them?"

"No." She pushed him back into cover and tapped her virt to warn Levi. *>Don't open. Don't*— Too late. When she looked again, the Rors had disappeared inside. "Shit."

"What's happening?" Griz whispered.

Where to begin? She pressed her back to the shuttle and wiped her clammy palms on her jeans. "Have you heard of the Mzarak Scouts?"

"No."

"They're bounty hunters, from Zrata."

"My homeworld? Why are they here?"

"The person I was going to see...I think they want to kill him."

If what Blackbeard told her was true, Levi was as good as dead now. What had even been the point of saving him? She peeked out again. One of the Rors exited *Caerus* and looked around. He raised his arm and descended the ramp. Levi followed, pale, staggering but alive. For now. The second Ror closed the procession. The three of them disappeared inside the flier and it took off, threading between the spacecrafts on the landing field.

"Can we follow them?" Vera asked.

Griz nodded, but when they reached his van, parked near

GALAXY GRIFTER

the service entrance, the flier with the Mzarak Scouts had disappeared. Huge toolboxes rattled against Halkeeth's tiny yellow racing flier, still stationed in the back of the van, as Griz drove across the tarmac past stationary spaceships. "They must've gone through the western exit," he said.

"No, look." She pointed through the passenger window at a Jaemlen-built, midsize freighter. The grey flier peeked from in its cargo hold before the hatch closed.

Griz slowed the van.

"Keep going." She didn't want the bounty hunters to notice them. "What gate is this?"

"L fifty-seven," Griz said.

Vera pulled up the spaceport's departures schedule on her virt and typed in the gate number. "They're leaving in thirty minutes."

Griz pulled over next to other utility vehicles parked near the western exit. "Should we call the police or spaceport security?" he asked.

"And say what? We can't prove he didn't willingly go with them."

"I guess they'd need a warrant from the Department of Xeno Affairs to search the ship." Griz scratched his ear. "But there must be a way to help your friend."

"Must there?" She'd sworn it had been the last time she helped Levi... Why was she even doing this? "Don't think there's much we can do now."

"I have a thought." Griz leaned into the back of the van, grabbed a black box, and started the engine.

"What are you doing?"

He drove back along the landing field and slowed near the Mzaraks' freighter. He lowered the window and opened the box, revealing two round pucks. "Neodymium magnets. They'll mess with their engine scan if I can get them in."

"What? Griz, wait." She touched his arm.

"You helped me and Halkeeth when we were in trouble. I think I can help your friend now." He leaned out of the window and shoved the magnets into the ship's left rocket engine. "Now they can't depart without a mechanic. And if they log a job with Lentatech, I'll assign it to myself."

"And then what? You want to get yourself killed?" She wouldn't allow it.

Griz drove for a few meters and parked behind another ship, where they'd be out of sight. "I'll just look around. They won't kill me, I'm a Ror."

"So?"

"Our faith forbids it."

"That literally never stopped Humans."

"It's different for Rors. Low birth rates. Our instinct to preserve our species is almost as strong as self-preservation."

She sighed. Levi was the biggest jerk in the universe and didn't deserve anyone risking their hide for him. But if there was something she could reasonably do and didn't... *Fucking conscience.* She sighed. "So, what is your plan, exactly?"

When a request came through Lentatech, Griz waited for several minutes before driving back to the Mzaraks' freighter. He parked the van, retrieved his massive toolbox, and headed up the freighter's ramp.

Vera climbed into the back of the van to stay hidden. Why was Griz so eager to help a stranger? Granted, he couldn't know what an asshole the stranger was. And Griz thought he was also helping *her*. She'd made a real friend here.

After a while, someone knocked on the van's window. She held her breath and the trunk clicked open.

"Griz." She exhaled.

"No sign of your friend in the living area. He might be locked in one of the cabins." Griz was visibly disappointed.

"Too bad, I guess." Her relief tasted of burnt coffee, but they'd done all they could.

"Could you disarm the locks if you had access to their control panel?"

She scratched her cheek. "Possibly, if they're only digitally locked."

"I said it may be an operating system glitch, and if we tell them you're a technician..."

Her pulse jumped. "You want me to go aboard that ship?"

"I can keep one of the Rors occupied in the engine room and check the rest of the ship. You'll distract the second Ror and disarm the doors."

"It's too dangerous. I can't risk your life." She didn't want to risk her own either. The Rors had looked for her. They may have known what she looked like.

"I think it's a good plan," Griz said.

She reached over to the passenger seat, grabbed her duffel, and dug a grey cap from under her wet hoodie. "Can you pass me that?" She pointed at one of Griz's tool cases. When he did, she peeled off the sticker with Lentatech's logo and stuck it onto the cap before putting it onto her head and tucking away her ponytail. "Right... If we run into any problems, we get straight out."

Chapter 32
Body, Head

If Levi had learned one thing from dying, it was that brawl bruisers and hangovers weren't the extent of Human suffering. Everything hurt: moving, not moving, breathing. Yet he was glad to be able to do these things. Lying on the sofa, he licked his dry lips and glanced at the kitchen. Too far to walk. "*Caerus*, I need water."

"I don't understand the request. Try again." Some things a ship couldn't do. Yet. He'd fix that once all this was over.

Levi almost looked forward to the redhead's return. As horrible as she was, she'd brought him back from the dead. He wondered what Amrie would've done. Cleaned out his account and left, most likely. His virt buzzed on the coffee table next to the sofa. Someone banged on the hatch outside.

"It's open." He brought one arm over his face, hoping the pose of aesthetic helplessness would persuade Vera to give him a drink.

"Levi Adder?" Her voice was unusually gruff and not hers at all.

He peeked from under his arm just as a huge Ror yanked him to standing.

"You alive." The Ror's claws ripped through Levi's shirt.

Levi raised his hands, choking on how much it hurt. "Let's talk this through, shall we?"

A second Ror, even taller but leaner, stepped from behind the first. "You're Levi Adder."

"I know who *I* am, but you've never introduced yourselves." Levi remembered Vera saying something about bounty-hunting Rors.

"You no dead? No tracker?" the thicker Ror growled.

"Oh, I've been dead, and would prefer not to go back there. Have the Breznis sent you?" Levi asked.

"We no work for Breznis. We buy your location," the Ror said.

"Who *do* you work for?"

The Rors exchanged glances.

"You come with us, or I break your back." The thicker Ror flung Levi to the floor toward the exit hatch. Then he pulled Levi up to standing again and pushed him out of the ship, down the ramp, and toward a grey flier.

The taller Ror went ahead and held the flier's door open. "Get in."

How gallant.

The flier was empty. If Levi felt more like himself, and less like a zombie, he would've slid through to the opposite door and made a run for it. In his current state, the threat

GALAXY GRIFTER

of a broken back kept him docile. He winced and shuffled onto the back seat. The taller Ror climbed in and sat next to him. The shorter one took the driver's seat and started the engine.

"You're bounty hunters?" Levi asked. Any information could help save him.

"Body, head, whatever client want," the tall Ror said, apparently lost in translation, but no less menacing.

"And what *does* your client want from me?"

"Who know about Operation Tetakoraa?" the Ror said.

Although he remembered that name from the Jaemlen–A'turi correspondence, Levi saw no need to show it. "What's Operation Tetakoraa?"

"Where you find blueprint?"

"What blueprint?"

The Ror's claws dug into Levi's shoulder, engulfing it in burning pain. "Blueprint you sell to Logic Interstellar."

"I stole it! I stole it from a pirate ship!" Levi yelled, and the Ror let go. Levi glanced at the bloodstains seeping through his already torn shirt. "I don't know where the pirates got it."

The flier slowed next to a midsize freighter and glided into its cargo hatch. The Rors stepped out and motioned for Levi to follow.

He gritted his teeth and forced himself out. "I was a hostage on that ship. There was a battle. I stole a shuttle to save myself and found the A'turi file by accident."

"You lie." The tall Ror slammed a heavy hand into Levi's back, causing him to lose his balance.

He plunged, face down, into a metal staircase. Stars flashed

277

before his eyes, followed by a fresh bout of pain, encasing his much-abused brain case.

"No kill him!" the second Ror growled. He rolled Levi over and pushed him to sitting.

Blood gushed into Levi's left eye. He closed it and touched his forehead. A bump swelled where he hit the stairs, with a gash down the middle. That was going to leave a scar. He pressed his sleeve to the cut. "Keep doing that and there won't be much I'll be able to tell you."

"You tell client." The thick Ror hauled Levi over his shoulder in one humiliating move and carried him up the stairs.

"Who's your client? I can pay you more than they're paying you." Dangling with his face against the Ror's back, hairy even through his shirt fabric, Levi fought back nausea. He would've been leaving a trail of vomit, if his stomach hadn't been empty for the past fifty hours, as per the cryogenesis instructions.

The Ror tossed him onto the floor in a small cabin with unfaced walls, a bunk, and a waste bucket and turned to leave.

"Wait." Levi scrambled to his feet. "We can come to an arrangement."

The Ror looked over his shoulder. "We honor our contract. The Mzaraks want no trouble."

Levi's arms sagged. "You work for the spooks then?"

"The spooks?"

"The unmarked warships that hunted me near Saturn?"

"Prepare for takeoff." The Ror stepped outside and shut the hatch behind him.

"Wait!" Levi gripped the handle. *Locked.* "We can talk about this!"

GALAXY GRIFTER

He banged on the hatch, shouting offers of money and information, but nobody seemed to be listening. After a while he sank to the floor and pressed his sleeve to his brow. Still bleeding.

Operation Tetakoraa, the spooks... He was fucked, he realized, as his mind drifted into darkness. What would they do to him?

Why had he taken that damn file?

Chapter 33
The Coffin

Levi sat on the cabin's floor with his back pressed against its hatch when an unfamiliar voice jogged him into consciousness.

"Anyone here?" it said.

Levi touched the gash in his brow, wondering if he was hearing things.

"Levi?" the voice said.

He shuffled away from the hatch. "Yes?"

It clicked and opened. A Ror poked his head in—a different Ror, smaller than the other two captors and dressed in blue trade attire. "I'm Griz, Vera's friend. I'll get you out." He pushed a large toolbox into the cabin and opened the box. "Get in. I told the Mzaraks I'm checking the wiring. One is on the engine room's floor, holding up a cylinder. Told him he can't put it down. The other is in the cockpit. We can get past if you're quiet."

Reluctantly, Levi obeyed, trying to shake the feeling that he was climbing into his own coffin. The wrenches at the

280

GALAXY GRIFTER

bottom of the box dug into his ribs as the Ror slammed the lid down. A very uncomfortable coffin. What followed was a bumpy ride with numerous stops and starts.

Where was this guy taking him? Levi needed to return to *Caerus*, to the safety of his ship and the shadow routes where the Mzaraks couldn't follow him. But...he was not on Blackjack, Xinlouyang Spaceport security wouldn't simply let him take off, and *Caerus* was the first place Mzaraks would look for him once they realized he was gone...Levi felt sick and asphyxiated. He gasped for air when the lid finally opened.

Vera knelt by the box. Her eyes shifted from his bashed face, to his ripped and bloodied shirt. Her face was stern, like it was taking her every bit of self-control not to explode. "Get out."

He sat up. They were in the back of some kind of vehicle. It jerked forward.

"Can you fly a manual?" Griz said from the driver's seat.

"This thing?" Levi pointed at a fluorescent abomination parked in the van's rear. It looked more like a toy than a real vehicle, and was undoubtedly used for some amateur sports.

Vera turned to Griz. "I thought you're flying."

"I'm not good like Halkeeth. I can stay to talk to the Mzaraks. It will give you more time." He drove through the spaceport's exit gate and did a U-turn.

"Are you out of your mind?" she asked.

"They will not kill me, I promise you." The Ror backed the van toward rows of containers and stopped.

"We're going together. No discussion."

Having figured out their plan, Levi scampered out of the box and opened the flier's door. "I'll fly."

Vera scoffed. "You look like you're about to pass out."

"I'm fine." He climbed into the pilot seat, unwilling to entrust his life to this dubious duo.

"They're coming." Griz pointed through the window at the grey flier, which headed toward them from the spaceport's gate.

"Then hurry!" Vera slapped the flier's roof and climbed in next to Levi. Griz squeezed into the back. Too cozy for comfort, it trumped being imprisoned with the waste bucket.

With the three of them inside, Levi steered the flier out of the van's trunk and between rows of container. Hopefully the abandoned van would distract the Mzaraks, if only for a minute. Approaching the flyway, he glanced at the rear display. No sign of the grey flier. He merged into the traffic headed toward the skyline of Xinlouyang.

Vera fidgeted with her virt. "Slow down, there are cameras."

He wiped the sweat from his brow. "Could your getaway ride be more overt?"

"You don't get to complain." She pulled up a text box.

He snatched her virt and tossed it out of the flier's window.

She glared at him. "What did you—"

"Who were you messaging?" he asked.

"My boyfriend, to let him know I'm alive."

"Too risky."

Griz ripped off his own virtEgo and disposed of it in the same manner.

Vera scowled. "That was unnecessary. Nobody accessed our devices. He's just being a dickhead."

GALAXY GRIFTER

"Can't be too careful." Levi turned off the flyway, and toward a high-rise shopping center. He landed on the rooftop and closed his eyes. No longer able to discern where in his body the pain was coming from (he was a personification of pain), he wished for a second he'd stayed dead.

"We should go to the police," Griz said from the back seat.

"We shouldn't. Watch the flier and holler if they turn up. I need meds and a new virt." Levi stepped out and headed into the mall.

Vera followed.

The bustle inside collapsed onto his aching head like a ton of bricks. He nearly retched from the smells coming out of the food court. A dark fog crept into his peripheral vision and he reached for a wall to steady himself.

She stopped next to him. "Are you okay?"

"No. Were those the bounty hunters you mentioned earlier?"

"I assume."

"How did they find me?"

"How should I know? Saw them when I was returning to pick the frame up. I tried to warn you, but—"

"And the third one?"

"Griz?" she asked. "He's my friend and has nothing to do with them."

"So he just happens to be a Ror?"

"Yes!" She raised her voice. "He saved your life and now we're both in the crapper thanks to you."

"Why?" Levi tore himself away from the wall and started toward an electronics store.

"Why what?" She caught up to him.

"Why did you and your *friend* get me out?" Inside the store, he approached a vending machine filled with gadgets and selected the latest virtEgo model.

Vera shuffled from foot to foot. "Because I'd just gone through hell bringing you back from the dead? And Griz... he's just a good person. And he doesn't know the kind of ass-hole you are."

"Good person?" He'd laugh if had the energy. Something didn't add up, but he was too ill to think.

A message popped up on the vending machine: *Please tap to pay or log in at the terminal.* He had nothing to tap with, so he keyed in the details of one of his many k-bit accounts.

Not enough funds to complete transaction.

Fuck. His money was running out quick. He logged into another account. This time the payment went through. The machine spat out a brand-new device.

Vera nudged him out of the way. "I need one too, thanks to you."

He stepped aside. She could pay for her own gadget—this was half her mess, as far as he was concerned, and he wasn't giving her another coin. As she did, he removed his from its packaging and set up his profile. It wasn't easy with shaky hands and blurred vision. "Where's the drugstore?"

"There." She pointed. "Quick, I want to make sure Griz is okay."

He staggered through the fog that engulfed the mall when something hit his side. Not a Ror, just a bulky Human. "Watch where you're going."

GALAXY GRIFTER

Vera appeared next to him and looped her arm through his, screwing her face up like she was touching dogshit. "You should be in a hospital."

"I should be in hyperspace." *With my* Caerus, *scamming creatures across the galaxy*, he added in his head. He couldn't return to *Caerus* now, as the Mzaraks were sure to be watching the ship. *Fuck.*

The next set of vending machines thankfully contained first aid supplies. He paid, popped a handful of pills, and leaned on the machine, using his virt camera as a mirror. He did look like shit, and the gash above his left eye would definitely leave a scar. With his teeth, he unscrewed the top from a tube of medical glue and tried to apply it to the laceration. It dripped onto his eyelid. *Double fuck.*

Vera took the tube from him. "Get down."

He spat out the cap into his fist, looked around to make sure nobody was watching his act of humiliation, and knelt. Her lips twitched as she applied the stinging substance to his wound and pinched it closed. Never before had a woman touched him with this much contempt. She handed the glue back and stuck a bandage on his forehead. "Let's go."

Rising, Levi realized whatever drugs he'd taken must be kicking in. Things didn't feel as wobbly as they did a moment ago. "What now?"

"You tell me. We're in this mess because of you, so you better have a plan to get us out of it."

"For starters, we need a better ride than the fluorescent monstrosity."

He bought a clean shirt from yet another vending machine

and they returned to the flier. Griz stood leaning against it—there didn't seem to be any Mzaraks in sight. That was either lucky or suspicious. He had a complex relationship with luck of late, so he opted for the latter.

An old Suix flier landed in the next parking spot and two teenage boys climbed out. Levi approached the one on the driver's side. "How much did your flier cost?"

The boy looked around as though doubting the question was directed at him. "Four and half grand, why?"

"Any problems?"

"No..."

"I'll take it from you for six. Cash in hand, we'll do the paperwork later."

"What, now? Nah...I don't think so." The boy glanced at his friend.

"Seven grand, and you can buy yourself a Levitas or a Fortis. No one will ever give you more for this junk."

The boy exchanged looks with his friend again and, after a protracted pause, nodded. Levi transferred the payment, and the boy transferred him the key to the Suix. Then the boys gathered their belongings and walked off into the shopping mall. Levi turned to Griz and Vera. "We need to split up."

"What?" Her eyes widened. "No way."

He beckoned to her and took her aside. "Your friend is right to say the Mzaraks wouldn't kill him *intentionally*. It's like they've got a species-wide mental block. But the more implicated he gets, the more likely he is to become collateral damage."

Vera looked around as though considering his words. "What do you suggest we do then?"

"We split up, and fast, before the Mzaraks find a way to check the flyway cameras."

"So, you'll just dump us here?"

"We'll reconvene—"

"No. I'm keen to keep Griz out of it, but the Mzaraks were already looking for me on Blackjack. I won't let you dispose of me like you did on the *Comet*."

Rolling his eyes hurt too. "I—"

"I'm going with you and you're telling me everything."

Inside, the Suix smelled of sweat and weed and was littered with cans and packaging. To Levi's relief, the autopilot was working.

Vera fastened her safety belt. "Are you sure Griz will be okay?"

"More okay than if he was with us." He set a destination at random.

The Ror agreed to the split-up faster than Vera did. The logic made sense to him. And Vera was glad to know that he would likely be safe.

"Where are we going?" she asked as the flier left its parking spot.

"Not to the spaceport. If I was a bounty hunter, that's where I'd be looking."

"What do the Mzaraks want from you?"

"Operation Tetakoraa."

"What's that?"

"Not a clue." He watched the flyway and the rays of the setting sun bouncing off the densely built skyscrapers. "Seems to be another part of the blueprints."

"These fucking blueprints! They've been nothing but trouble. You never even told me where you got them," she said, her tone urgent, insistent.

Funnily, that was the same thing that interested the Mzaraks.

"Out with it—who owned those blueprints?" she demanded.

"Jaemlen intelligence, I think." He watched her reaction.

Her confusion seemed genuine. "Jaemlen *what*? Why they fuck would they have A'turian blueprints?"

"No clue."

She exhaled. "Levi, this concerns me too. Where did you get them?" She held a pause. "For fuck's sake, I should have let them take you."

"You probably should have. Actually, why didn't you?"

She crossed her arms and turned away from him. "I already told you."

"Because you're a good person?"

"It's not a concept you're familiar with."

"Are you in love with me?"

She gagged, rather convincingly.

He pulled up at a charging station on Xinlouyang's outskirts, complete with a convenience store and coffee shop.

She looked out the window. "Where are we?"

"Fuck knows, but I haven't eaten in days. I'll tell you what's what once we fuel up." Levi parked the small transporter, carefully looking around the outside of the vehicle before exiting and making his way over to the store.

GALAXY GRIFTER

They bought coffee and protein pastries and sat at a table. He waited for her to take a bite and stood. "I'll use the bathroom."

She nodded, chewing.

He slowed by the restroom's door and glanced over his shoulder. She seemed preoccupied with her new virtEgo and he continued on, through the café's exit, into the Suix, and up onto the flyway.

Chapter 34
The Choice

Vera finished her pastry and dropped the empty wrapper onto the table. Her virt showed a dozen missed calls and messages from Niran, but she wasn't ready to contact him. What could she even say? *Sorry, baby, got caught up helping an interstellar criminal again, don't wait up!* No, she couldn't explain why she wasn't home, so she was just going to ignore Niran for now. Besides, she had other things to think about.

She typed *Operation Tetakoraa* into a search engine. The results it brought up looked irrelevant: *Tetakoraa* was the name of a Jaemlen mythical creature or goddess from centuries back. She was depicted with the amphibious head and upper body of a Jaemlen female and tentacles for legs, kind of like the Jaemlen version of a mermaid. But what did that have to do with the A'turi hyperdrive or Jaemlen intelligence? *Jaemlen fucking intelligence*—as if Mafia and bounty hunter gangs weren't enough. She shivered at the thought. She'd really messed things up for herself this time. All for a guy who'd dumped her in space like rubbish.

Where was he anyway?

She looked around the nearly empty service station café. An elderly couple ordered food at the counter. Had Levi passed out in the toilet? It wouldn't surprise her, given the state of him. Rolling her eyes, she headed to the restroom and stopped by the door, suddenly anxious at what she might find... or not find.

She pushed it open. The stalls stood empty.

Of course.

She left the toilet and looked out of the café's window. The Suix was gone.

She really didn't learn, did she? Vera threw her head back in a bitter laugh. The elderly couple stared at her. She deserved all their judgment and more.

Then she thought of Griz and the anxiety set back in. What if the Mzaraks found him? How could she have allowed him to get tangled in this? *Hate* no longer encapsulated the scope of the loathing she felt for herself. She tried calling Griz. No answer. Right, he had thrown his virt away too. Perhaps he hadn't yet gotten a new one. She tried Halkeeth.

She answered after several rings. "Vera, where are you? Griz is with me. He told me everything."

Vera let out a breath. "Is he okay?"

"Yes, we're at my flat. Where are *you*?"

"Listen, if the Mzaraks or anyone turn up looking for me, just give them my number and go to the police, okay?"

"Your number?"

"Yes, it's part of the plan. Please?"

"Okay, but—"

"Thanks, talk to you later." Vera hung up, her heart still

pounding. At least Griz was safe, but...what was she meant to do now? Call a cab, go to her apartment, and wait for some Rors to come and rip her to shreds? And what about Griz, Halkeeth, Niran, and her brother's family? None of them were safe while the bounty hunters were looking for her. And Fred...Fred had been right in so many ways. She could never understand his insistence to stay on Blackjack, but now she felt that people like her didn't belong in more polite society. She couldn't hold down a job and she endangered everyone she'd cared about. But at least Fred would probably be okay. The Mzaraks wouldn't possibly go after him...right? Her head was aching—if she inadvertently dragged her brother into this mess again, she couldn't live with herself.

She needed help. Someone who could get her out of here, without judging or asking too many questions. And right now, there was only one person she could think of who'd do that for her.

Slowly, she scrolled through her contact list. *June*. The call went straight to a recorded message. "This is June from Chin Up Carriers. I'm probably in hyperspace, but leave a message and I'll respond after landing."

Vera held her virt close to her mouth, making sure neither of the elderly people would hear her. "June, Vera here. Give me a call when you get this. Urgent. Bye."

Since she was calling folks in desperation, Vera figured she might as well call Niran after all. She found his contact and stared at it for a long time, bracing, grieving for what she was about to do. *This is your own fault*, she reminded herself and tapped the call icon.

GALAXY GRIFTER

He answered immediately. "Vera? Where are you?"

"I'm sorry, my virt broke."

"Broke? I've gone to your flat, you weren't home. I thought something happened on the way from the spaceport."

"Uhm...No...I just...I got caught up with something. Are you safe? Did anyone talk to you?"

"Talk to me? About what?"

"Some people from work were looking for me. Rors. I was wondering if they'd tried to contact you?"

"No...are you sure you're okay? Where are you?"

"A café. Niran, listen...I'm sorry."

"About what?"

"We"—the words caught in her throat—"we need to break up."

The silence on the other end had the gravity of a gas giant about to crush her.

Finally, he broke it. "Why?"

She closed her eyes, voicing a choice she never thought she'd make, "I'm returning to Blackjack."

Chapter 35
The Butcher

"I'm happy to consult you off the record, but I'm not available until Wednesday," the doctor on the other end of the call said.

Levi couldn't wait until Wednesday. "Is there someone else you can recommend?"

"Not off the top of my head. You'll need to check the registry," the doctor said.

Levi ended the call and landed the Suix in a flier yard in Western Xinlouyang—the least reputable part of the megalopolis. Used vehicles sprawled across the desert floor as far as the eye could see, like a graveyard of rusty metal. A short man in oil-stained overalls approached the Suix. "Are you buying or selling?"

"Both." Levi climbed out of the flier. "Also...do you happen to know a surgeon?"

"A surgeon?" The dealer scratched the back of his neck with a wrench.

GALAXY GRIFTER

"A nurse or a paramedic could do. Or anyone clued up on anatomy."

"I see." The dealer looked around and leaned forward. "I might know a surgeon."

Levi traded the Suix for an all-terrainer and followed the dealer's directions: the first building on the right, past the bazaar. The building turned out to be a five-story concrete apartment block. A grubby eatery on its ground floor boasted a handwritten sign: *Proper Protein*. A front for an illicit doctor? Fine. It didn't matter to him if the doc was on the up-and-up, as long as they could get that damn chip out of his neck. If his enemies found a way to reactivate it... He shivered at the thought.

Upon entry, Levi was greeted by the stench of burnt cooking oil and an elderly woman. She wore what looked like a floral dressing gown, with her hair done up in a messy bun. "Welcome. Just one?" She raised a finger.

"I'm, uh, not here to *eat*." He wondered if he came to the wrong place.

"Ah." The woman placed a BACK SOON sign on the counter and gestured for him to follow, past the empty tables and through a door labeled STAFF ONLY. They walked through a dirty kitchen and down a flight of stairs. The concrete basement was cold and lined with display counters like the deli section of a grocery store.

The woman stopped. "We have chicken, pork, and—"

"Shit."

A pig's head stared at him with dead, glassy eyes. The objects on display were animal parts, outlawed for the past century, since the rise of factory-grown meats.

"All fresh, of the highest quality," the woman said.

Levi backed up. "I was looking for a doctor."

"Oh...I will call my husband." The woman squeezed past him and disappeared behind another door on the opposite end of the basement. Levi studied the meat selection. While he felt no moral objection to the consumption of animals, the pieces on display elicited disgust.

The woman returned, followed by a stocky man with bushy eyebrows. He wiped his hands on his bloody apron and held one hand out to Levi. "I'm Hien, how are you?"

"You're a butcher?" Levi shook the man's hand. "I was told you're a surgeon."

"A butcher is a surgeon, just for dead flesh," Hien said. "Have you tried the real stuff? You won't want the factory trash after that."

"Maybe another time."

"If you want to sell a kidney, I can help with that too. I have six years of med school and equipment in the back room. Can even link you up with some buyers."

"And if I just wanted a foreign object removed?"

"I can do that." Hien waved his hand, inviting Levi through the door. They walked past a bloody animal carcass atop a metal table and into another room. This one had the same concrete walls as the previous area and a similar metal table, but thankfully this one displayed no traces of blood or meat. A bathroom was visible through an opened door in the back wall.

Hien offered Levi a chair, washed his hands, and retrieved a scalpel from a medical bag he laid out on the table.

GALAXY GRIFTER

Levi pressed his fingers to his neck until he felt the implant. The butcher's implied connection to the organs black market concerned him. What if the guy knocked him out and sold him for parts? He had to risk it—removing the tracker trumped caution.

"What you'll be removing is a small tech chip. It's embedded next to the artery, so please use caution with that knife. I could bleed out," he warned.

"You won't." Hien slammed a needle into Levi's neck. "This will put you to sleep. Your chip won't explode when I take it out, will it?"

Levi let out a bitter chuckle as the meds sent a wave of pleasant drowsiness over him. That wasn't something he could guarantee.

———————————— ● ————————————

After what seemed like hours, Levi roused from his medicated state.

"Here you go." Hien dropped the blood-covered chip into the palm of Levi's hand.

Levi let out a heavy breath and rushed into the bathroom to flush the darn thing down the toilet. "Track that, assholes." He glanced in the mirror. The bandage on his forehead, the dark circles around his eyes, and the fresh stitch below his stubbled jaw made for a pitiful sight, but things could've been far worse.

He returned to the operating room and transferred the butcher his payment. "As you may have guessed, bad people are after me."

Hien raised his large hands. "I ask no questions."

"You said you knew people. Think you know someone who can help me?"

"If you have money, I can sneak you past spaceport security and off the planet."

Levi cocked his head. "Handy. But I was hoping for a more permanent solution."

"Ah," the almost doctor said. "I do know someone who might be able to help... for the right price, of course."

—————————•—————————

Levi wandered slowly through the gloomy halls of an abandoned factory. Rusty machinery littered its floors. Sunbeams fought their way in through the sand-crusted windows and bounced off the joists that crisscrossed the tall ceiling. This place couldn't be good for his fresh wounds; the sooner he could get out of here, the better.

"Shealth? You in here? I want to commission a job."

Silence.

"The steak is out of the bag," he said—an odd passphrase Hien had taught him.

Silence. Perhaps Shealth wasn't home. Growing impatient, he turned toward the exit and fresh air, when a scaly trunk fell into his path from somewhere above. It slithered against his legs, coiling around him, until the Sehen's snakelike face came into view. The female reptilians were even larger than their male counterparts, and this one was a prime example of the female Sehen giant stature.

GALAXY GRIFTER

"I lisssten." Her eyes glowed yellow in the poorly lit hall.

"Shealth?" He pretended not to be intimidated by the reptilian's hospitality. "Hien, the butcher, told me you can help with a problem."

"Who'sss the problem?" The Sehen flicked her tongue mere centimeters from Levi's face.

"Mzarak Scouts—two Ror bounty hunters that are out to get me."

The Sehen tightened her hold on him. "You wantsss me to kill them?"

He drew in a labored breath. "No, I need information, and I want you to extract it."

"More complicated. Find and kill—quick and quietsss. Catch and torture—sssslow and loud. Exsssspensive."

"I have the money." Levi tried to move his arms, which were growing numb in the Sehen's hold.

Shealth tightened her rings. "Why ssshhhould I work for your money? I can make you beg me to takessss them."

"I don't doubt it. But my money's a small fraction of what you'll get if you help me." He gritted his teeth, his every muscle fighting against the pressure. That wouldn't stop the reptilian from squeezing his guts out like toothpaste if she decided to.

"How ssso?" she asked.

"Mzaraks are highly paid thugs, any coin you can knock from them is yours as long as I get my intel. You can take their ship too."

"Ssship? What kind?"

"A Jaemlen four-cabin freighter, about a decade old, at most."

Shealth loosened her grip. "Where isss they?"

"The Mzaraks? I last saw them at Xinlouyang Spaceport." He wriggled his limbs to try to restore circulation.

"Spaceport cameras. Shhhealth deportsss," she said, hinting that her presence on Seshat was illegal.

"We can lure them out," he said. "They're looking for me, so if we drop a hint..."

The problem with that idea was that it looked suspicious. He'd managed to successfully escape until now. Reappearing on their radar, or giving them an anonymous tip-off, would surely expose the trap. As bounty hunters, they'd be well-versed in such techniques. But if someone were to sell him out again...someone who knew about the Mzaraks. Like Blackbeard. Although Blackbeard would likely prefer to kill Levi himself. Mahru then, the Huxoran ship dealer that had sold *Caerus*.

"How would you feel about taking this party to Frigg?" Levi asked. "The sheriff is the only authority in New Aarhus and we can keep things quiet."

"That will cosssst," Shealth hissed. "But if I get that sssship, Ssshealth accepts."

Discreetly transporting Shealth and her slightly smaller associate, named Sahee, off Seshat did prove costly, depleting Levi of most of his funds—this last-ditch effort was going to leave him almost completely broke. At the very least, Hien's contraband system worked like an oiled machine. The two Sehens were driven to the spaceport in a refrigeration container packed with perishable foods and loaded onto a space freighter. The scanners didn't pick up on the live reptilians. Or maybe part of the payment went into ensuring they didn't. Levi traveled aboard the same ship as a paying passenger. *Caerus* would remain in Xinlouyang, until Mahru sold him out. Having to leave his darling behind after such a brief reunion pained him, but he had no choice. Once the Rors were taken care of and he could steal some shit to sell, he'd order a valet service to get *Caerus* shipped when the time came.

New Aarhus was a convincing spot for pretending to lie low. Its town center had more tractors than fliers. Levi strolled past low-rise wooden buildings and a fresh produce stall minded by a young boy in a wide-brimmed hat. The boy waved. Levi had been walking this route daily since landing on Frigg three days ago. There was no sign of the Rors.

He pulled up his virt and called his mother. When she answered, there was a rumbling noise in the background. "Levi? I'm sorry, it's windy, we've just come out for a walk."

"It's okay. I wanted to check if you received my present."

"The painting? I did. It's lovely, honey."

"The painter is the recently deceased Wasim Ohannes, the most trending contemporary artist," he said, sensing a *yes, but* in her voice.

"I've read about him," she said.

He'd have liked more enthusiasm. "You don't like it?"

"I do, it's just... You don't need to get us these extravagant presents. I'd rather just see *you*."

"I said I'll visit when I get the chance." He was growing tired of repeating himself.

"Listen, if something is wrong, your dad and I—"

"Nothing is wrong. I've got to go, Mum." He ended the call and walked into a pub that smelled of the freshly cut pinewood it was faced with. Farmers in muddy boots sat round tables. Old folks played the pokies in the corner.

A rotund bartender poured the whiskey. "You're not from here. A consultant of sorts?"

"Engineering." Levi gave a sour nod. If the Mzaraks didn't show, he'd need to dismiss Shealth...And then? What could even be his next move?

"You don't like it here?" the bartender guessed.

"Work's work. Not much else to do."

The bartender chuckled. "Have you seen the nature? The forests? That's why I've moved. Better than Earth, if you ask me."

"Have you been to Earth?" Levi would've placed the man's burry accent as Rebeccan. That made him think of the Breznis. Had the Ror told them he tricked their tracker? Would they be after him too?

"Nah. Too expensive," said the bartender. "And they wouldn't let a regular bloke like me stay, would they? Have you been?"

"In passing."

"And?"

"Almost as boring as Frigg. Just fancier."

The bartender laughed again. "I thought as much. Don't know why the government thinks they have a right to keep us off the world that we allegedly came from. Where are you from originally?"

"Eria," Levi lied. "But the job's kept me on the move this past decade."

"Eria? I heard it's a sinful cesspool. I'm from Rebecca myself, an industrial wasteland. Frigg is the place to be, I'm telling you. That's why the Jaemlens wanted a piece of it. I say they can't have it. It's ours."

Levi finished his drink and headed back to his motel, squinting in the last rays of the setting sun. He saw mountains far off in the distance—Levi had never been one for hiking for pleasure and didn't understand the allure of high terrain that wasn't a penthouse or his perfect ship. Nature was fine; tech was better. Turning the corner was a relief for his swollen eyes. He felt a pinprick on his upper arm...maybe the stress of the past few days was finally catching up to his poor body. He looked down. A dart's tail stuck out of his right shoulder.

Well, fuck me.

Darkness engulfed him.

Levi moaned and rolled onto his side. He blinked once, twice, and a room with oversized furniture came into focus. It took him another moment to realize he was aboard the Mzaraks' ship, on the floor of their living module. Sahee, Shealth's accomplice, rummaged through the contents of a kitchen freezer without looking at Levi.

Holding on to his head in fear it might crack open like an overripe walnut shell, Levi sat up. "What happened?"

Shealth, who was coiled in a massive armchair, raised her head. "The Rorssss took the bait."

He was meant to message her when the Mzaraks came, but he hadn't seen them approaching. "How did you—"

"Shealth don't trusssts ssstupid Human walking alone. We followsss you and watchess you."

That made him uneasy. "Where are the Mzaraks?"

"Dead."

"Why are they dead?" He tried to stand but felt too shaky.

"We killedsss them."

"The fuck, Shealth? The agreement was that you'd question them, not kill them." *That* was why most Humans avoided working with Sehens and why the Galactic Union refused to grant them membership.

"We quesssstioned them. Then killed them."

"What did they tell you?" He managed to scramble up to standing.

"We recordsss." Shealth slithered off the chair, into the cockpit, and started the playback of the recording. Pained screams projected from the speakers in walls, interrupted infrequently by alien speech fragments and the crunch of what Levi could only assume were Mzarak bones.

After several replays, he barely knew more than he'd started with. Who hired them? What was their end game? He was beginning to doubt his assumptions. "I thought you were meant to be good at extracting info."

"We cannot exssstract what they don't know." Shealth yawned, climbing back into the armchair.

"We extractsss money and weaponsss." Sahee pointed at a

GALAXY GRIFTER

dining table, surrounded by cushions instead of chairs.

Levi approached the table laden with guns and gadgets, and picked up a small black square with red veins—an A'turi data card.

In a single leap, Shealth landed next to him. "It's oursss. We agree you only takes informationssss."

"This *is* information," Levi said. "You can't decode it anyway, and it's not like you've given me anything else that's useful."

Shealth hissed, yellow eyes aglow, but said nothing more. Levi headed into the cockpit, hoping the ship's logs hadn't been cleared and played the last sent ansible message. He used his virt to translate the spoken Ror language:

"We confirmed the lead about Adder Levi on Frigg. Also received a lead on his accomplice involved in his escape—the Human female O'Mara Vera. Source has seen her on the asteroid in sector twenty-one. Confirm if you want us to follow lead after we recapture Adder Levi, or to proceed to Gleath to deliver the package collected in sector forty-three."

The message hadn't confirmed the identity of the Mzaraks' clients, but Gleath was the Jaemlen homeworld, the same planet that hosted the dreaded terraformation conference.

Levi spun the A'turi data card in his fingers. *This* must've been the package from sector 43 the Mzaraks had been referring to. What was on it? Another blueprint to replace the one he'd stolen? He doubted it. The Jaemlen warships that had pursued him were faster than what was thought possible. Perhaps Operation Tetakoraa was a collaboration between the two aquatic species to improve on the existing antimatter technology? Was that what he was holding? A blueprint for a new generation FTL engine?

305

Just as he was about to return to *Caerus*, pondering what this new discovery could mean for him, the Mzaraks' control panel bleeped with an incoming transmission. He didn't dare to answer, waiting for the caller to leave a message. They spoke a Gleathean Jaemlen dialect, confirming Levi's suspicions:

"Proceed straight to Gleath. We will investigate the lead on the asteroid ourselves."

———————————————•———————————————

Levi boarded *Caerus* and poured himself a drink, rolling the A'turi data card in his fingers. It gave him a feeling of déjà vu. But if the first card landed him in this mess, perhaps the second one could get him out. The only thing he learned about the Mzaraks' employers was their ansible code. He could contact them and tell them he had their file and use it to bargain for his life. But first he wanted to know what was on it. It'd give him additional leverage.

He slipped it into a storage compartment in his cockpit and scrolled through the contacts on his virt. The aliens referred to Vera as Levi's accomplice...Levi definitely felt a twinge of guilt about that one. He'd pretty much forced the stupid girl's hand, and now with the Mzaraks dead and him gone, she'd be the spooks' only lead. He didn't even have her new contact to warn her. But the message from the Rors suggested she returned to Blackjack, which gave him something to work with. So, he sat in his favorite seat behind *Caerus*'s rudder and called Ting, Blackjack's brothel madam.

She smiled at him from the virtual screen. "Are you in

trouble, young man?" She wore a high-collared top embroidered in red and black, with her hair up in a bun, a few loose strands to cover the scar behind her ear.

"Never out of it," he said with less mirth than before.

"How can I help?" she asked.

"You know the redhead that used to work at the pub, Vera O'Mara?"

"I heard she left Blackjack months ago."

"I'm thinking you'll find that she's back. I need you to get to her and tell her they know where she is and that she needs to leave, the sooner the better."

Ting arched her thin brows. " 'They know where she is and she needs to leave.' Is that all?"

"Yes..." He scratched the back of his head, which still ached after the tranquilizer. "No. Tell her to call me. Tell her I have a plan."

"Oh-kay." Ting disconnected and called him back two hours later. "Found your girl. She said to tell you to go fuck yourself. I assume you two have history. I don't think she's planning to leave, dear."

"Of course not." He gritted his teeth. He should've known Vera would be a pain in the ass, even about saving her own life.

Guess he was going back to fucking Blackjack. Again.

Chapter 36
Rusty

Levi banged the heel of his boot against the door of Blackjack Spaceport's ground control. A heavy crate weighed down his arms. The door cracked open and a small boy poked his head out. Yuri's hoarse voice sounded from inside the room. "Dima, who's there?"

The boy backed up, letting Levi step through. The old controller turned in his chair. "Levi? Have you met my grandson, Dima?"

"I have now. I brought you something." Levi bumped the crate. The liquor bottles inside clinked together. "Friggan moonshine. It's not Earthen single malt, but I'm told it's organic."

Yuri rose to his feet and took the crate from Levi, studying the assortment with the curiosity of unwrapping a long-awaited present. "What can I do for you?" he asked.

"Priority departure the minute I ask for it. And make sure nobody follows for at least thirty minutes."

GALAXY GRIFTER

"No problem." Yuri lifted one bottle and cradled it to his chest. "I can keep them on the ground for a while."

"I'll be back in an hour or two." Levi left the control room and strode past the spaceport's bothersome merchants, through the industrial zone, and onto Blackjack's Main Street with its clunking metal covering. The setting sun cast long, burgundy shadows, heightening his unease. He turned into an alley next to Stellar's sign and knocked on the door of Vera's old flat. A minute later it opened. Levi looked down expecting to see another child. Instead, a bare-chested adult Human male, no taller than the doorknob, gazed up at him.

"Is Vera here?" Levi asked.

"Who?"

"The redhead that lives... lived here."

"I've lived here for six months." The short man scratched his woolly stomach. "Fred, the fellow I rent from, is a red-head. Works at the bar next door."

Levi jogged toward Stellar before the little man finished talking. The sign on the door said CLOSED, but when he pushed it, it gave way.

Vera's large, bearded brother glanced up from the glass he was polishing.

A clunky android slid into Levi's path. A line of text rolled across its head: *Closed*.

"I need to talk to you, urgently." Levi stretched his neck to see past the robot.

Fred pretended not to notice at first. He swiped the glass two more times and waved at the robot. "Rusty, let him through."

The android backed off. Levi approached the bar. "Where's your sister?"

"Thought I told you to stay the fuck away from her?" Fred lowered the glass and the towel and rolled up a sleeve of his checked shirt.

"In as many words. But her life's in danger and—"

"How so?"

Levi exhaled. "If I said the Jaemlen government was out to get her, would it make any difference?"

"The Jaemlen government?" Fred rolled up his second sleeve.

"Can you just fucking call her? It's in *her* interest."

Fred stepped out from behind the bar, fists clenched. "She won't tell me why she left Seshat, but I know in my gut you're behind it."

Levi stepped back. "I'm trying to help her." What was this family's problem with him?

"Let me make myself clear—" Fred grabbed Levi and swung at him.

Levi ducked and reached for the blaster behind his back. He didn't come all this way to be manhandled by this glass-wiping lumberjack.

"Adder?"

Both men turned their heads.

Vera stood in the doorway backlit by the sunset's red glow. Her gaze slid across them and stopped on Levi's hand clutching the blaster he hadn't yet drawn. "Let him go, Fred."

Her brother's nostrils flared. "He's saying your life's in danger."

"He's full of shit. You know that."

GALAXY GRIFTER

"So you're not going to tell me what's happening?"

"I will, but you've got customers waiting." She pointed outside where the robot held back several tired-looking men.

"They can wait." Fred released Levi, who in turn left the blaster in his belt.

Vera touched her brother's arm. "We'll talk later. Rusty, we're open."

The robot wheeled away, allowing Vera and Levi to exit, pushing past the sweaty miners. Outside the sky was fading to black.

Levi raked his fingers through his hair. "The spooks know you're here. They'll come after you any day."

"Yeah, your hooker already told me."

"Ting's hooker, I—"

"Just fuck off before I tell Blackbeard to get rid of you." She crossed her arms, turning away from him.

"Blackbeard? You think he'll protect you from the Jaemlen fucking government?" He put his hand on her shoulder so she'd look at him.

She tossed his hand off. "You must be mad to think I'd want anything to do with you after—"

He caught up to her. "You may be pleased to know the Mzaraks are dead now."

Vera frowned. "Did you kill them?"

"You can say that."

"So you're a murderer too?"

"No." Why was she making this so difficult? "They weren't supposed to die. But they told the Jaemlens you're on Blackjack. I've got a plan, though."

311

"Congratulations, I won't be a part of it." She quickened her pace.

He gripped her arm. "So you'll just wait for them to show up?"

She brought her virt to her lips. "Rusty, come out here."

The android appeared in Stellar's doorway and rolled toward them.

"Get rid of him." She pointed.

The robot flailed its tentacle arms, the tips sparkling with an electric current.

Levi jumped back and raised his hands to shield himself. "Fine, I'm leaving. But don't blame me when you're dead."

Her frown deepened. It took him a second to realize she wasn't looking at him, but past him, into the dark street. He turned. A group of noisy lowlifes wandered into Stellar, but farther down the street...two...three Jaemlens in black bodysuits were headed toward them.

"Shit." Levi lurched back again as Rusty swiped at him, just missing.

"Rusty, abort." Vera raised her hand.

Levi grabbed her wrist and ran as fast as his legs allowed, tugging her behind him down the sparsely crowded streets.

Pew! Pew! Two white beams shot past them. Someone screamed.

Levi ducked in front of a parked all-terrainer. He pulled her down with him.

Blaster shots rattled against the old vehicle. Vera curled over as dust from the all-terrainer's hood settled on her back and shoulders.

GALAXY GRIFTER

When the shots ceased, Levi peeked out. Rusty trundled into the Jaemlens' path. They fired again, shots sparking like fireworks, reducing the android to a heap of smoking metal.

"Rusty!" Vera shrieked.

Levi sprang to his feet, pulling her up with him, and they sped across the road and into a side alley. Footsteps pounded the unpaved streets behind.

"We gotta get to the spaceport." He glanced back.

Hair tousled and eyes wild, Vera yanked her hand free and pushed passed him, through a door of a three-story building. With no hesitation, he followed her up a few flights of stairs and onto the roof, littered with empty cans, bottles, and cigarette butts.

Breathing heavily, they crouched by the parapet. Four Jaemlens jogged along the street below. The last held a huge black-and-red lizard on a leash. It reached to its master's waist in height and probed the air with a forked tongue. The Jaemlens slowed, letting the lizard forward.

Vera gasped. "Is that a...senhound?"

"Yep. We're fucked. They can sniff anyone out."

The senhound led the Jaemlens straight to the entrance of Vera and Levi's hideout. Two of them went inside with the senhound, and two remained by the doors.

"Great, we're trapped here now?" Levi stood and walked around the roof's perimeter. They were only several blocks away from the spaceport, but the building didn't even have a fire escape ladder.

Vera walked to the edge of the roof, glanced down, and took several steps back.

"Wait, you're planning to jump across?" He stepped into her path. The next building had to be at least three meters away.

She exhaled sharply. "Drunk kids do it for fun all the time."

Drunk kids did a lot of things. It didn't mean sober adults could. Yet, that seemed to be the only option.

"I'll go first." He bolted forward, lunged himself from the parapet, and landed on his feet on the other roof. He turned back and waved. He could probably catch her if she didn't make it.

She made it, landing on one knee. He offered her a hand. She slapped it away and winced as she stood. He ran for the trapdoor. Shut.

Vera limped across the roof, broke into a jog, and leaped to the next building. He followed. This was the last apartment block. The factory was right across the street, but too far to jump. Vera tugged on the handle of the trapdoor. It didn't open either.

"Stand back." Levi drew his blaster and fired at the hinges.

White beams battered against the rusted metal, further corroding it. When he yanked the handle, the door came off the hinges. He tossed it aside and they fled down more stairs.

They made it down to the street and ran for the spaceport. In front of the entrance Vera halted.

He nudged her forward. "Come on, there's nowhere on Blackjack to hide from a senhound."

"But Fred..."

"He'll be fine, it's *us* they're after." He pulled her through the sliding doors.

GALAXY GRIFTER

She looked around frantically and dug her heels into the floor. "I can't leave my brother."

"We don't have time for this!" He ran ahead, intending to escape from this rock with or without her.

A large, bald man stepped into his path. One of Blackbeard's thugs, the same one that had beat the crap out of Levi in Vera's apartment many months ago.

Levi swerved to the left, but the thug caught him and held him in a reverse bear hug, pushing the air from him.

Two others flanked Vera.

"Well, well, who have we here?" Arms crossed, Blackbeard marched into view. He stopped in front of Levi. "Going far?"

Levi writhed in the thug's embrace, trying to reach his blaster. "This is a *really* bad time, Blackbeard."

"I'm sure it is." Blackbeard leaned so close Levi could smell his rank breath.

Pew! The bald thug toppled to the floor, bringing Levi down with him. Blood oozed from his head wound.

"What the—" Blackbeard spun around, drawing his blaster. The remaining gangsters followed suit.

Four Jaemlens and one senhound raced toward them.

Blackbeard fired.

Levi scrambled from under the dead gangster, got hold of Vera's arm, and dragged her down the terminal. She no longer resisted. Shots whistled past and they fled to *Caerus*, dutifully waiting for them in the spaceport.

Once aboard, he locked the hatch and powered up, willing his beautiful ship to get to its top speed as soon as possible. "Yuri, I'm taking off!" he shouted into the ansible.

315

"Okay, okay." Yuri sounded flustered. "Who is shooting outside, you know?"

"No clue, but don't let them follow us."

Caerus started the countdown.

Ten, nine, eight.

"Sit down!" Levi yelled.

Vera strapped into the seat beside him.

Three, two, one . . .

The ship took off.

From the corner of his eye, Levi saw Vera turn a little green, jutting her jaw, teeth clenched. *Caerus* jumped into hyperspace, the force pulling them both to the back of their seats. In seconds, they were streaming through space. He smiled. They'd made it.

"We're on a shadow route now; they can't get us here."

With trembling hands, Vera undid her seat buckles, sprang up, and marched into the living area, pacing back and forth like a caged senhound.

He stood. "What's your problem? You should be glad you're alive and safe."

She stopped, fists clenched. "Glad? You just couldn't leave me alone, could you?"

"I saved your life down there."

"Saved it? You ruined it, you miserable fucker." She sucked air in through her teeth, as though no words could sum up her contempt.

He scoffed. "What was there to ruin? You realize I didn't *have* to drag my ass across the galaxy to warn you?"

"I wish you didn't. Every time you show up, someone tries

to kill me. If my brother is hurt, I—"

The ansible bleeped. Levi hit the icon, accepting the incoming call from Yuri.

"Levi, they left Blackjack shortly after you. I couldn't keep them on the ground for long."

"It's okay, I think we're clear," Levi said.

Vera walked up to the control panel. "Yuri, can you check if Fred is okay please?"

"Fred O'Mara, yes? Will check on him."

There was a sound of something smashing, then Blackbeard bellowed into the ansible. "Why the fuck were Jaemlen ninjas shooting at my men, Weasel?"

"Honestly, I wish I knew," Levi said.

"If you show your face here again—"

Levi turned the ansible off. He could guess the fate Blackbeard would promise him and didn't want to be the subject of further insults.

He stomped into the kitchen and poured himself a drink. Several minutes later, Yuri called back to confirm Vera's brother was alive, albeit angry. "Says someone destroyed his android."

Levi turned to Vera. "Happy? Now maybe some gratitude?"

Gloomy, she lowered onto the sofa and wrapped her arms around herself. "I saved your life twice on Seshat, and you—"

"Yeah, I left. I couldn't fathom you wanting to help me, when all you do is insult me, and it made me real fucking suspicious."

She huffed and looked away.

"Anyway, I've got a plan to help both of us."

"Enlighten me."

"The Mzaraks were taking an A'turi data card to the Jaemlens. The veins on the card look different; I'm assuming it's a different file. Maybe another blueprint for something even greater than the hyperdrive."

She shook her head. "This is what got us in trouble the first time."

"Yes, but this time I know their ansible channel and I can use the card as leverage."

"To blackmail them?"

"You catch on fast. But first I want to know what's on that file. I found somebody selling a cube, we—"

"Ah, so that's why you came for me." Her lips curved into a bitter smirk. "You needed me to decode another A'turi file."

"No. It's not like that."

She shook her head. "You're a piece of shit, Levi."

That was it. He'd had enough of her. Maybe he should've left her on Blackjack. He clenched his jaw and leaned over her. "You think your skills are so special? I could have asked any IT grad to do it. Like I said, I didn't *have* to drag my ass across the galaxy, so—"

"So why did you?" She held his angry gaze.

"I . . ." He faltered. Somehow that question caught him off guard. Failing to find the words, he stormed off into his bedroom and slammed the sliding door behind him.

He'd made a mistake coming for her, just like he did with Amrie.

Either way, it was too late to get rid of Vera. *Caerus* didn't

GALAXY GRIFTER

have a detachable unit. So, he faced the prospect of a very unpleasant journey.

He threw open his wardrobe and ran his fingers through the soft brown mink of a spare blanket. Even when he acted on impulse, it was usually rooted in practicality. Maybe he'd think straighter once he calmed down. For now, shutting off the torrent of insults would be a win. He took the blanket and a pillow from his bed and returned to the living area.

Vera sat on the couch, pouting, looking away from him.

He tossed the bedding beside her. "I don't need your help decoding. You can go back to Blackjack or wherever the hell you want, once we land. For now, you'll sleep here. You know where the bathroom is. There's food in the fridge and a virtual gym in the cargo hold."

She glanced at him, at the bedding, and blinked.

"I'm guessing you also want this back." He retrieved her virtual frame from behind the sofa and handed it over.

Her face softened as she studied the recurring image loop of her friends. "Where are we flying?" she asked quietly.

"Earth."

Chapter 37

Spyder

Moonlight glinted off the mica grains in the rough stone wall, but there wasn't time to admire the texture. A shadow swished past the disk of a moon, wings flapping audibly in the distance.

Panting, Vera ran along the castle's facade until she reached a window and started to climb. Once inside, she didn't bother lighting the torch. She had done this enough times to remember her way in the dark. Something squeaked underfoot and scurried away. *Fucking rats.* The throne room was enveloped in blue moonlight streaming through the large windows. Dust floated in the moonbeams. She struck a flint, creating a flurry of sparks, and set the kindling in the fireplace ablaze. It illuminated the room in warmer tones, reflecting off a sword fixed to the wall above the throne. She climbed up and pulled it down as a shrill cry pierced the silence. With the weapon heavy in her hand, she braced herself and dodged the toppling stones as the monster broke through the castle wall and lunged at her with full force. The creature resembled a Sehen, but five times the size and with thrice the heads. She ducked and lunged to the right. It missed her. The heads snarled, baring rows of carnivorous teeth. She maneuvered between them, swinging the sword. *Why did they make it so heavy?*

Wack! One of the heads rolled to the floor. The remaining two attacked with doubled zeal. *Slash!* She managed to get an eye. The creature squalled, reared, and crashed back down. Vera swerved from it, having to hold the sword with both hands now as her right arm tired. She made it into the beast's blind spot. *Hack!* Off came the second head. *One more to go.* She pivoted. A moment too late. The last head came crashing down on her, jaws wide open. Black enveloped her vision, and two big words hovered above her eyes:

YOU DIED.

"Fuck!" Vera yanked off the VR helmet. Sweat trickled down her face. The display showed a still of the now single-headed dragon that clenched its jaws around what used to be her character. Blood spewed in all directions.

Levi laughed behind her.

Startled, she spun around. "How long have you been standing there?"

He had barely spoken to her these past few days, spending most of the time in his cabin, coming out only to check the control panel and cook—something he did daily, despite the availability of ready-to-eats. The minimal contact was fine with her. She had nothing to say to him.

"Long enough to see you were playing in child mode." He grinned.

"And I suppose you've nailed the pro version?"

"Actually—"

"Unlike you, I haven't spent half my life playing VR games while planet-hopping aboard a fancy spaceship." She pulled off one of the controller gloves, her muscles tingling from the exertion created by gravitational manipulation.

"I didn't have a fancy ship for half my life and you're holding the sword all wrong. I can show you." He stepped toward the VR platform.

"No thanks." She pulled off the second glove, suddenly conscious of how sticky she felt. She'd prefer to get to the shower without him smelling her, even though the bathroom triggered traumatic flashbacks of having to bring him back from cryostasis.

A jolt passed through the ship, nearly knocking her off her feet. She glanced at Levi, his smug grin replaced with a concerned frown.

"That wasn't the VR, was it?" she asked.

"No." He turned and bolted up the stairs and out of the cargo hold.

She untangled herself from the gaming equipment and followed. The jolt could only mean two things: a mechanical fault or...they'd somehow fallen out of hyperspace and collided with a real object. In either case, *Caerus* should've notified them of the issue, and it was disconcerting that the typically ultra-reliable AI system was silent. Once she'd scrambled up the stairs, her second theory was confirmed. The viewport revealed they were hurtling through a narrow asteroid ring toward a green planet.

GALAXY GRIFTER

Another jolt knocked them both over.

"*Caerus*, what the hell?" Levi grabbed onto the controls. The ship didn't respond.

"Shut the computer down!" Vera screamed.

Levi strapped himself into the pilot seat and shut off the power. *Caerus* went dark and slowed, the inertia corrections lifting and spatial gravity taking over. Vera found herself floating in the dim cabin, lit only by emergency lights. Another jolt sent her up and forward. Levi caught her arm before she smashed into the viewport and helped her into the seat next to him.

She clicked the safety buckles. "Turn it back on."

Once the system powered up, she opened the console and typed frantically. "Something's overriding the input."

"There are two ships behind us." His eyes fixed on the lidar.

She popped open the control panel's lid and disconnected several cords. The ship went dark again. "There. You should be able to jump now, without the AI."

"Jump where? If we can't access the map—"

"Anywhere."

Levi steered *Caerus* into a U-turn, away from the green planet. The two ships came into view and fired at them. He swerved and accelerated. Vera shut her eyes. *Caerus* jumped into hyperspace.

"What now?" He pressed himself into his seat.

For the second time since they'd met, she saw true fear in his eyes.

"We need to stop," she said. "I need to figure out what's hijacking the computer."

"We can't exit hyperspace without a fucking map. We could—"

"Die, I know. But we won't be any less dead if we keep flying blind."

He looked at her, eyes glinting in the glow of the control panel.

"Do it." She'd lived through enough to know the anticipation of death was probably worse than the real thing.

He exhaled and hit the hyperdrive.

They fell through the white discus. On the other side, interstellar space welcomed them with glinting stars and nothing more. This time they exhaled simultaneously. They had no idea where they were, but there appeared to be no immediate dangers.

"Kill the engines. We'll hang out here for a while," she said.

"Can you fix it?" he asked, rubbing the dashboard of the control center tenderly. Vera sighed—this ship was probably the only thing in the universe Levi had ever actually cared about. She felt slightly bad that it might be damaged beyond repair. But their lives were higher on her list of concerns.

"I...I'll try to diagnose. We'll go from there."

───────────── • ─────────────

Working in zero gravity, using a very basic toolkit she found aboard the ship, proved quite the professional challenge. She used bandages from the first aid kit to tape the disconnected parts of the control panel to the glass of the viewport to prevent them from floating off.

GALAXY GRIFTER

"There." Vera poked a tiny screwdriver between two sets of chips inside the motherboard.

"What?" Levi unbuckled himself for a better view.

"This isn't supposed to be here."

"Then how did it get there?"

"Don't know." She removed the chips, carefully wiped off the thermal paste, and taped them to the glass, revealing a metallic button the width of a thumb. Vera's eyes went wide—no wonder they'd gotten off course. Vera picked at it with the screwdriver, but it seemed fixed in place with hair-thin wires, like tentacles. After a lengthy struggle, she freed up the parasite and held it in the palm of her hand. One of its eight legs had broken off but the rest was intact.

Levi cringed. "What is that?"

"A spyder. A minibot that implanted itself into the motherboard." She'd kept up with the tech industry news enough to recognize the gadget, but never expected she'd be holding one.

"And controlled my ship?"

"Changed its coordinates, most likely, in accordance with preset instructions."

"How'd it get in?"

She shrugged. "On Blackjack, I'm guessing. Might've snuck through the hatch when we were running from the Jaemlens."

"Get rid of it."

"No." She clutched it to her chest. This was the rarest and probably most expensive piece of technology she'd ever held. Plus, it was kind of cute, all small and shiny. "It's disabled and I'd like to keep it."

He grimaced. "Will the navigation work now that this thing is out?"

"We'll find out soon enough." She untaped the microchips from the glass. "If not, do you think anyone would pick up a distress signal out here?"

"I don't even know where 'here' is. This thing could've been messing with our route for days."

"No pressure then." She sighed and proceeded to reassemble the control panel.

Vera turned on the faucet and let streams of warm water run over her face. It felt good to finally wash off the sweat. Her head buzzed from the liquor she'd downed after *Caerus* confirmed its systems were operational, but her nervous system was grateful for the fuzziness. She stepped out, threw her washed garments into the dryer, and slipped into a T-shirt she had been forced to borrow from Levi. Had she planned to flee Blackjack under gunfire, she might have packed a change of clothes.

When she returned to the living area, Levi was sitting on the kitchen stool.

He moved a refilled glass toward her and raised his own. "Here's to the rest of this journey being...less eventful."

"Less eventful would be nice." The drink rolled down her throat like a small flame. The whole ordeal felt more like a dream with each sip, but it still wasn't enough to put her completely at ease.

GALAXY GRIFTER

She put the glass down. "Do you ever feel like you're merely delaying the inevitable?"

"If by 'inevitable' you mean death, yes. But that's the whole point."

"Do you ever get tired?"

"Of living?"

"Of running, hiding, and... everyone else."

He looked like he was considering. "Sometimes, I suppose. But the alternative would be worse. At least it's not boring, right?"

"I much prefer boring."

He snickered. "No you don't. You're a natural. You didn't even panic when we lost control of the ship. I panicked. Why didn't you?"

"I did, on the inside. But... a part of me felt it wasn't real. These kinds of things don't *happen* in real life. In VR sims, sure, along with mermaids and dragons. But not in reality."

"So you offhandedly disassociated to stay calm, found the spy bot, and fixed the ship? And you say you prefer boring?"

"Absolutely."

"What a waste of potential."

Her gaze met his and she felt an inexplicable urge to run her finger over the thin scar above his brow. But she hadn't drunk nearly enough for that and looked away. "There's no potential."

"The things you could do with a little imagination..." He emptied his glass and walked out of the living area.

When he hadn't returned fifteen minutes later, she realized he'd ditched her again, even if they still were aboard the same ship.

Chapter 38
Terra Mater

Caerus dove out of hyperspace next to a beautiful blue marble, veiled in a lacework of clouds.

Earth. *The* Earth.

Vera had seen it in countless holo-films, but physically being this close felt like entering a mythical realm. Her gaze locked on the swirling mass of blue and white that filled the viewport as she tried to make out the continents. Continents! These stretches of land reminded her of cereal slabs soaked in blue milk. She had never seen this much water!

A familiar queasiness broke her enchantment as *Caerus* prepared for landing.

"Will they even let us out of the spaceport?" she asked. Levi had asked her to fill out virtual arrival forms, but last she'd heard, visitors required an invitation or a permit, and permits weren't just given to anybody. A nobody like her didn't belong on Earth.

"They will." There wasn't a hint of doubt in his voice.

GALAXY GRIFTER

"You've been here before?"

"Yes."

They hadn't spoken much since the spyder incident. Like in the days before it, he had been markedly brief and courteous, as though merely tolerating her presence on *Caerus*. It should've been the other way around. She should've been the one tolerating him, but she'd grown tired of the game.

She tasted bile in her mouth as the ship descended through a milky-white layer of clouds and asked no further questions.

The clouds broke to reveal a colorful patchwork of the land below and, eventually, the landing field, similar to the ones on Rebecca and Seshat.

Levi unbuckled his safety belts. "*Caerus*, schedule departure for tomorrow night."

"Departure slots are available at six thirty and eight PM. Newruk time," the ship said.

"Book it for eight." He turned off the engine and faced Vera. "Will you go into the city before heading wherever it is you plan to go?"

She remembered he'd said he didn't need her help decoding and that she could go wherever she pleased. She hadn't planned where, but this was Earth. She couldn't believe she was here. "I'll see the city, if they'll let me."

"They'll let you."

He told her to follow him into the cargo hold, where they climbed into a small black flier. Levi piloted it through the hatch and past a leaf-shaped terminal building. She had seen it before, in videos about Earth. The stem and veins held vertical gardens, green, yellow, and brown. The rest of the building was glass.

A. Zaykova

Their flier queued behind a row of others. Humans in blue uniform appeared to be checking each one before letting it out the gate.

Vera tensed. "What are they looking for?"

"They're just welcoming officers. They think people want to be welcomed by a Human, and not a machine."

"Like live tellers at fancy supermarkets in Xinlouyang?"

"Exactly. Your virt." Levi held out his hand.

Vera glanced at the nearest welcoming officer and passed her virtEgo to Levi. The androgynous Human waved at the flier in front of them and approached their window.

They smiled. "Hello, and welcome. What brings you to Newruk today?"

Levi handed over their virts without answering.

The officer scanned and returned them both. "Have a great evening."

Vera looked down. Her virt displayed a visitor permit, valid for thirty days. "Have you lived on Earth?" She was sure these could only be given out via invitation by a citizen, an Earther.

"Maybe." Levi steered the flier through the security gate.

If he was an actual citizen, that would explain how he got her a permit, unless...

"Are you traveling on a fake ID?"

"Does it matter?"

She shrugged and looked out the window. At least Levi's dastardly ways were being used for something wonderful for once.

Newruk City was lush with vegetation—tall trees, real ones, in all sorts of varieties arranged in large parks. The air streaming through the open window tasted sweet; the oxygen

GALAXY GRIFTER

content was 100 percent organic. She noticed she had a light-headedness as she studied the tree crowns, tinged with warm colors, bright yellows, gleaming oranges, fiery reds.

"It's autumn," she guessed. She'd never seen an autumn before, but she'd read about it in some books about ancient Earth. Xinlouyang only experienced mild seasonal shifts in temperature. But it had no trees to change color.

The flyway wound past low, spaced-out buildings. They grew taller as they approached the city center. Still, they wouldn't compare with Xinlouyang's skyscrapers. A tiny population with plenty of space left no need for high-density architecture.

Levi landed on a green lawn near a stream of fast-running water. Upstream, a cascading waterfall rumbled off a cliff. Above it stood a sand-colored palace, with a colonnade and domed rooftops.

"The UCH headquarters." Levi pointed. "You wanna get out?"

The Universal Council for Humanity—their species' most iconic building.

She'd seen it in history lessons, textbooks, videos, and holograms. Under different circumstances she might have been enthused, but now...she felt lost.

Where would she go once he left her alone?

She opened the flier door, climbed out, and started walking downstream, away from the palace. She tasted salt in a gust of wind, which blew colorful leaves across the grass. She picked one up and ran her fingers over its yellow, waxy surface and jagged, toothy rims tinged with red.

Ahead, the descending sun painted the sky into similar

shades. The stream disappeared below a bridge that was crossed by walkers and runners. Mostly Human it seemed, but there were a few different species. She continued forward, realizing an endless body of water lay beyond. *The Atlantic Ocean*, she remembered. It was huge, sparkling in the sunlight.

She touched the railing of the bridge and filled her lungs with the wet and salty breeze. The blue-green mass of water heaved up and down like a breathing organism, and she adjusted her breaths to fall in time with it. It felt comforting, despite the cold air creeping through the thin fabric of her jacket. Most Humans never got to see an ocean.

She wondered what Earth was like before Terra Mater, the biggest conservation project in the history of Humankind, which retroformed Earth to its original state. Humans had been evacuated to Mars, and later dispersed through the galaxy. A few were allowed to return decades later, but most of the planet's surface became conservation land—a living museum of Humanity's cradle.

She thought about the videos she had watched of waste floating in the bay, and sunsets blocked out by toxic fumes. Had it ever been like Blackjack? She dismissed the thought. How could it be, with such vast, open spaces?

Levi stepped onto the bridge beside her.

"I thought you'd be gone by now." She tried to sound indifferent, to conceal her surprise.

He leaned on the railing. "Didn't realize you wanted me gone."

"When did it matter what I want?" She kept her gaze on the darkening water.

GALAXY GRIFTER

"You hungry?" he asked.

A hollowness inside her stomach suggested she was. And cold. She crossed her arms to try to warm her hands.

"Come." He touched her elbow and started toward the flier.

The voice of reason told her not to follow him, but where else could she go? She didn't even know how to get back to the spaceport. Taking one last look at the ocean, loud and ominous in the twilight, she followed.

They flew above the lights of Newruk, the most livable Human city, a status symbol, worthy of showing off to alien ambassadors.

"You won't tell me whether you're really an Earther?" she asked.

"Did you know the Shadow League was formed on the premise that the government shouldn't get to decide who lives on Earth and who doesn't?"

"Yeah...I guess."

"Do you agree with it?"

The lights and buildings grew sparse as they appeared to head away from the city center. "It's not up to me. Why? Do you agree?"

"I don't believe in government more broadly."

"Go figure you're an anarchist."

"An individualist. I don't care how others are governed, as long as I'm not." He landed the flier outside a quaint two-story building.

She searched her memory of what she'd read about Newruk, and the word *cottage* came to mind like a nod to a

333

distant past. It stood in a street with other similar cottages surrounded by more vegetation and lit by streetlamps. Elsewhere in the galaxy, the rich lived in glistening penthouses, while others, like James and his family, were content to squeeze into cramped apartments. But on Earth, wealth wasn't defined by Human-made luxury. The elite few had the entire planet to themselves, creating a perfect, classless society. It made sense that their urban design prioritized concepts like sustainability and community over indulgence.

Maybe the Shadow League had a point. She looked around. "Where are we?"

"Come on." He climbed out of the flier, altogether too familiar with the routine.

A hollowness gnawed the pit of her stomach. Something was wrong with this picture.

"What are you worried about?" He chuckled. "It's Earth, nothing interesting, and therefore dangerous, ever happens here."

That did nothing to reassure her. "It feels like you're visiting someone familiar. Who?" She stayed a step behind him as he walked to the door of the cottage.

"Family." He rang the doorbell.

An older woman in a floral tunic and fluffy slippers opened the door. Her hair, naturally grey and impeccably styled, framed her round face, which elongated in surprise as she flung herself forward, wrapping her arms around Levi's neck.

He returned her embrace. "Hi, Mum."

Vera's jaw dropped.

"Iris, who is it?" A man appeared in the doorway—tall and

GALAXY GRIFTER

slender, like a spitting image of Levi, though his thick, wavy hair was grey, and age had softened his sharp features. The man's expression warmed as his gaze fell on Levi.

Levi responded with a reserved nod and untangled himself from his mother. "Vera—Mum, Dad." He pointed to each of them.

Vera closed her mouth and offered a stifled smile in greeting. She wanted to say something, anything, but all words were lost.

"Lovely to meet you." Iris beamed. "Come inside, it's cold out."

———————————— • ————————————

Levi's parents' living room—Vera blinked a few times to ensure she was in his parents' living room and not in some bizarre dream—was nothing like *Caerus*'s extravagant interior. With floral curtains and beige carpet and furniture, it looked cozy and elegant at once and seemed to complement Iris's perfect hair and fluffy slippers.

"Are you hungry? We haven't had dinner yet." Iris let go of Levi's arm and turned to her husband. "John, come help me set dinner up. You kids can help yourself to fruit in the meantime." She pointed to a large bowl on the dining table and looked at Levi again, as though unable to walk away from him. She cupped his cheek and frowned. "Is that a scar?" She traced her fingers over his brow.

Levi removed his mother's hand from his face. "Just a scratch. I fell from the virtual gym platform."

She sighed and headed into the kitchen, beckoning for her husband to follow.

Once they both had left the room, Vera stared at Levi, who was digging in the fruit bowl. "What the fuck?" she mouthed.

He winked and tossed something round to her.

She caught it. Translucent fuzz covered the fruit's pinkish skin. She gave it a smell—fresh, citrusy, and bright, nothing like the cheaper Huxoran fruit she'd grown up with. She tried to remember the fruit's name and, failing to do so, headed to the sofa. A photo hung above it, depicting younger versions of Levi's parents and a boy of no more than ten with green eyes and a wide grin. He looked...so normal.

How did he grow into—

"How's work going, son?" John returned to the living room and loafed in the doorway.

"Same old." Levi plopped into an armchair.

Vera lowered onto the edge of the sofa still holding the fuzzy fruit.

John sat next to her. "How do you know—"

"Work," Levi said. "She's in the IT department."

<hr />

The dry red wine did little to alleviate the awkwardness at the dinner table. Levi hadn't bothered with explanations, leaving Vera to play the part of the girl "from the IT department."

An IT department of what? She cringed, taking another gulp. What did his parents think he did for a living?

Iris barely took her eyes off Levi and did most of the talking.

GALAXY GRIFTER

"The Stroeves decided to move back to Jerichon. Their house is for sale at the moment." She glanced at Vera. "More salad?"

"Sure." Vera decided keeping her mouth full was the best excuse to stay quiet.

Iris passed her the salad bowl. "Where are you from, Vera?"

She swallowed. "Xinlouyang city, Seshat."

"You have family there?"

"My brother and his wife and daughter. My parents are dead." She tried to preempt further questioning.

"Oh." Iris brought her hand over her mouth. "I'm so sorry."

"It's fine, it's been a while." Vera scooped up the salad, hoping the conversation would return to the Stroeves, whoever they were.

"An accident?" John asked.

Iris gave him a stern look.

"No, Mum got cancer when I was fourteen. Died a year later. And Dad..." Vera glanced at Levi, but he seemed preoccupied with his dinner plate. "Dad had a heart attack a few years back."

"That's terrible," Iris said. "You poor dear. So young too."

"It's fine really." Vera shoved a fork-full of salad into her mouth.

"Unbelievable that in this day and age illness still claims the lives of so many people," John said.

"Yeah..." Vera felt like a party pooper. It was Levi's fault, certainly, but his parents seemed friendly and no less perplexed by this visit than she was. "Dinner's delicious," she said.

"Thank you." Iris beamed like Sandabur's suns.

"Can see where Levi's culinary inclinations stem from."

Iris's eyes widened. "He cooks?"

"Uh…" Vera felt her cheeks warm again. She should've kept chewing.

Levi looked like he was suppressing a chuckle.

Iris crossed her arms. "You've never cooked for us. But why am I surprised? We hardly see you these days, and I barely know anything about you."

He treated her to his disarming smile. "What do you want to know, Mum?"

"Everything!" she exclaimed. "How long you're staying with us would be a good start."

"We've got a job in Fowlerton tomorrow, and then heading to Mars in the evening."

Iris's face dropped. "Tomorrow? I haven't seen you in over a year, and you're leaving tomorrow?"

"I'm sorry, but you know how work is. I promise, I'll take a proper holiday as soon as I'm able."

She shook her head. "You keep saying that, but we never see you."

John broke his thoughtful silence. "Do you have to travel as much for work, Vera?"

"She doesn't," Levi cut in. "You're seeing me now, Mum."

Iris exhaled. "I am, that's true. I'll take what I can, I suppose." She smiled again, still warm but visibly tired, and started to stack the empty dishes.

"I'll help." Levi stood and picked the stack up. "And, Mum, can you make up the guest bedroom for Vera?"

Chapter 39
Whiteware

The guest bedroom had a violet throw on a double bed and matching gauzy curtains. It looked both so garish and so cozy at the same time.

"The bathroom is across the hall," Iris said. "I've put the towels here for you."

"Thanks." Vera lowered onto the edge of the bed, next to the white towels.

"I'll be upstairs. Call me if there's anything at all you need." Iris held Vera's gaze as though insisting she meant it.

"Thank you."

"Good night." Iris rubbed Vera's shoulder and left the bedroom.

As soon as she was gone, Vera fell back on the bed, her head spinning with incomprehensible thoughts.

Levi, the swindling scumbag Levi, who owed money to the Pooch, who had mercilessly ditched her in space, who had almost gotten her killed multiple times, was born and raised on *Earth*. That made no sense. He had a living family here who was kind and generous, and who seemed beyond thrilled to see him. Which made even less sense. But there was something else that was making her almost queasy—the fact she begrudged him these things. Things she didn't and couldn't have.

She threw her boots off and tried to make herself comfortable but couldn't quite find the right angle to help her drift off. The fabric felt soft and cool, with a faint lavender smell, total luxury that she was not used to at all. She checked her virt but couldn't focus. There were a few messages from Fred, stating he'd had enough of her secrets and wouldn't speak to her ever again. She thought about responding, but had neither the energy nor anything to say in her defense. All that mattered was that he was alive and, as far as she could tell, safe.

She tapped through her nebula archives aimlessly until she came across an old video. She perked up slightly. In the video, she sat on Dad's lap, sucking her knuckles, snug against his big chest. How old was she here? Four? Five?

Next to Dad, her brothers grappled over a small toy, but sat to attention when Mum brought out the birthday cake, a green-and-blue monstrosity that was meant to reference some cartoon character.

They all sang happy birthday to James, but Fred blew out the candles before James had the chance to. James cuffed Fred on the head.

Dad stuck his arm between them. "Can't you two behave for two minutes?"

"He started it," James nagged.

GALAXY GRIFTER

"I'll finish it." Mum handed James a knife. "That's to cut the cake, not your brother."

Both boys found her statement highly amusing and started cackling so much that the first cut of cake became wildly uneven.

"Okay, that's that." Mum reached for the camera, smiling. The video ended.

It's been... ten years since Mum died. Vera realized she'd missed the anniversary; she used to note it religiously, taking time to talk to Fred about the good times, making sure they didn't forget even the tiniest details of her life. Now, she could barely remember Mum's voice except for the replicas in the videos.

She blinked back the tears and found herself falling into a darkness she wasn't ready for. Too much had happened lately. Perhaps more than she could handle. She stood and walked out the door.

In the bathroom, she ran cold water over her hands and wet her face. That felt better. She looked in the mirror: tired but resolved to keep her shit together.

That resolve wavered the minute she returned into the hall, still not ready to face the darkness that awaited in the quiet of the guest bedroom.

Fuck. Maybe she needed to leave? Find a hotel and book a flight out of here first thing in the morning. *But a flight to where exactly?* Where could she even find a place to call home now?

She spotted a strip of light underneath the door Iris had said was Levi's. Sighing, Vera knocked.

"Come in."

She pushed the door open.

His dimly lit room wasn't too dissimilar from the one she'd grown up in after her brothers had been forcibly removed from it to sleep in the living room. It had a practical and minimalist design with a desk by the window and a bed by the wall. Though Levi's room appeared bigger, and somehow sturdier. The bed looked solid and the desk might have been real wood, rather than the pressed metal she had on Blackjack.

Levi lounged on the bed, wearing a plain T-shirt and shorts. "What's up?"

"I..." *Felt sad and lonely?* She tried to think of something less stupid to say. Her gaze fell on a rectangular object in his hands, which she initially mistook for a virtEgo. "What is that?"

"A book." He held the object out to her.

"A paper one?" She stepped closer and picked the book up.

Heavy, compared to a virt, it had a grainy brown cover that said *Ovid, Metamorphoses* in block letters. She needed both hands to hold it open and turn the flimsy pages. The lines of text didn't follow her eye movements.

"It's not very comfortable, is it?" She brought the book near her face. It smelled... She wasn't sure what it smelled of, but it wasn't unpleasant.

"There's more upstairs," he said. "I can show you tomorrow."

"Thanks." She handed the book back.

"Did you want something?"

"No." She failed to find an excuse for a conversation. "Just don't feel like sleeping."

GALAXY GRIFTER

"It gets like that when your brain doesn't know what sun you're circling."

"Yeah." She turned to leave but glanced back from the door. "Your parents are nice."

He sat up. "Does that surprise you?"

"It does. I must've imagined you had a hard childhood."

"Not at all. It was quite a happy one."

"So you have no excuse?"

"None. Not everyone's a victim of their circumstances."

"Huh." Was that meant to be some kind of a dig at her? She faced the door again.

"They think I'm a consultant for a whiteware company."

A snicker escaped her. "Why?"

He motioned for her to shut the door.

She did and he scooted ninety degrees to press his back to the wall and make space for her. "Got involved in a tech grift eight years back," he said.

She sat on the opposite end of the bed, like a kid preparing for story time. She motioned for him to continue.

"The manufacturer thought they were getting a good courier deal, and we—I was working with a guy named Venji—thought we scored a cargo full of wearable gadgets. Only instead of gadgets, we landed half a dozen washing machines and as many fridges. Venji offloaded them and took off with the ship and the front payment. Without me." He ran his thumb over his book's pages and they rustled like a tiny flier engine. "I'd nowhere to go, so I used my last coins to get them shipped here. Who'd look for stolen fridges on Earth, at a professor's and an engineer's house?"

"What did you do with all that stuff in the end?"

"Told my folks I'd gotten a job with the company and sold them, to Mum's friends mostly. Venji was an idiot; fridges are a lucrative gig. The only problem is that Mum expects me to keep supplying everyone she knows with whiteware, believing they're entitled to a friends and family discount. I think she thinks she's helping me. And you saw how pushy she can be."

"So, what do you tell her?"

"I...used to buy them at retail price and resell them to her friends at a loss. Now I've got a regular customer discount, so I break even."

She pressed her hand to her mouth, not wanting to wake anyone with her laugh. However much she hated him, she was grateful for this distraction. When she finished, she wiped the tears from her eyes. "Why won't you just tell them you've changed jobs?"

"Then I'd need a new legend. And who knows what favors that might involve?"

She cracked up again. "You could tell them the truth. They're your parents."

"That I'm a thief? I'll pass, thanks." He kept his wry smile, but she noticed his jaw stiffen. He was ashamed of admitting it, which she understood because it didn't make *any* sense. Growing up on Earth, he would've known no need—he had fresh food, good education, loving family. Why throw that all away?

"Why are you a thief, Levi?"

He scoffed. "Why is the sky blue?"

GALAXY GRIFTER

"Something to do with light particle oscillation."

He grinned at her joke and for a second she wished that they'd met in another life, where she wasn't so jaded and he wasn't such an asshole.

She yawned and stretched as tiredness finally caught up with her. "I'm surprised you never said you're from here. Unlike you to miss a bragging opportunity."

"Being born somewhere is hardly an achievement."

"True, although unexpected, coming from you."

"Nor something to be embarrassed of."

"Huh?" Was that another dig at her?

"You said you were from Seshat at dinner."

"Ah." She remembered. "So, like a true Earthen snob, you've assumed I'm embarrassed of being from Blackjack?"

"Is there another reason?"

"Do your parents know of Blackjack?"

"Dunno."

"I bet I've saved myself at least fifteen minutes of explanations."

"Fair." He leaned forward and tossed the book he'd been holding. It landed on his desk with a thump. "How'd your folks end up on Blackjack anyway?"

"Don't know."

"You never asked?"

"People go to Blackjack to escape their history, not talk about it."

"And you have no guesses?"

"No." She sighed and scooted farther onto the bed. The wall felt cool against her back. "Mom was strict. Had us make

345

our beds, exercise, and learn stuff beyond the school curriculum. Dad used to call her 'Captain' as a joke, but...not really a joke. He'd sneak us candy and let us stay up late when she was working." She smiled at the memory. "Mum's motto was 'Be grateful for what you have, work hard to build on it, and mind your own business.' That implied asking less questions."

"Seems dictatorial."

She shook her head. "She was trying to protect us. You know how dangerous information can be."

"Isn't knowledge meant to be power?"

"On Earth, maybe. When you learn the wrong thing on Blackjack, someone makes sure it's the last thing you learn." She twisted her sleeve in thought. "I think Mum always planned for us to leave. Did you know many of those born on Blackjack don't even have IDs, like they don't exist? Our IDs were immaculate. Yet she'd never go off-world herself. Not even to see a doctor..." Vera swallowed. She hadn't realized it'd be so hard talking about something that happened so long ago.

"Why?"

"I didn't ask. Maybe I didn't want to know. I was a teen, scared of losing my mother. And maybe even more scared of finding out she might have done something that made it impossible for her to leave, even if her life depended on it. Dad never really..." She took a deep breath as her voice cracked, her eyes clouding with tears. "He never really got over her death."

"He got sick?"

"He drank. Never in front of us, but it was obvious. Without Mum there weren't rules to break. Guess we all rebelled

GALAXY GRIFTER

in our own way. I, for one, stopped exercising." She snickered, blinking away tears. "I guess I'd hoped he'd get better eventually. Seemed like an awful existence. And then, one day, he didn't come home."

"What happened?"

"Fred found him at Stellar with a blaster hole in his head. I suppose that's one way out."

"You think it was suicide?"

"Doesn't matter what I think. The local medic recorded it as such. Who could prove otherwise? We had more pressing problems. Dad had accumulated a massive debt on the books. We'd lose everything, our home, Stellar... The Pooch bought us out with a huge interest rate, and... and now I'm here." She sniffled and wiped her nose on her sleeve.

Not even her best friends had heard this sob story. It was strange to be pouring it out to the Weasel, of all people, but at least he wouldn't feel sorry for her. He wouldn't give a rat's ass, and that was good. Who cared what he thought anyway?

He scratched his neck, where the implant had been. "Is that why you took the Breznis' database?"

"Yes." And before that, she intended to steal his blueprint. Maybe she wasn't much better than him. She fanned herself with her hands, like it would make the hot tears roll back. "Turns out talking about my parents makes me ugly. I still can't believe I've met yours."

"Why?"

"You've never even mentioned them. Not once."

He looked out the window. With the blinds rolled up, it revealed shadows of trees against the moonlit, cloudy sky. "It's hard enough watching my own back. I'd rather no one knew about them," he said.

"Huh." Apparently, Levi Adder cared about someone other than himself. This night had been full of revelations. "Why'd you bring me here?"

His lips curled into a grin once more. "I know you're trouble, but I doubt you're a threat to a couple of pensioners. And maybe"—he held her gaze—"you're the closest thing I've got to a friend. Besides *Caerus*."

"Wow..." she whispered, running her fingers through her ponytail. "That's kind of pathetic. I don't feel the same. I have real friends and you make a lousy one."

"Well, you haven't made it easy either. You haven't said one nice thing to me since the day I met you."

"Why should I say nice things to you?"

"Exactly. You're mean and cold. Smart. Competent. But so judgmental."

She scoffed and he kept smiling until her cheeks burned. She narrowed her eyes. "You're diverting. You want something from me, don't you?"

He shook his head, as though clueless.

She extended her arm and gave him a shove. "You're a terrible person. What do you want from me?"

He took a moment to answer. "You'll say no. But you'll do it anyway."

"Do what?" She hated the sound of it.

"If my plan fails and the Jaemlens get me... you'll tell my parents I'm dead."

"What?"

GALAXY GRIFTER

"It will be cruel if they have no way of knowing."

"No."

"They'll believe you, now that they've met you."

"You're unbelievable." She scrambled to the edge of the bed. The hint of connection she'd imagined they'd shared popped like a soap bubble.

He caught her arm. "Is that such a terrible thing to ask?"

"You've no right." She pulled her arm free, but the darkness she'd been holding back engulfed her before she managed to stand. It passed through her in ugly sobs, and she covered her face with her hands.

She was so alone.

To her shock, Levi put his arm around her and pulled her toward him. "Shh, you'll wake everyone."

Wake everyone. Of course. He viewed her breakdown as an inconvenience.

"It's not fair. You don't deserve a family." That was a horrible thing to say, but she'd gone past caring. She tried to push him away, but he held tight, and she sobbed into his chest as though a faucet had blown off inside of her.

Gradually the outpour diminished, and her jagged breathing evened. It brought about a sense of relief. She opened her fist where she had been clutching his T-shirt. There was a wet patch next to it.

He loosened his hold on her.

She raised her head and her lips accidentally brushed against his neck. A warm pulse passed through her rib cage down into her abdomen. His muscles tensed. On instinct, her lips traveled farther up until they found his.

349

He pulled away. "We shouldn't."

"Just shut the fuck up." She straddled him.

His protest was short-lived and ceased once his hands found her flesh.

He felt and tasted comfortingly familiar. More familiar than he should've been after their stint on the *Comet*.

Had she thought of him since then? Of this? More often than she cared to admit.

Chapter 40
Road Trip

Her flames extinguished, Vera dozed on Levi's shoulder. Her porcelain-pale skin looked almost translucent in the moonlight, which streamed through his bedroom window.

She smelled of vetiver, sandalwood, and bergamot.

He'd noticed she'd been using his cologne for days, but only now realized he liked it on her. He liked her in his bed much more than he liked her hostility.

The spyder incident had reminded him why returning to Blackjack had not been a mistake, why it paid to keep her close. He'd brought her here as an appeal to her conscience, in case she thought of double-crossing him once more. But he hadn't intended to win her affection or...whatever *this* was. The last time he thought he'd seduced her had nearly cost him his life. What game was she playing now?

He gave her a nudge. "What's your deal, kid?"

She opened her sleepy eyes. "My deal?"

"What will you do once we get through this?"

"We probably won't." She rolled over, turning her back to him.

Optimistic... He rose on his elbow to glimpse her face. Had she resumed hating him? What for? "If you'd just given me the cube when I'd first asked for it, you could have avoided all this," he said.

"And still be stuck at Stellar with a debt I could never pay? No thanks."

That's right; she'd always had her own agenda.

"And on Seshat, why didn't you let the Mzaraks take me? What debt were you paying off then?"

She sat up, gaze drifting across the shadowy room. "You know...if you feel guilty for dragging me into this mess, you could apologize."

He grimaced. "Apologize? What for? Why would I feel guilty for your decisions?"

"Ugh." She scooted to the edge of the bed. "I think I prefer the guest room."

He wrapped his arm around her waist. "Stay."

The past few weeks had left him wired. For the first time in his life, he started having dreams he could only describe as nightmares—a hostage writhing in mortal agony as blood streamed from his slit throat onto the deck of a pirate ship's cargo hold. In some iterations of this dream, it was Levi and not Wendigo wielding the laser knife. In others, the throat being slit was his own. Sharing the bed with a warm Human with the right appendages provided a welcome distraction.

She pulled away from him. "I'm not your lapdog, Levi."

GALAXY GRIFTER

"Don't go. I'm sorry." He wasn't, but few people wanted the truth.

She remained still for a moment, averting her gaze, then sighed and lay back down beside him.

Because she believed him or because she didn't want to face her demons alone either? He pressed up against her, supposing it didn't matter.

———————●———————

Levi woke from the best sleep he'd had in weeks. The sun poured through his eyelids and Vera breathed rhythmically into his ear. He would've remained like that for a while if not for the rude realization that he had business to attend to.

He forced his eyes open and checked the time. Midday. "Shit."

She stirred and opened her eyes, almost golden in the yellow sunlight. "Morning to you too."

"We've overslept. I need to collect the cube. You can stay here if you want—"

"I'm coming with you. It's my problem as well and I need to know what's in that damn file."

"Then we leave now."

Now dragged on for more than an hour.

His mother insisted on feeding them breakfast and lunch at once and packed fruit and sandwiches for the trip. Just as well, since they wouldn't have a chance to eat until nightfall and the sandwiches did look amazing.

He took the food and his belongings to the flier. On his

353

way back, he overheard her through the kitchen window. "You've made up then?"

"Made what up?" Vera sounded confused.

"With Levi. I guessed you must've had a fight. I know he can be difficult, that boy. But he generally means well."

Clearly, Mum had noticed the disuse of the guest bedroom.

He sighed and stepped into the kitchen.

She stood with her back to the door and continued talking. "His father was like that when he was younger. Temperamental with the most fragile ego."

Vera met his gaze and bit her lip.

"He's right behind me, isn't he?" Iris turned and locked eyes with him. "It's only the truth, dear."

"Dad," Levi called into the living room. "Mum says you have a fragile ego."

"Shoosh!" She waved her arms. "You're leaving, and I still have to live with him."

Dad stuck his head through the door. "What's that?"

"We're leaving," Levi said.

His father crossed his arms. "If you must, then..."

"I'll be back in a few weeks, once this job's done."

"The fridges won't sell themselves," Vera blurted, and covered her mouth with her hand, failing to hide her amusement.

Levi gave her a glare and hugged his parents goodbye.

"Where to now?" Vera asked as soon as they'd shut the flier doors.

"A crop farm, eight hundred kilometers south of here." Levi started the engine.

She screwed up her face. "What's an A'turi cube doing on a crop farm?"

"Apparently the owner was a retired xenolinguistics professor. Kicked the bucket a few weeks back. The son's selling his stuff for extra coinage. Good timing, if you ask me."

Newruk's suburbs shrank to the size of miniature models and disappeared as he steered the flier up and away from the city he both loved and hated. The weather had improved from yesterday and the strait ahead glistened aquamarine.

He set up the autopilot and reclined in his seat. "Did I tell you I got lost at sea once? On Eria, in my uni days."

Vera detached herself from the window. "You went to university on Eria?"

"Yeah, the party planet. We hijacked a raft for someone's birthday—"

"What'd you study?"

"Interplanetary law."

She snickered. "How fitting."

"Never graduated."

"What happened?"

"With the raft?"

"With the university."

"I got kicked out after getting arrested, but I promise the raft story is better." His failed education was not where he'd planned to take this conversation. "None of us knew how to operate it and—"

"Wait." She raised her hand. "How did you get arrested? And why did you study on Eria if Earth's education is considered—"

"The best in the galaxy? Because I would've killed myself if I had to stay here any longer," he snapped, annoyed by her prodding. But they'd only just built a rapport, which he hoped to maintain.

"Why? You said you had a happy childhood."

"I did." He saw no reason for it to have been unhappy. "I guess I grew bored of it. You saw my parents with their perfect house and perfect jobs."

"I did." She crossed her arms. "And I think you're spoiled as fuck."

He shrugged. "Maybe I am, but when I'd imagined that kind of future, I wanted to jump off the Council Cliff. I couldn't live like that."

She didn't say anything, so he continued. "I got in all kinds of trouble as a kid. No test uncheated, no lie untold. I framed other children, watched them step in my traps, and shook them down for favors. But the adults kept giving me second chances."

He omitted that he'd had no friends, and that one kid had tried to kill themselves because of something Levi had said. He couldn't have imagined anything more pathetic. Yet the adults had expected remorse, so he had pretended to be remorseful. He'd yearned to get away from them all.

He squeezed the control wheel to dissipate the memories. "My folks weren't too fond of me moving to the galactic capital of hedonistic pursuits, but I'd convinced them. The first year was great. But eventually they refused to fund my lifestyle. So, I had to find alternative sources of income."

"Drugs?" she guessed.

GALAXY GRIFTER

"Drugs aren't worth as much as the secrets people want to keep."

"Blackmail?"

He nodded, pretending to study the dashboard. "A lot of rich kids, minor celebrities, and politicians holidayed on Eria. I learned that you don't need to be a lawyer to make mega coins. But...I bit off more than I could chew. Someone dobbed me in. I was young and stupid and I got caught." He sighed.

"And?"

He watched small clouds rush by outside, like ghosts of his past. "I was a nobody back then, but I've witnessed a lot of sketchy shit. The cops cut me a deal, and I sold out whomever I could. Got away with probation. But gangsters hold grudges. That was the first time someone tried to kill me." He rubbed his neck, remembering the garrote, and how his escape had been a lucky accident. "The cops' promise to protect me amounted to nothing, so...I asked someone else to deal with it. That landed me in debt and later, on Blackjack.

"Guess I found something I was good at." He raised his arm and picked a speck of dust from the flier's ceiling, waiting for her to come up with a snarky remark. Something about him not being *that* good given their current predicament. But she only scooted closer and he felt the warmth of her leg against his.

"Do you regret it?" she asked.

"Getting caught? Hell yeah."

"Just that?"

"What's done is done, right?"

"Right."

He looked out the window at the azure ripples that glinted in the westward-rolling sun as her thigh burned against his like a branding iron. Something pinched in his chest and the words rolled out without him meaning them to. "I regret my parents attending the trial. The expressions on their faces when I admitted to the charges…that's why I act like I've cleaned up, I guess."

"I get that." How could she? She never had a perfect future to waste, but her tone lacked sarcasm.

"I think Dad still believes I fucked things up for good. Not living up to my potential, whatever that is." He moved an inch away from her, feeling he'd said too much.

"You haven't sold enough fridges for him?" At least he could trust her to not let it get sappy.

"You won't let that go, will you?"

"Never." She beamed, flaunting her dimple.

The tightness released into a kind of giddiness and he raised the yoke, so the flier darted toward the water until he leveled it to glide along the water's surface.

Vera stuck her arm through the opened window, catching the spray. Her lips parted in childlike awe. Maybe Earth wasn't as bad as he was used to thinking?

A jagged coastline came into view ahead. He switched to autopilot again, allowing the flier to rise to a safe latitude and into the grey clouds that rested atop the hilly shore. These cleared farther inland, revealing forests and grasslands with blotches of lakes and rivers. Urban centers and farmland occupied less than one percent of Earth's surface.

GALAXY GRIFTER

"Look, animals." Vera pointed.

Levi leaned toward the passenger window to see what she was seeing. Little white blobs scattered across the field below like aphids on a leaf. "They're just sheep."

She pressed her face to the glass. "Can we go down?"

"Seriously?" He remembered that neither Blackjack nor Seshat had real fauna. "We're behind schedule."

"Just for a minute." She craned her neck as the dots disappeared from view.

"Too late, we've passed them."

"Go back."

"I'm not going back to look for sheep."

"Why not?"

He exhaled. "Listen, Earth is basically a wildlife reserve. How about next time, I'll take you to see better animals. Like...elephants or something."

"There won't be a next time," she pouted.

"Fine." He made a sharp turn and steered the flier toward the ground as though intending to crash it.

She held on to her seat but didn't utter a sound. The sheep scurried out of the way with loud bleats as the flier came to a halt in the middle of the flock.

She jumped out. "Look, babies."

A fat mother suckled two nearly fully grown lambs.

Levi clenched his jaw and leaned on the flier's roof. "If you get sheep shit on your shoes, I won't let you back in."

Fortunately, sheep weren't the most interactive animals and she agreed to leave several minutes later. Unfortunately, she spotted a herd of deer next and demanded another landing.

A. Zaykova

These guys didn't mind being touched, and Vera fed them the lunch his mother had packed for the road. They'd lost about an hour for these diversions, but Vera returned to the flier happy as a little kid.

"You haven't seen live animals before?" he asked.

"Not like this. I had a black kitten when I was eight. Someone had snuck it onto Blackjack and Dad named him Chernobyl. He wasn't very smart though; the neighbor poisoned him."

He cringed. "Are all your stories this morbid?"

"Not my fault everyone I cared for kept dying. Think I turned out okay despite it."

He shook his head and started the flier. "You most certainly did not."

Chapter 41
The Farmer

At dusk, the flier landed near a lone house in a field. Levi messaged the vendor and winked at Vera. "If anyone asks, I studied xenolinguistics at Aeolis University on Mars." They climbed out.

A shrill sound startled her as a black-and-white dog ran toward them across the field, barking.

"Cody, shut it!" The man that followed the dog looked like he walked off a film set and not out of a farmhouse. He stood about as tall as Levi, but with more shoulder span. His cropped hair and beard glowed gold in the setting sun. "You made it. Long trip?"

"Got held up." Levi gave Vera the side eye.

"Igor." The man held out his hand, bicep bulging below his shirtsleeve.

Levi shook it. Vera quit staring and introduced herself.

"Are you a xenolinguist too?" Igor gave her a firm handshake.

"Uh...no, I'm a programmer. Same thing but with

computer lang—" Vera gasped and froze as the dog's wet nose pressed into her hand.

Igor smiled and pulled the dog back. "He likes you." He retrieved a metallic cube from his jean pocket and handed it to Levi in exchange for payment.

Vera dared to pet Cody. When he responded with a playful tail wag, she knelt down and scratched behind his ears. "He's a sheepdog, isn't he?" She'd seen these in movies.

"He is, not that there are any sheep here." Igor ruffled Cody's neck.

"We saw some on the way," she said.

"There are flocks up north. But this is a grain farm, or at least it's meant to be. Just me, Cody, and Annabelle, the old mare."

"A horse?" Vera had never seen horses either.

"Her first time away from Seshat," Levi said, and she realized she must've sounded peculiar.

Igor glanced at the darkening sky. "That's a long way. I can show you the horse if you want."

Her heart beat a little faster. She side-eyed Levi, who'd probably try to tell her not to go.

"Go ahead." He leaned on the flier's roof, as though objections were futile.

Igor led her into the stables, where Annabelle met them with sad, giant eyes, more alien than any extraterrestrial Vera had seen.

"She was my dad's." Igor patted Annabelle's face. "I think she really misses him."

"I'm sorry for your loss."

GALAXY GRIFTER

"Thanks. He'd been sick for a while, but nothing truly prepares you for when it actually happens."

"It doesn't. I lost my parents a few years back." Vera placed her hand on the white patch between the huge eyes. The creature snorted at her, unfazed by another Human in its presence.

"I'm sorry. That sucks big time. I still talk to him, you know? I can almost imagine him answering."

"Of course." Vera heard of people doing that to cope with grief. She never could. She didn't know what her parents would say and trying made her feel foolish.

"Hey, listen." Igor rolled on the balls of his feet. "You guys could stay here for the night. It's a long way to either city and there's plenty of space in the house."

"That's kind of you, but we wouldn't impose like that."

"Pah, you'd be doing me a favor. I'm not used to this solitude. Took leave from the military just over a year ago to look after Dad." He sighed. "It's been quite an adjustment."

"I can imagine, but we've got somewhere to be by morning."

"Dinner then. When did you last eat? There's not a place around."

She wondered if she could sell the idea to Levi. After all, she did feed their snacks to the deer, and she liked the feel of this place. And she was liking Igor more and more. "I'll see what I can do."

———————•———————

A couple of hours later they sat by a bonfire, stomachs full of grilled protein and beer. Vera pressed her back against

Levi's chest, his arms wrapped around her, listening to sounds she had never heard before: the crackling of the flames, the chirping of crickets, and what she guessed were birdcalls.

Igor cracked open another beer can. "Glad you guys stayed. It's been a while since I've had company."

"Why don't you just sell the plot?" Levi asked in the same tone he'd asked why Vera hadn't left Blackjack when they'd first met. He made things sound uncomplicated.

Igor took a swig. "Selling it isn't a problem. Getting it back, if I ever decide to, might be."

"Rent it out then."

"I might, eventually. Once I fix things up a bit."

"Again, the tenants can do it in lieu of a few months' rent."

Vera lightly elbowed Levi in the ribs. *Shut up. The guy has his reasons.* But Levi couldn't hear her thoughts and only adjusted his posture.

Igor chuckled. "It's not just the farm that needs fixing. Consider it therapy. An ugly divorce followed by Dad's illness took their toll. But I'll get there."

"I'm sure you will. This place is beautiful." Vera squeezed Levi's hand before he said something insensitive again.

"It is." Igor nodded. "Grounding. What about you, Vera? You said you're a programmer. Who do you work for?"

"I freelance," she lied.

"Nice. Working on anything right now? I led a team of programmers in the defense force."

"Oh?" Vera sat up, detaching herself from Levi. She hadn't expected that.

GALAXY GRIFTER

"Still do some consulting remotely. Robotic applications mostly."

"Like...spyders?" She felt her pocket but remembered she'd left the device in the flier.

"No, more like the rescue bots they used in the Ylkvist disaster. Why, you've programmed spyders before?"

"No. Just read about them."

"Same principles. It's not a set-and-forget job. There are nuances depending on the tasks and the planetary conditions they're needed for. Wanna try?" He took his virt off before she responded and expanded it to full size. "I've got a simulation app here somewhere."

Vera shifted toward him.

Levi caught her arm. "Right now?"

"You think I'll get another chance to program military robots?" This was nonnegotiable.

Igor handed her his virt. "I've picked an easy one."

A hologram of a cat-sized, four-legged creature appeared on the ground next to the dying flame. Cody raised his head and growled.

"Easy, boy." Igor patted the dog's neck and turned to Vera. "Can you make this guy walk a full circle round the bonfire?"

Levi cringed. "Come on, we've gotta get back to town."

"She'll do it in fifteen minutes." Igor gave Vera a nudge. "Right?"

"We'll see." Her fingers already ran across the virtual keyboard. She turned off the projection, reducing the robot to an on-screen diagram. She didn't want them watching her trials and errors.

Levi stood. "I'll be in the bathroom. Then we leave." He walked off.

"Through the kitchen, second door to the left." Igor called after him.

"I'll find it."

Vera focused on the simulator. Several minutes later, she brought back the hologram. The robot trotted around the fire on bouncy legs.

"Good." Igor nodded.

The robot completed the circle, stopped, leaped into the air, and landed on all fours on the other side of the smoldering embers. Vera exhaled. She passed the test and then some.

Igor's face elongated. "Very good." He took the virt from her and perused the code. "Where did you study?"

"I'm self-taught." She clasped her hands together.

He looked up from the screen. "Well, if you're looking for something more permanent, I can pass a word to some people. They're always on the lookout for talent."

She smiled, more validated than she'd felt in weeks.

"What's your contact?" he asked.

She glanced over her shoulder toward the house. Levi hadn't returned yet. Was this too risky? She extracted her contact card from her virt and passed it to Igor.

He must've noticed her hesitation. "Your boyfriend won't mind, will he?"

"He's not my boyfriend." The words left her mouth before she could catch them.

Igor shrugged. "Cool. He's not a xenolinguist either."

She froze. Was this a trap? They should've never stayed here.

GALAXY GRIFTER

Igor slid her card into his virt, minimized the screen, and slapped it onto his wrist. "I've spent my entire childhood around xenolinguistics, so I know what they look like."

She didn't move, eyes fixed on him, wondering whether to try to run for the flier or call out.

Igor swigged his beer. "I'm guessing he's dealing with some underground space-tech resells. Not that I care. It's none of my business while I'm in reserve. Just wanted to make sure you're aware he's not who he says he is."

She exhaled halfway. Was he really saying this out of concern for *her*?

"How long have you known him for?" Igor asked.

"A long time."

"Well, then, you should be fine. You look smart enough to take care of yourself. Right?"

"Right."

"And, Vera, I'm serious about there being opportunities for your skills. Just keep your record tidy."

"Thanks."

The house door creaked and Levi walked down the porch.

She jumped to her feet. "I'm ready to go if you are." She smiled, trying to seem calm.

Levi sauntered toward them. "Did you do it?"

"Oh, she did it, all right." Igor rose to his feet. "You missed the fun."

"Gutted." With a deadpan expression, Levi wrapped his arm around Vera's waist and looked down at her. "We're leaving then?"

"Yes."

They started toward the flier. It seemed like a cold farewell for such a warm reception. Vera looked back. Igor carried a rubbish bag, leading Cody toward the farmhouse.

"Hey, Igor." She waited until he looked at her. "I hope you fix the farm and...vice versa."

He smiled broadly and waved. "I will. Hope to see you back for more beer and robots."

Once inside the flier, Levi set the autopilot for Newruk. "Back for beer and robots? What was that about?"

She chuckled. "Human connection. You wouldn't get it."

"I wouldn't get it?" He gave her a dirty glance as the flier rose above the dark landscape.

"Please tell me you didn't steal anything."

He moved away from her. "You think I'm some kind of klepto?"

"You snooped around the house, didn't you?"

"What makes you think that?"

"You spent a quarter of an hour in the toilet? Are you suddenly pee shy?"

"Dinner was undercooked, so..." He shook his head and looked away from her.

"You didn't find anything?"

"Nothing interesting."

"Good."

"Still think Igor is a suspicious motherfucker." He reclined the back of his seat and lay back with his arms behind his head.

"Why?"

"I don't like blues. What kind of moron would want to work for an army?"

GALAXY GRIFTER

"I don't know. One that doesn't make a living off professional crime?"

He snorted at that and looked away.

"Come on, I thought he seemed like a good guy." She clung on to that impression. The galaxy couldn't be full of assholes only.

Levi scoffed. "Based on what? The fact that he looks like an action figure?"

She giggled, remembering Iris's comment about his fragile ego. "He *is* very handsome."

"If you're into beefcake, sure."

"He's got a masters in infotech."

"Rare catch, a nerdy beefcake. Too bad he likes guys or I could take you back to that farm." The muscles in his jaw twitched.

"Maybe I'd take you up on that if you and I didn't have bigger squid to fry," she said.

"I can fry them without you." He dropped his seat farther down and closed his eyes, steadying his breath, pretending to be asleep.

She watched him in the glow of the dashboard, then leaned over and kissed him on the corner of his mouth. Tomorrow he'd probably ditch her in outer space again, but tonight, he was all she had. He didn't move, but when she tried to settle back into her seat, he pulled her on top of him.

Chapter 42
Fried Squid

Levi parked his flier at the end of the line queuing for the security check at the spaceport gate. No longer trusting things going well, he felt an urgency to leave Earth. Hyperspace seemed safer. Monochrome in the predawn lights of the terminal, Vera sat on the passenger seat, looking into the distance, one leg tucked underneath her. He projected a map of the galaxy into the space between them and flicked it with his finger. It spun like a roulette wheel. "Want to pick a destination?" he asked. Their next move depended on what they'd find on the alien card, but they still needed to set a course for somewhere.

"Seshat," she said, without touching the map.

"Don't know what you see in that rock, but okay. At least it's far enough to give us time to decode the files." He'd have preferred Sandabur—he needed a holiday more than ever, not that he could afford it after spending all his funds on the Sehens.

GALAXY GRIFTER

By the time a pink dawn lapped at Newruk's horizon, *Caerus* hurtled through hyperspace, on a shadow route to Seshat. Vera unbuckled as soon as the onboard assistant allowed it, and set up the cube and her virt on the kitchen bench. Levi plonked the A'turi data card atop the metal box, hoping it actually contained new information. Admittedly, his plan to blackmail the Jaemlen spooks had many holes, but it was better than no plan.

She tapped the virtual keys projected onto the marble countertop. "There are two files on here. I'll start with the smaller one."

She seemed different since the night at his parents' house. For one, she no longer yelled insults at him—a welcome improvement. He liked to think he possessed certain talents, but to attribute the transformation to her getting laid seemed like a hyperbole. It looked more like transcendence. Not the nervous clutching at straws he had seen on Seshat nor the suicidal resignation he'd found in her on Blackjack, but a calm and collected acceptance. He didn't feel that way at all, and it awed and frightened him.

He stepped behind the high stool she was sitting on and burrowed his face into her copper strands, still smelling of last night's bonfire. It would be tempting to think they'd finally landed on the same page—temporary allies. But he couldn't dismiss the possibility of her playing her own game, like she had done with the blueprint. What could she do now? Sell him out to the spooks?

He walked around the corner of the bench and placed his hand on hers. A test to see what she'd do. She didn't jerk away but looked at him with puzzlement.

371

"I'm glad you're here." He held eye contact.

"I'm not," she said, and resumed work.

It infuriated him. Physically she'd been affectionate enough, but never with her words.

Like she was always angry for something he didn't do. He clenched his teeth and walked one circle round the kitchen island. *You must love playing the victim. You're the one who came into my bed.* He wanted to say something hurtful, but they had a long trip ahead and it'd be smarter to stay quiet, to enjoy her nonverbally, and find a way to get back at her later. If they lived. Yet he couldn't help himself. "You're not better than me."

She looked at him again, this time thoughtful. "Maybe you're right. Maybe we both had it coming."

That frustrated him in a whole new way. "To hell with your defeatism and what we had coming. With my luck and your brilliance—"

"My brilliance?"

"Just fucking own it. We'll be fine, that's that." He started toward the bedroom, deciding he needed time away from her.

"I won't argue as long as you don't ask me to trust a word you say."

He stopped and considered a fresh thought. What if she didn't hate him but intentionally held back? "Trust is for losers," he said. "Extraordinary lives are built on leaps of doubt." He turned around, cursing the contradictory feelings she aroused in him. "I want you."

Her lips betrayed a hint of a dimpled smile. "Right here?"

"All over this ship. But we can start here."

GALAXY GRIFTER

———————————— • ————————————

"Wake up." Vera's voice sounded urgent, and as soon as he opened his eyes, she shoved a virtual document into his face. Her hands were shaking. "Read this."

After hours spent aboard *Caerus*, the A'turian translation was beginning to take shape. The Supayuyan text contained many gaps, but the scraps of lines and paragraphs suggested this document wasn't a technical one. The opening page indicated it to be an agreement of sorts, a memorandum on an Operation Tetakoraa. It spoke of some dispute, of terraformation and of... missiles.

Vera's face was white. "This is bad. This is so bad."

He shrugged, still hoping the intel would give him some kind of leverage. "Let's wait to read the whole thing before drawing conclusions."

Hours later, the conclusions proved devastating.

Operation Tetakoraa was a Jaemlen plan to wage war within the galaxy.

Levi had been correct in assuming that the Jaemlens and the A'turi had collaborated on some new technology. Only it wasn't a new generation of engines, as he'd previously thought. The antimatter blueprints were used to design weapons of mass destruction, more powerful than all the nuclear bombs in the galaxy.

If used, they would spell the end of any species that encountered them. And it seemed like the plan was to use them against Humanity.

"We have to tell someone." Vera paced between the

cockpit and the kitchen, dressed in his T-shirt, rolling its hem between her fingers. Her transcendence evaporated quicker than counterfeit perfume.

He leaned on the kitchen bench, rereading the part of the document that detailed the launch of an antimatter missile into Seshat, and frowned. "Do you think this could be a hoax?"

She stopped in her tracks. "Like the blueprint and the spyder?"

He shrugged. His hope of negotiating with the spooks got sucked out the porthole. "Surely they'd have changed plans once their document went missing?"

"*We need to tell someone,*" she repeated louder, resuming her pacing.

"We'll send a tip to the cops and UCH as soon as we're planetside," he said. It wasn't possible to send files via ansible, and he didn't want to be implicated in a conflict of this scale by calling Starpol.

"How long until…" She opened and closed her mouth as though physically unable to finish the question.

He checked the time stamp in the document—$9.37565e+8$ seconds post treaty signing—and tapped the converter key. "Nine hours and twenty-two minutes."

"Fuck." She tugged on her shirt's collar like she was short for breath.

Fuck indeed. They would never make it in time, which left the ansible as the only option. That would involve a very unpleasant dialogue with the authorities and likely be followed with his incarceration in some lunar correction facility.

GALAXY GRIFTER

But the destruction of Seshat was bad news for Humanity and, therefore, his business.

He picked up the virtual document, approached the control panel, and hit the emergency icon. Vera followed him into the cockpit and pressed her back to the ship's hatch.

The ansible crackled. "Starpol, please state your emergency."

"I'd like to report a threat of a terrorist attack," Levi said.

"Please tell me your name and ID number," the operator said.

"Is that important? Someone wants to blow up an entire planet in the next nine hours!" Sure, they'd probably find some way to track him, but he wouldn't just hand them his identity on a platter.

"You can make the report anonymously," the operator said.

"Great. We discovered two documents on a device belonging to a member of the Jaemlen government," Levi said. "One of the documents appears to be an agreement between Jaemlen and A'turi officials to launch an antimatter missile into Seshat, third planet of the Ra system. They will demand the UCH to surrender Frigg and Sandabur to the Jaemlen and the A'turi governments respectively, because they believe Humanity doesn't need so many aquatic planets. The second document is in A'turian and we haven't had time to translate it. I believe it is a blueprint for the antimatter bomb they are planning to use. Oh, and it says they'll bomb Earth too if their demands aren't satisfied." Levi found that last fragment particularly concerning.

"Can you read out the first document word for word please?" the operator asked.

Levi read the text, including the time stamps and the missile

375

carrier's route coordinates. These corresponded with none of the main routes, which suggested the terrorists were using an alternate map. An A'turi shadow map, perhaps.

"Are you able to send me these documents or deliver them to your nearest police station?" the operator asked.

"We're in hyperspace."

"What is your nearest Union port?"

"Seshat, but we'll never make it in time."

"Can you reroute to another port? Alternatively give me your coordinates and I can dispatch the nearest patrol vessel."

Vera leaned over the ansible. "What are you going to do about the missile?"

"I'm forwarding this conversation to the appropriate team who will make a decision on further actions."

"Will the people of Seshat be evacuated?" she asked.

"Your report is being taken very seriously. I cannot say at this point what action will be taken."

"Can you call my brother James O'Mara? He's in Xinlouy-ang, I need to talk to him."

"I'm sorry, I cannot. Can you please state your coordinates?"

They exchanged glances again, and Levi shook his head. They were on a shadow route and he couldn't give out these details to the government.

Vera leaned over the ansible again. "Please, this is import-ant, I need to—"

Levi touched her hand and ended the transmission. She was being irrational. Nobody could evacuate an entire planet's population in nine hours based on an anonymous report, and nobody would allow her to spread panic.

GALAXY GRIFTER

"They're not going to do anything, are they?" she whispered.

He shrugged. "They can try to intercept the carrier based on the coordinates we've given."

"And if they don't?"

He didn't answer. An A'turi ship would likely be heavily shielded, and there were no guarantees it wouldn't jump to some backup route. If it exited hyperspace anywhere near a planet, even if Humans shot down the missile, the results would be catastrophic.

Tears poured from her eyes. "Why did they have to choose Seshat?"

"Because it's too dry for them and because it's one of our key manufacturing hubs."

"He has a two-year-old."

"Who?"

"My brother." The faucet turned on again, like it had at his parents' house, her body trembled from the sobs.

It annoyed him, even if he logically knew her reaction was not inappropriate. He tried to imagine Vera's niece and a billion others perishing in an attack that would make nuclear bombs seem like flea bites. He didn't know these people. Was he supposed to feel sad for them? He searched for that emotion and came up empty. Instead, he felt angry. Angry for Humanity's inevitable loss of status as a result of the attack. The limitations this would create for his freedom of movement.

This couldn't have come out of nowhere. The governments wore amicable facades, but the stew must've gone bad a while back. Was Frigg just the last straw? Had the luxury resorts along Sandabur's endless coastline been a longtime bone in the Jaemlens' throats? Had they decided to use it as a bargaining chip in the alliance with the A'turi?

"Why do the Jaemlens think we'd give up our planets to them? That Humanity won't fight back?"

She wiped her eyes with her hands, but the tears kept rolling. "Against antimatter bombs? That's more powerful than GU's entire nuclear potential. And they said if their demands aren't met, Earth would be next. The UCH won't risk this. Not their precious Earth."

"If the UCH indulge them, who knows what they'll demand next? They don't get to banish us to some arid corner of the galaxy!"

Yet a part of him knew she was right. This was the end of GU. An ugly divorce. Huxorans and Rors would be forced to choose sides. The galaxy hung on the verge of chaos.

Fuck that.

He opened the shadow map and studied it for a long time. Then he typed in the coordinates from the A'turi document and drew a line connecting their route with *Caerus*'s. "We may be able to reach them before Starpol."

She glanced up at him, a glimmer of hope in her red, puffy eyes.

"But even in the best-case scenario, it's suicide." He showed her the point where the two routes intersected. "It's just two light-years away from Seshat, but this is the earliest we can get ahead of them."

She tilted her head. "So we reach them and then what?"

He raked his fingers through his hair, trying to think of a better solution than the one that had originally occurred to him.

GALAXY GRIFTER

Her face softened with the realization. "You want to ram the A'turi spaceship?"

"Not if we don't have to. They'll pulverize us before we get close. We need to engage the hyperdrive while docked to the A'turi ship or inside it." That way *Caerus* would slice through the A'turi ship like a missile, hopefully detonating their engines and the bomb they were carrying.

"Why would they let us dock?"

"I have a hunch A'turi aren't immune to bullshit. Guess we'll conduct a little science experiment to test that hypothesis." He mustered a grin.

She looked at him with utmost incredulity.

He straightened his face, knowing this was his last chance to back out. "We don't have to do it. We never caused this and it's not up to—"

"We're doing it." She wiped the remaining tears off her face. "If there's the slightest chance we can stop this madness, I'll take it."

He exhaled, fighting the sinking sensation inside, and entered the new coordinates into the terminal. Survival was not an objective.

———————————— • ————————————

They spent the next few hours in glum silence. What was there to discuss? In the intended scenario they'd intercept the A'turi missile carrier and die trying to stop it. In the more likely scenario, they'd never find the A'turi ship, and would either be arrested at any of the Human ports, or return to

Blackjack to live as fugitives until sold out to the new Jaemlen and A'turi overlords.

On the bright side, there were no more tears. His plan seemed to reinstate Vera's resoluteness. She bustled in the kitchen and made them coffee. His tasted of the imminent doom. At least he'd die doing what no Human had done before.

"What if we don't go into the A'turi ship?" She leaned on the counter, as though reading his thoughts. "What's the likely radius of the explosion?"

"Large enough to take out a planet, according to the memo. Although I imagine the vacuum would condense it. What are you thinking?"

"There's a flier in your cargo hold." She glanced at the hall-way leading toward the stairs. "I initially thought we could drop the data cards off in the flier like a message in a bottle, so Humanity has a chance to protect itself, should the A'turi try this again. But... if the radius of the radio signal is bigger than the radius of the explosion..."

"You want *us* to stay in the flier too?" he guessed, immediately rejecting the idea.

"Yes. We could set up an encrypted exchange between the flier and *Caerus* and unencrypted forwarding to the A'turi ship." She drew two arches in the air, mimicking the paths of the signals. "The transmission will look like it's coming directly from *Caerus*. That should buy us some time. Maybe enough for the authorities to get here?"

Levi shook his head. "I won't let you turn *Caerus* into a remote-controlled dummy. If it must self-destruct to save some dumb planet, it deserves to do so with its captain on board."

GALAXY GRIFTER

"It's just a ship, Levi."

"To *you*." He pushed his cup aside, nearly spilling its contents. "You don't get it." He marched to the cockpit and dropped into the pilot seat, intent on remaining there until the bitter, glorious end.

She approached quietly and sat next to him. "If I don't get it, explain to me. What is it that makes *Caerus* worth dying for?"

He shrugged. "It's home..." But it was more than that. A part of himself, without which he might as well have been just another lowlife, drifting by without purpose.

"Let's see..." She looked thoughtful, tapping the smooth control panel with her fingernails, an annoying, uneven rhythm. She spoke again, before he could tell her to cut it out. "You hate conformity and being controlled, right? So in a galaxy governed by others' rules and expectations, you've built this entity that is entirely yours and for you."

His shoulders relaxed slightly. *Close enough.* "I haven't just built it, I've risked my life filling it with all the best things the galaxy has to offer."

"Risking your life is different from choosing imminent suicide." She leaned back in the navigator seat. "I'd risked my life to get off Blackjack and I'd give it up in a heartbeat to save my brothers. Yes, even, the oldest one." She rolled her eyes, her tone tinged with humor. "He can be a bit of a jerk, but still. But I wouldn't climb into their funeral pyre. It wouldn't bring them back. Trust me, I know a thing or two about loss." Her gaze drifted to the viewport, settling on the endless darkness of hyperspace.

And there it was, the damn self-preservation instinct. A

possibility of survival, no matter how small, always won over pride, greed, revenge...

She turned to him again. "Look, you've built something great here. But if we survive, you could build it again."

He scoffed. "You know there's slim chance of that, right? We're off a standard route, there are no guarantees someone will actually find us."

"But there *is* a chance, right?" Her eyes glistened with hope and determination.

He didn't want to dissuade her.

While Vera set up the remote and encrypted access to *Caerus*, Levi tried to keep busy with cooking. Normally he found it relaxing. Currently, he was trying to think of the smoked protein steaks as anything but his last supper. With his lifestyle, all his suppers had the potential to become his last and he didn't want it to feel dramatic. In the end, everything tasted wrong, and he came to the conclusion he had no appetite.

Vera appeared not to suffer from this infliction. She cleaned her plate, then carried her digital frame to the flier.

Making sure she'd left, he returned to the cockpit and knelt beside the control panel. "It will be over in seconds," he whispered, as if talking to a child, or a pet, perhaps. "At least you will never have to rot in a junkyard." He stroked the cold surface. Deep inside he knew the ship didn't care. It wasn't a living, thinking entity. Not really. So why did this feel like betrayal of the highest order?

GALAXY GRIFTER

When Vera didn't return five minutes later, he took the stairs to the cargo hold and found her just standing there, next to the flier, clutching her virtEgo.

She whirled as though he startled her, then asked, "Will you record a message for your family, in case we don't make it?"

He tapped his fingers on the flier's roof, thinking it over. "Maybe just a note for the authorities to tell them I'm dead." Talking about the end diminished his resolve. And he needed all of it to lie to the A'turi. "You?"

"I tried. I can't do it." She lowered her virt with an exhale. "They make it look easy in movies."

"I think I should stay aboard, just in case anything goes wrong, or they don't fall for your encrypted signal. But you should go in the flier. There will be more oxygen with just the one of us, almost doubles your time and chances."

Her face hardened. "No way. If you're staying aboard, then I'm staying."

"Why?" She'd just told him she wouldn't jump into a funeral pyre even for family. And despite what they'd been through over the last few days, they were not *that* close.

She sighed. "Have you ever been stranded in outer space with no FTL engine, no ansible, or ability to change anything, all alone like a fucking speck of dust in the vacuum?"

Oops...He'd never really thought about how waking up in the *Comet*'s detached module had impacted her.

"Because I have, and it fucking sucks, Levi." Her voice was high and accusatory. "So it's either both of us, or none of us."

Twenty minutes passed before *Caerus*'s lidar detected another vessel. Several minutes later, it transmitted the visual to Levi and Vera. They watched the huge A'turi ship through a virt screen on the flier's dashboard, thousands of kilometers away. The ship had an arrow-shaped bow and five directional rockets growing from its rear like tentacles. It carried two smaller rockets below its belly. The missiles. It hadn't yet tried to shoot *Caerus* down. That was promising.

Knowing he couldn't afford hesitation, Levi requested contact. The ansible crackled, connecting, but nobody responded.

"Hello?" He waited for the second's lag. "If you can hear me, I want to say I know exactly what your plan is. I have your missiles' blueprint and I'll sell it to the Human government unless you buy it first. Ten million kilo-bitcoins to keep me quiet."

Silence.

Next to him, Vera shook her head. "They won't bite."

A white beam shot from the A'turi ship, closely missing *Caerus*.

"Go ahead and kill me. The blueprint is on a nebula drive and will go public. You'll blow up Seshat. You'll probably get Frigg and Sandabur. But somebody will figure out how to match your strength soon enough. And then the whole galaxy will implode, you included." He waited out a pause, wondering if the Earthen authorities would ever act on his bluff. "I don't care who wins. I just want my money. But if it's all the same to you, I'm leaving hyperspace in five, four, three—"

A single word came from the ansible. "Dock." The voice

GALAXY GRIFTER

was hollow and clearly synthesized. A hatch opened above the missiles like a side mouth.

Levi guided *Caerus* toward it.

"We won't have a signal inside the ship. Activate hyperdrive in five, four, three..."

The visual on his virt disappeared.

"What the—" Vera frantically tapped her virt.

"Shit!" He should've stayed aboard *Caerus* after all. "Are they jamming us?"

"I don't—"

The visual returned for a second and disappeared once more: They exchanged glances.

"I think it's our position," she said. "The A'turi ship is just blocking the radio waves due to its size, and given it's likely filled with water..."

Levi grabbed the flier's controls and steered it up at full speed. Maybe if he moved around relative to the spaceships, the signal would return. Vera kept tapping the settings on her virtEgo.

The visual returned, revealing the A'turi ship's hatch, still open, mere meters from *Caerus*'s cameras. Levi's chest squeezed from the devastation at what he was about to do, but knew he had to, now or never.

You were a damn good ship, Caerus. *The best ship there's ever been or will be,* he thought, willing his silent words to span the distance.

Out loud he said, "*Caerus*, jump."

Obediently, the ship engaged its hyperdrive for the very last time. Levi's gaze remained fixed on the visual, his muscles

385

trembling from the focus. As *Caerus* surged through the airlock, Levi caught a glimpse of the A'turi ship's interior, glowing red, like the cube. Then the visual cut.

He glanced down, realizing Vera was squeezing his hand.

"Did we do it?" she asked.

That's when he saw a white flash through the flier's window.

With the hyperdrive engaged, *Caerus* would have torn through the belly of the alien spaceship. Antimatter from the ship's mangled engines had set off a chain reaction of annihilation, as they had planned. The explosion grew tendrils and bloomed like a flower before dying out.

A distress beacon flickered on the dashboard of a small, black flier, stranded in hyperspace, mere thousands of kilometers away from an explosion massive enough to destroy a planet. Once the afterglow fizzled out, Levi closed his eyes. "Rest well, old friend."

Vera pressed her shoulder into his. "I'm sorry. I know you loved *Caerus*."

"I—" He tried to speak, but no words would come. He couldn't even remotely express how much the ship had meant to him. It was like someone'd sliced open his rib cage and scraped it bare. And yet... *Caerus* had gone out with a bang, while they still had problems. The flier had no faster-than-light capabilities; they were off a main route with a limited supply of oxygen.

"You think Starpol will find us?" Vera asked, gently steering the conversation away.

GALAXY GRIFTER

"You know my level of trust in the government. You would've lasted twice as long if you had let me stay aboard *Caerus*."

"Don't be stupid," she said. "You think I'd let you ditch me in space again?"

He snickered and wrapped his arm around her. As he switched off all the warning signals blinking on the control panel, leaving only the beacon, he thought that he should have left her on Earth, found someone else to do the translation. She'd hardly seen anything beyond Blackjack and didn't even know what she was capable of. It seemed like an awful waste.

They stayed silent for a while, and he thought she'd fallen asleep tucked against him, until she stirred and said, "It's not the worst way to go."

It wasn't. Yet it still felt wrong. "I'm sorry." The words tasted foreign in his mouth, as he was more used to faking them.

She looked up at him and shrugged. "Not every day you get to die saving the world."

"The last thing I'd expect of myself, actually. Although I always knew I'd die in space. Only...I'd imagined being aboard *Caerus* and alone."

"Oh, I'm sorry for ruining your morbid fantasy with my presence." She laughed.

"Eh, it's kind of nice actually. Only..."

"What?" She peeked into his face.

"Nothing." They fell into silence once more, losing track of the passage of time.

"You reckon if we...if things were different, we could be friends?" It was the dumbest thing he'd ever said, and when she looked at him, her expression suggested as much. Then she reached up and kissed him.

This was, by far, not the worst way to go. He leaned into the feeling, until a flash in his peripheral vision made him pull away from her. "Is that a ship?" He stared into the darkness. A moment later, a Human warship came into view.

Her gaze slid from him to the ship and back again. "You don't look all too happy."

He turned the control panel back on, preparing to make contact. "I've only just embraced the idea of dying a hero. Now, they'll throw me in prison."

Chapter 43
Cheeseballs and Huxifruit

Vera and Levi stepped off a commercial passenger hauler and queued for the customs check-in at Xinlouyang Spaceport. A Huxoran baby wailed somewhere ahead, a shrill, squeaking sound. An elderly Human couple bickered behind them.

Levi leaned in to Vera's ear. "They have no clue Seshat would be a charred nugget if it weren't for us."

"The blues said they had it under control, we only meddled." She scanned her virt and walked through the cylindrical security machine.

He followed. A web of red lights flickered across his face and body and morphed into a holographic welcome message. He joined her inside the terminal with colorful shop fronts. "The blues say a lot of things."

She smiled. "Thank you."

"For?" He'd come to expect her sarcasm.

"You kind of saved the world," she said seriously.

He chuckled, unable to see himself as that kind of guy, even if it were, technically, true.

"No, really." She kept a straight face. "I have family and friends on Seshat. You don't. You didn't have to risk your life."

"Yeah, well, I kind of hated the idea of being ruled by wet overlords. Otherwise you're right, there isn't much on Seshat worth saving."

"Oh yeah? So why did you come here?"

She had a point. The soldiers brought them back to Earth for questioning, but he didn't want to stay there once they released him. His homeworld triggered all kinds of feelings. And given he had no ship and nowhere else to be . . . "Because you did." It was true, even if it made no sense.

She gave him a skeptical once-over. "Since when are you such a cheeseball?" She walked on without awaiting a response. "Speaking of cheese . . . I'm starving."

"Then let's get out of here already," he said. "Go somewhere nice to celebrate being alive."

She pointed at a sign. "Pendo's Pizza is round the corner. I've been craving it for weeks."

He cringed. "You do know they're made on a food printer?"

"Amazing, right?" She headed for the pizza kiosk inside the spaceport.

Amazing was not a word he'd use for this junk food, but it seemed he had no say in the matter.

Moments later, she slapped a greasy plate and a can of beer onto a high table and took a hunk out of the colorful slice the size of her face. "Mmm." She closed her eyes and smiled.

GALAXY GRIFTER

They would need to work on her culinary preferences. Among other things.

He took a cautious bite of his own slice. "Surprisingly tolerable." He wiped his fingers on a paper serviette. "You know what bothers me?"

"Huxifruit on pizza?" She picked at a piece of something green on her slice. "They're polarizing, but I'm kind of into it."

"No. The fact the blues let us go."

"Hm?"

"I mean, the days of questioning were punishment enough, but... didn't think I'd get off that easily. Especially after they'd read out the list of the laws I apparently broke." He fiddled with the top of his beer can.

"You gave them unbelievable evidence against two entire governments, the Breznis, and whoever else. And you did just save a planet, whether or not they want to admit it."

"Admit what?" he scoffed. "They're going to pretend it never happened."

"I can see their reasoning. Most Jaemlens would have no idea about the planned terrorist attack. Their government denounced it. It's just one radical faction gone rogue." She bit off another mouthful, puffing her cheeks like a hamster. "Imagine the panic and tensions that would ensue if people thought otherwise."

"Whatever. I didn't think it would end with us signing some nondisclosure docs, that's all."

"Well, imagine they'd locked us up and the documents turned up in the public domain. That would get messy."

391

"The documents?" He narrowed his eyes. "Wait, are you saying you've blackmailed the UCH's intelligence service into letting us go?"

"Not blackmailed, just...gave us a bit of leverage. You know I had nothing uploaded, I merely hinted at the possibility."

He stared at her with newfound admiration, determined that he needed to keep her close. At least for now. "Why didn't I think of that?"

"Maybe I'm the smart one in this tandem?" She winked. "Although I did learn from you."

He laughed. "So I'm not just a pretty face? Maybe the blues are the ones that got off easy. Ever wondered how much coinage could be made from this...leverage?"

She choked on her beer. "You're joking, right? We barely made it alive out of your last get-rich scheme. I didn't blackmail them, I've negotiated a way to ensure our safety. Leave it at that."

He dropped his head back, but she was right of course. "I'm kidding, I'm done with it."

"Done?" She arched an eyebrow.

"With the schemes. Not every day you get a clean slate. Besides, it's a rigged game. Anytime you break big, you spend more trying to clean up after yourself. And I'm sick of buying washing machines for my parents' friends. I'm done." He banged the can on the table to punctuate his point.

She reached for his hand. "That's suspiciously sensible of you."

"Maybe that's what happens once you roll over thirty? The

GALAXY GRIFTER

only problem is that I've no clue what else to do with my life." The idea of having to look for a real job filled him with more dread than a Sehen's embrace.

"You'll figure it out." She walked around the table and kissed him on the cheek. "Come on." She took his hand and led him down the terminal, checking the mail on her virt. Not far from the exit, she stopped by an ad selling secondhand spaceships. She tapped the sign and a catalog of holographic models appeared above it. She glanced at him. "Any thoughts on these?"

He sighed. "I'm in no position to replace *Caerus*. The blues refused to compensate me for it, and if I'm to rely on a legal income...it may take a while."

She scrolled through the holograms. "I was actually thinking of getting one for myself."

"For you? Can you afford it?"

"Like you said, there's money in blackmailing the government." She grinned.

His eyes widened. "You didn't?"

"Of course not. You think I'm mad?"

More often than not. He chose not to voice this.

"But they did offer me a job. Which means I'll be able to do a hire-purchase." Now she was talking straight.

He stepped back. "A job? With the military?"

"Programming robots and stuff at Xinlouyang's Ministry of Defense's office. Apparently Igor put a word in. Also by 'offer,' I mean they strongly implied it was in my best interest to take it, not that I'd want to decline."

"Programming robots?" His breath quickened. He came to

this shithole for her and she didn't consider this detail worth mentioning? "When were you planning on telling me?"

"Now? I was waiting for the paperwork to come through. I...didn't want to get my own hopes up." She peered into his face. "What's wrong?"

He breathed deeply, trying to rationalize his anger. "It's just that...you'll be working for the blues and I'm..."

"Just some guy with a clean slate. Which you're intending to keep clean, right?"

"Right."

"So, we can still..." She looked around as though searching for the right word. "We can still be friends."

"Friends?" He remembered what he'd said to her in the flier when he thought they were going to die, when he wondered what could have been if they didn't, and how she kissed him in response.

She must've thought of it too, because she averted her gaze, trying to hold in a smile. The dimple on her right cheek betrayed her. She took his hand, once again, and led him through the sliding door, out of Xinlouyang Spaceport.

The story continues in...

Book TWO of Blackjack Interstellar

ACKNOWLEDGMENTS

Writing may seem like a solitary endeavor, but I've learned it takes a village to publish a book. My village is made up of amazing people from across the globe, and I'm endlessly grateful to them for helping me make this dream come true.

Firstly, to my husband, for his patience, for cheering me through the highs and for holding me through the lows.

To Olya Ostasheva, for agreeing to be my guinea pig and reading parts of this book long before it was even a book. It gave me the courage to take it further.

To my beta readers, who generously shared their time and insights: Rayner Ye, S. C. Jensen, T. K. Toppin, Nik Bright, B. S. H. Garcia, S. L. Wibrow, Jack K. Boyles, and Jessica Aragon. You're all such talented authors, and I wouldn't have gotten this far without you.

To my editor, Stephanie Lippitt Clark, for believing in this story and for being so fantastic to work with.

To my agent, Bethany Weaver, for welcoming me to the Weaver Literary Agency team and always having writers' best interests at heart.

To the team at Orbit for making this book the best it could be and getting it into readers' hands.

Acknowledgments

To Sean Monaghan at SpecFicNZ and to Samantha Wekstein at the Manuscript Academy for their thoughtful first-pages assessments; to Rachel Grosvenor for helping me with the query package; and to K. J. Harrowick at WriteHive for her manuscript assessment—your input is truly appreciated.

To everyone who provided feedback on the early drafts via TheNextBigWriter website and elsewhere—I grew so much in my craft because of you!

To my Crime Queriers group, for their much-needed support, camaraderie, and for being an awesome bunch of humans. I'm looking forward to collecting all your books on my shelf!

Finally, to my family—my mum, now among the stars, my dad, my grandparents, my brother, my sweet munchkin of a child—to my friends who have been here for me, and to the broader writers and readers community: you make it all worthwhile.

MEET THE AUTHOR

Anzhelika Moiseeva

A. Zaykova's short fiction and poetry have appeared in multiple magazines and anthologies including *Etherea*, *Leading Edge*, and *The Future Fire*. She holds a bachelor's degree in communications and has a decade's experience writing and managing media for the New Zealand government. A. Zaykova is a member of several writers' associations and communities, has worked as the press office head for Worldcon, and has managed social media for SpecFicNZ. She now lives in Australia.

Find out more about A. Zaykova and other Orbit authors by registering for the free monthly newsletter at orbitbooks.net.

www.ingramcontent.com/pod-product-compliance
Lightning Source LLC
LaVergne TN
LVHW031938140625
813765LV00005B/133